THE PRESIDENT'S DAUGHTER

THE PRESIDENT'S DAUGHTER

MICKY O'BRADY

Table of Contents

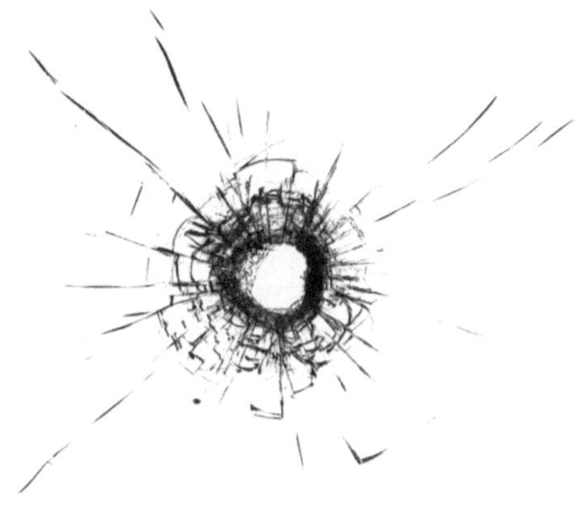

CHAPTER ONE

Inauguration

"Are you prepared to take the Oath, Senator?"

The Chief Justice's voice carries over the gigantic speakers, drowning out the applause of the crowd in front of us and turning their cheers into an awed silence.

This is it.

My dad takes a step forward and raises his right hand, radiating an aura of professionalism and seriousness. Next to me, Mom straightens up as if she was the one being sworn into office. I bet she has her game face on, happy smile frozen to perfection.

"Please repeat after me. I, Leopold Forrester, solemnly swear—"

Every single member of the audience below us falls silent and hangs on Dad's every word as he repeats the Chief Justice's oath. Me, I know the few lines by heart. I just hoped I'd never hear Dad say them.

"To preserve, protect, and defend the constitution of the

1

United States, so help me God."

As if they were a living entity, hundreds of "Leo Forrester for President" signs pick up on their enthusiastic wiggles and jiggles as the Chief Justice shakes Dad's hand. "Congratulations, Mr. President."

Below the Capitol's balcony, the crowd erupts into even bigger applause. People leap to their feet and cheer, waving their little American flags through the air as if they wanted to hail Air Force One. It's a sea of red, white, and blue as far as I can see.

The Chief Justice congratulates the new First Lady—aka my mom. Then he turns around, smiles at me and extends his hand.

I wish I didn't have to take it.

I wish it was a year ago and I didn't get into that damn car.

I wish… It doesn't matter.

Adjusting my crutches, I shift my weight onto my healthy right leg and take the Chief Justice's hand, forcing a smile that I hope looks only half as fake as it feels. As soon as he lets go, my mother hooks her arm into mine and pulls me forward to meet Dad at the balustrade. For a moment, I consider resisting, but it wouldn't do any good other than getting me into trouble.

We're separated from the audience by a Plexiglas barrier and an impressive line of wide-shouldered and serious-faced security guards. Hundreds of TV cameras point at us, recording every angle of Dad's Inauguration for eternity. A giant American flag waves above us all, its shadow whipping across the crowd as the fabric ripples in the wind.

I keep my forced smile and awkwardly wave down at the masses, while my parents… Well, enthusiasm is radiating off them like heat from the sun.

It doesn't touch me at all.

The music starts and the cannons fire their obligatory salute. While the marching band keeps playing, Dad stands on the podium, waving to the audience in front of the Capitol building.

"Alix. Smile." My mother pushes this out between her teeth. She has this freaky ability to talk through a smile without moving her mouth.

I don't roll my eyes. I don't give a snappy comment. I just force the corners of my mouth up some more.

Eventually, Dad turns away from the audience to lead us toward the town car. My parents are on a tight schedule for the rest of the day.

Once he's next to me, I look up at him, trying to catch his eye.

"Congratula—"

Dad pushes past me to shake somebody else's hand.

Right.

I swallow hard.

Of course things would be the same, no matter if the cameras were rolling, or not.

I feel for a good hold with my crutches before I force my sluggish left leg in the other direction and take a few careful hobble-steps toward my ever-present wheelchair.

Being the new First Daughter has its upsides: A Secret Service agent dressed in a black suit pushes my wheelie over to me. It looks tiny next to him. I have to crane my neck to meet his eyes— or rather his pitch-black sunglasses—and when I do, all he does is cock an eyebrow at me.

Suits me, I don't really want to talk either.

I let myself fall into my wheelchair, hoping nobody sees the relief on my face when the stabbing pain in my leg turns down to bearable burning.

Sunglass-guy pushes me past all the excited faces toward the limousine that's supposed to bring me back home.

My parents don't want poor little Alix to be too exhausted.

Or rather, Dad probably doesn't want to be seen with poor little Alix.

Sometimes I still wonder how he and I could go from two peas in a pod to… whatever we are now. Surely not father and daughter. We haven't been that since I became a cripple.

Oh, sorry: person with mobility impairment. My shrink says I shouldn't put myself down, but it's tough to stick to less offensive terms since the first newspaper headline I saw after that fateful day is still burned into my mind: *Senator's Daughter Crippled in Serious Car Accident.* Right.

My cheeks burn and I lower my gaze.

At this point, Sunglass-guy wheels me past the masses toward the black town car, turning my wheelchair around so I can say goodbye to my parents. Both my dad and mom followed us at a slow pace. Dad must have shaken a million hands already.

Mom bends down and kisses my hair.

"Have Linda make you some food, okay? And eat it," she adds under her breath. She knows very well I won't. No appetite.

She lets her hand linger on my shoulder, massaging through the fabric. "And please take one of the pain killers, sweetie. You know where they are."

Mom usually isn't so much into public displays of affection, but over the last year, we've gotten better at it. Plus, this is politics now. The new President and First Lady—and the First Daughter, for that matter—need to project the image of a happy family, no matter the individual family members' mood.

And I really don't want to know what Dad is thinking.

The one second he doesn't have his features under control, it's right there: The distant stare, as if he was trying hard to remember how life with a healthy daughter was. That stare's been there every day since the seat belt broke and I flew into the town car's windshield, shattering part of my spine.

Anything in my life I took for granted was ripped away from me the second I came close to dying crashing into that windshield: The ability to walk without a crutch. The unconditional faith and trust that nothing bad will ever happen to me. The sense of adventure each new day held.

Oh yeah, and also my dad's confidence in me. Me, the fragile, tender, delicate thing.

Ugh.

Dad's blank stare is gone as quickly as it came, replaced by a smile. Not the smile he used to have with me, the one that made me feel special, the one that never left, even when I screwed up. No, this is the official smile.

The *President's* smile.

He squeezes my shoulder once. "We'll see you later, Alix."

"Sure," I say, keeping my eyes down. *Or not.*

Dad drops his hand fast, like he can't stand touching me, but I'm still pretty sure that this little caress of his handicapped daughter in her wheelchair has already bought him some votes from the right wing for whatever election comes next.

That's all that counts, right?

I huff to myself.

A year ago, my life would've still been considered normal for a sixteen-year-old, at least from my point of view. Going to school, taking a couple of advanced college classes to keep me from getting bored, working on one or two of my inorganic chemistry experiments, maybe even spending some time researching bioluminescent plants. Nerdy? Sure, but for me the usual.

If I had it my way, I'd be in one of Harvard's libraries right now or programming computer code in my dorm room. Goodbye to that future. I knew the moment Dad entered the race that any chance of "normal" I might've had was gone; I just never imagined that would also apply to our relationship.

Whatever. Self-pity has never helped anybody, yet it seems to be all I've left.

Sunglass-guy turns my wheelchair around and gets the limousine's door for me. Using all the strength I have, I push myself up into a standing position, for a moment so distracted by my misery I forget about my left leg. Before I can realize my mistake, my weak knee buckles underneath me and my body responds to the siren call of gravity, a force of exactly nine-point-eight-one meter per second squared about to introduce my face to the asphalt.

Sunglass-guy lunges forward, his quick grasp saving me from toppling over.

"Whoa—thanks!" With all the cameras on me, there's no doubt I would've become an instant viral internet sensation, and not the fun kind. I'm awkward on my best day, and I never said that day was today.

Sunglass-guy nods once, but keeps his hand wrapped around my biceps until I'm seated in the car. Can't say I mind it at this point. After sixteen years with two healthy legs, it's not the easiest task to be reduced to one healthy and one basically useless leg. The last year was rough. I'm still taking too many things for granted, like being able to shift weight onto my left leg. Sucks getting used to being a crip—

Sigh.

My hands shake when I buckle myself in, but for a whole different reason.

Deep breaths, Alix.

Nothing is going to happen. Just because I'm in another town car doesn't mean we'll have an accident. This seat belt will hold.

Tackling that resistant buckle like a physics problem, I talk myself through the process that used to be second nature, at least before flashbacks and a shattered spine.

With a click, I buckle myself in, mind and logic winning over panic and memories, and not a moment later, the car creeps forward at a snail's pace. Although the way out of the area in front of the Capitol building is cleared, Sunglass-guy is taking it easy. Nobody wants to see the First Daughter flee the scene, or her driver smash into an overeager journalist.

I crane my neck and look out the window. Sam must be somewhere close by; he'd be his dad's shadow on a day like this. Unfortunately, shadows are tough to spot on a cloudy day, so no luck. Disappointed, I lean back into the soft cushioned seats and take a deep breath. I would've loved to at least sneak a peek at him.

As soon as we're moving and the noise of the crowd becomes more a rumbling in the background, all tension leaves my body. I chuckle once to myself. Well, considering this was my first major outing after months of physical therapy, I held up pretty well.

My gaze drifts and follows the people we pass, then the houses and the stopped traffic, not seeing a thing. It all blurs together into colors and nothingness, until I realize we're driving into the wrong direction.

"Excuse me?" I lean a bit toward the center to catch Sunglass-guy's attention in the rearview mirror. "I'm not supposed to go to the White House. I need to get home, please." *Home* as is for another few days before my parents have settled enough to have me move into the White House with them, that is. I wish I could stay at home, but no. Since Dad vetoed Harvard, it was either a boarding school in Switzerland *to work on my college credits*, or coming to the White House, and that decision was easy. I can work on my credits from here, I don't need a Swiss boarding school. Would look bad on my CV, as if I needed academic help. *Puh-*

lease.

Silence is the only answer I get from the front. That and the limousine speeding up.

I try again. "I'm not going to the White House ceremony, I'm supposed to—"

We turn the corner into the underground parking garage close to the White House perimeter so sharply, I'm thrown against the door. My shoulder hits the frame and a little squeak breaks free from my throat. "Ow! Geez!"

The car doesn't slow. As if Sunglass-guy had confused the pedals, he instead speeds us up, circling us down the ramp at a dizzying velocity.

I know what's going to happen before my body reacts to the sensation of being thrown into my seatbelt. From one second to another, my heart beats so fast it's close to not pumping any blood at all. The outskirts of my vision turn black, and none of the wheezy breaths I take are bringing enough oxygen to my lungs.

"Oh, no."

Of course, the erratic driving would trigger memories of my accident.

Flying glass, screeching metal, blinding pain.

"Stop," I croak, one hand at my throat. "Stop."

We don't stop. Nope. We keep spiraling downwards farther and farther, until we hit an empty level.

But still we don't slow down.

Not even when we're approaching the wall at the far end.

Holy cow! He must be crazy.

Sunglass-guy accelerates even more, inertia pushing me into the seat and bile up my throat.

"Wallwallwallwallwall!" I lift my hands to brace myself for the impact as the engine whines in a high pitch and races us toward the wall.

This cannot be happening.

Finally, fate is going to finish the job she started a year ago: I'm going to die. Ironically, it's again in one of Dad's cars.

Some sick little voice inside my head counts down the seconds until impact for me. Who knew that was a feature that came with imminent death?

Four, three, two, one... I hold my breath, arms outstretched, pushing myself back into the seat and preparing for the inevitable impact—

And with a flash of light, we drive *right through the wall.*

One second later, the limousine comes to a screeching and sudden halt. Inertia throws me forward into my seatbelt so hard, an *oomph*-sound leaves my throat.

The engine's hum fades, giving way to an eerie stillness that sends shivers down my spine.

What in the name of all that's holy just happened here?

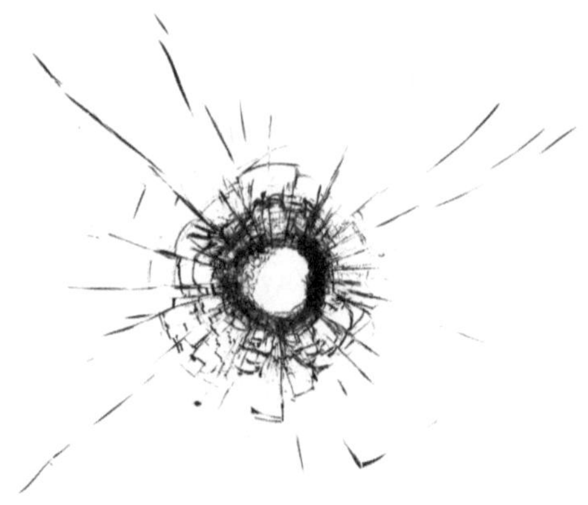

CHAPTER TWO

Game Changer

My mind is trapped somewhere between the horrors of reliving my accident and the wonders of surviving breaking through a wall. Or driving through it. Or whatever happened.

Fate didn't claim me, for the second time.

Every breath I suck in is rapid and shallow. My hands shake. A drop of sweat trickles its way down my neck.

In the front, Sunglass-guy exits the car as if nothing happened.

The door on my left opens and he holds out his hand for me, waiting.

And waiting.

My chest cramps from the force of my pounding heart. Yeah, no. I'm not taking his hand, sorry, not sorry. Not going to.

Sunglass-guy sighs and squeezes his wide frame into the rear of the limousine. Before I know it, I'm unbuckled and cradled in his arms like a baby.

Excuse me? "Let go! I can—" The rest of my protest gets stuck in my throat as soon as my head clears the frame.

Our sleek, black car is parked parallel to the wall in front of three traffic cones in the middle of a big office room, complete with polished wooden floors, an old-fashioned looking huge desk with file cabinets on one side, and a couch, chair, and coffee table on the other.

Skid marks scar the otherwise spotless floors, all more or less on top of each other, and all coming from… the completely intact wall behind the limousine.

My mouth drops open.

"What the heck is going on here?" Despite being so close, I doubt Sunglass-guy heard me.

He lowers me onto the couch, and I push myself farther back into the cushions, creating distance.

"What. Is. Going. On. Here," I repeat, but don't get rewarded with an answer. Great. That makes me feel better, really.

With a few long strides, this mountain of a man crosses the room toward a door on the far end of the room and presses a button next to it.

"She's here."

She's here. Could we be any more ominous if we tried? I stuff my hands under my thighs, but they keep shaking.

Sunglass-guy moves aside the moment the door opens and a lone figure steps into the office.

I don't know what I expected. Dr. Evil? An Alien? A Man in Black?

Nope. It's a guy, maybe early twenties if that, dressed in casual jeans and a loose Abercrombie sweater. His dark blond hair is tousled and messy. Could be carefully styled into a bed-head or just unkempt, tough to say.

He comes straight toward me, smile wide and eyes bright, both hands outstretched. "Alix. I'm so happy to finally meet you. I hope the trip here—" His brows scrunch together as he gives me the once-over. "Dimitri." He sighs. "What did you do to her?"

Sunglass-guy shrugs. "Nothing."

"*Nothing* as in you didn't give her a heads-up for the wall?"

Another shrug.

Abercrombie-guy rolls his eyes and focuses on me again, pulling both my hands out from under my thighs to shake them.

"Anyway. Alix, welcome to the Eagle's Lair, your new workplace."

Uhh, what?

He looks at me all expectantly for a moment before realization dawns on his face. He drops one of my hands and smacks himself into the forehead. "I'm sorry, I'm sorry. I'm two steps ahead mentally. I've read so much about you I forgot you know nothing about me. Ian Donckers. I'm with the PRICS-Division. We'll be working together."

Pricks wha—

His smile catches me off guard—warm and genuine, it lights up his whole face. Wait, he's actually happy to see *me*? Why?

Before I can ponder that puzzling question, I make the rookie mistake of meeting his gaze. Green eyes. Like, impossibly green eyes. And now my face is burning, because apparently my body has forgotten how to act normal around attractive people. Not that I was the life of the party before my accident, but maybe that year at home didn't help my social skills.

Luckily for me Abercrombie-guy—Ian Donckers—talks over my mortifying blush.

"I know you must have a lot of questions, but maybe it would be easier if I explained a little before we get that tackled. Something to drink?"

"S-sure. Cherry Coke? Please?" My voice does an unhealthy squeak at the end of the sentence I wish it didn't do, but that's me, Awkward-Alix. Hi, nice to meet you.

With a couple of long strides, Donckers walks around the coffee table and across the room to the opposite side of our pseudo-crash entrance. Instead of opening a fridge though he places his palm on what looks like an ordinary glass panel integrated into the wall. The surface illuminates with a soft blue glow, creating intricate patterns across his skin.

My jaw drops. "Is that—"

"Biometric security, correct." His eyes light up with an enthusiasm that makes him unfairly adorable. "Fingerprints aren't foolproof. Neither are palm prints. This system analyzes blood-flow patterns, micro-movements, and even electrical signals from nerve endings. Impossible to fool with synthetic prints."

My inner tech nerd brings out the confetti gun. That's cutting edge—no, beyond that! "Bioelectric signal detection… Are you using some kind of quantum tunneling microscope? Or how else would you get—"

He turns to me with such joy on his face I momentarily forget how to finish my sentence. "Exactly! Most people miss that completely!" He runs a hand through his hair, looking both excited and slightly sheepish. "I actually developed a new type of scanning technology that combines quantum sensing with AI processing. It can map the three-dimensional structure of tissue down to the cellular level."

No way! "But the processing power needed for real-time analysis…" I tilt my head and tap my chin, mind racing through calculations. "Unless you figured out a way to—"

"Compress the quantum data streams using neural networks?" He nods, looking at me like I'm the most fascinating person he's ever met. "You, Alix Forrester, are living up to your reputation. I read about the Manshield Hypothesis you disproved during the World Math Olympics when you were what, twelve or so? Your approach was truly fascinating."

Wait, people actually know me for that stupid Math Olympics? He *knows* me for *that*? Sam said I rocked it, but no one at my school even acknowledged I won. It was too nerdy for a school that thrived on football and cheerleading.

A soft whir interrupts my thoughts and a panel below the palm reader pops open. I honestly hadn't seen it before, it blended into the wall. Ian Donckers fishes for a Coke and a water and closes the panel door again.

A small little laugh bursts from my throat.

"What?" He cocks a curious eyebrow at me.

"You have the most sophisticated biometric security for a fancy fridge?" Talk about overkill, anybody?

Donckers smirks and shrugs his shoulders. "We use it elsewhere, too, but this was the first place I tried it out when I developed it. Seemed appropriate, since somebody was guzzling my water. Dimitri." He coughs out the last word, then shoots a glance over at the ginormous bodyguard.

All Sunglass-guy does is raise an eyebrow. Guess he doesn't feel too guilty.

I accept the Cherry Coke from Donckers, trying very hard to not notice how our fingers brush during the handoff.

"But anyway, I digress," he says, rubbing the back of his neck, "sorry. Got carried away. It's not often somebody actually understands the technical aspects. Most people's eyes glaze over the moment I mention quantum anything."

I pop open my Coke and decide to put on my big girl pants and not talk around the issue. "So you thought abducting the newly-elected President's daughter and driving her into an underground dungeon would be cool so you'd have somebody to chat about this?"

Donckers flinches. "Well. No. Apologies. An unfortunate side effect of our location." He sighs. "Let me give you an intro to the next four years of your life and help you understand. This is the Eagle's Lair, home of PRICS, which stands for Presidential Reconnaissance and Information Collection Service." He counts off every letter on the fingers of his right hand.

PRICS.

I cut an eye at him. "PRICS. You're kidding me." Who comes up with an acronym like that? I'm sure there's an app for that, for crying out loud.

He wrinkles his nose. "I know, right? Give me five minutes and I'd have ten better names than that, even without tasking AI, but anyway. We're a secret organization and a covert branch of the Secret Service with the sole and single purpose of making the President's life safer. Yes, I know, we already protect your father with bodyguards etcetera; but what we do—what you will do— they can't. We—you—can find out information, straight from the source, and help the President where they can't. And of, course, we have much better tech gadgets." He winks at me.

A secret branch of the Secret Service.

Hidden under the White House.

Part of me wants to dismiss it as fake, but then my gaze darts to the wall that's in one freakin' piece and over to the fancy fridge on the other wall. Location and high-tech gadgets suggest government, so I'm okay buying that part of his story, but…

The part he said about me, about me helping the President? *Me*, helping Dad?

A dry chuckle breaks free from my throat.

Right.

People have come up with better ideas for being punk'd.

Donckers' forehead scrunches up. "What?"

I don't even know where to start. "The word *helping* implies action, and I don't know if you've noticed, but that ship has sailed for me." I nod toward the car where Sunglass— *Dimitri* has unloaded my wheelchair from the trunk. "And even if that didn't matter, I'm not the right person for the Secret Service. My dad doesn't discuss his work with me." And at this point, he wouldn't put enough faith in me to make it through the day on my own, let alone work for the Secret Service.

I take a sip of my Coke, hoping it will push down the lump of inadequacy lodged in my throat.

Donckers leans forward, resting his forearms on his legs. "Alix, no, that's not it. We have the Secret Service for active protection. We need you simply because you are you. You're our biggest asset, our inconspicuous pair of eyes nobody expects. We're playing on your alibi as First Daughter. Not even your father will know that you're with us. All we need you to do is keep an eye on him—or his visitors—when we need you to. You are our connection between Leo Forrester, the President, and Leo Forrester, the private person." He gestures around the room. "This was all built for you. Well, not you specifically, but decades ago for the current President's kid or kids, as long as they're over sixteen and willing to join. This term it's going to be you, Alix."

A small flutter comes to life deep down in my chest. Me watching over Dad… He used to be the most important person in my life, and maybe… maybe it's pathetic, but *maybe* if he saw me more and realized that inside I was still the same old Alix, even if the outside was weak and broken…

The flutter is getting bigger, warmer.

We were such a great team before my accident. Maybe we could get back to that. He could be proud of me again, and not just ashamed of his little handicapped daughter. Heck, I'd be happy if he didn't see me as a failure anymore. If I took this job—

Wait. What did Donckers say? I cock my head. "My dad won't know I'm with the Secret Service?"

"No. His reflex would be to protect you and keep you out of the loop, and that's exactly what we can't have. We need you because you have 24/7 access to him. You can go where Secret Service can't. You can ask questions and pick his brain, all without arising suspicion. And you can accompany him on trips to gather information. That, by the way is the emphasis here: Gathering information. Inconspicuously, because"—he lifts his fingers for an air quote—"you're *just a teenager*. But then, also his daughter."

I huff to myself. Great. So no matter what I do for him, he'll still be babying useless little me. "How can that even be legal?" Recruiting me without Dad's knowledge, that's so spy-movie.

"It's a legal grey zone, but make no mistake, it is perfectly legit. We couldn't exist otherwise. And, Alix, we're not putting you in danger. All we need is passive acquisition, you listening, you keeping an eye out when you accompany your father on trips. You're perfect for us. A genius-level First Daughter—of course you'd be interested in your father's work and ask questions, and that's exactly the kind of intel we might one day need to help protect your father."

Meaning, I'm special? Yeah, I wish. Special was when I was about to embark on my PhD. Now special means Dad wants to cut my meal in pieces for me. Acid burns up my throat, as every time when my thoughts drift into this direction. It's not easy turning from a teen-prodigy into a moody cripple, but I've done it spectacularly well.

The longer I'm silent, the more Donckers relaxes back into the cushions of his chair, taking a sip of his tea.

"Intrigued?" His voice is warm and soft, soothing somehow.

Something inside of me cramps up and breaks open. Dang it. I nod.

His lips curl up on one side, giving him a mischievous expression. "I knew it would be up your alley. And you needn't worry. Like I said, you're not going to be an active field agent, we'd get in a buttload of trouble if we exposed the First Daughter to anything dangerous. It's all brain work, Alix." He taps a finger against his temple. "That's your thing. But we also have a bonus for you." He opens a small drawer inside the coffee table and takes out a file folder, laying it down in the middle between us. "This is my treatment plan for you. You work for us, we fix your leg."

My mouth drops open. "Fix my—?"

"Correct."

I refuse to let the tiny spark of hope grow bigger. "But it's irreparable damage to the spinal cord."

"An implanted microchip. This is top secret and the newest of the new. We're the government, Alix. And we're good. Well, *I'm* good." The slight blush creeping up his neck makes him look quite endearing. Stop it, Alix. Focus on the tech, not the tech expert.

He gives the folder a slight shove toward me, a welcome reason to drop my gaze from his before I blush worse than he does.

I take the folder and flip it open. Page after page is filled with medical descriptions and reports of my spine and leg, some of them I understand, some I don't. Having a mom who's a doctor only gets you so far in terms of absorbing medical knowledge, despite being really good at science.

On my first cursory glance, I'd say everything is here. Reports, scans, results.

A shiver runs down my back. "Where'd you get that?"

"Please." Donckers huffs. "We deal with intelligence. A

medical record isn't a problem."

Oh. Well, true.

I turn toward the last pages. A microchip, a splint… and four little words that make my heart skip a beat, no matter how cool I'm trying to play it: Final strength 99-100%

I let go of a slow breath through pursed lips. "Where's the catch?"

"No catch." Donckers shakes his head. "You work for us, we fix you. If you want to. You don't work for us we drop you off at home with a mild sedative that will make you forget this encounter. Matrix-style."

And then I won't get my leg fixed. There's the catch. "That's blackmail."

"No, that's the secrecy of our job and our technology. Unfortunately." The way he says it, I believe him, he's sorry. Doesn't change the choice I have to make, though.

I close my eyes, still holding on to the folder as if it was the Holy Grail.

Donckers taps my knee twice, and I open my eyes. "More info, to help you make up your mind. Data helps, right?" He gives me a small encouraging smile, and when I nod, carries on. "Agent Waterhouse is the head of PRICS and our immediate supervisor in the Secret Service." He nods at the wall behind his desk. Only now do I notice a framed, official looking picture of my dad with a plaque on the bottom, complete with his name, title, and the Presidential Seal.

The picture Donckers referred to is about a foot below Dad's, showing a man in his mid-fifties with eyes so watery and droopy he reminds me of a sad beagle. The permanent scowl frozen into his features deepens the lines that crisscross his face like the Amazon River, adding to that impression.

Floyd Waterhouse, Director, PRICS, it reads under the picture.

Donckers folds his hands on top of his knees. "We'll both be reporting to Waterhouse, but most of the time, it'll just be you and me. Well, every day basically, since I'll be with you under the pretense of being your teacher."

My jaw drops. "Wait, you're going to be my teacher?" Not the old guy Dad introduced me to a while ago, the teacher who didn't even know what CRISPR was when he asked about the paper I was reading, but Donckers? Green-eyes Donckers? I blush, but so does he.

"Uhh, yes. Me. Usually it would be Waterhouse training our PRICS-Agents, but with your genius-level we needed to crank it up, and that would be me."

"But you're barely older—"

"Twenty-one. And I invented the biometric security. The Holographic Wall." He gestures toward the high-tech fridge, then the intact wall behind the car. "And most of your chip." Another nod indicates the medical chart on the table in front of me.

Whoops. My cheeks burn. Never judge a book by its cover. One should think I had internalized that lesson, but maybe I'm becoming a bit rusty when it comes to being open-minded.

I suck in my lower lip. "Sorry."

"No need to apologize. You and I both know what being underestimated feels like." He takes a sip of his water, and I do the same with my Coke. *Awkward.* I don't think anyone would underestimate me right now, that's how low I've sunken over the last year, pulled down by the weight of Dad's candidacy. I knew there were going to be sacrifices along the way, I just never imagined I was one of them.

Your dad's late. He sent a car to pick you up.

Yeah, and after the accident, he couldn't even see how much I needed some kind of control, some kind of success. No. Despite me begging to go, he pulled me from Harvard. *The White House will be perfect for your needs,* he said. *That, or the Swiss boarding school.*

Right.

My needs. As if he knew at this point what they were. Hint: It's not a wheelchair accessible room and automatic doors.

Losing Dad's support ranks at a clear ten out of ten on those stupid pain scales the doctors shoved in my face every day after my accident, and it broke something inside me. Exit confidence; enter fear. I'm scared where I wasn't scared before, worried life is going to slip away from me, and then I'm gone—*boom*. Done. Nothing is guaranteed in life, not even life itself.

Not even the love from your family.

Ironically, while Dad kept me home to be closer, I'm still not getting much of a family. Dad's too busy, and Mom… we're getting better, but we're nowhere near where I was with Dad.

Donckers leans back into his seat. "You're going to love PRICS, Alix. It should be right up your alley. Imagine all the gadgets, all the options right at your fingertips." He wiggles his fingers at me. "We're set up deep under the White House. A secret passage connects our classroom with the Eagle's Lair down here, where we'll do most of your training and your treatment plus the physical therapy afterwards, for that matter." He points at the chart between us.

"Also, political sciences, code reading, covert operation training, theoretical tactical training—need I say more? You're going to *love* it." He smiles. The enthusiasm radiating off him is contagious.

I haven't loved anything for a long while now, but I can't help but smile back. Maybe… maybe I am going to love it. What did my life have to offer since the accident?

Nothing.

Nothing but frustration and feeling like I didn't only lose the ability to walk, but also to live.

I take a deep breath, filling my lungs with air for the first time in what feels like months. "It'll help my dad?"

"PRICS is invaluable to the President. To the outside, you're 'just' the President's daughter and living your 'normal' life, but you'll be collecting information when we need you to. We're banking on you being our spy on the inside. We can't do this without you."

I'll take that as a yes.

Helping Dad.

Being important to him again and not just a raging disappointment. Which, yes, I know, is more his issue than mine, but I can't help feel the same. I'm disappointed in me as well, but the simple thought of helping Dad sparks something inside of me that's been dead for the better part of last year.

It's absolutely crazy.

Impossible.

A game changer.

I look straight up into the expectant green eyes across from me.

Definitely a game changer.

One more deep breath.

"I'm in."

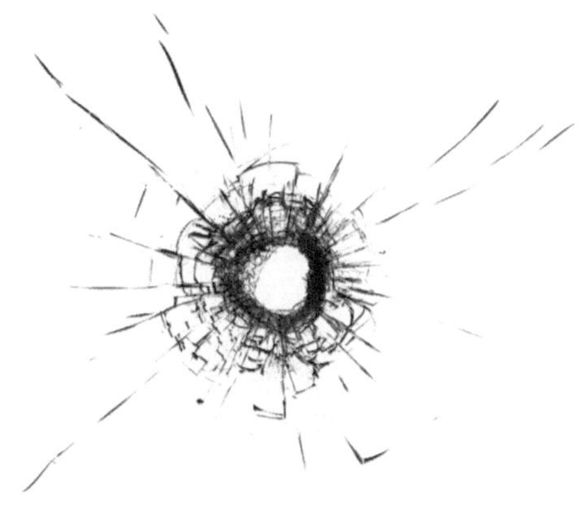

CHAPTER THREE

Determination

Three hours later, I'd take the spy gig any time of the day even if it came without benefits and against the will of my complete family.

Anything is better than going to a ball. In a dress. On crutches.

Alas, I'm ready to party.

Yay.

Donckers and Dimitri dropped me off back home about half an hour after I signed my life over to PRICS, and Dimitri, from now on my official personal Secret Service agent and shadow 24/7, is going to pick me up for the Inauguration Ball in less than ten minutes.

Maybe I should treat this as my first mission and just get through it, because… I'm a spy now. *Agent Forrester, Secret Service agent.*

Whoa. Unbelievable. And quite the ego-boost, I gotta say. The last year has cost me much of my vibe. Funny how that goes once external validation is gone. I give myself a thumbs-up in the mirror: Not a typical spy, but not too bad either. Linda has done her best to work my hair into some kind of fancy do that definitely beats my usual brown, rather limp ponytail. A dash of the so far unused perfume Mom got me for my last birthday surrounds me with a scent of lilacs.

The Inauguration Ball is a big deal, which is the only reason why I'm not fighting wearing a dress too much. I tried to talk Mom and Linda out of it, but didn't stand a chance. And, at least somewhere in the back of my mind, I agree with them. Not because I want to dress up, but because if I don't, it'll be another score for Gianna, and another loss for me.

I blow a raspberry at the mirror.

Gianna.

I'm afraid there's no way around her and her flawless persona tonight, no matter what. I wish I had more practice with public events, but I don't. Months of rehab kept me out of fundraising and campaigning, and while I would love to outshine Gianna at least somewhere, this isn't it. Because Gianna will be perfect, as always.

The President's daughter? That's the oddball over there, but look at the Vice President's daughter, now she's a confident young lady...

I make a face at myself.

Whatever.

The doorbell rings. My ride's here.

Grabbing my crutches, I hobble downstairs, ignoring Dimitri's outstretched hand. I got this. Linda gives me one small kiss on the forehead before she closes the door behind me. I'm going to miss her when I move to the White House, and for the umpteenth time, I wish she'd come with us. She's been our housekeeper since before I was born. She's more a grandma to me than anything else.

Dimitri and I spend most of the drive to the Inauguration Ball in silence. Here we are, two members of the secret PRICS-Division, one of us a silent mountain of a man, the other a teenager. I shake my head to myself. *A legal grey-zone. Off presidential access—so secret, not even the President knows about it.*

That part sucks. Dad won't even know what I'm doing for him. Still. If I can help him, I will. Just because he lost all faith in me doesn't mean I lost of all of mine in him.

No, not quite. I've got his back.

Dimitri throws a look at me via the rearview mirror. "Tonight, and whenever we're out of the White House, you can move freely and do all you want to, but I'll stay one step behind you, or lead the way when out in the open. I'll clear the bathrooms before you go in and will wait outside until you are done. Under no circumstances are you going to leave my sight. Questions?"

First Daughter Safety 1-0-1, alright. "Okay, sounds good to me." I think I'm going to like Dimitri. Anybody who dishes it out straight is on my good side. What is he anyway, in his late twenties? Tough to say with that aura of scruffiness around him, but yeah, probably late twenties.

Dimitri nods curtly. "Good."

I guess I'll get used to all that First-Daughter stuff when it actually happens.

Not even a minute later, we pull up in front of the Washington Convention Center. The press is everywhere, turning the night into a thunderstorm of flash photography. I swallow hard. That's a tad too much attention for me. I'd prefer to never see a single newspaper report with my picture in it ever again.

Presidential Candidate's Daughter in Critical Condition after Accident.

Senator Forrester's Daughter's Spine Broken: Paralyzed Forever?

As if he had read my thoughts, Dimitri drives us to the rear entrance protected by at least a million Secret Service agents in black suits with scowls on their faces. But: At least no press.

Dimitri gets out, walks over to the curbside, holds open the door for me, and helps me get out without looking like a dork. The crutches tend to have that effect on me. All agents step aside for us, be it because of me or because of Dimitri, and a minute later, he has supported me through a metal detector and we're in, at my first official event as the United States' First Daughter and soon-to-be-spy for the Secret Service.

The inside of the WCC is so beautifully decorated, it takes my breath away. It looks regal, somehow. I must say, the Presidential Inaugural Committee did a fantastic job.

American flags embellish everything. White curtains are drawn back on all doors and windows, giving the whole inside the appearance of a castle rather than a convention center. The stage at the far end has the Presidential Seal and Dad's name on the blue wall behind it as well as on the floor.

It's crowded already and people are in a good mood. Music plays, inviting guests to dance, and most of those who do hold on to a glass of something. My entrance is mostly unnoticed—or that's what I think until someone yells my name.

"Alix! Alix!"

My stomach lurches with anticipation when I look around, trying to find the owner of the voice I'd recognize anywhere. Eventually, I see a hand waving out of the crowd about five meters away.

Yes! "Sam," I yell and wave back to him. Unhooking myself

from Dimitri's support, I limp toward Sam on a single crutch. My beacon of light. I was so hoping to see him here.

Sam opens his arms for me and I fall into his tight hug. Makes my night, for sure. He smells good, a little bit spicy, but with a certain sweetness to it. Very Sam-like. Always with a whiff of butterscotch, for whatever reason.

I pull away before I enjoy his embrace for too long and it becomes awkward. "Wow, Sam." I scan him over from head to toe. "You clean up nicely." And that's an understatement. Sam is a good lookin' guy by default, but in his tuxedo… He looks like a younger version of his dad, Oliver Brooks, my father's oldest friend and newly minted Chief of Staff. Like his father, he has the same impressive height and presence that makes people stop and notice. But while he has his dad's striking features, his mom's genes show through, too—in his warm, brown skin tone and the unruly waves that never quite stay where he wants them to.

Sam tugs on his dress jacket, a lopsided grin popping up on his face. "Whatcha gonna do? I guess I better get used to suits anyway if I want to get a foot in the door."

"Still planning to be a Junior Intern?" I ask. Typical Sam-thing: Full-steam ahead.

"Well, I'd prefer to be a full-fledged Intern, but that's not going to happen until the summer. Gotta be eighteen." He rolls his eyes. "But on the other hand, I want to get a feel for the White House and a head start so I can rock this thing once I'm official." He cracks his knuckles, and the lopsided grin turns into a full-blown version, complete with dimples in both cheeks. My heart stumbles a bit.

Sam is the biggest reason why I regret not being on the campaign trail, and the biggest plus of not moving off to Harvard. Or the boarding school, for that matter.

I adjust my crutch. Should've taken both. "You're really

putting pre-Law on pause in exchange for interning? You got into Georgetown, Sam." Thanks to early decision and a perfect GPA, Sam's life would be mapped out already, if it wasn't for the minor distraction of Dad's presidency. But then again, it was kind of clear he couldn't let that opportunity pass. Having been with the campaign since the early beginning, Sam worked his way up to becoming one of our dads' most valuable staff members. Cue dinners at our place when his and my dad were working late and Sam's mom couldn't pick him up.

Sam waves my comment off. "Yeah, I know. My mom got all excited when that letter came. But honestly? I'm almost eighteen, and I've been working at the campaign for so long, it's part of my life. Plus, your dad just got elected President of the United States. *President!*" His eyes take on a far-away expression, one I'm only too familiar with when he talks about my dad. My rudimentary psych skills have long analyzed Sam's fixation on Dad. Easy. To Sam, Dad has become the role model his own father couldn't be; not after a divorce and leaving Sam and his older sister without a good-bye and without a single hello or phone call for over a year.

Bridges burned during that year, and only lately have they begun to rebuild them, one weight-bearing pillar at a time.

So yes, for the last couple of years, Dad has been the mentor Sam's been missing. Would be nice though if he were less fan-boyish toward my dad, and maybe more toward me.

My face bursts into flames.

I didn't just think that.

Sam raises a shoulder, thank God oblivious to the thoughts running through my head. "This is the experience of a lifetime for me. For the next years, I'm going to be closer than a shadow to your dad. That's worth way more in terms of experience than I'd be getting by attending pre-law. Also looks better on my CV." He grins and so do I, although it's forced.

Strikes me as a bit unfair that my resume just took a severe hit from the same thing that's boosting Sam's, but—

"Ah, Alix! Good to see you, girl." Somebody claps my shoulder from behind so hard, only Sam's quick reaction and hold on my arm keep me from losing balance.

James DiBiaso, newly elected Vice President, greets me with a face-splitting beam showing way too many teeth. In the hand not assaulting my shoulder he cradles a glass of champagne. Right behind him follows a blonde girl my age in a tight, curve-hugging black dress that emphasizes every curve of her voluptuous body like she stepped off the pages of a magazine.

That moment in front of my mirror when I thought I looked if not *good*, then at least okay?

Gone.

Gianna DiBiaso smiles in my direction, but I don't fall for it. Her eyes are on Sam, not on me.

I straighten up, tightening the arm that I've put through his for support. Pathetic, I know, but I can't help it. This little move is all the powerplay I got.

Surprisingly, not only does Gianna look good tonight; even her dad looks energetic and fit—not easy to pull off given his age and all the stress of the last campaign months. I guess the white hair is courtesy of raising two kids into adulthood and then having latecomer Gianna. She'd suck the life out of anyone.

The new VP gives me a careful hug, which is difficult, because Sam still hasn't let go of me. Compared to Sam, DiBiaso doesn't smell half as nice. Some old man aftershave mixed with something strong like whiskey.

I'm not a big fan of hugging people, with the exception being Sam, who's allowed to hug me any time of the day. With DiBiaso, a handshake would have been fine with me.

And that's exactly what I get from Gianna—*after* she pulls

Sam into a hug that lasts way too long. "Good to see you, Sam," she purrs so low it's close to inaudible through the background noise.

"You too, Gianna," Sam replies a tad too friendly for my taste, and while I would like to look and see if he's giving her the same smile I got when I came in, her dad's hold on my shoulders keeps me from that.

"So good to see you here, Alix. Really. Gianna and I missed you at so many of these events." While DiBiaso actually looks like he means what he says, Gianna hasn't taken her eyes off Sam so far, or even acknowledged my presence besides that cool handshake. Maybe she doesn't like me because her dad does and always has, ever since the beginning of the campaign. She probably has spoiled-princess-syndrome, or something.

DiBiaso overacts a dramatic sigh. "What a day, isn't it? You must be so proud of your dad. He's done a phenomenal job winning the American people. You and I know how much time went into this."

My smile falters a bit. Oh, don't I know it.

"But: he has won in a landslide. We basically own Congress now."

Exactly what Dad said. "Yes, Mr. Vice President, you do own Congress now."

"Oh, come on, Alix, 'Mr. Vice President?' You can still call me James. We've known each other for a while now." He taps me playfully on the nose. I fight the urge to recoil. Seriously? What am I, five?

Next to Sam, Gianna suppresses a smile.

Before I can come up with an answer that isn't disrespectful, some older gentleman sticks his hand in DiBiaso's face. "Mr. Vice President, it's an honor. George McFeeble, one of your biggest supporters. If I may?"

And just like that, Mr. McFeeble has directed the VP's attention away from me and toward his smart phone: Selfie-time.

The music transitions to a faster beat, energizing the crowd around us. We're possibly the only ones not dancing, not that I could, but—

"May I have this dance?" Gianna curtsies in front of Sam, a bright sparkle in her eyes I know mine could never give off.

Sam chuckles, and I basically die right there and then.

"My Lady," he answers, working on a Southern drawl, "I appreciate the offer, but for tonight I'm taken." Casually, he lays his other hand over mine hooked through his arm, and it's all I can do to not twitch from the sudden jolt of electricity shooting through me.

Gianna smooths her dress down her hips, emphasizing her curves. "What a pity, Sam. You deserve to have some fun too, you know?" She gives me a cool glance replaced by a much warmer and cuter smile when she looks back at Sam. "Next time?"

Sam nods once. "Next time."

DiBiaso and his biggest supporter weave their way through the crowd toward the bar at the other end of the room. Gianna throws a glance after them before she takes two quick, dancing steps and wraps her arms around Sam's neck. "Don't be a stranger."

He hugs her back with one arm, smiling under his breath. "You know I won't."

To my astonishment, Gianna wraps me into an embrace too—only not a tight one with lots of body contact like with Sam, but one of those pseudo-embraces, with about a mile between us.

Still, it's close enough for her to whisper in my ear. "You better make the best out of your time here, Alix. I'd be so much better at this than you are, and we both know it." Before I have a chance to even register what that's supposed to mean, she pulls back with an exaggerated girlie kiss into the air next to my cheek. She throws her hair over her shoulder, turns on her heels, and is swallowed by the dancing audience a second later.

I stare after her, open mouthed. What in the name of...?

Sam's quiet laugh breaks the tension. "It's okay. You can let go, she's gone." He gives my hand a little nudge.

"Huh?" I blink twice. What?

Ever so gently, Sam loosens my fingers clenched around his forearm. "Still don't like her, do you?" he asks quietly.

I blush. How embarrassing. "No. Not really. Feeling's mutual though." I'm pretty sure she hates me. Or no, not true. I'm so far out of her league, she doesn't even take me seriously. That's more like it.

Sam huffs. "Well, guess we both have one DiBiaso we don't care for that much." He pats my loosened hand again, and while all I want is to enjoy the sensation of his skin on mine, his phrasing ruins that for me.

One DiBiaso we don't care for that much.

Him and the VP don't get along at all for whatever reason—but does that mean he does care for the *other* DiBiaso, I.e., for Gianna?

Please no. He can't be into Gianna. Not after he... Oh, whatever. He held my hand *once*, one day after dinner at our place a couple of months ago.

Once.

Sometimes I think I made it all up, but I have witnesses.

Mom saw it.

Dad saw it, right before they both jumped back into work mode.

Sam held my hand once and never again.

Yeah, that doesn't exactly grant me girlfriend rights. It's more like support by a friend than a romantic gesture. Just my luck.

I'm in the middle of a mental huge cringe when Sam tugs on my arm twice. "Your dad's going to arrive pretty soon. We should go backstage."

For our family's great entrance. The First Family of the United States.

Yay. So excited.

Sam leads me through the crowd and toward the little door hidden behind blue curtains and guarded by more Secret Service agents. One curt nod of Dimitri's is all the *open sesame* we need, and then we're in, quiet hallway and smell of sweaty socks included. And we're not a moment too early.

Down the hallway, maybe thirty meters away from us, the presidential entourage marches in our direction: an armada of black-suited agents, a red dot of color—Mom in her evening gown—and smack in the middle a head of short brown-grey hair that makes Dad look *distinguished*, as Linda says.

All that's missing is a slo-mo shot to establish their super-hero status.

Once they reach the area close to the stage entrance it's pretty crowded in this narrow hallway.

"Alix, Sam. Sorry it took us so long to make it here, we were running late since someone broke through the perimeter during our walk to the White House. Naked, by the way." My mother tucks a lock of hair back into her do.

Come again? I probably didn't hear that right. "Excuse me, what exactly happened?"

Of course I get ignored. Dad straightens his tie and holds out a hand to Sam. "Sam, good to see you," he says over my head. "Thanks for coming here tonight and taking care of Alix." They shake hands and Sam's face splits into a wide grin at the same time as mine falls.

Taking care of Alix. Rather *babysitting* Alix.

"Anytime, and my pleasure as always, Mr. President."

Dad laughs. "Well, that title will take some getting used to." He winks at Sam, not at me. "By the way, Sam, Alix, meet Floyd Waterhouse, he's the head of the Secret Service. Everybody else here you should know." He steps aside, and there he is. Droopy eyes in a sad beagle's face.

The head of PRICS.

My boss.

Although my left leg already hurts like someone tried to chop it off, I straighten.

First impressions count.

Completely unaware of Waterhouse's significance, Sam extends a hand, already the professional he's going to officially become one day. "Of course, Mr. President. Mr. Waterhouse, nice to meet you."

"Likewise." His voice is a growl more than anything else.

"Alix, Mr. Waterhouse also organized and vetted a new teacher for you." Impressive how Dad can school his face into a mask of neutrality. I'm sure he wasn't happy after he hand-selected that older gentleman with the lack of knowledge in current genetic engineering.

Borrowing from Sam's professionalism, I shake Waterhouse's hand. "Thank you, Mr. Waterhouse. I appreciate that." *Especially those green eyes.*

A muscle in Waterhouse's jaw ticks. "Of course. A genius to take care of a genius." His stare bores into me like a drill into plywood, and all of a sudden, I feel like I messed up already.

Fast, purposeful steps approach from the side. "Mr. President?" Everybody's attention shifts to the tall, bald-shaved African-American man in his late forties, who rocks his tuxedo just as well as his son.

"Oliver," Dad says with a sigh. "Can't it wait?"

"Only if you'd like to postpone running the office effectively." Oliver holds a clipboard and paper under my dad's nose, and while I know it annoys him, at least it frees me from the looks and attention I don't know how to handle.

Dad raises an eyebrow. "We can't do that electronically?"

Oliver shrugs. "Wet signature."

"Alright then. Pen?" Dad holds his hand open, waiting.

"Uhh…" Patting his pockets, the other man grimaces. "Somewhere. Somewhere. Just had it a minute ago…"

Dad sighs again and takes his own pen from his inside pocket, imported from France and super expensive. "Never mind." He signs and hands the clipboard back to Oliver, who also reaches for the pen.

Wrong move.

Dad snatches it from Oliver's grasp. "Mine, Oliver. Get your own." He shoves it back into his pocket with a pointed glance at his Chief of Staff. Like an old couple, those two. What Oliver lacks in terms of focus, Dad makes up times ten. They work well together though. Oliver's ADHD combined with my dad's OCD makes for a pretty intense work environment, but also for a very effective one.

"Excuse me, Mr. President?" Jenna Altman, our newly-minted press secretary, pushes through the crowd of staff and agents. "I've got Tim Ribbons here, from the L.A. Times. You promised him an exclusive about the first six hours as an inaugurated president?" She holds an older gentleman by the sleeve of his black suit, his other hand wrapped around the handle of an expensive looking camera with a huge lens on it.

Oliver steps aside and gives Sam a small smile, the only acknowledgment to the fact his son is part of this entourage.

Dad doesn't miss a beat. "Of course, Mr. Ribbons." He

shakes the reporter's hand, although I bet he doesn't remember anything about that exclusive Jenna mentioned. And he doesn't have to, that's what he's got *people* for these days.

"An honor to meet you, Mr. President, and congratulations." Tim Ribbons beams at my dad. "A couple of questions maybe? Before your speech? And then I'll catch up with you later again?"

"Of course." Dad is all business. To me, it's obvious how his shields go up as soon as a reporter is close by. He's still the open, friendly person they all know, but to me, he's like a computer with an anti-virus program running in the background: A tad slower with his responses as his brain filters the questions and comes up with the politically correct answers. Nerdy comparison, but true.

"Perfect, perfect. So, as president-elect, what have you been focusing on that you will continue now, even today on the day of your inauguration, if possible?"

Dad tugs on his jacket, straightening it. "Ah, Tim, you know my personal pet peeve, the Genetic Testing Bill. I'm glad we finally got it off the table. The American public is safer for it. Now I want to focus on gender-equal pay and support for families with disabilities—"

"Because of your daughter's condition?" Tim Ribbons cocks his head to the side, shooting me a sideways glance.

Oh dear.

Warmth creeps up my neck, bringing my cheeks to what most likely is a splotchy flaming red. *My condition.*

Sam stiffens the slightest bit, the muscles in his forearm tightening under my hand. Tim Ribbons is the only one in this group who doesn't realize the ginormity of the double-edged blooper he just landed. Oliver's expression turns blank as always with this topic.

The slight pause before Dad's answer isn't noticeable to

anyone besides his closest circle, us. "Mr. Ribbons." Dad's smile is friendly. Deadly, but friendly. "My daughter's condition, as you put it, has nothing to do with my plans to give support to those in need. As you might recall, it's been on my agenda for years."

Ever since he got more than a glimpse into Sam's family life without Oliver.

Tim Ribbons pivots: "Of course, Mr. President. But speaking of your daughter—Alix, I'm glad to hear you're staying at the White House. As the First Daughter, you're going to be in the center of our political heart—"

Like a police officer stopping traffic Dad holds up a hand. "Exactly. She'll take the time to recover and learn, but let's not focus on Alix."

"Why not, Mr. President?"

Because he's embarrassed by me.

"Because I think a young woman like her needs some time away from the spotlight."

Translation: *because he's embarrassed by me.* I dig my fingers into Sam's arm. Hard.

Tim Ribbons gives me a friendly smile. "But I assume Alix will be accompanying you on trips here and there? Nothing's more educational than traveling and—"

"Mr. Ribbons, Alix is far from a condition that would let her travel. She's too delicate at the mo—"

"Dad!" My mouth drops open. What the heck? "I'm not—"

A flicker of... *something* crosses Dad's perfect political mask. With one quick step, he's in front of me, both hands on my shoulders, head bent low and close, his back to the reporter. "Alix, you know how I meant it."

I shake my head. "No, I don't. I'm not weak. I can walk, and it'll get better. I—"

There's that odd flicker again. "Of course you're going to get better." His voice drops lower, barely audible over the muffled beats of the music from behind the wall. "But I want you to take it easy. Rest. Stay out of trouble. Focus on getting better, okay?" I get a smile, the one that comes with an extra serving of pity.

And I don't want it.

Dad used to give me wings. For the last year, all he's done is pluck them out, one feather at a time.

One more try. "Dad, I could travel with you. I'd love it." And, if I'm not mistaken, that's what PRICS wants me to do eventually anyway.

For one short, heavenly moment, a glimpse of the old Dad shines through: A spark of the same mischief and spirit that made us such a good team before—and then it's gone. He squares his shoulders some more to block off Ribbons and the others. It's only him and me now—well, and Sam, but to Dad he's family.

"Alix, I really don't think this is such a good idea. I—"

"Mr. President?" Jenna lays a gentle hand on his shoulder. "We should get you up on stage. You too, Alix."

Dad deflates. "Of course." He gives me one more sad smile. "We'll discuss it later, okay?"

Later. Of course.

Without as much as another look at me, he brushes past his security detail clearing the way up to the stage for him, taking two steps at once.

"Move, Alix." Mom presses her hand into my lower back. The three of us need to line up for Dad's speech.

"See you up there," Sam whispers and lets go of my arm. He's the lucky one, he can stay out of view with the rest of the staff. I'm the one who has to show her happy face to the American public.

"Alix." Mom's bringing out her nagging tone. Apparently,

she's more eager than me to get up there.

"On my way," I hiss over my shoulder and limp up the narrow steps. Gosh, seriously, it's not as if—

One moment of distraction, and my crutch glides off the edge of the step. Carried forward by inertia and my weight, I crash into the stairs with a deafening thud, my crutch performing its very own drum solo on the way down.

Before I can realize I've fallen, at least three pairs of hands are on me, yanking me back up to standing.

"Are you all right?"

"Alix—"

"Does anything hurt?"

Dimitri. Sam. Mom.

I shake my head. "N—no, I'm fine." My voice comes out in a mortified croak. Somebody gives me my crutch, but it might as well be a giant neon sign pointing to my humiliation. My face burns as I try to avoid eye contact with anyone and everyone. Stellar performance, Alix. I slipped and face-planted on my way up to the stage, nothing says *dignified First Daughter* like that, does it? At least I wasn't out in the spotlight yet. Small mercies.

"Alix!" That's Dad, flying down the stairs. "Alix! Are you okay? Does anything hurt?" He pats down my shoulders and arms as if he was the medical professional, not Mom.

I straighten and pull away. "Dad, I'm fine. I just slipped, no big deal."

"No big deal?" Dad's eyes widen. "You could've injured yourself even more." He looks over my hand. "Sam."

"Mr. President?"

Dad takes my hand and drops it on Sam's arm. "Alix won't be coming out onto the stage. Do me a favor, keep her out of view up there, keep her seated, and make sure she doesn't fall again."

"Yes, Mr. President."

Now wait a second! Anger surges through me. "Dad! I can come out. Nothing happened. I just slipped! No big deal!" Forgotten is my trepidation about facing the American public—it's different now. He can't drop me like that.

Dad's gaze hardens. "No discussion, Alix. I'm not taking any risks." And with that, he turns around and climbs the stairs to the stage with the energy of a lifetime.

He really means it. The First Family—without their daughter.

Sam lets go of a breath. "Come on, Alix." To nobody's surprise besides maybe my dad's, we make it up to the little area next to the stage without any problems. "You want to sit—"

"No." I shake my head.

"But your dad—"

My jaw tightens. "Don't. Care." I slipped. People do that all the time. No need to freak out, no need to treat me like I couldn't walk. Well, technically he's right, but still. Hurt cramps around my chest. The old Dad would've never done that. Cut me out like that. The old Dad would've proudly paraded his daughter. The new one… not so much.

Sam sighs. "Okay then."

A booming voice announces Dad over the PA.

"Ladies and Gentlemen, the President of the United States!"

Like a sports star who just won a championship, Dad greets the enthusiastic crowd with lots of waving and we-did-it-gestures before he takes the microphone for his speech. For now, my mom stays with Sam and me in the background, together with most of the essential staff.

The audience below us laughs and cheers, but I don't. I'm not listening. For one, I'm still mad. For another, I don't have to. All his speeches have taken apart the Genetic Testing Bill, all have emphasized America's strength and morale as a leader of the free world, and I've liked them all.

But he never asked my opinion. Probably didn't want to *exhaust me* too much.

The audience's applause comes so sudden I all but jerk. Off to the side, Matt Decker pumps a victorious fist, which means Dad didn't mess up his speech too much or added any of his own jokes. As his speechwriter, Matt hates that.

Dad turns around, waving in our direction. Our cue.

"You stay, Alix." Mom adjusts her dress, and then she struts out onto the stage and takes Dad's outstretched hand, just like we were told during the prep: The First Family supporting their husband and father.

Only that it's not the First Family.

It's the First Couple, their daughter forgotten in a corner behind them as they laugh and wave down into the crowd. I'm clinging to my crutch and Sam as if they were my lifelines.

My parents hug, laugh and wave, like they did a million times during fundraisers and campaigning. All without me.

My cheeks cramp up from the strength it takes to keep the corners of my mouth turned upwards. The gap between us isn't just palpable, it's visible. It's on display for the whole world to see.

The audience is still going crazy with applause, so my parents take position in the center of the stage, right where the Presidential Seal is embedded in the ground.

With a *click*, the lights on stage turn off and I'm left in the dark.

Metaphor for my life.

The only spotlight is directed on my parents on the dance floor. They get into position, and three seconds later, they sway and move to the music.

Like an uninvolved bystander, I watch the scene unfold in front of me, staring out of the dark and into the light down at the man who used to be my dad, but isn't anymore.

My parents dance, radiating happiness and success, while I—

Sam wraps his arm around my shoulders. "Come on, Alix." He gently steers me toward the treacherous stairs and helps me down, this time without too much embarrassment on my part. Maintaining his hold, he keeps his arm around my shoulders and gives them a reassuring squeeze. "Your dad's been under a lot of stress, Alix," he murmurs into my ear. "He's just worried about you. It's gonna get better."

Only I've lost hope.

Interesting how people can change. How *everything* can change in one little moment. My old life didn't know any limits. My new life does: they're as hard as a windshield before it shatters. That's something I learned they didn't teach in books.

At any given time, everything could be over, the candle snuffed out without as much as a warning.

Boom. You're gone.

I was so naïve before. I felt safe.

As if. *Nothing* is safe, nothing and nobody. Never.

I press my jaws together so hard my molars make a cracking sound.

Safety is such a finicky little thing. In theory, we're all safe here in America. Yeah, in theory.

Theoretically, my dad should have picked me up that day. He didn't, so one of the town cars came.

Theoretically, we should have taken the route Dad and I always took. Tons of traffic, so we detoured.

Theoretically, the seatbelt should have held, and yet it didn't.

That's when it started. That's when the kink in Dad's and my relationship started. Not later, with the Harvard-debacle, but when he sat at my bedside, stone-faced, staring at the cast and contraptions that held my body together. When I wasn't perfect anymore.

"Alix," Sam whispers and squeezes my shoulders once more. I don't think he knows what this little gesture means.

Or, maybe he does.

Sam knows everything. *Everything.* He was there from moment zero, when I thought my life would end. He was the one talking to me and keeping me awake after the accident, telling me all would be fine, although I could feel very well that wouldn't be the case. He was the one holding my hand in the ambulance when nobody else was there, and later, he was the one who handed me the tissues when Dad hadn't checked in with me in over a week and they told me I'd never walk independently again.

Sam knows all the dirty details. Sam saw all the tears.

"Alix," he repeats. "It's gonna get better. I believe it with all my heart."

Any response I might've had to his probably misplaced optimism drowns in even more applause. The Secret Service agents ready themselves to have my parents leave the room: off they go to the next Inauguration Ball. Lots of men in dark suits with earpieces clear a path for them, every single one of them looking serious, like they mean business.

I'm now a part of that world: Secret Service, security, espionage.

Supporting the President—the father—who has lost his faith in me.

I wrap my hand around the crutch with so much force, my knuckles turn white.

If I had a button to switch off all the anger, frustration, and boy, that stupid self-pity, I'd push that button so hard it might break.

Alas, I don't have that.

What I do have, and what I intend to use, is hope.

I'm going to walk again.

I'm going to walk again, and I will get over this bump in the road of my life and go to Harvard, on my own. Dad *will* see me for myself again.

He will.

The cheering and noise around me dies down to a degree, which is exactly when I snap out of my self-motivational talk only to realize… my parents have left.

Without saying goodbye.

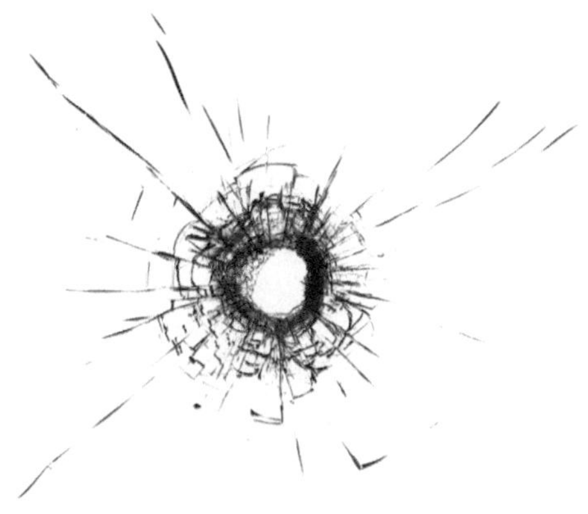

CHAPTER FOUR

Too Much, Too Soon

"Honey, are you sure you don't want me to drop you off at class?" It's the twentieth time Mom asks me the same question, and the answer is still the same.

I suppress a sigh and annoyed eye roll. "Mom, it's fine, seriously. Dimitri can push the wheelie if I get tired, and we're taking the elevator." I shove the eggs and bacon from left to right on my plate. My stomach growls, demanding to be fed, but I ignore it. I've probably lost what, ten pounds since the accident? Happens.

If I still had an appetite, I'd love living in the White House on the other hand: We have our own chef, which means awesome breakfasts and dinners, although I could never complain about Linda's cooking.

Overall, while I've only been here a couple of days, I've discovered that life in the White House is about the same as at home, minus the privacy. Two nights ago, a nightmare woke me up screaming, and who suddenly stood inside my room?

Yup, Dimitri: suit jacket open, right hand under his left armpit, ready to draw his gun.

Needless to say, I snapped my mouth shut as quickly as I could, but I'm pretty sure the damage to my reputation was already done. Thank you, Mom and Dad, for putting me in the room farthest away from you. In normal families, the *parents* actually check on their PTSD'ed screaming daughter—not the bodyguard.

Across the table, Mom sighs, murmuring to herself. "That's the ten o'clock, then lunch with the Garrison Foundation, then discussion of school health at three. Oh, where's that… got it." She tugs a paper down into her slim briefcase before she snaps it shut and walks around the table.

"Bye, sweetie. Have fun. Get smart. Well, get smarter." She gives me a quick kiss on the forehead and off she goes, the heels of her shoes not making a sound on the fluffy carpet. And that would be what a busy First Lady looks like.

If she knew what I was up to today, she'd not let me leave her sight.

Spinal surgery. Spy training.

Actually, no. She'd probably quiz Donckers on the chip and insist on watching the procedure.

I suck in my lower lip.

Dad on the other hand… tough to say. The old Dad would've given me thumbs-up and told me I'll be great, as long as I put my mind to it and stayed safe. The new Dad would echo the exact same thoughts I had when Donckers offered me the job: Not spy material.

Oh, wait: the new Dad would never know, because we never get to see each other. How many times did our paths cross since the inauguration? Three? Four? Can't be more than five, max.

Something else always had priority: new staff that needed welcoming, a crisis somewhere in Eastern Europe, or insert-problem-of-the-day here. All good reasons, but somehow… somehow I can't shake the feeling he doesn't *want* to see me.

And that thought hurts.

I drop my fork onto my plate. Whom am I kidding? I won't eat anyway.

And before I fall back into the dark chasm of self-pity and sadness, I push my chair back and fish for my crutches. Whatever. Today is the first day of my new life.

Learn. Get better. Move on to bigger and better things and become somebody Dad can be proud of again.

Yeah, Alix. Stop embracing your defeatist mindset and toughen up. It's not about how many times you fall, but about how many times you get up. Right?

Right.

I wish it wasn't easier said than done.

Dimitri waits for me in front of the residence, his designated station while I'm inside. I fall into the wheelie while he clicks the crutches into their holder. So far, he hasn't said a thing about my nightmare. No smirk, no comment, no funny glance. Instead, he pushes me to the elevator as my silent, non-judgmental companion.

We make it downstairs and down the hallway to a room adjacent to the official West Wing, marked "Classroom 1."

After a crisp knock, Dimitri opens the door for me to roll through before he follows into a moderately small classroom, maybe the size of my new bedroom here. The space somehow manages to be both cozy and intimidating—like somebody compressed an entire science department into one room. A sleek whiteboard on wheels stands sentinel at the far end, partially obscuring a massive world map dominating the wall where my room has its ornamental fireplace. The right side houses everything I hold dear in my life, the floor-to-ceiling shelves crammed with everything science, from beakers to state-of-the-art microscopes. My inner nerd cheers at the sight of a cabinet marked with a bright red sticker that screams "DANGER! CHEMICALS!" in all caps. A solitary student desk sits toward the left, positioned to catch both the morning light streaming through tall windows and the view of the beautiful White House Gardens beyond the terrace doors.

"You must be Alix. Welcome, I'm Jason Miller, your teacher. Come on in."

Uhh…?

There, atop a bigger desk in front of my smaller one, sits Ian Donckers. Or—well, yeah, that's definitely him, even with this new look that makes my brain short-circuit for a moment. His previously short dark blond hair is now dyed an intense black, which somehow makes his bright green eyes even more striking. He's also traded in his clean-shaven face for a goatee. For whatever reason it doesn't make him look pretentious, just the opposite. He rocks it. To top it off, gone is the casual Abercrombie sweater, replaced by a very well-fitting tailored black suit. The absence of a tie and the one undone top button reveal just enough skin to be distracting, and I hate that I notice these details. None of them are important.

But boy, do they kick my heart into a weird somersault-mode.

Whoa. Easy there, tiger. It's, like, two square centimeters of skin. Relax.

Donckers gives me the hint of a smile and lift of one eyebrow, and I could swear that wink acts as a catalyst to some kind of chemical reaction inside my body, or else I wouldn't know how to explain this strange sensation shooting through my stomach—

Aaand my cheeks just turned supernova.

Dimitri closes the door behind us. The second the outside world of the White House is shut out, Donckers drops his pretense and waves at me.

"Hey, Alix. Good to see you again. Sorry about this, but it's part of my alias while we're working together. So you're calling me…?" He wiggles his brows expectantly.

The supernova decides my face is not enough and takes over my whole body. "Uhh…"

Dang it. Caught staring instead of paying attention. Fantastic start. I busy myself with sliding out of the wheelchair and behind my desk as if it was the most difficult task in the world.

Dimitri takes position by the door, legs spread in a wide stance, arms crossed behind his back. Everybody is so professional. Besides me, that is. *The President's Daughter? That's the odd-ball who makes googly eyes at her teacher.*

I roll my eyes at myself, then sigh and decide to fake it until I make it. Pseudo-professionalism, here I come, because I won't give in to embarrassment. "Sorry. Call it nerves or catching me off-guard." There. I sold that well. *So* professional!

Donckers closes his book. "Fair enough. And not to be overly critical or nagging from the get-go, but consider this your first lesson: listen. Always. You don't need to understand everything you hear, you just need to listen and memorize. Little tidbits of information can prove invaluable when added on to a bigger pile of information, and you'll only find out its true worth then. In our line of work nothing can be dismissed and everything is important. You need to remember names, facts, situations, and pick up on abnormalities in a heartbeat. That's now all going to be part of your job. Memorizing is a muscle that needs to be flexed. Want to try it again?" He gives me a smile so open and encouraging, so expectant and warm, I snap my eyes closed.

It's that or *literally* turning supernova.

Okay. Okay. I picture rolling into the classroom again. *"Welcome,"* he said, *"Jason Smith"* no, no—something common, but no *th* in it. Jason Miller—I got it! I blow on my cuticles, faking nonchalance. "You're Jason Miller, my new teacher. Nice to meet you, Mr. Miller." Funny how the supernova tunes it down once my brain is working. It's not quite so hot in here anymore.

Donckers slow claps. "There you go. Nicely done. You're our ears and eyes, so make good use of the tools you have."

He scoots back farther onto his desk and grabs a little thermos. The scent wafting over is heavenly, sweet and spicy, and just right. Better than food.

Donckers follows my gaze to his thermos. Wordlessly, he bends sideways, pulls a second cup out of a drawer in his desk, fills it from his thermos, and hands it over to me.

"Chai?"

"Love to." I lean forward and take the cup out of his hands. For a short moment, our fingers connect, like when he handed me the Cherry Coke on the day we met. It's the softest brush of skin over skin and nothing really worth mentioning, but still a tiny surge shoots through my hand and settles in the center of my stomach, bringing something to a flutter.

Which is why I only hear part of his last sentence. I curse under my breath. "Excuse me, Mr. Donckers, would you repeat that please?" Embarrassing, *again*. Blanking out—twice—is so not me. I look down into the tea as if I wanted to read a fortune out of it.

"No 'Mr. Donckers,' Alix. Just call me Ian, okay? The

teacher-job is just an alibi. We're a team. If other people are around, stick to Mr. Miller, or Jason, but otherwise Ian it is."

"Ian it is," I say, trying out the name rolling off my tongue. It fits him.

"Yup, that's me." He fake-salutes. "Now, before I get you down to the PRICS Lair to get the chip implanted we should—"

A screeching, ear-bursting sound blasts through the room, so loud I jerk and hit myself in the face with the back of my hands.

"What the—" Ian slides down behind his desk in one smooth motion, pressing a button on a keychain dangling from his belt. The same second, the lights dim and the windows darken on their own, but not only that: noise from the hallway outside the closed door has become muffled, almost muted. The poster of the human nervous system framed next to the door turns into a screen, showing exactly what's going on in the hallway in front of our classroom. The whiteboard up front goes through the same transformation and turns into a huge screen. Yikes. I will never ever dare put a marker to that board.

A message scrolls over the screen, written in bright red letters and blinking for emphasis. *"Priority One Communication. Priority One Communication. Priority One Communication."*

My eyes dart from the tinted windows to Ian and back to the screen. "What's going on?" I squeak. Obviously something is happening, but—

"Waterhouse." It sounds more like a curse than anything else.

Another press of a button, and the sad beagle face is right in front of me, projected onto the former whiteboard.

"Agent Donckers. Agent Forrester." Waterhouse nods. "We have a situation."

Agent Forrester.

"What's going on, sir?" Despite his colloquial tone, Ian stands ramrod straight.

Waterhouse sighs. "In about fifteen minutes, the President is walking into the Green Room to welcome a group of young entrepreneurs to the White House. One of them is Josiah Lucas." The bags under Waterhouse's pale eyes twitch once.

Ian balls a fist. "Crap," he curses under his breath, sucking in his lower lip. "How could we grant him visitation rights? The CEO of MetaGeneSolutions, seriously?"

MetaGeneSolutions? Why does that ring a bell?

Waterhouse scoots closer to the camera. "Believe me, Agent, when he applied for the Entrepreneur-Reception last term, he wasn't even on our radar." Waterhouse pinches the bridge of his nose. "Obviously that has changed in recent history, especially with the President holding his own against the Genetic Testing Bill."

Whoa. Now I know. Josiah Lucas, the CEO of the one company that manufactures the genetic screening test needed for that awful bill Dad hates with all his soul.

A portrait photo of a man who's been in the news almost more often than Dad over the last couple of months replaces Waterhouse's image: mid-forties, sleek, black hair gelled back into an Elvis-do, a friendly smile and dimples. Three seconds later, the image is gone, and Waterhouse back.

Ugh. Not an improvement.

His eyes narrow to slits. "The President, as a man of his word, insists on keeping up the previous President's promise and greeting the group in the Green Room, but that's a disaster in the making. Lucas brought a photographer. Any picture of the President with him even in the same frame—"

"Is going to make the President look like he played the American people by denouncing the Genetic Testing Bill during the election, only to now go back on his word after he won the election." Ian works a hand through his hair. "Not good."

"Not good at all. We can't withdraw the invitation only for Lucas, or it will look like we pick and choose the freedom to visit the White House depending on somebody's political beliefs. I don't think I need to mention the repercussions this will cause President Forrester."

Repercussions? Wait, what?

Ian paces in front of the screen, a mesmerizing back and forth of exactly three steps left, then three steps back. "Is the President aware that Lucas is here?"

"Yes."

"Wait a second." I lean over my desk. "Are you sure?" Because I'm sure that Dad is not a fan of anything about the Genetic Testing Bill, least of all the company that started it all.

Waterhouse's cool gaze hits me like an ice-bucket-challenge in the face.

"Yes, Agent Forrester. I'm very sure. Your father won't back down because of one inconvenient guest, and that's a quote."

Yeah, sounds like my dad all right. Heat creeps into my cheeks as I sink lower into my seat again. "Okay," I peep one octave higher than my normal voice. "Just checking."

Waterhouse's jaw tightens. "A low-blow like that this early in the term... The President's not going to recover from it. Luckily for us, his schedule is tight. The Green Room will happen during a ten-minute window before he's meeting the Minister of Defense back in the Oval Office. Agent Donckers, Alix must get Lucas out of the Green Room for exactly those ten minutes. She has to keep him away from her father, or else the President can kiss public support good-bye for the remainder of his first and then most likely last term. A puppet without power."

"What?" Ian's head whips up. "That's impossible. This isn't part of Alix's job description, and she hasn't even been on duty for ten minutes—"

"Do I look like I care about that?" Waterhouse's not-pretty face turns into a snarl. "You wanted this job. You begged for it. Now make it work. Agent Forrester's a PRICS-Agent and she's intelligent from what I hear, or else I wouldn't have needed to hire your smart ass to teach hers! Make. It. Work."

Oh my God. Me? They need me? I don't even know what to do. I don't have a clue about anything, not what I'm allowed to do, nor what I should be doing, nor hell, *freakin' anything*!

Ian stops pacing and steps closer to the screen. "In all fairness, sir, without any introduction this is a step too big for day one—"

The glare turns icy, dropping the temperature in the room by several degrees. "Are you saying you are unable to comply with a direct order, Agent?"

Oh, dear.

Ian suppresses a wince and pulls his shoulders back. "No, sir. I was merely attempting to—"

"Good then." Waterhouse checks his wrist. "Lucas is passing through the White House metal detectors as we speak and will be in the Green Room together with his group in less than five minutes. You'd better think of something, Agent. If I don't have confirmation of him leaving the White House within fifteen minutes from now, your promotion is going to be very short lived."

If I ever heard a threat, this is it.

Same goes for Ian. "Yes, sir. We'll do our best." He clenches his teeth.

"You better. Oh, and, Agent Donckers, before I forget it. You stay out of this one. It's a high media event, and I can't have your picture float through newspapers all the way to Little Springs. Agent Forrester is on her own."

Ian flinches while Waterhouse types something off-screen, his image flashing once before it's replaced by the Seal of the Secret

Service.

Silence.

That… didn't just happen.

My mind spins in circles, unable to come up with something that makes sense. Waterhouse can't be putting Dad's political life in my hands and my hands alone, can he?

Ian is frozen in front of the white board-turned-screen, chewing on his lower lip. Without looking, he finds the keychain dangling from his belt and presses a button. Within two or three seconds, the screen turns back into a whiteboard, the windows lighten up, and the monitor next to the door morphs back into a poster. Even the noise from the hallway, all the chatter and steps, fills the air again.

Ian still hasn't moved.

"Uhh, Ian?" I don't feel well. At all.

His shoulders heave up and down once before he spins around on his heels. "Alix, into your wheelchair."

"My wheel—"

"Now!"

He rolls my pink wheelie around and locks it in place. Before I know it, my crutches are clicked into the holders and Ian wraps his hands around both of mine, pulling me up to standing. I squeal once and, in an attempt to cover for the sudden change in balance, stumble forward onto my good leg—and directly into Ian's chest.

Whoops.

For a moment, neither of us moves.

My heart's hammering against my chest, or it could be his, I couldn't tell.

Ian's green gaze finds and locks with mine.

It feels pretty warm in here, like, for real.

His grip on my hands is strong and soft at the same time, and the skin on the back of his hands way smoother than mine.

Of course, *my* hands start sweating the second I think about his touch on me.

Keeping me close to his body, he turns until the back of my knees hit the seat of my wheelie and buckle, but even after my butt hits the cushion, he won't let go of my hands. Time stretches into an eternity, yet it doesn't last long enough.

"Ian." Dimitri's deep baritone breaks the spell. "T-minus nine minutes if you want to keep your job."

Ian blinks twice. "Right. *Right.*" He drops my hand and turns the wheelie by its handlebars. "Time to protect our president from a ruined reputation. We'll come up with… well, *something* on the way."

He spins me around and pushes me toward the door Dimitri opens for us.

My chest tightens. The room starts to shrink, the walls creeping closer with each heartbeat. I can't do this. How am I supposed to keep Lucas from meeting Dad? I have no freakin' clue how to to do that!

I force air into my lungs—and pick up on the most unnecessary detail given that I'm *this* close to a panic attack: Spring soap.

Ian smelled like spring soap.

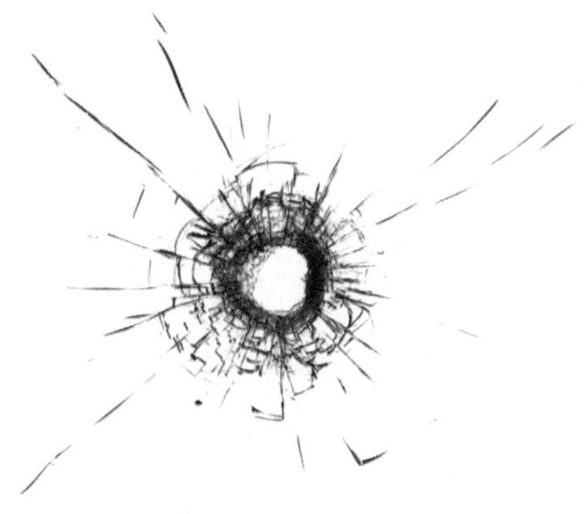

CHAPTER FIVE

Diversion

Ian wheels me through the hallways of the White House as if we had all the time in the world. Nobody would assume we're in a hurry, unless they looked closely. Then they'd see the small, crisp maneuvers Ian makes to guide us smoothly through oncoming human traffic, or the slight increase in speed to make sure we don't get stuck behind somebody.

Acid roils inside my stomach. I'm not good at improvising. *Get Lucas out of that room*, Waterhouse said—well, duh, but how? I can't very well walk up to him and ask him to leave with me.

Ian evades a flock of interns. It's not much farther to the Green Room, and—

"Alix, listen," Ian whispers so close to my ear I jump from the warmth of his breath against my skin. "Your best tactic is to come up with a convincing lie when you see Lucas, something like—"

My stomachs cramps up. "I'm not good at lying," I bite out over my shoulder, trying to keep my voice down and my face turned forward, because if I looked left, there wouldn't be an inch between Ian's and my face.

"You're kidding me," Ian shout-whispers. "You're a teenager. It's in your job description!"

"Then I probably didn't get a copy of that," I hiss at him and cross my arms in front of my chest. Sorry, but I turn tomato and get nervous when I'm lying. Sue me.

Ian chuckles, a sound so warm and deep it brings goosebumps to my skin. "Okay, then don't lie."

"Huh? But how am I supposed to—"

"Tell him you're a scientist yourself. Your reputation precedes you. People know that about you. Ask him questions, get him to talk, guide him out of the room. Stick to the truth as much as possible and distract people. Have a cover story."

Oh.

A mind exercise.

I can do that.

A weight is lifted off my shoulders. I can talk science all day long, Josiah Lucas or not. But wait: "What if he doesn't want to talk to me?" Humoring a teenager versus meeting the President— tough choice. *Not.*

"Lay it on thick. If he doesn't want to talk to you, make your disappointment obvious. There's press there, not just his photographer. If he doesn't want a negative story, he'll talk to the President's daughter." Ian stops in front of the last corner before the Green Room. "You gonna be okay?"

I wouldn't call it being okay. "Chances are, I can distract him and get him out of there." Get him talking about genetic splicing methods, ask him to draw up an explanation for me, take him to the East Room next door and pretend I'm looking for paper and a pen, while Dad enters the Green Room: Disaster averted.

Not a great plan, but hopefully one I can execute. After all,

I'm the President's daughter, not just any teen. That should put a bit more weight behind my request to talk to him. Right?

Ian squeezes my shoulder once. "Exactly, distraction. That's the spirit. Sorry we don't have more time, this isn't ideal. Anyway, good luck, Alix. You can do this." And *poof* he's gone.

I'm on my own.

Okay then. Time to complete this mission, Agent Forrester.

I give my wheels a good push maneuvering around the corner, when a large body bumps into me. Their foot gets stuck behind my left wheel and spins me around, the force of the pull precariously tipping me to the right.

"Ugh," I grunt, throwing my weight in the other direction to avoid sprawling to the ground.

"Oh, crap," curses the guy, folders spilling out of his arms and hitting the floor with a splat, papers all over the place.

Before I have a chance to get my wheelie back under control, Ian is there, taming the wild beast I'm sitting in into submission.

I swallow dry. "Th-thanks." Complete a mission? I can't even drive around a corner alone. *Not spy-material.*

"Man, Alix, so sorry. Didn't see you there." The guy who ran into me—Yoshi Nagakawa, Dad's Deputy Chief of Staff—rubs his neck and grimaces. "You all right? Is your leg hurting? Can you move it?" Yoshi turns red. "I mean, is it worse than before? Seriously, so sorry."

Sigh. Talk about awkward. "No worries, Yoshi. It's all right." *If I can please get going now.* I throw a quick glance toward the Green Room. Doors are open. A couple of people there. Relaxed atmosphere. Good. That means Dad isn't there yet.

Ian must've seen my quick check. "Let me help you." He bends down and collects at least half of the scattered papers in one scoop, giving them to Yoshi, who smacks his forehead with the other hand.

"Man, where are my manners? Thank you—you're Alix's teacher, right? Yoshi Nagakawa."

"Jason Miller. Yes, Alix's teacher. Did we get everything there?" He nods at the papers crumbled in Yoshi's hands, the unspoken implication to move on in the air.

Yoshi nods, sorting them quickly and listing them off. "Duty Roster, New Employees. Got them. Where's the... ah, Genetic Testing—"

Ugh. Gone is the urgency to leave. Those three words, a knife to Dad's heart, and therefore to mine too. "Not again. Please tell me it's still off the table." Or else Dad's going to be in an even worse mood during dinner, and it's already apocalyptic. Bad enough, he's about to meet the MetaGeneSolutions-CEO—if I can't prevent it, that is.

Yoshi flinches. "Yeah, wish I could. The Republicans made a few minor changes and re-introduced it. This thing bounces back to us like a stupid rubber ball, only now it comes with a rider to make it more palatable for us: Financing for families with handicapped dependents."

Ouch. That's the carrot they're dangling in front of Dad's nose.

Yoshi rolls his eyes. "It's not as if we hadn't tried getting that kind of support through Congress for years, and now of all times we're about to get it—*if* we agree to the Genetic Testing Bill."

"And I totally believe you should, just to get that rider," a female voice comes from behind me, causing my stomach to cramp.

I close my eyes. Just what's been missing to make my day. Seriously, is everything and everybody against me today? Fate, hello? Some support would be nice.

"Ah, Gianna," Yoshi says, way friendlier and much more patiently than I ever would, "you think so?"

"Of course." She nods, the blond curls bobbing around her head. "You won't be able to stop the Genetic Testing Bill forever. It's the future. Plus, this way at least you get the rider." She shrugs. "But then, what do I know." Brushing a strand of hair out of her face, she turns toward Ian, her bright blue eyes kicking up a notch in their intensity.

Somebody laughs out loud inside the Green Room.

Shoot. I need to get going, and I have way too many balls in the air here with Yoshi and now too-good-for-me Gianna, who of course is oblivious to my discomfort—or she's bathing in it. Quite possible. My awkwardness serves as her fuel, usually.

"Oh, hello." She beams at Ian. "I don't believe we've met before. Gianna DiBiaso, the Vice President's daughter." She holds out her hand and I'm sure she's pushing her chest out even more than before, for emphasis.

Aww, come on, there's no way anybody—

"Delighted," Ian says with a mischievous cock of his eyebrow, "Jason Miller, Alix's teacher."

"A pleasure," Gianna purrs.

"All mine," Ian replies, and I'm about to puke before something inside of me turns cold and ugly.

I grip the wheels so hard my knuckles turn white. "Real smart, Gianna. Obviously, you haven't thought about the ramifications of the Genetic Testing Bill." Gosh, why do I even bother? Shutting up might make her leave quicker, but then... *gah*, I can't let this one go.

Gianna cocks her head at me. "What?"

I shrug, doing my best to sit straight. "Mandatory gene screening at birth. No big deal if it's about preventing illness, I'm all for it. Very big deal if your genome is used to predict if you have a risk or tendency to become violent. Anti-social. *Boom*— you're labeled a risk to society and you haven't even had the chance for an undisturbed development. So—"

"This Bill will make America safer—"

"Or it will ruin the lives of hundreds of thousands who are innocent, yet found guilty at birth!" I'm completely on Dad's side with this bill. I've got his back, even though I can't say he has mine at the moment.

Gianna glares at me. "Yeah? We can arrest them right there, before anything happens. If it's for the country's safety, who cares?"

My mouth drops open. "Do you even hear yourself? You sure you read the bill? And understood it? Because—"

"You can bet—"

Somebody pushes past us: *White dress shirt, white suit, black tie, black hair gelled back.* "Excuse me, please."

Josiah Lucas.

He enters the Green Room down the hallway without a second look at any of us.

Oh, shoot.

My eyes dart back and forth from him to Gianna.

Time to face the battle.

Ian squeezes my shoulder once—for everybody else the signal to calm down with Gianna, for me the signal to get going, or I can add screwing up Dad's political career to my CV.

"Ladies." Yoshi is right in-between Gianna and me, both hands outstretched toward us as if he was the referee in a boxing match. "Let Congress handle the verbal battling." He rubs his palms together. "Anyway, gotta get going. Uhh, sorry again, Alix. Nice meeting you, Jason. Gianna."

Ian nods a short acknowledgement and Yoshi scurries off, not a second too early.

Behind us, Dimitri clears his throat.

"Right," Ian says, "Alix, you finish your history assignment and I'll meet you in the classroom. Hurry up, we've wasted enough time."

No kidding.

"I'm on it." I *think.*

Gianna places a hand on Ian's forearm as he turns to leave. "I'll come with you. Same direction. By the way, I'm probably going to join you in class one of these days. My private teacher is leaving for a conference."

If I hadn't rolled in the opposite direction already, I'd flatten her toes with the wheelie and all the weight I carry, real and emotional.

To Ian's credit, he doesn't even flinch. Instead, he keeps on walking, forcing Gianna to follow him—because his hand is covering hers on his arm. "Well, I can talk to Marcus and see where you're at in your studies. Why don't you tell me—"

He leads Gianna around a corner and out of sight, although not out of mind. Never out of mind, I'd be stupid if I let her—

Another loud burst of laughter inside the Green Room.

Priorities, Alix.

I force all thoughts about Ian's hand on Gianna's out of my head and push my wheelie toward the Green Room.

Showtime.

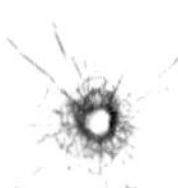

The problem with improvisation is that it's tackling an unknown with too many variables to be predictable. Not my thing. There's a reason I prefer science, and it's not the bubble-volcano experiment from first grade. And it's fair enough to say that if I'd ever been as insufficiently prepped for a quiz as I am for this mission, I wouldn't be taking advanced college classes at my age.

With one last push to my wheels, I enter the Green Room.

For a moment, all eyes are on me—or at least that's what it feels like. Could be because people know I'm the President's daughter, or because I'm in a wheelchair. Either would do it.

Biting down so hard my jaw hurts, I ignore the stares, and pretend I have every right to be here. Where's Lucas?

Ahh, close to the windows, sipping on a glass of OJ and easy to spot despite the maybe twenty or twenty-five other people in the room. While some guests admire the paintings hung on the green walls or check out the expensive plates in the heavy wood-lined vitrines, most stand around in their best attire, holding glasses of various liquids and chatting. So does Lucas, only he has cornered one of the Secret Service agents—a stern-faced tall man, whose nose, bent at an odd angle that speaks of an old break, twitches with barely concealed impatience. Given that all agents are heavily trained in hand-to hand combat I can't help but wonder about whoever managed to leave that permanent mark on his face. The agent clearly isn't thrilled about the company. Looking at him, if I were Lucas, I'd take the hint and leave him in peace.

I keep on rolling forward, making sure my wheels don't get caught on the thick carpet in the middle of the room. Happened the first time I was here, during my getting-to-know-the-White-House-tour before we moved in.

People make room for me without as much as acknowledging me, but at least they don't ask me what I'm doing here either.

Yeah, you don't ask that to the President's daughter. Or to somebody in a wheelchair.

Eventually, I stop in front of the fireplace close to the window and Lucas, but face the painting hung above the mantelpiece, pretending to study it.

Commence alibi.

My heart's beating at an unhealthy frequency of one-sixty

beats per minute, and it shows, I'm sure.

Deer caught in headlight?

Hi, it's me!

I take a deep breath.

Okay.

Okay.

I can do this.

Ask him about genetic splicing; ask him about genetic splicing…

Behind me, Lucas says to the agent, "No, it's easy. Takes less than thirty seconds to work once ingested."

"Eaten?" asks the agent, skeptical.

"Doesn't matter. Dilute it, sprinkle it, that's the beauty of it." He laughs. "Manufactured in one of our East-European daughter companies by the way. For medical purposes."

Yes! That's my in! Medical stuff!

Oliver enters the Green Room from the Treaty Room, scanning the crowd. Crap. My countdown has been officially initiated. If he sees me…

Initiate meeting. I spin my wheelchair around. "Oh, you must be—"

Either Lucas has moved closer or I've spun too far toward the right, but the footrest of my wheelie catches him in the shin. Like I got him with a taser, he jerks back. The juice in his glass sloshes around once… twice… and spills over onto his white dress shirt and suit, staining them bright yellow.

"What the—!" Lucas stares down at his shirt, and so do I, mouth open.

Oh, shoot.

That's not what I planned.

"I'm so sorry, I didn't think—"

"Obviously," he snarls, handing the half-emptied glass to the less than thrilled Secret Service agent.

My face burns. "My apologies. I just heard you talk about medical stuff, and… you're Josiah Lucas, right?" *Adding excited grin now*, probably the fakest I've ever done. "I've always wanted to ask you about—"

Lucas' jaw tightens. "Excuse me, but I don't have the time right now." He starts wiping down his shirt with a cloth hankie he produces from his pocket together with a small pillbox he pushes into the agent's hands. "Hold that."

The agent wrinkles his crooked nose. Looks like we're both equally unhappy about the situation.

Okay.

I can still save this.

"If you'd like me to, I can show you the bathroom. It's for employees only, but—"

"I'm fine," he grumbles.

Ouch.

Across the room, Oliver shakes hands, but cranes his neck at the commotion here in the back, the one I'm causing.

One more try.

"No, seriously, I'm so sorry. Let me get you there so you can clean up." *And so that you're out of Dad's hair.*

"I said I'm fine!" The stain on his shirt isn't going anywhere.

"But with that shirt… And the President will be here any minute."

"Exactly. And that's why I'm not leaving. If you'd excuse me?" He shoots me a glance that's meant to kill before he strides past, buttoning his jacket closed to hide the stain.

Oh, shoot.

Crap, crap, crap.

A drop of sweat runs down my neck, making me shiver.

Not good. Not good at all.

I totally screwed that up. What am I supposed to do now?

Lucas is still in here and it can't be much longer.

So much for having Dad's back. I—

Wait.

Waterhouse said to get Lucas out of the Green Room, but there's another way to keep them apart: Don't let Dad enter the Green Room.

A heat wave runs through my veins, followed by another cold shiver.

It's not what I would have chosen, but I guess the choice was just taken from me.

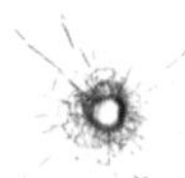

Never have I wheeled through a room this fast before, carpets and other obstacles be damned. When I first I entered the room, I pretended I had every right to be here, now it's a much tougher job to sell after that embarrassing scene with Lucas.

My only hope is nobody will mention it to Dad.

I roll past a handful of seriously overdressed people, and unfortunately also past Lucas again—who's been cornered by Oliver. It won't take me much longer than ten seconds to be out of Oliver's periphery, but those ten seconds are pure torture. I prefer to keep that tough-as-steel-look aimed at Lucas, not me.

"Mr. Lucas."

"Mr. Brooks."

No love lost there.

My right wheel catches against the corner of a coffee table. Stupid non-ADA-compliant furniture, stupid—

One quick glance up to Oliver while I wiggle back and forth to free myself. Good. He's not bothered with me. Lucas shakes hands with him and gives him a little gift box.

My wheel is freed, and I shoot straight ahead.

"Full signature, please, if you don't—"

And *zoom*, I'm past Oliver and out of the immediate danger zone. Wouldn't be surprised if I left skid marks on the floor as I turn left into the hallway toward the State Dining Room. I can cut through there and should be able to catch Dad if he's on his way from the West Wing. He'd always take the West Colonnade. He wouldn't walk indoors if he had the choice.

Luckily for me, Secret Service agents are stationed in front of every door—the ones leading into the State Dining Room and out of the State Dining Room. Talk about wheelchair accessibility: Agents opening the doors for me will do the trick.

As soon as I'm out on the Colonnade, I see them: Dad, two Secret Service agents, and Jenna Altman, the Press Secretary.

And: Sam.

My heart skips a little beat for a different reason than performance anxiety.

One quick glance to my watch: Dad's meeting starts in eight minutes. I'm not a second too early.

I need eight minutes of his time, or at least seven. Knowing him, he wouldn't want to be late to the Minister of Defense, so he'd skip the Green Room and go right back to the West Wing.

A dry swallow works itself down my throat. Why is this so hard?

Ten meters in front of me, Dad cocks his head to the side, his eyebrows diving down into a disapproving V.

That's why it's so hard.

Still, I keep on rolling forward until I meet Dad and his entourage in the middle of the Colonnade, large office windows to my right, white columns to my left. Behind them, birds tweet in the gardens, giving the illusion of peace which bursts into a thousand splinters the moment Dad scowls at me.

"Alix."

Commence next fake smile, not a tad better than the last. "Hey, Dad. Uhh, can I have a moment? Please?" I add.

Dad opens his mouth, most likely to tell me no, but Sam has pulled Whittaker to the side already, and the Secret Service agents follow suit, giving us privacy.

"What is it, Alix? I'm busy." Dad frowns, annoyance flickering across his face. The short high I get from Sam's quick wink and tiny encouraging nod crashes down to the ground, burning.

"I know, and I'm sorry. I was just wondering if—"

"Wait, why are you not in class? It's the middle of the morning." He crosses his arms in front of his chest.

My face starts flaming like a lighthouse. "I... Mr. Miller is pretty easy going."

Wrong thing to say. I notice my mistake the second the words leave my mouth. Dad's lips press into a thin line, a muscle in his jaw ticking. I'm about to get my butt handed to me.

"Alix, I—"

And then he stops, one hand balled into a fist. I don't think he realizes he's doing that. "You know, never mind." The hand relaxes and pats my shoulder awkwardly. "It's okay, Alix. If you need time off and can't focus on studying, it's fine. It's fine." His voice is tired. Resigned. "Maybe I expected too much from you, keeping up your studies despite everything. It's... fine."

Say what? "No, Dad. It's—"

"I would just ask you to stay with your security detail, honey. If something ha— I mean, if you fell again... I don't want you to be alone." One more pat.

"I'm not falling." Cue flashback to Yoshi almost running me over. My cheeks heat up another ten degrees. "And even if I did, no big deal—"

"No, it is. It's not like it was before, Alix. And... I want you to stay with your agent." Two fingers pinch the bridge of his nose. He sounds… beaten. "So please, just get back with your security detail and stay safe. I don't care if you decide to study or not."

And with that, he sidesteps me and keeps on walking down the Colonnade, Altman and the agents falling into step with him. Only Sam stays back, torn between following our Commander in Chief or picking up what's left of me.

I give him a short wave of my hand. Leave.

"Sorry," he mouths and takes off after Dad.

My stomach roils, bringing a wave of nausea.

I don't care if you study or not.

That's not my dad. Because my dad would never say that. He'd be proud of everything I did, of every nerdy, geeky, dorky tidbit of information I could find in the farthest corners of my mind. He'd be encouraging me to become better, to always reach up to the stars, to never stop improving.

Tears prick my eyes as my throat closes off to anything but a wheezy breath.

He's given up on me.

I've disappointed him as a daughter, and now I'm failing him as a spy.

Keeping my eyes from blinking and the tears from falling, I stare straight out into the gardens and their deceptive beauty while I let Dad walk right into his political death.

Maybe I don't care either.

No, not true. I'll always care about my dad, no matter what.

In front of a distant fence, a line of visitors waiting for admission to the White House Tour moves a little. Two boys play ball; people take selfies and laugh. Such a normal scene. Such a normal life.

One of the boys throws the ball a tad too high and it almost makes it over the fence.

And *boom*, an epiphany strikes.

Like a shot of lightning hit me, I'm back in the game, fired up, heart thudding and pumping blood to every cell in my body.

"Whoa! He threw something over the fence!" I yell, pointing at the line of visitors.

Once more, louder. "He threw something over the fence!" I'm totally selling this, pushed forward in my chair, arm and finger outstretched, eyes wide, breathing wildly.

But I'd be lying if I said I expected the reaction of the next ten seconds. Not to that proportion.

For the shortest moment, the two Secret Service agents freeze before their heads whip around to me, my outstretched arm, and then toward the fence.

They spring into action.

One of them all but tackles Dad, pushing his head and body down into a bent-over position while keeping himself between him and the Gardens.

"Lockdown! White House lockdown! *Now*," the other agent barks into his sleeve microphone. "Object over fence! Repeat: Immediate lockdown, object over fence!"

Wait—lockdown? The sound of my pulse swells inside my ears. He's putting the White House on *lockdown*? What about just bringing Dad to safety and away from the Green Room?

The second agent sprints over, shielding Dad from the other side. "*Trailblazer* West Colonnade, accounted, returning. *Trailblazer* returning." He grabs Altman and Sam by the arm, pulling them in my direction. "*Timber Wolf* and *Typist* accounted," he growls into the mike and turns to me. "You too."

"I got her." Dimitri's deep baritone makes the agent look up in surprise, and me too. Where'd he come from that quickly? "*Trouble* accounted," he mutters into his microphone.

A short acknowledging nod, and the other agent lets go of my handlebars, focusing on shielding my dad, as they hurry him and everybody else to the next doors and inside the building.

"Alix!" Sam tries to turn around to me, but the agent has no mercy.

"Move, sir!" He grabs Sam by the shoulder and all but shoves him through the doors, the last I see of him a face of worry—for me.

Dad on the other hand… Yeah, not even a glance in my direction as the agents usher him inside.

"Let's go," Dimitri says, swiftly turning me around and pushing me back toward the entrance I came from. To my right, dozens of men clad in black suits spill out into the gardens, some with dogs on leashes, some even in full SWAT-gear and… bomb squad attire?

"Oh no," I breathe.

"Full lockdown mode," Dimitri says. "Search for the object, nobody leaves or enters the White House until cleared. The President stays in the basement and Situation Room until the White House is emptied."

Meaning, he won't be meeting Josiah Lucas. That's what I wanted, right?

We enter the hallway again and barely avoid getting knocked over by about a dozen Secret Service agents, all running back and forth, checking rooms, directing visitors, talking into their sleeve microphones. The Press has swarmed out from their office downstairs, taking pictures of frightened visitors and angry agents trying to do their job without distraction.

My stomach roils again, the nausea back, and stronger.

Dad won't be meeting Josiah Lucas.

But I'm in a buttload of trouble.

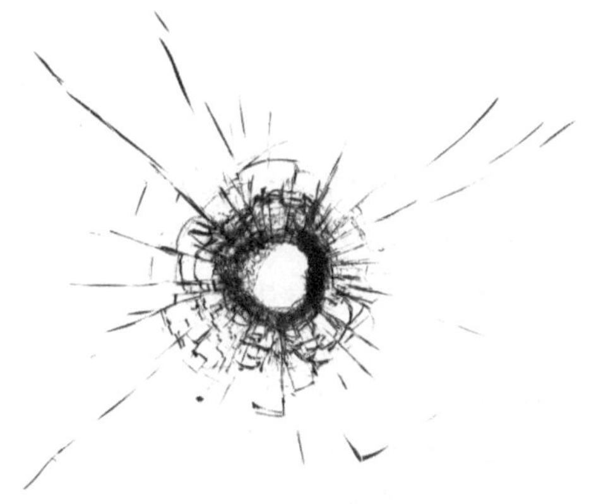

CHAPTER SIX

Surgery

"What the hell happened out there?"

Ian slides off his desk the moment Dimitri closes the classroom door behind us. "I had visual, but no audio." He holds up a thin, transparent sheet of sorts and waves it. "*Lockdown,* Alix?"

"I, uhh… It didn't go as planned." No kidding. I single-handedly derailed the functionality of the White House. Scared the Secret Service into sending a bomb squad into the Gardens. Inconvenienced hundreds. Employees, visitors…

Ian stares at me for a second before the corners of his lips twitch up. "Well, at least we don't have to worry about an alibi for your surgery. Nobody is going to come looking for us during a lockdown." He grins. "Come to think about it, a bit overplayed, but you completed the assignment, Agent. Not bad."

Also, not the way I would have phrased it. "Dad's going to kill me." He really is. And Sam will probably think I'm the biggest moron on the planet when they find nothing in front of that fence, then review the tapes, only to find—wait for it—nothing there either.

"I don't think so. Believe me, object over fence happens more often than you'd think. So do false alarms, and the Secret Service prefers a false alarm and safety over no alarm and ignorance. You'll be fine."

Speaking of. I peek up at him from under my lashes. "Say… would Waterhouse really have fired you?" Had I not been in absolute panic-mode I'd have processed Waterhouse's threats and Dimitri's warning better and sooner, but alas, it appears I'm only human.

Ian sighs. "Well. He isn't the biggest fan of me replacing him."

…or I wouldn't need your smart ass to teach hers.

"But he wasn't quite… *suited* for the job?" I ask.

"Waterhouse is a superb agent, but you can't talk quantum mechanics to him." Ian shrugs. "I on the other hand love quantum mechanics—"

"Same here, as you know!" I give him a super-dorky thumbs-up I regret the moment I do it, but Ian doesn't seem to have minded it.

"Which is one reason why I really, really wanted this job." He grins.

"What's the other?"

"Huh?" He raises a questioning eyebrow.

"The other reason why you wanted this job?"

For a long moment he looks right through me before he blinks quickly. "Ah, that. Never mind. You know what, we should get moving." He holds up the letter-sized transparent sheet. "We have about three hours before they lift the lockdown, and I intend to use them. Give me your hand."

Uhh—?

Ian kneels next to me and takes my hand in his like we did this every day. Thing is, he might be holding somebody's hand every day. I definitely don't. All the tiny hairs on my body raise in response to his touch, and my stomach doesn't waste a second either, turning one-eighty on me. Gone is the roiling and nausea, and hel-lo butterflies. Ian flattens my hand onto the sheet under his.

"DNA-secured Ultra-Thin Information Pads, or DUTI-pads, as I like to call them. Useless in anyone else's hands besides the owner's. And this one is yours now." He lifts his hand from mine. "See?"

Graphics and letters come to life under my palm, but I'm so not looking at that. Only at my hand, the one that feels cold after Ian's touch is gone. Bleh. So cliché.

"Works like an iPad, only better. We'll be using it during class. Keep on bringing your backpack and books though, better for your alibi." Ian tilts his head, waiting for my response.

"C-cool," I stammer. Brain, I'd appreciate you keeping those hormones under control. Thank you. Yours, Alix.

"Right?" He beams, then stands up and takes the crutches from behind the wheelie, handing them to me. "We're going down to the Lair. The wheelchair stays here."

He holds the world map to the side for me, pointing at one of the wooden panels in the mantelpiece of the old fireplace hidden behind it. "This is one of the secret entrances to get to the Eagle's Lair. A holographic wall protects it, which is why you need to place your hand right here for it to recognize you as one of ours and open."

Ian waves me over and keeps talking while I work myself into a standing position on my crutches, avoiding any weight on my useless left leg. Surgery can't happen early enough.

"If you haven't guessed it yet, another secret entrance is in your room, a couple of floors right on top of us. Same fireplace, same panel."

Well, good thing I'm in the East Bedroom then and connected to PRICS. Coming to think about it, I doubt it was coincidence. I wonder how they convinced my parents to put me in that room, or maybe they happily put me in the room farthest away from them all on their own with the mood I've been in for the last months.

And after my performance today, Dad's going be thrilled I'm as far away as possible.

Ian takes me by the elbow. "I advise against taking this as a shortcut from your room though: It's only for emergencies. If the First Daughter vanishes out of her room and the guarded residence, all hell is going to break loose. If we disappear from here, we have an easier time with Alibis." He taps the wooden panel twice, waiting for me.

"Biometric?" I ask.

Ian nods. "Second use for it. After the fridge, of course."

"Priorities, right?"

Ian chuckles. "Exactly."

I place my palm onto the part of the trim that doesn't look distinguished to me, although that's probably the point. As soon as my skin touches it, a surge of warmth spreads through my hand, without light or sound. Fascinating to know what's happening right now, how I'm being analyzed. Science FTW!

Half a second later, a three by two-foot opening appears in the wall next to the fireplace, mostly hidden behind the map of the world. Until now, my day has been pretty crappy, but this… It makes me smile. "Seriously nice invention, Ian." Truly awesome, actually, at least from my geek point of view. "Plural, to be fair. Palm reader and Holographic Wall."

Ian gives me a very polite bow. "Thank you, ma'am, much appreciated." He motions for me to step in. "Oh, by the way, to make it even cooler, the holographic projection is solid, unless set on disperse, like when you drove through the wall down in the Lair. What I want to say is, don't try to run through it."

I roll my eyes. "That risk is low."

"For now." He gives me an evaluating glance. "Are you ready? Not too tired, no second thoughts?"

I snort. Second thoughts?

This is my one make-up shot at life, and I'm not going to waste it.

I shake my head and push my chin forward. "No, I'm ready." And even if I wasn't, I'm not chickening out.

I step through the opening, taking care to keep my crutches close and not go sprawling down the narrow staircase that opens beneath my feet. It's a long, *long*, zigzagging staircase with a high metal railing toward the middle of it. The shaft is lined in unfinished concrete, giving it an industrial touch. At least the stairs' surface is smoothed out and even, or else I'd be getting stuck with the rubber foot of my crutches.

Ian follows me. "And just FYI, Dimitri stays up here today to account for us during the lockdown. Usually, when the secret entrance is sealed from the inside, it automatically opens the door to the terrace, so anyone who might see us walk into our classroom but doesn't see us if they follow us in there would think we exited toward the White House Gardens."

Behind us, a faint hum starts, and the holographic wall pops back up.

"Give me the summary of what happened in the Green Room and the Colonnades, if you don't mind." With that, Ian lays his hand around my waist, and because I'm me I stiffen and a little squeak breaks from my throat.

Ian clears his throat. "Just making sure you don't crash down the stairs. I'm planning on fixing one thing today, not several. So, what do you say? Let's go?" He keeps his hand perfectly still against my waist.

"Yeah," I rasp. "Let's go." About time at least one reason for my awkwardness gets surgically improved. Pity we can't do that for the rest, but maybe, just maybe, I'll eventually learn to live with it.

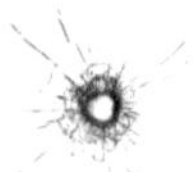

If I thought Ian's office was all that made up the Eagle's Lair, I was wrong.

Once I've made it down one hundred and fifty freakin' steps to the ninth sub-level to an ancient-looking, dusty storage room at the end of the stairs—only there to explain the stairway if anybody found it accidentally, as per Ian—and gone through another holographic wall right into the office I first met Ian in, I'm in for a surprise.

A whole maze of uber-bright, white, non-descriptive and boring hallways is hidden behind his office. I didn't expect that at all. We pass dozens of doors before we enter a medical suite complete with an examination table in the center, a moveable OR lamp on the ceiling, a crash cart, and whatnot.

Goosebumps and a nice serving of nausea assault me the second the medicinal smell hits my nose.

Blinding pain, needles digging for veins, shouting around me, and the sure knowledge that this is it, I'm going to die.

Ian pushes his palm into the small of my back, gently so. "Minor procedure, Alix. You'll do fine. No need to get worried." His voice is a reassuring soft murmur. "Come on, Dr. Soong will explain it to you."

"Okay," I squeak and force my body back into motion. Great. Now he's also a mind reader. I shuffle forward, but after a million stairs my legs are wobbly.

No stamina.

No use of my leg.

And that has to change. It just *has* to.

"Alix." A man in his sixties with salt-and-pepper hair and thick-rimmed glasses greets me with a friendly clap on the shoulder, mindful of my crutches. "Finally meeting our guinea pig for the neural chip Ian designed. I'm Dr. Soong. I'll be handling your procedure today. Oh, you might see me wandering the halls upstairs—I'm also the White House medical director." He leans in conspiratorially. "But let's pretend you don't know that yet, so shh…!"

Dr. Soong launches right into explanations about the procedure, and while it's all super exciting, I have a hard time processing it. It's not that I have a problem understanding his medical lingo, it's more that my heart is hammering at hummingbird-speed and every breath I take is fast and flat.

Anybody think I'm nervous?

A small incision, microscopic insertion of the microchip, a couple of stitches, done.

Sounds good to me. Even if he was sawing open my spine and turning me into Frankenstein, I would do it. I'm not going to stay the sad girl in the wheelchair to Dad.

I want to walk again.

I want to stop being so dang sorry for myself I can't see further than my crutches reach.

Meaning, I want to *live* again.

So I let Dr. Soong position me curled up in a modified fetal position on the table, let him push up my shirt and clean the area with antiseptic, and let him numb me up around my lower spine.

Interestingly, my body is there, reacting with goosebumps to the cold disinfectant, but in my head, I'm somewhere else.

I don't feel the needle go in.

I don't care about the slight sting, the pressure.

I don't even mind Dr. Soong's humming during the procedure.

All I do is go to my happy place, to the place where I could do no wrong, where life didn't seem to constantly slip from my grasp.

Eventually Dr. Soong places a small Band-Aid over my back. "All done, Alix. The procedure was a success." He helps me to a sitting position with careful, practiced movements. "A minimally invasive incision right at the site of your nerve trauma. The microchip is already emitting calibrated pulses of NeuroStym radiation."

I whistle through my teeth. "I'm a pioneer of science." NeuroStym is so new, and so theoretical—or so I thought—it's tough to believe that's actually what's helping my nerves recover and regrow.

Dr. Soong's eyes twinkle. "Indeed you are. Early trials suggest neural regeneration rates that dwarf conventional treatments, but you'll be our first human trial to prove that theory."

"Happy to be the guinea pig." Thrilled, to be honest.

Dr. Soong flashes a thumbs-up. "We're looking at weeks for noticeable changes, but hey—we're making medical history here." He gestures to my back with a mix of professional pride and scientific excitement. "I'll get you fitted with a new therapeutic brace. It'll give us a plausible cover story for your improvement. Plus, your nervous system needs the support while it regenerates."

He holds up a finger, signaling me to stay put, then turns toward the door on the right. The moment he cracks it open—

"... throwing her into this half-cocked and unprepared! You're setting her up for failure!" Ian's voice thunders through the gap. "—this isn't just desk work, this is active duty! You can't seriously—"

Dr. Soong winces and quickly snags something from just inside the doorway before pulling it shut. "Ah, sorry. Seems like our resident genius is having a moment. Our boy tends to get... intensely protective of his, uhh, projects." His smile turns apologetic. "Which, right now, is you. He'll get over it."

Yeah. Whenever the waves die down from the stupidest blunder any newbie ever took.

My face burns. At least Ian isn't too angry with me, more at Waterhouse, I hope.

The doctor holds up a fancy-looking splint. "Your new tool. Wear it every day. I can't have your mother get curious about your faster-than-expected recovery and insist on a CT or MRI. She'd discover the chip in no time." He loosens the Velcro around the black plastic, about to wrap it around my leg, when Ian reaches over his shoulder and takes it.

"I got it, Doc."

I jerk. Didn't even hear the door close. Or open, for that matter.

Dr. Soong pats his shoulder. "Alright then, you came up with the idea, after all. See you later, Alix." He waves at me and then he's gone, the white double-door swinging closed behind him.

Ian turns the splint in his hands, quiet for a good ten seconds. Then, he sighs. "You know, maybe once it has worked we can get that chip out to the general public. I'd love that." He bends down and fits the splint to my leg. "But we'll have to see. Right now, it's Top Secret. Military." A hint of something bitter creeps into his voice.

He tightens the Velcro and adjusts the little wheels and angles around my calf until everything feels snug. "I took that from your wheelchair's pouch." He straightens and pulls my cell out of his back pocket, taps the screen and holds it in front of my face. Once face recognition has kicked in, he nods. "I'm putting in my number and save it under 'Mr. Miller'. Please, and that's a no-brainer, don't text or leave voice messages with sensitive information. Give me a hint and I'll figure it out, whatever it is." He looks over the rim of the phone, and when I nod, so does he before returning his attention to the device in his hands.

"Cool. I'm also installing a bunch of security updates, but I'd still appreciate if you didn't lose your phone. You should also carry it with you at all times. In case of an emergency, when I need you down in the Lair, I'll text you."

"Or call me." I wiggle my thumb and pinky next to my ear.

"I'll try not to. I won't know the situation you're in, and since we have already established coming up with a spontaneous lie isn't your forté, a text will give you more time to improvise."

Well, duh. Makes sense. I'll need that time. "Okay. Okay. What do I tell my parents? And what phrasing are you using so I know what to do?" *Attention—super-secret task ahead* might not be wise to use.

Ian keeps on typing. "The text will say something along the lines of 'please read page 112', so—"

"Ah. Smooth." I wave my hand like the coolest, most blasé teen in town. Fake it until you make it, right? "112—the European equivalent of 911."

Ian grins. "Exactly. The right mix of obvious to you and inconspicuous to everybody else. But anyway, you tell them whatever works. Late assignment, forgot something—or nothing at all and you just come down here."

Oh, like that's going to fly in the middle of the night. I'm never late with assignments. If I forgot something, I can pick it up in the morning. And just sneaking out… Nope. I need something watertight, something that's already battle-proofed. "What would you tell yours?" Another thought comes to mind. "Do yours actually know what you're doing? Your parents? I mean, with PRICS being secret and all that?"

My questions wipe the grin right off his face. For a moment, a hint of vulnerability flickers across his features. It makes him look so much younger, more like me, not like the genius guy who invented the Holographic Wall and got promoted to teaching me *because it takes a genius to teach a genius.*

"I… haven't spoken to them in a while." He hands me the phone and scoots up on the table next to me, keeping his eyes trained on the floor.

"As in 'too busy to call', or…?"

He gives a dry laugh devoid of humor. "More as in 'everything's top secret'. My work, me…"

My brows scrunch together. "Huh?" How can he be top secret?

Ian sighs. "Alix, the holographic projector… it's one of a kind. It gives our military a huge advantage. And it's complicated. Like, *really* complicated and complex. When I signed my life over to the FBI, all my files about it had to be destroyed for security reasons. Nothing was left. The only hard drive with the data on it was here." He taps his temple. "That makes me very valuable. And also a liability. Let's just say me socializing is not encouraged."

"You mean, with people outside the Secret Service—or with your parents?" Both seems a bit strict, I mean, even James Bond and Ethan Hunt have somewhat of a private life. Kind of. I *think.*

Ian scoots a tad farther back, hands balled to fists and knuckles white in his lap. "With… Well, they…" He pauses, then tries again. "I haven't…" He shakes his head. "You know, it doesn't matter. It's a once-in-a-lifetime opportunity and I'm honored by the trust and hope the FBI put in me. The genius kid, who's going to come up with all these solutions to their problems, the inventor-on-call for all things computer and military use. That's what they hired me for before Waterhouse promoted me to work with you."

Riiight.

I don't have to be a spy-in-training to figure out there's more to the story. Neither do I have to be a psychologist to know he doesn't want to talk about it. So I do what anybody with a bit of common sense would do: I change the topic. Sometimes I surprise even myself with my level of maturity.

I rock to the left, bumping my shoulder into his. The slightly teasing move comes natural, somehow. "Know what? I think I just realized they couldn't have come up with a better name. PRICS truly fits them." Whatever is going on with Ian's level of secrecy, it doesn't sound like fun.

Ian laughs out once, and damn if I didn't make me proud that it was my one-liner that did it. "Now that you mention it, I have to agree." One more chuckle that makes me feel all proud. "But anyway. Since we're on that topic, an FYI. Eventually your father's term or terms will be over, and you'll be dismissed from the Service. Of course you know you're not allowed to talk about anything PRICS-related to anybody at that point, but mainly… you're not allowed to talk about me."

My eyebrows shoot up under my hairline. "You?" My face warms. Why would he think I'd talk about him? I—

His cheeks color in the slightest red. "Yeah. Me. You're one of only a handful of people who know who I truly am. It's that watertight." There's that bitter tone again.

I bump my shoulder into him once more, for emphasis, and wiggle my eyebrows. "Guess I'm special, huh?"

Ian whips his head around.

Pause.

A slow nod.

"Yeah," he drags out, green eyes pinning me to the spot. "I guess you are."

Air lodges in my throat as his gaze holds mine captive. "Uhh—"

A flicker of awareness crosses Ian's face and within a split-second he slides off the table so fast, the whole thing wobbles.

Yikes, Alix. Maybe tone it down a notch?

When exactly did I start treating my teachers like they were buddies? Oh, right: When they were not much older than me and looked like Ian.

Ian clears his throat. "But anyway. We probably should go back upstairs. The first lockdown of your White House career should be over soon."

I groan, even though I'm appreciating him brushing over that awkward moment. "What did Waterhouse say?" Because I definitely heard loud and clearly what Ian said.

"Grumpy as always, but admitted he'd rather have the media write about the lockdown than about Lucas and your father in the same room." He pauses, looks down at the ground, then up at me from under his eye lashes. "We should really go back upstairs." The apple in his throat bobs up and down once before he straightens his chin up and holds his arms out for me. "Come on down."

Down as in…?

Ian cocks his head to the side, arms outstretched, waiting. "You shouldn't put stress on your spine."

Oh.

Wait. Are we doing this?

Apparently we are.

Okay then. I lean forward and drop my hands onto his shoulders. With one small step back, Ian makes room for me, supporting me all the way off the examination table, keeping me close to his body and from moving my back too much. The scent of spring soap surrounds me, and for a moment, all I see are those green eyes of his. My insides tighten—and then my feet hit the ground and Ian lets go of me, the moment gone.

I don't think any of my previous teachers would have helped me like that, and I wouldn't have wanted them to help me like that either.

So, what do I make of that?

I suck in my lower lip. "Uhh, thank you. For… for coming up with that chip, I mean." Way to go, Alix. They probably already pasted my picture next to the definition of awkward on Wikipedia.

"My pleasure, Alix," Ian says slowly, his words carrying a weight I can't quite decipher. "My pleasure."

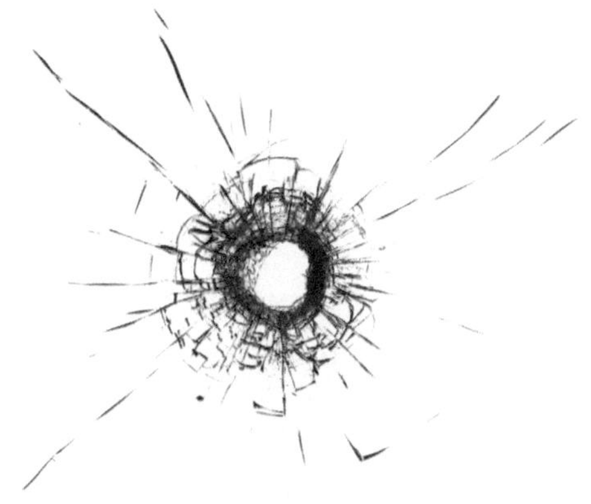

CHAPTER SEVEN

For Better or Worse

When I wake up the next morning, the memory of my successful procedure has me floating on cloud nine.

Look at that, I'd forgotten what happiness felt like. What being trusted feels like. Maybe Soong snuck something into my injection when I wasn't looking. I swing my legs over the edge of my bed and wobble over to the bathroom on my crutches. Somehow, the left leg feels lighter today, or maybe that's just my imagination. Placebo-effect.

Meh, who cares? Somewhere attached to my spinal cord is a little chip diligently working its magic on me. "Abracadabra," I murmur, giving myself a thumbs-up in the mirror a second later once my butt is planted firmly on the high chair in front of the sink.

Like I was on a mission, I get ready for school—well, PRICS—and wheel into the dining room.

"Alix."

Poof.

Cloud nine gets caught by a hurricane-sized storm and ripped apart.

Dad's sitting at the head of the breakfast table, iPad and newspapers scattered around his plate, eggs and bacon already gone from it. He might look relaxed with his coffee mug in one hand and the iPad in the other, but to anybody who knows him, the warning signs scream to be careful.

So I am.

I roll to my spot at the long end of the table, on my best behavior. "Good morning, Dad." I know this mood, the barely-controlled tension and stress boiling under the surface. For the past year since my accident, Dad's been a spring coiled too tight, about to explode at any given moment. Welcome to a life under the spotlight of politics.

He sets the mug down. "What was that yesterday?"

Here we go.

I serve myself some eggs. Some actually make it onto my plate. "I wanted to ask you—"

"That's not what I meant."

Yeah, I figured. My face predictably turns an unhealthy red. "I saw that one boy throw something over the fence, and remember how they said in the security briefing to let us know if we saw something unusual?"

A muscle in his jaw thrums—and then relaxes. He takes a sip of coffee, and I can all but see him counting down from twenty. When he talks, his voice is even. Calm. On the surface, at least. "I remember. But I hope you also remember that that's exactly why I don't want you out and about. You shouldn't put yourself in a situation that could become dangerous and you can't handle alone." He points at my wheelchair. "We've lost enough to that thing already."

The relief that he isn't chewing me out for calling a non-existent threat is so short-lived it doesn't even take a single breath before it dies.

Once upon a time, I thought the pain of his disappointment would lessen as the weeks flowed by, but no. His verbal knife is slicing me open the same every time, deeper and deeper, until one day I'll fall into pieces.

"I can handle myself alone." I stare down into my eggs. I'm not *that* broken.

He sighs. "I'm just saying that we should maybe make sure everything around here is easier to access with a wheelchair, and until then you should maybe stay away from—"

My head whips up. "Oh, come on, Dad. I'll be fine. I'm learning to walk better on crutches. I'm getting stronger already. And remember how you always told me to take all hurdles in my way? That's—"

Dad throws his napkin onto the table, anger flickering across his face. "That was before—"

He snaps his mouth shut, lips pressed into a thin line.

Before I turned into his special-needs daughter.

"Before we moved to the White House," he finishes.

Of course.

Damn it, that hurt. None of this is my fault, and I'm doing the best I can to show him *I'm not freakin' broken*. Still, tears that weren't there a second ago clog my throat, refusing to be swallowed. The food on my plate turns blurry, but before the first tear can fall, Dad pushes his chair back.

Pause.

"I… I'll be downstairs. I have work to do."

He walks out on me and closes the door behind him.

"Yeah," I whisper, "same here."

But no matter what Ian throws at me, it can't be as tough as convincing Dad I'm still the same me, wheelchair or not.

That is a task I'm not sure I can handle.

Like yesterday, Ian waits for me in the classroom. Dimitri wheels me in, but after I've pushed myself out of the wheelie and behind my desk, he takes position in the hallway, leaving me alone with Ian.

The air is filled with a slight scent of his soap and aftershave, and for a moment, I'm back pressed against his chest after he helped me off the surgery table. My heart misfires twice, dipping my stomach into a roller coaster nosedive.

Get a grip, Alix. That guy is your teacher.

I drop my gaze down onto the floor, hoping my cheeks don't show the familiar warmth tingling all the way down to my fingertips and toes.

To my utter relief, Ian busies himself with his drawer. He takes out another cup and fills it with tea from his thermos before he brings it over for me.

The weight Dad dropped onto my shoulders lifts a little.

He holds out his cup, waiting. I clunk my cup against his, and we grin at each other like only true nerds can. The smell of freshly brewed chai with a hint of Ian's scent clinging to it… I like it. A nice mix.

"Cheers, Trouble," Ian says, raising his mug at me.

"Trouble?" I scald myself when I swallow too fast.

Ian slides back onto his desk, like he did yesterday. "You haven't figured it out yet?" He shakes his head in mock disappointment. "See, you didn't listen. Tah-tah. That's in your job description. You've heard at least one other person call you Trouble. Not just me."

No way. No one calls me Trouble. I didn't hear anything. I'm pretty sure I would have picked up on that.

Ian sees my frown and explains. "Dimitri uses it all the time. It's your callsign. The Secret Service christened you 'Trouble.'"

Oh no.

That's my call sign? The colonnades—that's where Dimitri used it. I thought it meant trouble was happening, but it makes sense. Dad, Jenna Altman, Sam: *Trailblazer, Typist, Timber Wolf.*

Trouble.

I cross my arms on the desk, rest my head on top of them, and groan. That callsign is going to stick with me for the rest of the term. I can practically see the heads turning when Dimitri announces *Trouble moving* or whatever—and then dorky little me hobbles or wheels around the corner. Yeah. Me. Trouble. Obviously.

I let my head hit the desk. "Can't I get Brainiac? Maybe Smartypants? *Anything* else? *Please?*" I whine into my table. Anything is better than Trouble.

Ian chuckles. "This Presidency got assigned the letter T, so no. Your father is *Trailblazer*, your mom *Therapist*."

Without looking up, I lift a finger. "Tachyon. I'll take that."

A snort bursts from Ian's throat, even though he tries to cover it up with a cough. "Moving faster than light. I see what you did there, Alix."

"Ain't nobody gonna say I didn't have a sense of humor," I mumble into my arm.

"Don't worry about that callsign. The Secret Service knows you're PRICS—well, at least the upper brass knows. They know PRICS kids mean trouble for whoever crosses them wrong. Your callsign is actually a compliment."

I'm slowly lifting my head up. "A compliment?" Talking about living up to the pressure. "Do my parents know?"

"Of course they know. Your father signs off on all the callsigns. I heard he was very pleased with yours."

Dad liked the callsign? Yeah, I bet. Trouble is all I caused him in the last couple of months.

Ian interrupts my self-pity. "Anyway, situation report. That's our way to start the day before we begin quote-unquote spy school." He scoots farther up onto his desk and activates a DUTI-pad. "It's a short report today, the term's still young. We don't have any activities tracked yet besides two credible threats against your father's life the Secret Service picked up on, and—"

"What?" I cough, swallowing my tea and burning myself for the second time in five minutes, then cover my mouth with my sleeve. "Two threats against my dad?"

Ian cringes. "It sounds worse than it is. These things happen. All the time. Ninety-nine percent turn out to be nothing. The Secret Service and FBI hunt down the other one percent. It's nothing, Alix."

"Nothing?" There are *death threats* against my dad! I wouldn't call that nothing!

"Look, one of them was traced down and eliminated, i.e., taken in. A religious fanatic claiming the president was actually a demon. He was planning an, uhh, rather deadly exorcism. Hence, we got him." He cringes again. "But like I said—"

"What about the other one?"

"Huh?"

"You said there were two threats." My fingers drum a rhythm onto the desk. I heard him. Clearly.

Ian sighs. "The other one… the FBI and Secret Service are working on it."

My blood pressure drops. "That… that doesn't sound good."

"It's not bad either. Look, most of the time nothing happens, I'm telling you. We're all here to prevent exactly those kinds of things. This little tidbit of information we had wasn't enough yet to find the perpetrator, which usually means there is none."

There's none, or he's too good to be that obvious, and Ian must know it too. That he dismisses this... He doesn't want to worry me.

Oh, dear.

I wrap my fingers around the hot mug until they sting. Before I fall down the bottomless pit of worry and fear that's become my second home, Ian hands me my DUTI-pad. "Spy-time, Alix. Just let me know if I'm going too fast."

Only because I'm still mentally hyperventilating do I not roll my eyes at his comment, and five minutes later, I'm glad for it. For the first time in years, I actually have to pay attention. Those times in school when I thought I knew it all? Gone.

Ian's style is fast-paced and spiked with information.

We start with coding—writing code, recognizing and deciphering code, coming up with my own code—and boy, am I glad I'm good with numbers. To me, it feels like I can barely grasp the more complicated codes, the ones relying on mathematical formulas and equations, but Ian still seems to be pleased with me. He's the one juggling them like an artist though. Not me, and while I'd love to blame the four years he has on me for that, I doubt that's it. Ian is a natural.

It's kind of cool.

When we take a break from coding, we start with languages. Basic Chinese and basic Russian, spiced up with some other languages I've never had interest in but that could be important given the current political landscape, depending on where I'm accompanying Dad to.

If I'm accompanying him somewhere, that is. Last time I checked he didn't sound that enthusiastic.

Languages are a tad more problematic. The grammar is easy,

and I can also do a moderately good job remembering the vocabulary, but pronouncing words in a foreign language is not my forte.

Ian cringes a lot when he hears me talk.

"Remind me to never send you on a mission where you need to speak in a foreign language," he says after another butchered attempt of mine to say "Where is the bathroom?" in Swahili.

Well, I agree with him. I also hope he never sends me on a mission where I would need to speak anything else but English. I wouldn't do well at all, and that thought more than scares me, especially after Ian leads me through the current political landscape. Mind blowing.

Seriously.

Mind. Blowing.

The connections, favors, games, and—sometimes illegal—activities going on around us without anybody noticing…

It's like a soap opera, and not a good one.

I soak it all up like a sponge.

One of these days, any of the stuff Ian is teaching me might make a difference to Dad's safety, might save him from people who want to kill him.

I need every ounce of knowledge I can get, because I won't let him down.

He might think I'm fragile, but I'm not.

I'm strong enough for the both of us.

The first couple of weeks pass in no time, and I'm loving them.

Before my accident, I always had a goal to reach: study this, work on that, get into Harvard, get my PhD before twenty… Well, the accident and Dad took that from me, and since then

I've been drifting aimlessly.

Until now.

In the mornings, I look forward to seeing Ian and to starting class, no matter what he challenges me with: Continuum and quantum mechanics, advanced cell biology, physical and analytical chemistry—I love it all.

I love it, but thing is, I don't love it as much as my spy-classes. They're the icing on the cake and what I can't get enough of. Call it a new purpose in life, whatever, but Ian and those classes, they recharge my batteries. Every day I'm expecting Dad to notice I'm doing better. One of these days, he must pick up I'm smiling more. I'm eating more.

Alas, he's usually too busy or in a bad mood, and today is no different. Thank you, Genetic Testing Bill.

"Damn it!" Dad slams his fist onto the table, barely missing the iPad he's reading on. "It's like they're playing ball with us." His fingers jab at something on the screen.

Genetic Testing Bill: America's Savior from Crime?

I raise an eyebrow. Catchy headline.

"Genetic Testing Bill?" My mother dabs at her mouth with her napkin.

Dad pushes his chair back and gets up. "Oliver sent a memo. I need to go downstairs. Be back later." He balls up his napkin and drops it onto his seat. My mom throws me a meaningful glance. *Later* means in about fifteen hours. Mom and I have begun to figure out how this whole President business works. Living where you work means no time off. Ever.

If he's not down in the West Wing until late, Dad's brooding over something work-related up in the residence, and even if we still got along like peanut butter and jelly, I'd give him and his mood a wide berth.

If only he knew I'm working on helping him, every single

day. Cue the sappy music.

This morning in class, Ian greets me with the obligatory cup of chai, but instead of the wide smile he tends to have for me, he seems preoccupied.

"I hope you had a solid breakfast today, Trouble. We're sending you on a live exercise."

The sip of tea doesn't make it down my throat. I choke, coughing violently, barely covering my mouth with the crook of my elbow. Why can't he wait until I've swallowed?

"A… what?" I wheeze, tears in my eyes. He can't have meant that. I'm nowhere near ready, I've screwed up the last, I—

"Don't worry," Ian says, "it is, to quote Waterhouse, nothing you can't handle. And it isn't," he adds quickly. "You'll be fine."

Oh, really? Then why does that reassurance do nothing to make me feel better, nothing at all?

The cup in my hands shakes on its own account. Can't possibly be from my hands. No way.

Ian slides off his desk, drags a chair over to me, and straddles it across from my desk. "Alix, I said don't worry about it. I wouldn't have let you take this job if I didn't know you can handle it." He hesitates for the shortest moment, then reaches across the desk and wraps his hands around mine holding the cup.

If he thought it would calm me, he was wrong.

The heat of the cup is nothing compared to the heat of his skin on mine. Nothing.

I shake my head to clear it. Pull yourself together, Alix. What the heck is wrong with you?

"You said my work was information retrieval only," I squeak in a high voice that doesn't sound like me at all.

Ian flinches. "I did. And it is. Kind of. The order comes from Waterhouse directly. He's interpreting the PRICS charter quite fluidly these days." His jaw clenches, the movement drawing attention to the sharp line around it. He brushes his thumb over the back of my hand—probably unconsciously, but each tiny movement sends sparks up my arm. I try to focus on his words, but he's close enough I can make out a starburst of amber in his green eyes, like a nebula expanding through space. Mesmerizing.

My heart skips a tiny little beat at the same time Ian gives my hands a squeeze… and then lets go.

Right.

I rush a sip of tea, the faint hint of Ian's spring soap clinging to my hands. Goosebumps. All the way down to my spine.

I ignore them.

Ian gets up and keeps talking. "This time, you're prepared and ready for it. We're using the skills you learned so far, so it should be a good practice exercise. This afternoon at thirteen-hundred hours, the Minister of Defense of the United Provinces of Talevir is coming to meet with your father."

My eyes widen. "The Minister of Defense? Didn't you tell me how he has this anti-American background?" I remember that lecture vividly; it kept me from sleeping well for about two or three nights, until we talked about counter-terrorism protocols.

"Yes. Exactly that Minister of Defense, Atlas Varen. This is a one-time opportunity for us. The FBI has certain… *assets* in place, but decided to put a tracker on him, especially after the latest intel we got." He carefully aligns the DUTI-pad with the corners of his desk.

My hands feel clammy. "Latest intel?" Why don't I like that sound?

More aligning of the pad already perfectly parallel to the desk. "Well… The Secret Service still hasn't gotten anywhere with the death threat to your father I mentioned a couple of weeks ago."

My whole body locks into a stiff rod. "You think… You think

Varen could be out to kill my dad?"

Ian winces. "I wouldn't phrase it like that. We don't trust him. We want to rule him out as a *potential* assassin."

"No kidding!" What about not letting him close to Dad? On second thought, what about taking him into prison while we have him here? A shiver runs down my body until it hits my core, freezing me. "What if he is trying to kill Dad now? Today?" I should have been nicer; I should have—

"Trouble, don't worry. It's not like that. It's a precaution. Yes, we're assuming he's meeting with radical groups and supporting anti-American terror camps, but we don't have any intel he's planning something. And: It would be a huge advantage to have position on someone like Varen—which is where you'll come in—especially if he is connected to terrorist camps. We know his location; we hopefully will know theirs. The problem is that he comes with the highest security detail we'll allow for a foreign dignitary on American soil. Neither the FBI nor the Secret Service will be able to tag him, even though they're securing his stay here. They cannot risk it. If they get caught, it'll be a major scandal and most likely spark the anti-American cells to make a move against us and even target your father."

Ian points at me. "And that's why we need you: Waterhouse ordered us to get you in and implant the tracker on Varen for us. Quick in and out. You'll meet him and place the bug on him without noticing—mission accomplished. Let's go over the details." He gets up again and grabs another one if his DUTI-pads while I try not to panic.

Implant a tracker on a foreign Minister? Of a country that isn't exactly friendly with the US? And who might want to kill my dad? How do you even *implant* a stupid tracker?

A wheezy breath leaves my throat.

No pressure. No pressure at all.

There's a million ways I can mess this up. Varen is one of the most dangerous men in the world—I could be causing an international incident and maybe even terror cells to unleash their attacks onto America... or Dad.

Oh, crap.

What if I mess up, and he...

I blow air out through pursed lips. Obviously I can't mess up. At all.

Yeah, again: absolutely no pressure.

Ian sighs and regards me with a certain pity. "I know. Waterhouse is throwing quite the jobs at us, but..." He lifts one shoulder. "One could argue it's not a true active mission, Alix. It's an attempt to get intel. There's absolutely no risk for you, or I wouldn't allow it. The PRICS charter forbids it, regardless of what Waterhouse comes up with."

My heart skips a beat. No matter his reassurance, I can't shake the feeling I'm biting off a whole chunk more than I can chew. "Ian... I'm not good at that. Meeting people, acting, I..." Closing my eyes, I take a deep breath. "This is a bit short notice. We can't even work out a plan until he arrives in"—I check my watch and swallow dry—"less than two hours."

Oh, double-crap.

Ian ignores the panic radiating from me and sets a little box in front of me. "This is the tracking device you're going to plant on Varen. Have a look at it. It might change your mind."

The box is tiny, like one of those you would expect expensive earrings or other jewelry in, only it holds a tiny vial squished into a lot of foam to keep it safe. I lift out the vial, hands still jittery. On the bottom sits a tiny, maybe needle-pin sized spike, and that's it.

"No way," I breathe, looking at Ian with wide eyes. "Is this a genome tracker? *Biology Unlimited* had an article about the theoretical use of messenger-RNA alteration for tracking use, but they said the degradation rate made it impossible to maintain a signal for more than an hour. You must have—" My cheeks flush as I catch myself geeking out, but Ian's expression makes me pause.

His eyes light up with that half-smile that makes my pulse skip. "Go on. How would you solve that?"

I pretend like I was thinking for a moment, because I totally didn't lie awake at night after reading that article. Did not. And if I did, I wouldn't have thought about how to solve that exact problem, because who'd do that just for beeps and giggles? Right?

I tap my index finger against my lower lip. "Huh. Artificial nucleotides to modify the ribosomes? For self-replicating proteins?"

The pride in his expression sends warmth through my chest and makes that sleepness night totally worthwhile in retrospect. "Brilliant. If anybody would recognize and figure out a genome tracker, it was going to be you. Oh, and we modified it so that it comes with a microscopically thin glove for your index finger. All you need to do is get in there and shake Varen's hand, and the injection unit will insert the tracker into his skin and bloodstream. After a couple of hours, it'll have copied itself into enough of his cells that we can monitor him."

And keeping an eye on him means more safety for Dad.

I drop my head onto my desk, still clinging to the little jewelry box.

Go in, shake hands, get out.

Sounds easy.

Well, not easy-easy, but doable.

Find an excuse to see Dad, greet the most dangerous man in the world, inject a tracking device, and don't get my dad killed.

Sounds definitely not doable, and more like a recipe for

disaster.

I groan. "Love the tech. Hate the job." A jittery breath works its way out my narrowed throat.

Ian stays silent, but his silence speaks loud enough. This is why I joined PRICS. Not because of its cool tech—okay, maybe that was part of it, but still—but because Dad needs me. Because I can actually do something to protect him.

The fear doesn't vanish, but determination pushes through it. I sit up straight.

"Okay." My heart still pounds, but with less panic, and more purpose. "Show me again how this works."

Because no one—*no one*—threatens Dad when I'm around.

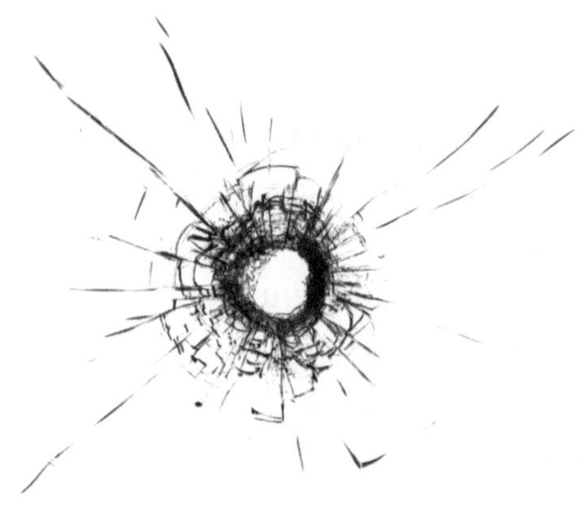

CHAPTER EIGHT

Different Kind of Failure

About one hour later, I'm more or less sufficiently prepped for my, uhh, *mission*.

On my right index finger, I'm wearing a microscopically thin glove with the tracker injection unit at its tip, and I'm trying to remember really hard that I shouldn't scratch myself with said finger or I will auto-inoculate myself. Life as a spy is tough.

We know Varen is going to be in the Oval Office with my dad in about fifteen minutes. Our plan is for me to go over there with the official excuse of wanting to ask Dad for access to the White House Library Room—good for studying—while "accidentally" meeting Varen, introducing myself, and inoculating him with a handshake. Mission accomplished.

Easy-peasy.

Or not.

It took Ian only the last hour to convince me that if I fail, I'll only fail to inject the tracker, and not cause an international

102

incident or get Dad killed. Now, isn't that reassuring?

"Take the crutches, not the wheelchair, Alix. For one, we want people to see you getting better and using the brace. For another, it gives you more flexibility of movement and you'll need that." Ian hands me the crutches, making sure I've got a good grip on them before he releases my arm. Appreciate that, because leg getting better or not, if the wooziness is any indication, I'm probably pale as a ghost.

Ian holds me by the shoulders and squeezes them. "You'll do fine. If anything feels wrong, you abort; you come back. No biggie, okay?" His expression takes on a mask of begrudging acceptance that he covers up quickly with a smile.

"Now go, Agent Forrester. Show them what a PRICS-member can do." He gives me two thumbs up and opens the classroom door for me.

I pass by Dimitri, who's still guarding us from the hallway where he'll stay. I need to take advantage of being a teenager: I have to be inconspicuous and non-threatening, and that doesn't work well with Dimitri scowling over my shoulder.

When I walk past him, he gives me the tiniest nod.

This is what being knighted must feel like.

Maybe I won't screw this up. Maybe I can get it done.

No, correction: I *will* get it done. I'll have to.

It takes me longer than normal because hobbling on crutches while paying attention to not accidentally poking myself with the auto injector is kind of tough. Plus, despite the new splint being awesome, it doesn't make my knees wobble any less. Even my healthy leg feels buttery.

A few minutes of ungainly maneuvering later I arrive at the Secretary's Office, the official entrance to the Oval Office. Mrs. Houser, my dad's chief secretary, has her desk there. She acts as a buffer between Dad and all visitors—the dragon to his dungeon as he likes to joke. No one gets into the Oval Office without Mrs. Houser clearing them and then announcing that person to Dad. Plus, from what I've heard, the small desk in the corner is for Sam. Pays off to be the Chief of Staff's son: I doubt the other Interns have a desk this close to the action.

My hands are sweaty as I knock on the doorframe. Deep breath. "Knock, knock. Incoming."

I step inside and as I do my mind slips into performance mode: A hundred percent in the game, sharp, focused, and ready to go. This is real. Not a test I could retake if I messed up. *Real.*

Mrs. Houser sits at her desk typing away on her keyboard, as most of the time. She looks up from her desk when I come in, a sweet smile on her face the moment she recognizes me. "Alix, how are you? It's been a while. Are they keeping you busy with homeschooling? I heard your dad say he got you one of those extra-smart teachers." Her smile grows wider.

I like Mrs. Houser. Like almost everyone else, she has been with Dad's team since the campaign. She is so soft spoken that I sometimes have a hard time hearing her, and in the beginning of the campaign, I wondered how she could survive between my loud and energetic dad and the equally energetic, but slightly more chaotic Oliver Brooks. It's easy though: she calms them down.

"Hi, Mrs. Houser. Indeed he did—I can't complain. Mr. Miller is keeping me pretty busy, but I feel like my GPA got a nice boost since I started with him." I nod toward the closed doors of the Oval Office. "Is my dad in, by any chance?"

Mrs. Houser nods and clicks on something on her computer. "Like you needed a GPA-booster, Alix. And yes, he's in, but he is seeing a guest right now. It's probably not the best timing. Just come back this afternoon, okay? He should be here any time after fourteen-hundred hours."

Uh-oh.

I can't really leave right now, not if I want to complete my mission.

A cold bead of sweat runs down my neck, joining the ones already collected between my shoulder blades.

And then I've got an idea.

Improvising, right now.

"Oh, that's all right, Mrs. Houser. It's not that important anyway. But since I'm here: I was wondering if you could do me a favor. Remember the cake pops you made for everyone for Election Day? The ones you put an 'X' on so they would look like a vote for Dad? I would love to learn how to make them. Would you mind giving me the recipe? Please?"

She leans back into her chair, one hand over her heart. "Those were good, weren't they? Almond-Marzipan flavored. That's a good recipe to start with, Alix, not too difficult." She looks at the computer again. "Ok, give me a second, I'll write it down for you. All you need is—"

She takes an expensive looking pen of the same brand Dad likes to use and starts writing down instructions. Normally I'd ask her to just dictate the recipe into my phone, but today I need her to spend the time writing it out. So, over the next couple of minutes, I ask and Mrs. Houser explains step by step how to make cake pops. Quite complicated. If she ever expects me to show results from this, I'm in deep.

Before I run out of questions, the door to the Oval Office opens and I forget to breathe.

Oliver comes out first, his tie actually tightened around his neck for a change. A distinguished-looking, middle-aged man in an impeccable suit follows him and shakes his hand—that must be Varen.

My dad is the last one to step out of his office, showing the mask of friendly neutrality that is his political game face—until he sees me.

From one second to the next, his face loses color.

"Excuse me." He pushes past Oliver and Varen without as much as a glance at them. Before I can even get a word out, he grabs me by the elbow and turns me around so that I face the exit door toward the West Wing and away from Varen.

"Alix. What do you think you're doing here?" he hisses at me. His fingers dig into my arm, pinching me.

A chill rises from inside my chest, burrowing itself deep.

That's not like my dad. He's never pushy or physical with me; he only hurts with words, and even that only unintentionally. I hope.

"I... I just... The Library, I just wanted to ask you—"

"Look, I'm happy you feel up for increasing your studies again, but this is no place for you." He throws one glance over his shoulder towards Varen and Oliver, then scans the office behind me. "And you're here alone again. No security detail. We talked about this. You need somebody to—"

I yank my arm free. "I don't need anybody, Dad. Don't overreact. I just wanted to ask—"

"And I want you to walk out of here right now. I'm disappointed you're ignoring my ord—" His lips pinch together. "My request. It's simple enough, Alix. I don't ask much of you, but please go back to class and find your security detail."

With his last words, he turns on his heels and leaves me standing there, alone.

Ignored.

Dad.

What... what's that about? I could always visit him, no matter what, where, or when. This is new.

Mrs. Houser and Oliver look at me with pity in their eyes,

the final straw that makes this rejection real.

Dad is kicking me out of his office in front of everyone, and neither have I done anything to deserve that, nor done anything to defend myself. Can't very well start an argument in front of everybody, and he knows it. In fact, I could bet it's what he's banking on: my maturity.

Hot tears rush to my eyes, but for a change, their source is anger, not self-pity. Not sure if that's an improvement, because I can't cry now, no matter the reason. I can't lose control in front of everybody.

I slowly turn around, focused intensely on my steps. My hands wrapped around my crutches are cold, just like my heart, frozen into a solid block of ice. I wish Sam was here to—

No.

I'd be even more embarrassed.

Without any further words to me, Dad returns to Varen and thanks him for coming to the White House.

Varen.

My mission.

Another sting inside my chest, and this one from failure of a different kind.

I place one foot in front of the other; it's as if I'm not even touching the ground, but falling through it. Here I thought I was so clever keeping Mrs. Houser talking until Varen came out, but turns out I'm nothing but a fool when it comes to predicting or directing Dad's behavior.

I should never have signed up for PRICS. What an idiotic idea. I'm failing as a daughter, and I'm failing as a spy.

Doing my best to fight off the tears threatening to fall down my cheeks, I don't even hear Oliver and Varen approaching from behind, making their way to Varen's security detail in the lobby.

The moment Varen passes me, his right foot brushes my left

crutch. It's not much, but it's enough that both of us felt it.

Maybe it's desperation, maybe it's Ian's training, or maybe it's out of spite because of Dad's words, I don't know.

All I know is that I use this chance.

I give a little surprised yelp, let my crutch slide away from me, and fall down right in front of one of the most dangerous men in the world.

"Oh, *skrachtni*! I'm so sorry," Varen calls out while taking a surprised step back as though to not step on me. "I didn't watch where I was going. Are you all right?"

I grimace like I'm in pain and hold my braced leg with my left hand, massaging it. "Oh no, sir, I'm sorry. I should've cleared the way sooner. I know I'm slow. Let me just get out of your way."

I pretend to try to get up in the most complicated way ever, and I'm only half pretending.

Am still not using that index finger…

Varen holds out his hand for me. "Here. Let me help you."

I give him the most thankful smile I have and grab his outstretched hand with my right unoccupied one. With one big tug, he gets me up to standing, while I… while I release the tracker into the back of his right hand.

Gotcha.

Oliver scrambles past us, picks up my crutches from the floor and hands them to me. "You okay, Alix? Or should I call the Doc?" He looks worried. It's probably not high up on his list to have the foreign dignitary knock over the President's daughter— or rather the President's daughter being in the way of the foreign dignitary, especially with somebody like Varen.

"I'm okay. No worries." I offer him a weak smile and turn back to Varen. "Again, I'm very sorry, sir. I'm still not as quick with these as I could be." I nod toward the crutches supporting me once again, and smile. "Thanks for your help, I appreciate that." Where I'm finding the balls to talk to him, I don't know.

"No problem. And I'm sorry for running into you like that. I also should have watched out better." His lips curve into a polite smile, yet his eyes stay cold and dark, sizing me up like he was memorizing every inch of my face, assessing me.

The chill inside my chest gets a hold of my soul, numbing it down to my core.

Menace.

A wheezy breath leaves my throat—and Varen's attention shifts back to Oliver instead of me.

That man… He's dangerous. Evil.

I hope he never ever finds out what I did to him just now.

Oliver leads Varen past me. "Let's get you back to Limo One, sir, it should be ready for you."

He leads the way out of the secretary's office into the lobby, followed by Varen. For a short moment, I think I catch a curvy blonde walking past them in the hallway, but she's gone as quickly as she came.

With Varen out of the office, the temperature in the room rises noticeably from freezing to above zero centigrade again, if only barely. I ready myself on my crutches but make the mistake of looking back to say goodbye to Mrs. Houser.

Dad still stands next to his secretary's desk before he pivots on his heels and walks into the Oval Office.

Only it wasn't fast enough to hide the vacant expression on his face.

As if I didn't even exist.

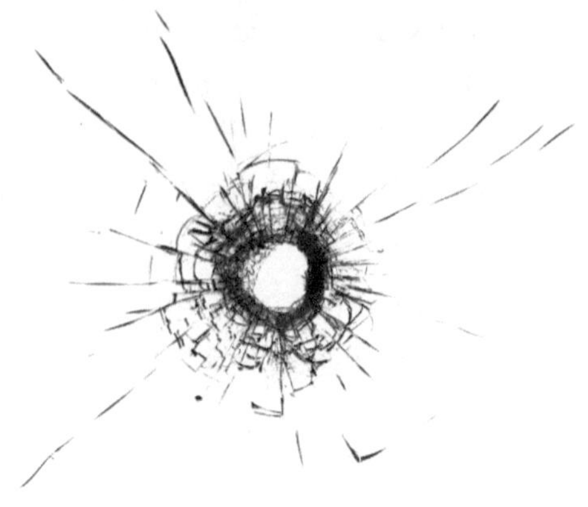

CHAPTER NINE

Way Down We Go

Dad's behavior has flipped some kind of switch inside me. I'm mad, but in a very, very confusing kind of way. I still feel the sting of his public rejection like quicksand trying to pull me under and drown me, only that now I'm wearing a flotation device made out of anger.

I want to cry and at the same time throw my crutches at somebody, or at least… I don't know, scream. Release that pressure around my soul *somehow*.

How I make it to the classroom I don't know, but the moment I reach it and see Dimitri in front of it, the tiniest bit of that pressure lifts off my chest. The classroom. Here's my safe spot, a secret hide-away where I can finally vent.

Dimitri shoots me a questioning glance before he opens the door, and despite me still being in a busy hallway, I give him a small nod in response.

Yeah, I did it.

The quickest flicker of pride lights up on his face, nothing anybody besides Ian and me would notice, but it's there.

Funny how that tiny acknowledgement makes me lift my chin before I enter the classroom.

Ian is sitting on his desk as usual, twisting around the moment the door opens—but instead of the privacy I was hoping for, my safe haven has been invaded.

Adding insult to injury is a busty blonde I've seen way too frequently for my liking, accompanied by a middle-aged man in a suit.

Probably a teacher—and Gianna.

Gianna beams at Ian, one hand on his forearm like they were best friends.

I stop dead in my tracks. My safe haven, invaded by the enemy.

Something changes in Ian's face before he has himself under control and his attention back at the man in front of him.

"Anyway, Marcus. I think it's a great idea to combine resources, but Alix is up to advanced college and some post-grad classes, and I wouldn't want Gianna to be left behind. It's probably best if we call in your substitute when you're gone."

Gianna's face falls.

Ian slides down the desk, claps the other man's shoulder, and starts guiding him toward the door. "Next time maybe."

Marcus sighs. "All right then, I was hoping reports about Alix's level of education were exaggerated—no offense, Alix." He nods at me when Ian leads him past me.

"None taken," I croak, voice cracking at the end. I want him out of here. I want *them* out of here. There's only so much I can do to keep all my emotions contained, and I'm reaching my max.

Gianna doesn't spare me as much as a glance when she all but struts past me and out of the room. "If you ever have something more… *suitable* for me, let me know, okay?" There it is again, the Gianna-purr, maybe this time with an undercurrent of something close to annoyance, but still.

I bite down so hard, my jaw cracks.

Can she please get out of here, in the name of all that's holy?

Finally, Ian closes the door behind Gianna and her teacher. He hurries over to me and lays both hands on my shoulders. "Alix?"

Everything I wanted to say is stuck in my throat, held back by a lump the size of a boulder. I'm afraid once I open my mouth I'm either going to scream or cry, or maybe both, and neither option would make me look sane.

"Alix?" he asks again, holding me a bit away from him and checking me from head to toe.

"Alix, talk to me. You look like crap. What happened?"

A weird sound leaves my throat, a mix of huff, snort, and wail. The moment it escapes, I wish I could take it back, but the damage is done.

Ian's eyebrows shoot up under his hairline. He looks me over head to toe, takes in my fingers wrapped around my crutches in a death grip, my stiff spine—and exhales softly. "I'm sorry," he says, brushing his thumbs over my shoulders. "I thought—"

"He just—" I start, my voice cracking. "He didn't even give me a chance to—"

Ian's face falls. "I'm really sorry. That's the thing with missions and assignments, there's always the element of surprise."

I huff. "Surprise, right. He acted like I was nothing."

Ian furrows his brows. "Wow. That's unexpected, especially when in the Oval Office."

"No kidding! Who treats somebody else like they're invisible? Or a nuisance?" Even Sam spends more time with my dad than I am! And I bet he gets more positive interactions per day than I have in the last months!

"You tried your best. It's okay." Ian squeezes my upper arms, then resumes the calming circling of his thumbs across my shoulders. The gesture is comforting—too comforting. It weakens the walls I've erected around that messy heap of emotions, and I can't have that. Weak walls equal overspill, and overspill equals losing it. Not going to happen.

So I pinch my eyes closed and suck a deep breath in. "No, it's not okay! I'm trying here, I really am!"

"Hey. Don't worry about it. You didn't get it done, no big deal. We were the FBI's last shot anyway, and they can't complain if we can't pull off what they couldn't handle in the first place. No big deal, Alix."

Huh? I pop my eyes open. "What do you mean?"

Ian stops the mesmerizing twirl of his thumbs. "What do *you* mean? Are we talking about the tracker?"

Geez! I shake my head. "No! I implanted the tracker! The tracker is in: Right hand. It's in!" I sniffle after the last word.

Ian's jaw drops. "Say *what*? You implanted the tracker? You did it? You did it, Alix! I *knew* it!" In one fluid motion he pulls me into his arms, crushing me against him in the biggest hug I've ever received. "I knew it! I—"

That's when he realizes I'm not breathing.

That's also when both of us are probably realizing that we're very, very close for a teacher and his student. As in, *very* close.

My cheek rests against Ian's chest, and while I'm stiff as a board and still holding on to my crutches, his arms are wrapped around my upper body and his cheek is pressed against the top of my head.

Neither of us moves—or breathes—for a good five or ten seconds.

Then, I swear I hear Ian swallow hard before he slowly pulls away from me, keeping me at a good arms' length. Something flares in his eyes when he looks at me, gone as quickly as it came.

He clears his throat. "So, wait, what have we even been talking about? What am I missing?"

I open my mouth and snap it closed again. "My—" Can't say it out loud. Verbalizing it would mean feeling like a disappointment all over again, and I'm not ready for that.

Ian understands me without words. "Ah. Your father."

"Yeah," I whisper. That guy. And dang it, a single anger-sadness-fueled tear slips past my eyelids. Traitor.

"Hey." Ian gently wipes the tear from my cheek, and that small, tender gesture makes it even worse somehow.

Walls? Crumbling.

"Need a minute," I choke out and look up to the ceiling to keep the tears from falling.

A low groan rumbles from Ian's throat, the fingers on both my shoulders digging into my shirt. "Alix…"

I sniffle. "Almost there…" Who am I kidding. My lungs burn, my stomach is roiling with acid from Dad's behavior, my heart is racing like crazy, and my skin tingles where Ian touches me. To say I'm a hot mess would be an understatement.

"Alix…" he says again, with a desperate undertone this time, before he whispers low under his breath. "Aww, damn it."

He pulls me closer—but stops halfway, held back by an invisible line. Something darkens in his eyes as awareness spreads between us. We're still way too close for a teacher and his student, way too close. He must know that too. I can feel his fingers cramp into my arms, opening and closing as if they were fighting a silent battle. For a second neither of us moves.

Tic-tock.

I give a small nod, the faintest possible, just in case I'm reading him wrong—

A low sound leaves his throat, and then, with one big pull, I'm back against his chest.

Yeah, that invisible line? Pretty sure we've kind of crossed it.

And this time, I melt into his embrace.

He cradles me and ever so softly rocks me back and forth, a gentle sway in the emotional turmoil of my mind. His one hand keeps me tight to his body, the other he sneaks up to the back of my head, guiding it against his shoulder, ever so slightly messing my hair.

And somehow, he grounds me.

I'd forgotten how good a hug can feel. How warm. How healing.

Ian's embrace protects me and builds me up from the inside out. What would take me an hour of crying under my blanket, his hug begins to fix right away. He's the rock keeping me steady, the hand reaching into my darkness—

Hand reaching into my darkness?

What the heck, Forrester? Pathetic much?

Definitely pathetic, and might as well add my favorites, girlish and confused.

Yes, also definitely confused. Because… a bajillion emotions assault me at once, and I'm pretty sure I shouldn't feel any of them.

I shouldn't feel any of them with Ian. *My teacher.*

This is more than the warmth I feel when Sam is around.

More than when he held my hand that one time.

More than—

I squeeze my eyes shut so hard it hurts. Ridiculous. That's not me. I'm not a girly-girl. I'm a logical thinker, a scientist. Not a hormonal teen.

But the difference between Ian's soft touch, this contrast between his caring and Dad's ignorance, is glaring.

Ian holds me, rocks me, murmurs encouraging words in my ear, and lets me be.

Exactly what I need—or better, exactly what I needed about a minute ago. As if my mind had shifted into a different mode, the memory of Dad's rejection is being overwritten. With every second that passes, I become more and more aware of every part of my body pressed into Ian's—and every part of his body pressed into mine.

My cheek rests against his, his scent fills my nose with every breath I take, and if I concentrate on how I'm molded against his chest, I can feel his heartbeat reverberate all the way into my body, racing as fast as mine.

As if realizing that made it stumble, my heart pitter-patters once.

Ian adjusts his hold, his breath falling against my ear in waves.

Holy cow.

My eyes pop open wide.

What is going on here? What am I doing?

I'm pretty sure this is forbidden. The hug. The butterflies. *The butterflies!*

I shouldn't have butterflies. For the last two years, I wanted Sam to hold me like this—

Sam.

Guilt washes over me like a Tsunami-wave.

I shouldn't be in Ian's arms. I like Sam. Ian is my teacher-slash-tutor-slash-colleague and four years older than me. *Four years.* He's an adult by all means, and me, I'm... not. Even if we were closer in age, which obviously we're not, I'd make a fool out of myself: I'm pretty sure guys prefer the more classic attractive beauties with lots of boobs, and that description isn't really me.

Gianna, a nasty voice whispers inside the back of my head, *they go for girls like Gianna.*

Ian sways me back and forth gently. "Better?" His goatee scratches over my cheek as he whispers into my ear, heating it close to the point of spontaneous combustion.

I bite my lower lip.

What an idiotic, hormonal teenager I am.

One more deep inhale, and I pull away from Ian.

"Thanks, Ian." I give him a weak smile. "All better now." And I'm not even lying.

"Anytime." He tucks a strand of hair behind my ear and peeks at me from beneath his lashes. "In case nobody has ever told you that, but… your strength in facing challenges, it's remarkable." A small smile flickers across his face as he drops his voice to a whisper. "And it takes my breath away."

Over the next hour and a half, Ian debriefs me—well, after I'm back to normal and holding a cup of his chai in my hands. Despite the proverbial dagger of inadequacy Dad shot through my heart, it still beats stronger when Ian is more than thrilled about my improv skills. Maybe I did do something right after all by signing up for PRICS.

"That was one great move, Alix. Seriously. Well played." He frowns right after. "But honestly, I have no idea why your father reacted the way he did. So far, he's well known for his open-office policy with all White House employees. And we have dozens of agents stationed all through the West Wing. Even if you fell, there would've been help. Maybe he just had a bad day."

Or a bad year.

I stare into the tea. "Yeah, maybe." I clench my teeth together so hard they hurt.

"Alix?" Ian cocks his head to the side.

"Huh?"

He slides off his desk and squats down in front of mine, arms crossed on the wooden surface, warm gaze on me. "What do you need?"

My mouth opens—and then closes again. What do I need? "I—"

"I mean it. What do you need?" His gaze holds mine captive, its intensity breaking yet another wall inside of me, the one that held all of last year's ugliness at bay, the free falling, the old life being ripped away from me and turned into this downwards spiral of helpless flailing to regain my footing.

What do I need?

Such a simple question with such a convoluted answer.

I need control, safety.

I need to feel like I'm doing something right.

I need to know I'm still worth something.

"Alix?" Ian's voice is soft, carrying all the empathy I'm missing from Dad.

Emotions clog my throat, cutting off my words. All I can do is whisper. "I don't know." Because admitting the truth to Ian, how insecure I am, how much I've lost my self-worth, would mean destroying his opinion of me. He's the only one who still thinks I'm the old Alix, the one who disproved the Mansfield Hypothesis, the one who had life all figured out. He still has faith in me. Au contraire to Dad, Ian doesn't think I'm broken. Weak. A failure.

And I'm going to keep it that way.

Scraping together all the strength and determination I have, I make a conscious decision to step off this emotional rollercoaster and rip my annual pass in two.

I need to toughen up.

Easier said than done, but good plan. Good plan.

Ian sighs and rests his chin on top of his crossed arms on my desk, gaze searching mine intensely, evaluating me. "Okay then." He nods to himself. "I've got an idea."

"You do?"

"Yup." He all but jumps up and takes my hand, pulling me out of my chair, a mischievous smile on his face. "Time to exercise my freedom as the head of PRICS. If Waterhouse can bend the rules, so can we."

He lets go of my hand, walks to the map of the world, and opens the secret passageway. "After you." Fumbling for my crutches, I squeeze through the hole in the wall and follow him downstairs to the Eagle's Lair. He's got an idea. Okay then.

About nine floors later, I really wish they had an elevator here.

Before I can fall into the couch and catch my breath, Ian holds open the door at the right side of the room close to his desk. "Nuh-uh. This way." He throws a thumb over his shoulder toward the bowels of the Lair.

Oh. "What else's here?" Besides the medical treatment room I've been to.

Ian leads me down the maze of blinding white corridors. "Tons. You'll get to know most of it eventually. We have almost everything. Not much personnel usually, but we can man it ourselves. A shooting range. Lab. Even a holding cell."

Okay. Not what I expected down here.

"Plus, we have this baby here." He holds one half of a wide double-door open for me and—

My barely revived spirits drop to a new low.

A gymnasium.

Not the type of idea I imagined he had, not at all.

The countdown to Ian realizing what a klutz I am has been initiated.

Most of the floor is covered with thin red or green mats, like those used during martial arts classes. In one corner of the room, a boxing ring is set up next to the wall. Lots of crates with boxing gloves and pads line the other wall, while several heavy bags dangle from contraptions mounted to the ceiling.

Ian turns toward me, working a hand through his hair. "Look. I can't help you with your father, Alix. At least not the way I'd like to. What I can do is… well, let's call it *adjusting your physical therapy goals*, because if we name it self-defense, I'm getting myself into pretty deep waters, you not being an active agent and all." He shrugs and blushes, that same hand scratching the back of his head.

"Self-defense?" I squeak.

"Exactly." He steps closer, so close I get a nose of his Ian-scent. "I can imagine what it looks like inside of here." His finger taps the center of my forehead. "Physical therapy would strengthen your body, but Krav Maga… it'll also strengthen your mind." That same finger brushes over my forehead toward a strand of hair he tugs behind my ear.

The sound of my pulse swells in my ears, roaring like a wild river.

"Okay," I breathe. Okay.

Not what I imagined, but okay.

I can handle it.

I *will* handle it.

The image of two ice-cold eyes pops back into my mind, the face they belong to assessing me, remembering me.

I shudder.

Self-defense sounds *great*.

Ian clears his throat and drops his gaze, pointing to a smaller door to the right without looking at it. "There should be workout clothing for you over there. Let's go and get changed and meet back here."

I'm not sure if I saw his cheeks redden or not. Maybe? Yeah, I think so. After readjusting my crutches, I file that information for later and hobble toward the door he pointed out, my forehead burning with the memory of his touch.

Oh, dear…

Keep it together, Forrester.

It takes me twice as long as Ian to get myself into the black yoga pants and shirt, mainly because I have to get the brace off and then on again, but maybe also because… Stalling isn't bad, is it?

Strengthen my mind… but what about my ego when I make a fool out of myself in front of Ian? Just saying, I was never the first to be picked for a team in PE. More like the last…

Eventually, I'm done changing and go back outside. I'm thankful the shirt provided is black, because I'm sure I'm showing sweat stains already, just from nervousness.

Ian is on the mat, going through a couple of kicks and punches to the air, not having seen me step out. Like me, he's in an all-black outfit—martial arts pants and a tight shirt that shows off his chest and arm muscles. He moves smoothly, somehow different than he did when wearing his suit, with a coiled power, like a panther ready to strike, prowling, evading, then bursting forward with some kind of fancy kick or strike.

Gone is the geek who talks about Physics. This is a man who knows how to fight.

For a moment, I stop and watch. Ian pulls off a combination of kicks and punches, and I envy him.

His confidence.

His skills.

His strength.

Ian spins for a high kick, long lean muscles flexed all over his body.

With a loud *clang*, my right crutch falls to the floor. Ian finishes his kick and, now that I gave myself away, waves at me to come over.

I hope he didn't see me staring at him.

My crutches leave little indentations on the mat when I wobble over. Ian grabs something from a bin next to the heavy bags before he jogs back to me.

"I know this deviates from what we discussed when I recruited you. Heck, it deviates from protocol." He frowns and sighs. "But: as we've seen since you joined PRICS, we won't know the situations you might find yourself in. Especially with Waterhouse spicing it up for us… you need to be able to defend yourself—no matter how."

Yeah, right. Maybe I could knock somebody out with my crutches. "Sure. I'll be up to a black belt level in no time." I can't keep the sarcasm out of my voice. Even if the accident never happened, I wouldn't be good at this.

"The level doesn't matter. It's a mental thing more than anything else. Surprising your opponent and never giving up, that's what makes you stronger. Everything else? That's bonus."

That little tidbit of hope thrown out to me, he starts me with a couple of warm up moves that make me break out in sweat in no time. Aww, man…! I should be studying behind a desk now. Even languages would be welcome at this point, because athletic stuff is so far out my comfort zone it's ridiculous.

Once he considers me sufficiently warmed up, Ian shows me how to make a fist and how to punch without injuring myself.

"The first two knuckles are the strongest. The others—"

I raise my hand just like in school. "Break. Read that in—"

"A journal. I know you did." A hint of delight touches his expression but is gone in an instant. I must have imagined it. And really, I should stop quoting journals.

As soon as we start going over actual physical work—fighting stance, shadow boxing—it's clear to me quoting journals isn't my only problem. My strength in this will be theoretical rather than practical application. Ian gives me encouraging comments, but honestly, he probably has to stretch to find anything positive.

So much for strengthening my mind.

Still, he advances me from shadow boxing to hitting an actual focus mitt with the hand that isn't supporting my weight with my crutch.

First, he holds it still, letting me hit against a resting target, but eventually, he starts moving it after each of my punches, making me follow him. It takes me forever, but after a while, I work out a rhythm. It's simple physics, and once my brain gets its neurons firing accordingly, I actually hit it better, despite my left leg locked in the brace and supported by the crutch. Most surprisingly, I like it. Makes me feel energized and strong, like I haven't for a long time—or ever.

Look at that. Maybe Ian's idea wasn't a bad one after all.

"Nice, Alix," he says when I deliver a good punch, his words raising me up as if I could fly.

We get faster and faster. First Ian waits seconds between my punches, but then he moves the glove so fast, I barely have time to think, and that's probably the point.

Not even a minute later, he adds a second glove for me to hit, and without thinking, I drop my crutch and start throwing punches with both hands.

A power rush surges through me unlike anything I've ever felt. With every punch I deliver, I get stronger: Despite my breath coming out in gasps and my knuckles starting to hurt from dozens of impacts they're not used to, I put more weight behind the punches and rotate my hips more, like Ian showed me.

Eventually, Ian drops his mitts, a wide grin on his face. He uses the back of his hand to wipe the sweat off his forehead. "Who said you weren't made for this, Alix? Those were awesome punches! And notice something else?" He pointedly looks down at my bad leg and then over at my crutch on the floor out of reach. "No crutches, Alix. *No crutches.* You didn't only stand without your crutches, you *punched* me *while you stood.* You stood!" He beams at me as my mouth drops open.

No crutches.

Ian grabs me by my shoulders, giving me a proud shake. "You stood without crutches! Granted, you were a bit wobbly here and there, but you didn't even notice your crutches were missing because you were focusing on the task. That's a *giant* step, Alix!"

I stare at him open-mouthed.

Ian's right. It's a huge step—no, a *giant* step, as he said.

"I stood." My voice rises at the end, as if it was a question—but it's not. It's a fact. I stood. "I really stood. And moved. On my own." The last time I did that was before the accident. I blink three, four, five times, but my crutch still lies on the floor instead of being glued to my hand.

A light, triumphant laugh burst from my throat. "I stood! Woooh!" I throw my arms up and pump them.

"You did!" Ian grins and holds up his hand for a high-five.

Me, ever the dork, tries to hit it mid-victory air punches. Of course, and probably predictable by anybody but myself I miss his hand, my momentum of committing to the move carrying me forward and into a stumble. "Whoa—!"

Before gravity and inertia can do their thing, Ian catches me. We collide in a tangle of limbs as he wraps his arms instinctively around me, stabilizing me.

"Ngh," I grunt.

Ian chuckles in response, the sound reverberating through me. "I got you, Trouble. You moved, but let's give it a bit more time for jumping, will ya?"

His words dance down my neck, and boy, if that doesn't make me aware of how close we are, I don't know what is. Oh, wait, I do know. Every breath he takes I feel in my body, every square centimeter of my body in contact with his is tingling and burning. Sensory overload, right here.

This whole moment lasts maybe a second, maybe two, before my mental faculties come back online and I take the only way out of this embarrassing situation. Clearing my throat, I pull away from Ian.

"Thank you," I say, "thank you for coming up with that microchip. Thank you for believing in me. And thank you for training me." My face might be burning, but never have I spoken truer words. Gone is the numbness from before, instead replaced by something feathery light dancing around in my chest, bouncing like an overexcited rubber ball. For the second time in less than two hours, tears prick at my eyes, but this time they're happy tears, and they don't fall.

I stood.

I stood, and after standing comes walking, after walking comes running, and after running comes a dad who can't simply dismiss me anymore.

Ian's wide smile lights up his whole face. "No need to thank me, Trouble. I'm an inventor—well, at least according to my job description before PRICS. *Of course* I'm doing all these things for you, not just because part of it is my job, but also because I genuinely feel like you deserve this chance. You'll be great at all things espionage. And the fact that you've improved stability in your leg shows that the micro radiation is already stimulating the growth factors, probably mostly neurotrophins—"

The next words slip out before I can stop them. "Aww. Talk science to me, baby," I say, then slap a hand in front of my mouth. Stupid! So stupid! "Sorry. Sorry! Didn't mean it like that! It's just been an exhausting morning and maybe I didn't eat enough or drink enough and I'm dehydrated, and also you're, like, the only one even mentioning anything beyond biology one, and when you do it really makes me happy, and since it's my leg it also…" I let my voice trail off. Embarrassment mode? Engaged!

"It also makes you happy, I get it. And no hard feelings. I'll gladly talk science to you. I know it makes your day." The way he says it, all calm with a little shrug to his shoulders, like, *no biggie, I know you, that's the way you are and that's cool by me…*

The flame lighting up my face drops lower and ignites something inside my chest, something wholesome and soothing, yet utterly exiting.

Ian shoves his hands into his pockets. "Now, let's keep this newest improvement on the down low. I agree with Dr. Soong. If your mom hears about your unexpected progress, she'll have you inside an MRI-scanner faster than I can falsify those images and erase the chip from them, and there goes that secret invention." He shudders. "I'd be in so deep, I—"

A deafening, whining alarm sound blares over the ceiling-mounted speakers.

I twitch at the same time as Ian curses. "Damn it! Can't we catch a break? *Seriously?*"

Adrenaline shoots through my veins. "What is it? What's going on?" Alarms? Is somebody attacking the White House? Dad?

"Proximity Alert." Ian curses once more. "Someone is coming to our classroom—and we're not where we're supposed to be. We're in deep."

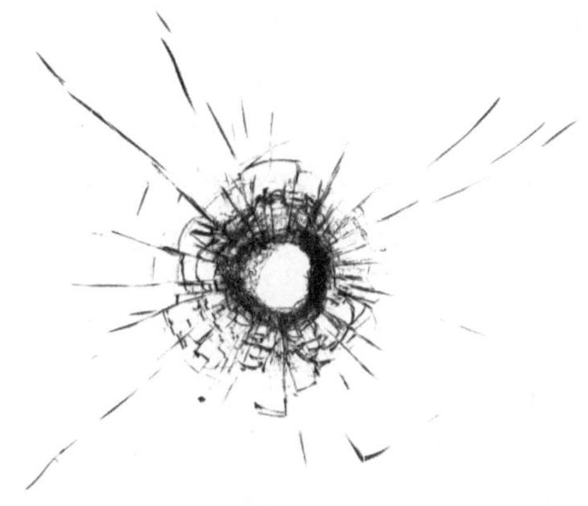

CHAPTER TEN

Rug Pulled

"I'm sorry about this, but time is of the essence!"

Before I know what's happening, Ian sweeps me off my feet to carry me horizontally across his arms, while bolting for the exit. He pivots sideways to protect me from ramming my head or body into the wall as he shoulders them open.

I squeak as he slips on the smooth floors, but he catches his balance and keeps sprinting down the hallway at a mad speed.

But he's going in the wrong direction.

"Ian—"

"Yes?" His breath comes out choppy, but I'd probably have stopped breathing if I had to run and carry him, so there's that.

"You're going in the wrong direction! The office and the stairs are—"

"Can't take them. We might be late, can't be seen exiting from the passage." He races us around another corner at a pace that has me wrap a second arm around his neck for safety and cling to him like a little baby monkey. It feels way too intimate, but I would also like to not drop, please. That being said, his hold on me is no less intimate with one of his hands pretty high up my waist and the other up my thigh, both gripping me tightly.

I don't even have time figure out how I feel about that before he crams us into an elevator so narrow Dwayne The Rock Johnson wouldn't fit.

"You'll have to stand now. Hold on to something." He pants, setting me down and stabilizing me with one hand while swiping a card in front of the elevator's reader.

The doors ram shut with a resounding metallic *bang*.

"Geez," I hiss, pulling my arms in. That thing could amputate somebody! "That's— Ngh!" The elevator shoots up so abruptly and fast I stumble into Ian, not that I had any room to move anywhere else. Ian captures me by the shoulders, then wraps one arm around me while pressing the palm of the other hand against a palm reader in the elevator's side panel.

An integrated DUTI-pad springs to life, showing a view of the hallway in front of our classroom and a tall person in a suit approaching our door. A red circle appears around his face, lighting up a moment later with a line of text popping up:

"Identification: Forrester, Leopold, POTUS."

My dad?

"Shoot," Ian curses. "Alix, follow my lead, okay?"

Follow his lead? Like—

The elevator stops with yet another forceful jerk, the kind that if I wasn't still kind of glued to Ian, would've thrown me to the floor. The doors open with a quiet hiss—and Ian guides me out of a massive old American Elm tree in the gardens, within view of my classroom, but hidden behind bushes.

No way.

Zip!

As soon as we're out of the elevator, the door closes behind us leaving nothing but a regular tree trunk, complete with bark, branches and leaves.

"Fascinating," I murmur while unwrapping myself from Ian. That's why it was such a narrow elevator. It must be the Holographic—

"Right. Let's talk about that later. Now I need you to do as I do. *Now*, Alix!" Ian pulls me with him and away from the tree.

Oh. Of course. Dad.

Instead of rushing us over to the classroom as I expected, Ian changes his approach. Gone is the hurry from before, instead he holds on to my left arm, supporting and guiding me across the lawn, careful step for careful step.

"Easy, Trouble, slow it down. You have to sell it. Lean on me," he whispers into my ear.

Right he is.

Bad leg.

I slow down my newly discovered limping walk a second before Dad steps out of our classroom behind two of his security guards. "We're clear, sir," a third one says after checking something on some kind of screen in his hands.

Dad nods—with an actual smile on his face.

A sharp pain slices through my chest, tearing open all the cuts that Ian just patched up so carefully.

Dad looks nothing like in the Oval Office. Nothing.

Gone is the vacant look, the frustration, the disappointment.

Instead he *smiles*. Like nothing happened.

It's kind of freaky.

"Good morning." He shields his eyes against the sun with the back of his hand.

That's when he notices my hand on Ian's arm.

And the smile freezes.

Ian holds out his right. "Good morning, Mr. President. An honor, Jason Miller, Alix's teacher."

It feels like forever until Dad takes Ian's hand. "It's only now hitting me that I was the one signing off on your position, Mr. Miller. I wasn't aware we had placed somebody so… young into such a responsible position. Especially considering Alix's level of education."

My jaw drops open. I didn't hear that correctly, did I? No nice to meet you, no pleasantries—he went straight for the kill shot? What the—

Ian accepts the challenge without the blink of an eye. "Yes, Mr. President, I know I'm young. I also have an IQ of one-seventy-six and will be more than capable of getting Alix back to the level she needs to succeed at Harvard."

Bam.

Touchdown.

Dad gives Ian's hand another agonizing slow shake, never taking his eyes off him. "I'm glad to hear that. Let me know if you need anything for her classes. After all, I control the school budget."

The two of them share a forced laugh, while I'm waiting for the earth to open and swallow me up. Whole, please.

Dad scans over me, brows crunching together. "Alix, why are you sweaty? And no school attire? For either of you?"

Oh, crap. Earth, now would be a good time, actually. "Well, I—"

Ian is quicker than me, by a million lightyears. "We just went over some physical therapy exercises between classes so that Alix doesn't sit for too long and gets that leg moving with her new splint. She's making good progress." He looks at me like a proud teacher, giving my dad a thumbs up.

All I do is nod like a bobble head.

Dad cocks an eyebrow. "Mr. Waterhouse failed to mention you also held a PT license. Is there anything you can't do, Mr. Miller?"

The breath I was about to take catches in my throat.

Ian on the other hand doesn't even flinch. "Possibly, but it won't matter for this position. My PT license is one of the reasons I was hired for this job. Two birds, one stone, you know?"

Both of them force out another laugh, and before Dad can unleash another array of questions, his third bodyguard with the screen in his hands looks up. "Incoming times two, sir."

Dad's shoulders pull back as if he'd gotten a reminder to stand straight.

I'm about to wonder what the agent is talking about when an intern steps out from our classroom behind my dad, Sam in his shadow.

Sam. Impeccable in his suit. Stunning, actually. The material hugs his athletic frame, making him seem even taller—and he's taller than his and my dad already. The whole look with the suit, and his hair styled in a more professional way than during the campaign trail makes him look quite yummy. I'd—

A wave of guilt crashes over me. I hugged Ian twice today, and to say I liked it would be an understatement. The guilt cranks it up, twisting my stomach into an unhealthy knot of emotions from all over the place, which is ridiculous, because Sam and I aren't a couple.

Still: One look at me and he must know what I've done. That I hugged Ian.

That I liked it.

The intern in front of Sam nervously tugs on his tie. "Uhh, the… Mr. President, the… I mean, I—" His face loses color when he realizes he's butchering it. Badly.

Sam on the other hand is on home turf with my dad. "Sir, the Secretary of State is ready for you in the Mural Room." Sam nods at Dad and winks at me with a slight smile around his lips, the one that shows only one dimple—the one that feels like a kick to my chest, speeding my heart up and making it fly.

Devil, you must've designed the teenage body.

Sam's eyes fall on my hand on Ian's arm, and as with Dad, his brows furrow.

This time I'm quicker. Out of reflex, I all but yank my arm out of Ian's, and for a second or two I'm standing freely and unassisted, without holding on to Ian at all—until I realize what a huge mistake I just made.

I *cannot* let go.

I don't have a crutch—it's still down in the gymnasium.

I blew my cover.

Lightning fast I shoot my arm back around Ian's and cover the whole episode with a little stumble.

"Oops, sorry," I say, hoping it looks and sounds convincing. Ian supports me more, but I can't tell if that's because he thinks I need it or because he's, well, playing along. Luckily for me, neither Dad nor Sam seem to have picked up on my faux pas, although Sam isn't looking anywhere else but at me.

Ian pats my hand hooked into his arm. "You should sit down, Alix. You've had enough exercising for today." He guides me toward our classroom.

"I agree." Dad's tone drops the temperature to right about freezing. He tucks his wrinkle-free suit jacket down and into shape. "Especially with that extra trip to the Oval Office this morning."

Zzzing.

There we go.

I knew it was only a matter of time.

A strange tension creeps into Dad's features. "That was the second time I found Alix away from her studies and where she wasn't supposed to be. Mr. Miller, I'd appreciate it, if—" His eyes become unfocused and glaze over for a second, then it's gone. "Never mind." He turns his attention back on me, the faint smile on his lips I've come to hate so much. "Alix, if you can't keep up your studies, I understand. If you need more breaks, more rest. The boarding school would be perfect for—"

I jerk to attention. "Don't even say it out loud, Dad. Not going to happen." Why, oh why, does he have to bring it up? Is it that hard to have me around? That hard to look at me?

Another tug on his jacket. "Judging by your current behavior I doubt your academic success is going to live up to what you could've achieved at the boarding school with the right treatment—no offense, Mr. Miller."

"None taken," Ian mumbles.

"Alix, all I'm asking is you take that into consideration. They're able to specifically cater to cases like—"

Oh, hell no. "I'm not a case, Dad! Stop saying stuff like that! I'm doing well, and I think there's improvement—"

"I've said it before and I mean it. I still think the boarding school is better for you." He casts an eye at Ian. "But since your mother and you voted against that decision and for you coming here, and I'm a man of democracy... But please, Alix, don't overdo it." He gestures down to my leg. "You know what the doctors said, and... no matter the PT, I don't want you to have false hope." A forced smile flickers across his face. False hope— wait, so he'd rather give up than hope? Give up on me?

"In any case. Mr. Miller, Alix needs a slow approach at the moment, and one that is constantly supervised. I will lower my expectations in terms of academics, but I'd at least expect her to stay out of the West Wing. I... I don't think it's professional for the

President to have his daughter around during business hours." Said the man's whose best friend's son has a desk next to the Oval Office.

The fissure in my chest rips open again, spewing blood like he'd hit an artery.

"But, sir, it was only—"

"It doesn't matter, Mr. Miller. I'd appreciate your cooperation in this matter."

With that, Dad turns around and walks out of the classroom, maybe not even knowing he has a proverbial target sign painted on his back, but surely not knowing what I already did to keep him safe.

What I would do, what I *could* do, if he took me seriously.

Alas, he's leaving Ian and me in the middle of the classroom, open mouthed and stunned.

The intern does his best to stay close to Dad, while Sam sneaks past me like a shadow. His hand brushes across mine and squeezes it once. "He doesn't—"

"Sam," my dad calls from the hallway, "Mural Room it was?"

Sam jerks up straight. "Yes, sir. Mural Room." He shoots me an apologetic glance and hurries out to follow Dad.

The door closes, leaving Ian and me alone again.

Our gazes meet, his as wide as mine. "What was that about?" Ian whispers.

My dad's ginormous ego? His inability to cope with my injuries? His disappointment in his not-perfect-anymore-daughter?

Pick one.

"Your guess is as good as mine." My voice is rough. Raw.

"He dissed us." Ian shakes his head, flabbergasted. "He totally dissed us. Lower his expectations in terms of academics? Does he know you at all?"

I wave him off. Welcome to erratic-Dad-behavior 101. "It

doesn't matter. We'll deal with it when we have to." What else is there to do? All the hope I had a mere ten minutes ago, all that is gone again.

Hot—cold. Hot—cold. I never know what to expect, and I get disappointed every single time. Maybe at this point that's my fault. What do they say? Doing the same thing over and over and expecting a different result is the definition of insanity?

Then maybe I should stop expecting Dad to change or act the way I want him to.

I fall into my seat behind my desk and cross my arms in front of my chest. Professionalism. Right. It's not *professional* for the President to have his daughter in the Oval Office. Sure. I'd win any bet it wasn't about *professionalism*. Deep down inside I know that. It was about me.

Ian's hand comes into my line of vision, holding a mug with a steaming liquid.

"It helps. And I'm telling you that as much as I'm telling myself. I can't get over the way he dissed us. He dissed *you*." Ian shakes his head.

I take the tea out of his hand, inhaling the mix of chai and Ian like an addict taking a sniff. "At this point I would say my dad has issues." One please take note, that for once I'm not blaming myself.

"Yeah, maybe. Something feels off with him." Ian's voice is soft as he slides behind his desk for a change. "Give me five minutes to forge the PT license and add it to my file at Human Resources, and then…" He sighs. "Then we'll continue PRICS training."

Because what else is there to do?

No matter what my dad thinks of Ian or me, we're here to protect him.

It's our job.

Too funny, because it seems more like I was the one needing

protection from him.

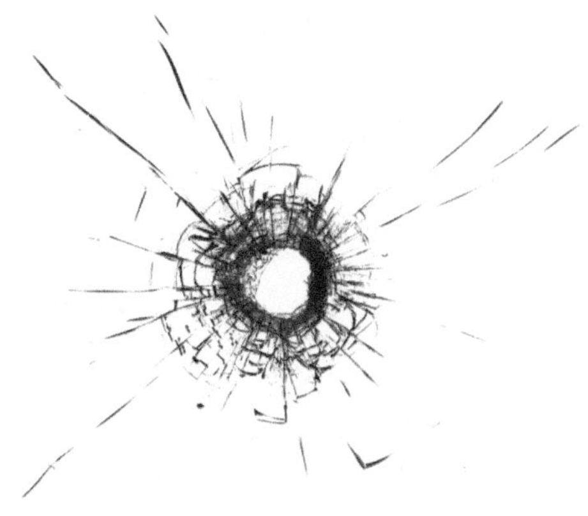

CHAPTER ELEVEN

Cards are Dealt

The next morning, I wake up early with every muscle in my body hurting and my heart as heavy as when I fell asleep. Maybe the PRICS charter has considered the psychological impact of meeting your dad's potential deadly enemies, but it surely hasn't taken the President's rejection of his own daughter into consideration, or has it now?

Whatever.

Resilience is not about taking a punch, it's about recovery, and I refuse to let Dad drag me down. Period.

I push the blanket back and swing my legs out of the bed. Ouch, sore. Come here, my little crutches.

For the first time ever, I'm kind of happy to use them on my way to the bathroom. Jell-O has nothing on the wiggliness of my arms. What a spy I am: ten minutes of punching and I'm reduced to a shaking mess the day after. Maybe that's the reason PRICS kids usually don't do any of the action-stuff.

The shower does a good job reviving me, so that once I'm ready for breakfast I'm pretty sure I'm wearing a mask of friendly neutrality compared to the scowl I'd rather show.

Professionalism.

Pfft.

I wobble down the center hallway, for once thankful for the thick carpet softening my steps and silencing my walk. Maybe I'm dragging my leg a bit, but dang, it's sore. When I pass the living room on my right, I pick up on Dad's voice from behind the slightly opened door.

"You've got to get a grip on it, Ol. I'm getting worried. At this point the repercussions for everybody involved—"

"I know, I know, but…"

Oh. Oliver. I'm about to pass the living room when Dad speaks again.

"I'm paying Sam now."

Sam? What's up with Sam? I stop dead in my tracks.

Oliver blows out a heavy puff of air. "Leo, don't get in trouble, he's a junior intern. I'll—"

"He's my private hire, and he'll work for it, no worries." He pauses. "Unless you want me to—"

"God, no! No. No. Thank you, but no. You know what happens when you give me options. Temptation is my enemy."

Soft steps approach the door. "Okay then. We'll keep the deal up for now and your salary low until—" The door opens a tad wider.

Oops.

I throw myself forward and into motion. Don't want to be caught eavesdropping—don't want to be caught by *Dad*, period. With a couple of fast hobbles, I make it into the West Sitting Hall and out of view. Here's to hope Dad and Oliver will go downstairs already. Neither of them sounded cheerful—har, har, good one—and I'd rather go through Mom's inquisitions about school than face Dad, no matter his mood.

But alas, fate throws me a bone: Instead of my mom, Sam is sitting at our dining table.

Sam.

That little bout of dizziness, that's from… walking too fast. Yup.

Sam looks up from his newspaper when he hears me coming in, gracing me with a smile that lights up the room and kicks my heart into a little stumble. The sparks in his eyes give him a mischievous, boyish charm somehow, like he and I were in on a secret nobody else knew.

"Good morning, Sunshine." He bows his head and pushes back his chair. Next thing I know, he's taken both crutches from me and hooked my arm into his until my hand rests on his arm in exactly the same way as it did on Ian's yesterday. The heat radiating from his body brings a whiff of his butterscotch scent with it, which in return sends a shiver down my spine and settles in my stomach. Predictably, my cheeks heat up, but luckily for me, Sam doesn't notice it. Instead, he helps me get to my place at the table.

I barely catch the last part of his sentence.

"… so Dad told me to wait for your mom to get me those papers, and then I'm off again."

Sam pushes my chair closer and takes the seat next to me, leaning onto the table and supporting his head with his hand. He's wearing a grey tie I would've called boring if it wasn't Sam wearing it. He makes it look good. Fantastic, actually.

"So, how's school going?" he asks softly, a little trace of something in his voice I can't quite identify.

"Meh, you know. School." This is me trying to sound appropriately bored. What did Ian say? Stay close to the truth or let them make assumptions. I don't really want to lie to Sam of all people, so I go with more information than less.

"Mr. Miller is really smart though. I've gotta give it to my parents and Human Resources, he was a good choice. Finally someone I don't have to dumb it down for, you know?" I smile at Sam and playfully punch his arm.

He wiggles his eyebrows at me, his smile turning even more mischievous. "You can always talk science to me if you want. You know that, right, Alix?"

If I didn't know better, I could swear he sounded worried.

"Yeah, I know." We've always been good at that. Easy. Sam's not as much into science as I am, but for a future lawyer, he's doing a really good job keeping track.

I point a finger in the general direction of the West Wing. "You've got to work and learn though, and I have to get through physical therapy. I'm seriously sore this morning."

Emphasizing my point, I stretch my good leg and make a painful groaning sound.

Sam's cheeks turn a healthy red. "Right. Sore."

I shoot him a confused glance. "Very much so, yes."

He reaches across under the table until he has my thigh. "Yeah? It's sore? Does *this* make it worse?" He squishes my thigh between his fingers until I burst out laughing. It hurts, it really does, but it also tickles.

I rock forward laughing and almost land face first on my plate. Sam is still squishing my thigh, moving his hand up and down my leg and evading me when I try to get rid of his. We both giggle like crazy, until Mom appears in the doorway.

"Children, children, can I never leave you alone? Alix, sit up straight. Sam, I got the papers. Give them to my husband; it should be all he needs." She hands Sam the papers.

My thigh feels cold where Sam's hand had squeezed it.

Maybe I should get my brain checked.

"Thank you, Dr. Forrester." Sam takes the papers. He gets up, pushes his chair back under the table, and playfully taps me on the shoulder. "Hope you enjoy *school* today."

He walks out of the room before I have a chance to make sense of that odd intonation. Reading between the lines isn't quite my specialty, so, is there something else he meant by that? Does he know school isn't school?

Lost in thought, I shove some bacon and scrambled eggs into my mouth.

"Glad to see you eat a bit more, sweetie." Mom presses a kiss on top of my head, then smooths down my hair. "Maybe tonight we can watch a movie together? You and me?" The hope in her voice makes it rise up in the end, a tad awkward.

Movies? Mom and I? Doing something that doesn't serve a purpose?

"Sure?" It sounds more like a question than a reply, but that's because I'm not sure I'm understanding her correctly.

"Wonderful. Looking forward to it." I get another kiss to my head, my temple this time, and then she's gone, already on her phone on the way down to her office.

A movie. Mom and me. A real mother-daughter-thing. We haven't done anything since… well, since I was ten and it became clear I wasn't developing in the same direction as she did. For her, giving lectures and talks at medical conferences, or being on TV since Dad became involved in higher politics, is the greatest thing ever. For me, not so much. It's the quickest way to make me break out in hives.

Ever since I flew into that windshield though things have changed. *She* has changed. Not that we were as close as Dad—
Yeah.
That.

I drop my head onto the table next to my plate, groaning, pretty sure I'm hearing the light laughter of fate as she extends her middle finger at me.

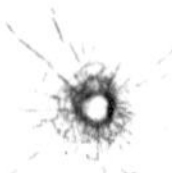

For the next four weeks, I bury myself in work.

I study harder, I read more, and I practice Krav Maga like a madwoman.

The more I focus on improving my skills, the less I have to think about my messed-up life, and the more I study and work with Ian, the more I feel like part of a team again, like I'm doing something useful.

Finally.

Ian and I, we have our own inside jokes we're cracking, and once I even got Dimitri to smile. Being in class with Ian is what gets me out of bed in the morning, and our work together is the reason I'm developing something close to an appetite again.

Of course, my mom has her own theory. "The White House is doing you good, sweetie. Nothing better than family to help you heal."

Well, yeah, only it's not my biological family, it's my adopted one, my PRICS family, because my biological one…

Two days ago, Ian suggested I give it a try with Dad during lunch down in the cafeteria, and see how it goes.

Not well is the short version.

Oh, we did talk, it's not as if he ignored me, but he never dropped the presidential façade. We ate together for fifteen minutes, and not once did he become my dad.

I don't know what's wrong with him.

Here I am, trying, and all I get is the distant-relative-treatment. The worried looks, like I'm too fragile for life. The conversations that barely scratch the surface of our relationship.

Ugh, ugh, ugh—and: Whatever.

If anything, it helped me change my approach when it comes to PRICS.

Yes, I'm supposed to *add a layer of protection* for Dad, as Ian phrased it, and I'm going to do that. It's why I signed up and what I signed up for. But… I'm not doing this in the hopes of impressing him anymore.

No. I'm done with that.

I'm doing it for me.

The time for continuing where we left off has passed, and maybe it had passed already on the day he threw me out of the Oval Office.

I'm doing it for me, because heck, it feels *good* mastering what Ian throws at me, no matter if Dad knows about my success or not.

That's why I'm pushing myself to work as hard as I've never in my life worked before. And Ian makes it easy for me to forget everything else besides PRICS. Whenever I've learned a new skill, he throws something else at me, expecting me to follow. Even I need to make sure I don't lose track of what we're studying—and that's a new experience for me.

Au contraire to the humiliation during Krav Maga. That feeling I know too well.

"Again," Ian commands from across the mat when I push myself up into a standing position, swinging my bad leg like a pirate with a wooden peg until I'm upright again. Yay for standing and wobbly-walking with my splint—boo for still not pulling off any ninja-moves.

"But I just—"

"Again, Alix." Ian's hand moves closer to the light switch. "You're overthinking. Let your reflexes take over."

I groan, and the corners of Dimitri's mouth twitch up the slightest. The bulky, padded suit he's stuffed himself into makes him look like a sumo wrestler, and the helmet adds another level of scariness.

"And remember: I want to see you follow him and bring him down. Don't stop until he's neutralized."

Seriously?

I'm already out of breath. I wipe my hair out of my face. "But—"

"Nope." Aaand he switches off the light.

It's amazing how silent darkness can be.

The second the lights are off, the whole room seems to grow into unknown vast dimensions, the only noise being the creaking of the floorboards as Ian walks toward us to the center of the room.

Well, that and my ragged breathing. It's pitch black and I can't see *anything*.

Before I have time to react, two large arms wrap around my midsection, holding me from the front above my arms. A small surprised gasp escapes me, as I drop my weight, aka, squat down as Ian taught me. Only, I'm too late. Like a toy, Dimitri picks me up, turns me sideways and smacks me into the mat.

"Ow," I groan as the lights flash back to life. My back. My side. My everything.

"Trouble," Ian gently scolds me as he walks over, "that was your third attempt." What he doesn't say is that the other two were not an iota better. It's implied though.

With a sigh he squats down next to me. "Let's break it down. You're thinking too much. You—"

I take his outstretched hand and let him pull me up to sitting. "I'm *not* thinking. That's my problem. My head's empty as soon as Dimitri grabs me. I don't know what to do."

Ian's brows scrunch together. "But we've been over the elements of this a hundred times. You know how to drop your weight, how to throw a knee, how to break the hold. You know all that stuff. You just have to let your reflexes take over."

Annoyed, I blow a raspberry. "Yeah, well, that's not working so well for me."

Dimitri hooks his hands under my arms and lifts me up to standing as if I weighed nothing. "May I suggest we switch it up for Alix?"

"Switch it up? How?" Ian stands up and brushes his hands off his thighs.

"We teach reflexes because for most people their brain won't be fast enough. Might be different for Alix."

Ian's eyes light up. "We don't teach her instinctive moves, but logical ones?"

My gaze darts back and forth between Ian and Dimitri. What the what?

"I like it." Ian rubs his hands together. "Dimitri. Slow."

Both step off to the side, away from me. Ian points at Dimitri. "He takes me into a bear hug from the front and pins my arms."

Dimitri complies, squishing Ian like a stuffed animal to his chest.

"What's the problem here?" Ian's voice is strained, thanks to Dimitri's hold.

"You can't breathe. He has control over you."

"Correct. He can lift me up, like he did with you. So what's your first move?"

"Make it difficult for him." I stand up straighter. Problem-solving.

Ian drops his weight into a half-squat. At the same time, he shoots his trapped hands forward against Dimitri's hips, creating distance between the two. "Much more difficult to lift me up like this. What's my problem now?"

Easy. "He's still holding on to you."

Ian grins. "Exactly. So let's loosen him up." In slow motion, he lifts his non-weightbearing leg, draws his knee up and rams it forward, straight into Dimitri's groin.

"Ouch," I mumble.

"Yeah, ouch, but your most effective shot. Hurts like… well, a lot. Another close-distance defense?"

"Uhh…"

"Think, Alix. Now!"

"Elbow!"

Ian delivers a slow-mo elbow to Dimitri's face. "Works, because I hit him in the groin, and he bent forward. Next!"

"Another one!"

"Next!"

"Ano—"

He rolls his eyes. "Come on, Trouble. He's lined up nicely. So nicely actually, it's an invitation." He taps a finger against Dimitri's face guard, right where the nose is.

I flinch. "Head butt?"

"Uh huh. Done correctly, one of your most effective close-range weapons. Hardest part of your skull"—he taps his forehead—"against the most vulnerable of his." He taps the plastic face guard around the area of Dimitri's nose again. "It's not only the impact, it's the whiplash too. Not good for neuronal connections, it disrupts them—*click*, lights out. Simple biomechanics."

Ian pats Dimitri's shoulder twice until he lets go. "Time to practice."

Grr.

In theory, this sounds doable. In theory.

"What I want you to do this time, is think your way through it. I don't care if the move is perfect, I want you to focus on one problem of the attack at a time and find a counter-attack, okay?" Ian has one hand on my shoulder, gaze glued to mine.

I drop mine to the ground. Ian's eyes, they do things to me, things I don't… I don't necessarily want to think about. "Uhh, yes. Understood."

Dimitri lines up in front of me. "Half speed."

"Half—" I don't get to finish my sentence. Half speed for Dimitri is double for me.

His arms wrap around my body, squeezing me, about to lift me—

Oh, hell no.

I don't want to be lifted. I drop my weight. Must keep him away from me. As Ian showed me, I ram my palms forward into his hips and keep my elbows close to my body. Distance. Good.

Dimitri moves in again—okay, fine. Serves me well. I yank up my right knee and throw it forward with all my might.

With a satisfying dull *smack,* it connects with Dimitri's groin—not that it did anything with the padded suit he's wearing, but still.

"Yes! That's it, Trouble! Keep it up, keep it up!" Out of the corner of my eye, I see Ian pump a fist. Nothing better to motivate me than somebody believing in me. *Hint, hint,* Dad.

My brain tackles this like a physics problem. Velocity, angle of the impact, flexibility of the spine—*boom!*

My helmeted forehead crashes into Dimitri's face shield, the impact throwing his head back.

"Ng-uh," he grunts—and lets go of me!

I throw my arms up in the air. "Woohoo! I did it! I did it!" The ultimate proof that mind over, uhh, reflexes works! Put your mind to it and there is nothing—

Dimitri rams into me with the power of a steam train. Inertia and the force of the impact carry my arms forward as my body doubles over the shoulder sunk into it.

We hit the mat with a thundering *wham* that drives all air form my lungs. Like a true ninja on a mission Dimitri does… *something*, and before I know it, he has me in a choke hold.

"Never stop or give up before your opponent is down," he mutters into my ear, giving his arms a little squeeze for emphasis. "The fight isn't over until it's over. No matter how good or how bleak the situation, you finish the fight." One more squeeze, and I cough.

"'Kay," I choke out. Life lesson right there. Maybe that one should overrule the mind-over-reflex-one. Pride comes before the fall, so much for my premature celebration.

Dimitri releases me and springs to his feet. Damn ninja-moves, seriously.

Ian slow-claps from the edge of the mat, walking over to us with a wide grin. "Nice, Trouble. Much better than before. Use your brain and—"

"Tell it not to stop until the fight is done. I know." I massage my throat and sit up.

Ian holds out a hand and helps me up. "Exactly. There may be a time where I'm not there. Where Dimitri isn't there. Keep your emotions locked out. Fear. Panic. Relief. Analyze the situation and act accordingly." He hasn't let go of my hand and it brings my lungs close to failure and my heart to a spasm.

Keep your emotions locked out.

Good one, I can't even do that when it's not about life and death.

Still holding my hand. Like it's no big deal.

But it is. It's a really big deal. It's such a big deal I don't know what to do with it.

Still holding my hand.

Ian arches an eyebrow. "Hear me? Analyze the situation and

act accordingly."

Analyze and act accordingly.

Still holding my hand.

Analyze and act accordingly.

Right.

That's my specialty, isn't it?

Only, it isn't in all aspects of life.

Analyze and act accordingly.

Still holding my hand.

Analyze and act accordingly.

Still holding my hand.

I chomp down on the inside of my cheek, although the pain does nothing to clear my mind of the idiotic idea taking shape inside it.

So screw it: I close my fingers over Ian's. Gentle. Soft. And, in the most ballsy move I've ever pulled, I look straight into his eyes. "I am."

Ian takes a sharp breath in as his gaze shoots down to our hands and then up right into my eyes.

One second passes.

Another one.

A third one, followed by a loud swallow.

Still holding my hand. "I'm glad you are."

A series of shivers spreads across my skin.

Whatever I'm doing here, I'm playing with fire.

And I'm bound to get burned.

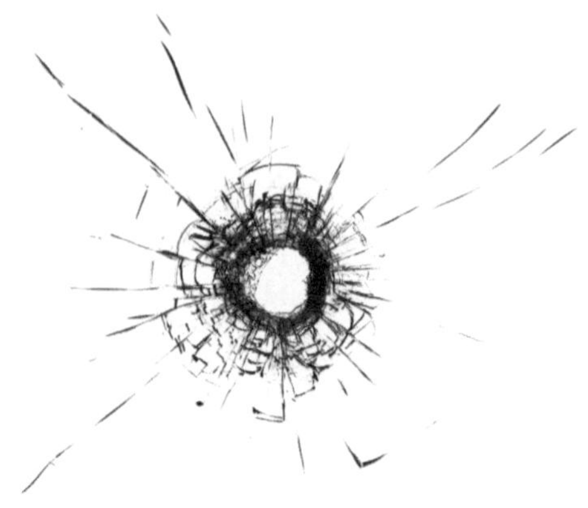

CHAPTER TWELVE

Unexpected

A couple of weeks later, at least my Krav Maga skills have improved, *au contraire* to my relationship with Dad. I can't bridge the gap that's opened up between us, and it bugs the heck out of me. It's—as always—not for lack of trying on my part, even though I've gone from *desperately* trying to *trying out of scientific curiosity*: Maybe today will be the day where things change. No? Oh well. Data logged for future reference, move on.

I must say, this approach is much better for my mental health.

Sometimes I wonder if he knows his disappointment in me has hurt me more than the accident, but I don't think he does. Or well, at least I hope so, or else it would bring his behavior to a whole new level of crappiness. I'm *this* close to throwing that into his face one of these days, but to be honest… I haven't found the courage yet.

Today has been an exhausting day with about a dozen new Krav Maga drills, hours of political history, and not nearly enough chai to regain my strength from either. To top it off, it's dinnertime.

I should have more of an appetite, but sitting across my parents at the dinner table while Dad's grumpier than usual thanks to some setback with the ever-present Genetic Testing Bill and its rider is not really setting the mood for me. Our chef has served a delicious filet mignon with baby asparagus, but I'd rather be in my room already, especially with Mom rambling on about a new project she took on as First Lady, trying to get Dad and me involved and talking.

"… and that's how we want to boost vaccination rates in underserved areas. What do you think, Alix?"

"Huh?" I look up from my plate. I'm not used to being asked for my opinion anymore, although yes, to her credit, Mom has been trying. Funny how my parents' positions changed in the last year.

Mom raises an eyebrow.

"Excuse me, I meant." Grunting sounds don't count as a reply, she always says.

Satisfied, she nods once. "I was asking you if—"

"I think you should drop it, Bethany." Dad wipes his mouth with his napkin, only to pick up the fork once more and continue his meal.

"Not at all, Leo. Alix would be perfect for this project with the CDC."

"I think she should take it easy. We're putting too much on her shoulders already, don't you think?"

Ouch.

Ouch, and enough! I slam my fist onto the table. "Dad! For crying out loud, I'm not fragile! My shoulders can handle it; my brain can handle it; *I* can handle it!" Granted, I only got part of the conversation, but can we stop putting me down and start lifting me up? The resignation in Dad's voice isn't imaginary or my sensitivity either. It's *there*!

Both my parents stare at me as if I'd grown a second head.

My mom recovers first, ever the diplomate. "What if we divided it between her and Gianna?"

Oh, hell to the no, no matter what the question.

"Bethany—" Dad starts.

"Mom!" I'm about to protest, when my cell next to me on the table vibrates and my iPhone's home screen activates with a pop-up:

Read page 112, please.

I cough and wheeze on my inhale—Ian's signal for an emergency meeting at PRICS.

Crap.

Crap, and so not good right now.

How do I get out of here, given that I'm sitting in a room with the two people who are absolutely not allowed to know what I'm up to?

Mom looks over to me when she hears me cough. "You all right, sweetie? Or do I need to Heimlich you?" She winks at me as she hands me my glass of water.

I take a sip and breathe easier. If she's making bad medical jokes, I may have a chance to get out of here—she's in a good mood, despite Dad crossing her plans for me. I wipe my mouth on my napkin to gain another second while coming up with a plan.

"No, Mom, but thank you for suggesting it. If I ever need a Heimlich maneuver, you'll be the first to know." I give her a dorky thumbs-up. Playing along is paramount now. "Oh, but speaking of 'first to know': do you mind if I went down to the classroom for a while longer tonight? Mr. Miller gave me this big assignment, and I think I'm really making good progress, but whenever I try to get to it up in my room, I get distracted. I need to get it done though, so I thought I'd do it downstairs to keep myself focused, and since Dad wants me to be more in my classroom anyway apparently…" Sorry, couldn't keep that one back. Did he ever think about asking *me* how I felt about the CDC-project?

I look from Mom to Dad, keeping my innocent-daughter-smile up while trying to not show how much I *really* need to leave. Like, right now. I can't have a veto from either of them. While I could access PRICS via the secret entrance and stairways hidden behind my bedroom's fireplace, I would prefer not to. My parents know I'm home, so if they check on me and I'm gone… It's a risk I don't want to take.

Dad's right eyebrow cocks up. "Is Mr. Miller going to be there?"

"Uhh…" Good question. I mean, yes, but should I say that?

Dad tilts his head, waiting, that annoying pseudo-smile on his face that doesn't reach his eyes. He isn't happy—but about what? Not happy that I'm going to burden myself with more work, weak little me? Not happy if Ian is there, or if he isn't?

I decide to go with a maybe. "Possible." I shrug. "He often works late."

"I see." He takes another bite of food without even looking at the plate. His gaze stays on me, evaluating me, burning through me.

Mom sighs. "All right, Alix. While your dad and I would obviously prefer you up here for a quiet evening, if you need to work on this assignment, get it finished and show Mr. Miller how it's done." There it is, the competitive edge she doesn't only have for her own projects, but for all of mine too.

Today, it comes in handy. No matter Dad's opinion, I knew

she wouldn't be able to stand the idea of her genius daughter not finishing an assignment on time. Oh, the shame.

"Thanks, Mom, that was really bugging me. Do you mind if…?" I let my question hang in the air, drop my napkin on the table and fish for my crutches next to my chair.

"Oh no, that's quite all right, there is no dessert today anyway." She waves her hand in my direction, dismissing me.

Dad doesn't say a word, yet his gaze burns into my back until I close the door to the dining room behind me.

I give it my best to make it out of the residence as quickly as I can, crutches and hobbling and all. Dimitri falls in step with me, as always.

"Wheelchair?"

I shake my head. "No. Easier to maneuver on crutches." Plus, Ian said to skip the wheelie as much as possible, since the chip seems to be doing its job and we need to work on the alibi of the brace improving my leg. Can't say I mind complying with that suggestion.

"Do you know…?" I whisper over to Dimitri. The only response I get is a short shake of his head coupled with a worried look around if anyone overheard me.

When we enter Ian's office down in the Eagle's Lair, he's sitting behind his desk, focused on something on one of his DUTI-pads. He doesn't even look up when we come in, and points to the couch.

"Have a seat. Give me a second."

"Sure," I croak. I've no idea what's going on, and it translates into a weird nervousness. Still, I sit and sink into the deceivingly comfortable couch, considering I'm probably waiting for bad news. I rest my crutches next to me and lean into the pillows, waiting.

After another two minutes, Ian grabs a DUTI-pad and crosses the room. Gone is the playful look he usually carries. This is business. He falls into his usual chair across from me and throws the DUTI-pad onto the table.

"What do you know about lev-metaminozole, Alix?"

"Lev-metaminozole?" Not the kind of question I expected. I shrug. "Not that much, just main-stream media knowledge. Designed as a drug against seizures and turned into a party drug with a pretty high demand for a couple of months. Vanished from the market when people died after only mild overdoses. Apparently, it overwhelms certain enzymes in the brain stem and suppresses the need to breathe, correct? I think they all died of asphyxia within minutes of taking the drug."

Lev-metaminozole had come in from the Eastern European area somewhere. Its street name was "breathless", and people assumed it was because its effects were so stunning it made you, well, breathless. Turned out they rather named it after its biggest side effect, and once the media had picked up on all those deaths and made the dangers well known, the drug evaporated, its place taken again by good old XTC.

Ian gives me a quick small smile and nod.

"Correct. We haven't had any drug busts with it for over a year now, and we thought it was gone for good. Well, it still probably is, at least in the grand scheme of things, but..." He falls back into the cushions and runs a hand over his face absentmindedly.

"Well, there's no good way of saying it, so I might just as well get it over with: we think your father has been the target of a lev-metaminozole poisoning intended to kill him."

The words hit like a physical blow. *"What?"* My stomach

lurches and I bolt upright.

I didn't hear that right.

The room tilts. No, no, no—this can't be happening, it can't be! Static fills my ears.

Dad…! He—

No, wait, *wait*. I saw Dad alive and well about five minutes ago.

My breath escapes in a shaky rush. "Ian, this is insane. I just saw him before I came down and he was fine. Your intel has to be wrong."

Of course, the information is flawed. Obviously, Dad is alive!

Ian holds his hands up. "Yes, I know that, I know that. The reason we're having this meeting is because while the assassin did *not* succeed in killing your father. They almost killed Yoshi Nagakawa instead."

Yoshi? Wait, *Yoshi*? Almost killed?

I cover my mouth with my palm, muffling the strangled sound trying to escape. Yoshi… "Is he okay?" Ten seconds ago, I thought this was a misunderstanding, now, not so much anymore. An abyss opens up under me. If Yoshi got hurt, if someone got close enough to hurt the White House Deputy Chief of Staff, who is to say that person couldn't hurt my dad?

"What happened?" I whisper from behind my hand.

Ian takes a deep breath. "Yoshi is okay. Mostly. He took your father's limo to an event downtown. On the way over there, he opened up one of those little water bottles your father insists on having in the mini bar, you know? Well, he drank some of that water. When the driver pulled over at their destination and opened the door for him, they found Nagakawa seizing in the back. 911 got him into the hospital in time, but he's still intubated and on a breathing machine. They found close to deadly levels of lev-metaminozole in his blood. He didn't stand a chance—besides a slight acidic sting to it, the drug is tasteless."

Oh my goodness. Poor Yoshi—and what a close call for both, him and Dad. It could have easily been Dad drinking from that bottle, he usually has one or two of those on every limo ride. He's a fan of staying hydrated and has the limo stacked with tons of those little pink-and-blue-striped bottles, his favorite brand, ordered from France.

I let myself fall backward into the couch. My core muscles refuse to support me. "How do we know Dad was the target for sure?" A cold fist clamps around my heart. "Who could've done it?" *And why wasn't I there to protect Dad?* The fist clamps harder. "Who knows about Yoshi? What else do *we* know?" I want to know everything. Need to know everything. Data grounds me, and boy, do I need to be grounded right now.

"We are ninety-nine percent sure your father was the intended target. It happened with water, which usually only your father drinks, and it happened in your father's limousine. He was supposed to take it to a meeting regarding the rider for the Genetic Testing Bill, but he was needed in the Situation Room last minute and couldn't go. That's why he sent Yoshi and let him use the limo alone for the first time ever, to get to the meeting and take his place. As a general rule, if you poison water in the President's limousine, you're not out to get his Deputy Chief of Staff."

Ian messes through his hair, shaking his head. "In terms of what else we know, it's not much. There were no prints on the bottle—on any bottle—and nothing out of the ordinary happened to or with his limousine. No repairs, no detailing, nothing. We're waiting for the results of a DNA screen, but preliminary results show no DNA that we didn't expect in this limo. That's pretty bad news for us. It means either the assassin is very smart and careful and didn't leave any DNA behind, or whoever the assassin is, is from your father's circle of trust."

Boom. That bomb hits me right into the gut.

Dad's circle of trust; one of us? That thought is more than scary.

"Oh my God," I whisper. My hands shake, and not even folding them keeps them steady when the implication of what Ian said sinks in.

No: When it sinks in completely.

My face must be as white as Ian's by now. We're two ghosts looking at each other.

"It also means whoever did this is still around and will probably try again, am I right?" It's a logical conclusion: if you risk getting caught trying to kill POTUS, you're crazy or desperate enough to try again until you succeed.

Ian blinks slowly once, nodding. "Yes, that's the assumption we're working under. Alix, listen…" He adjusts himself in his seat, fingers sifting through his hair once more. Now I know why he looks so tousled this evening. He sighs. "There's one thing I haven't told you yet. One thing that makes this a real mess."

My heart drops down to my feet.

"What?" I croak. Maybe I don't want to know.

Ian sighs again, buying himself time. "There's been one minor change from the limousine's routine. It's not big enough that we definitely know we have our killer, but it's big enough for us to investigate. Amando, the chauffeur, is the one who usually fills the minibar as part of his responsibilities with Limo One. Well, he was out for two days, and so… As the Chief of Staff Oliver Brooks reassigned the task… to Sam. Sam took over, Alix. Sam filled the minibar with the poisoned water bottles his father gave him."

I tilt my head to the left, frowning. Okay, Oliver gave Sam a job, and Sam filled the minibar, so what? We should question them if they saw—

The gears click into place and my thoughts come to a screeching halt.

Sometimes, I'm surprisingly slow.

"No." I don't even say it out loud, I only whisper it. "No." I shake my head violently until I get dizzy. "Nu-uh. I know what you're thinking and what the Secret Service must be thinking, but nu-uh, neither nor. Oliver didn't mess with those bottles, and neither did Sam." That's not possible. Not my dad's oldest friend. Not *Sam*, of all people.

Ian frowns, and for the shortest moment, I fear he's going to tell me they've taken Oliver or Sam into custody already, but no: If they had anything substantial on them, they'd be under lock and key by now and this conversation would be going differently.

Ian sighs. "Believe me, that's what I thought, but it's our only lead. Nothing else came up so far. We have orders from headquarters to start investigating the Brookses as of tonight. We're up to Condition Orange, and the only reason we're not up to Red is that we're hoping to draw the assassin out, and not push them into hiding."

I still don't think I'm processing this right. My brain has slowed down to first gear, unable to focus on what Ian tells me.

"Assassin… Wait, what? You… They're really thinking it was either Oliver or Sam? Why… I mean, how—"

From his usual position in the corner of the room, Dimitri pushes his earpiece farther into his ear, listening for a moment, before he looks up at Ian. "The Secret Service has just begun to brief the President."

Ian acknowledges the information with a quick nod. "Here's what's going to happen. Only your father will know about the poisoned bottles—well, and Yoshi Nagakawa, obviously. The Secret Service will keep this on the down low. They'll increase all of your father's security until we catch the assassin. There's a lot to it, not only visible manpower. We'll also crank up surveillance at all critical points with camera feeds. Your father will wear a tracking device so we know his whereabouts 24/7, even if separated from his security detail. While doing that, they will also keep their eyes on Oliver Brooks—again, inconspicuously so, as to not alarm him they're onto him." He holds up a hand before I can argue.

"Problem is, they can't do that for Sam. He's a junior intern without an assigned security detail, so he'd definitely notice a new agent following him around, and we can't have him become suspicious and… warn his father, or be warned himself." At least Ian has the decency to look uncomfortable with that last sentence.

I rub a palm across my eyes. "Ian, seriously—"

"Yes, Alix, seriously. And that's not all. Our biggest job is not merely reacting to what happened by increasing security, but actively preventing another attempt. We *need* to find that assassin, Alix—whoever it is, Oliver, Sam, someone else. It might be the same person whose threat we didn't catch all those weeks ago, or it might not, but we need to find them as quickly as possible, and we need to be smart about it. And if we can't find the assassin, then we need to rule out suspects to focus all our efforts on the one goal of preventing another assassination attempt on our President."

He leans forward in his chair, green eyes fixed on mine.

"Training is over, Alix. Waterhouse gave the green light. We're activating you."

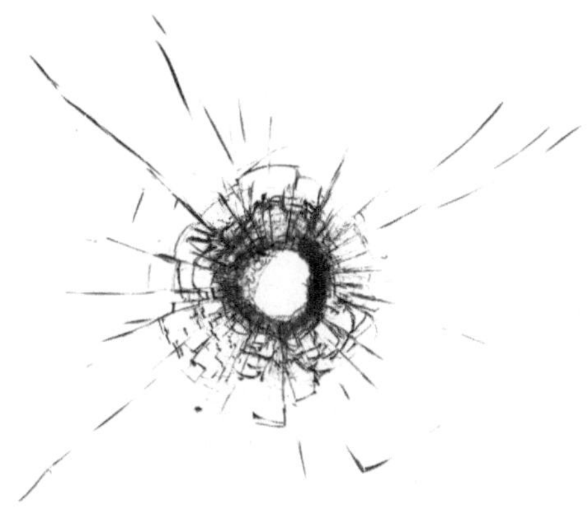

CHAPTER THIRTEEN

Shell-Shocked

"Here. Drink."

Ian pushes a cool glass into my numb hands. When I don't react, he sighs and kneels in front of me.

"Alix, you'll do fine." One of his hands comes to lie on my knee, its warmth breaking through the spell that has me. The glass shakes as I lift it to my mouth to take a sip of the cool liquid. Cherry Coke.

"Sam didn't do it, Ian." My voice is barely audible and rough, like I screamed my heart out a minute before. Sam didn't do it, and neither did Oliver. They love Dad, as weird as it sounds, but they do. They'd *never* try to kill him.

Ian squeezes my knee once, smoothing his thumb over it, the movement so much more reassuring than the frown that crosses his face. "Alix, you understand why we have to follow that lead though, right? I mean—"

161

"Yeah. Yeah, I do." Of course I do. I grimace and rub my palm across my eyes. "It's just that Yoshi's in the hospital because someone tried to kill Dad. *Kill* him! And the only lead we have is Sam and Oliver. *And* you're activating me. I seriously don't know what to think." I look down into the Coke—well, I pretend to. In truth I'm keeping my eyes on Ian's hand on my leg and the mesmerizing rhythm of his thumb. I have to look up if there's any kind of anatomical connection between the knee and one's stomach. It seems there shouldn't be, but if I go by what I'm feeling, there must be. If not that, then to the toes, because mine are positively curling.

My vision blurs. Oh, how much I'd rather focus on *this* and not the scary reality of what just happened. *Anything* but thinking about an assassination attempt on Dad.

Tempting—but not an option.

I tear my gaze away. "I need a minute to digest this."

"I know," Ian replies calmly. "I know. Our first priority is to keep your father safe, and right now that means we'll take advantage of your more than unique position. You're close to everybody involved, that's what's going to help us here."

He gives me a small smile, never breaking his mesmerizing rhythm on my knee. "Lev-metaminozole is still out there, and with the right contacts and a bit of effort, anyone could get it given enough time. Could've been Sam, could've been Oliver. Could've been neither, but somebody else. No matter what, the Secret Service will upgrade the President's detail and keep an eye on Oliver. We need you as Sam's friend. In no way are we expecting you to jump in front of a bullet for him; that's not what this is about. We need you as Sam's friend. If he is—should be— the assassin or a part of the attempt somehow, he'll be on high alert and careful whenever the Secret Service is around. You're the inconspicuous *in* for us, his friend, with whom he doesn't have to keep his shields up. The likelihood that he's going to let something slip with you is way higher, especially because you're trained by us to pick up on it, Trouble. You're the perfect mix. Innocent in his eyes, an asset in ours." He squeezes my knee. "Anything is considered a success. If you stay close to Sam and prevent another attack if he indeed is the assassin. If you find out anything useful about Oliver through him. If you catch Sam doing anything suspicious—"

I try to interrupt, but Ian lifts his free hand. "I know you don't think it was him, but please, you've got to keep an open mind. It's about the President's safety. We *cannot* afford to overlook anything."

I close my mouth again and nod. He's right, but that doesn't mean I have to like it. Waterhouse might primarily put me on this mission so I can catch an assassin, but to me, it's about that as much as it is about clearing Sam's name. Sam didn't do it— not Sam, not my best friend, not him. I would bet my life Oliver has nothing to do with this either, but him the Secret Service will take care of.

I take another sip of my Coke, and finally, my spirits regain some of their strength. This is what I was trained for. Dad needs my protection, and so does Sam. Waterhouse is activating me, and well, he's probably in for a surprise. Sam isn't alone in this. He's got me in his corner. I won't let them start a witch-hunt. I'll do whatever it takes to clear his name. If that means I have to find the real assassin, then so be it. I have all the PRICS resources I need, plus a couple of months of training under my belt, and most importantly, I have a brain I'm not afraid to use.

I can get Sam out of this mess, and hopefully his dad as well. Oh, and keep mine from getting assassinated. Yes. That, too.

Ian sighs and pushes himself off my leg to stand. Dang it. It was nicer when he still touched me.

"Starting tomorrow, you'll get closer to Sam. We can talk about alibis and the details later, but it's paramount you stay under the radar. Sam can't know what you're up to. If he is"— he corrects himself when he sees my facial expression—"*turns out to be* the assassin, we can't afford to warn him. If he isn't, we can't afford the true assassin realizing we know Nagakawa's hospitalization wasn't an accidental seizure. It'll take him or her a day or two to realize that plan isn't working. That means, we want that person in custody before he comes up with a Plan B."

There's a flaw in that logic. "But if he doesn't know we're on to him, won't he wait for Dad to drink the lev-metaminozole?" He has that death-trap in place, so…

Ian shakes his head. "Tomorrow morning, the Secret Service will be conducting a surprise in-service exercise for the incoming agents to the White House." He uses two fingers for air-quotes. "All presidential state cars will get a total security overhaul, and that includes replacement of everything possible, from fluid for the windshield wipers, to oil, to moveable parts in the limousine. Laptops, the blood reserves—and the drinks."

Makes sense. "So that's when the assassin will know Plan A didn't work, and he or she might move on to Plan B."

Ian sits in his chair again, green eyes focused on me "Correct. That's why we want you to keep an additional eye on Sam. But keep in mind, we also want to stay under the Secret Service's radar. Most of them don't know about PRICS. Their clearance level isn't high enough. I'd prefer if it stayed that way."

I nod, breaking eye contact and focusing on the glass of Coke that I turn between my hands. "What about Dad?"

"That's going to be the tough part." Ian crosses his legs as if he needed a barrier between me for what he was about to say.

I know what's coming before he opens his mouth. "I have to keep an eye on him too." No matter if he thinks I can't even tie my own shoelaces anymore.

"I'm sorry, Trouble," Ian says quietly. "It's not the easiest task given all that happened, but we need you closer to your father. You're our inside guy. Gal, I mean. Especially when he's home in the residence and the agents are standing watch outside of it. You're our eyes right at the source. Your father needs you closer—although he doesn't know it yet."

I take a deep breath and set the Coke down on the couch table before wiping my hands on my thighs.

No, he doesn't know it yet, but even if he did, I doubt he'd take me seriously.

When I make it back to the residence after another hour of briefing, details, and discussion of protocol, I peek into the living room. Mom sits on the couch, alone. The TV is on and while she's looking at it, she's staring right through it. By now, they must have told her about the assassination attempt on Dad and what really happened to Yoshi.

For the first time in years, my heart truly goes out to my mother. She looks… lost in the flickering light of the television. We're not a cuddly family, but I wish I could go over and hug her. Of course I can't—for one, we've barely started doing that again over the last year and it's still awkward, and for another, she'd know that I know about the attempted murder of my dad-slash-her-husband.

So I take a half step around the door. "Mom? I'm back. Heading to bed. Good night."

My mom twitches. Boy, she must've been far away in her mind, not that I can't imagine why. She turns around to face me and it takes all the self-control I have to not flinch or jerk back:

she looks horrible: Dark circles under her eyes like she cried, her usually pristine makeup smudged. I never noticed how many wrinkles she has—or maybe she didn't have them until tonight, I couldn't tell.

Yep, they told her about the attempt all right.

She tries to lift the corners of her mouth into a smile. Yeah. She fails that, completely. "Oh, Alix, I didn't hear you there. Sure, darling, go to bed, it's late. We've all had a difficult day." She turns to face the TV again and I know I'm dismissed. Dad is nowhere to be seen on my way to my bedroom, so I assume he's still in the Situation Room getting briefed. I wonder how he took the news. I also wonder if they told him about Sam and Oliver, but I don't think so. Ian said the Secret Service's tactic would be getting the assassin to be overconfident thinking they weren't on to them, and drawing them out. We both think it is risky for Dad, but the Secret Service wants to handle it that way and keep the information contained. Not sure what I think about that or that nothing was made or will be made public either, since this is a matter of national security. Jenna Altman will include a small one-liner about the Deputy Chief of Staff being hospitalized for a seizure into her press briefing, and that's it.

All those thoughts keep running around my head when I go back to my room. I get ready for bed, and tuck myself in, eyes wide open and my mind still running in circles.

It's not until a couple of minutes later when I realize I walked across half the room without my brace on.

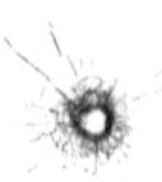

The next morning, we meet in our classroom the same time as always. I didn't see either Mom or Dad this morning and I don't have a problem with that at all. I haven't really worked on a tactic how to get close enough to Dad again that I can do my job—that he'll let me do my job.

Ian starts with a situation report, and not much is new. The press swallowed the fake story about Yoshi's illness. He's off the breathing machine and conscious this morning. One worry off my chest.

Security has been increased as discussed, but during the night, the Secret Service hasn't come any closer to finding the assassin, so our plan of trailing Sam is still on. First though, Ian and I run through the data we got from headquarters: DNA screens, chemical analysis and video surveillance reports.

All the stuff I learned—in PRICS and in school—has a real-life application. A shudder runs down my back. Perspective. Who cares about quantum mechanics? Writing papers, handing them in on time, taking quizzes… Nothing could be less important. *This* on the other hand… this is true responsibility. It's relevant. Important. It *matters*. I'm dealing with lives, and that thought alone is enough pressure to focus more than a hundred percent on whichever document Ian gives me.

The whole morning and most of the afternoon we're looking for a needle in a haystack, for anything the Secret Service could've overlooked and that could be worth something to us—but nothing. If I want to clear Sam's name, this is not the way that's going to happen. What a frustrating waste of my time.

Ian is about to show something on the white board pulling double-duty as a screen, when the alarm blares from the speakers.

This time I know the sound: we're getting a visitor.

Ian's gaze flies up to the monitor showing Dimitri's back to us in the hallway as always, but also a tall figure approaching. A circle pops up around his face, identifying him as "Brooks, Sam'mear, junior intern." And just like that, the atmosphere in our classroom has shifted.

"Well, at least we don't have to sprint up here this time," Ian says drily while pressing the button that converts our surroundings into a regular classroom again. Spy school? You wouldn't know it looking at this room.

After a couple of seconds, Dimitri opens the door and Sam comes in, tie not quite in place and the top button of his dress shirt opened underneath. I wonder if he knows he has a target painted on his back.

The second Sam's gaze falls on me, a smile comes to life on his face.

"Hi, Sam," Ian and I say simultaneously.

Despite the assassination attempt and everything around it, a tiny giggle escapes me. Ian and I, we've done this a couple of times already. Guess we vibe at the same frequency.

Sam's smile grows forced, so I backpedal.

"Hi," I say again, giving him a small wave.

His features soften. "Sorry for the interruption, but your dad asked me to tell you to be early for dinner today. He has an opening and would like to have dinner with all of us before he has to go back down to the office."

My jaw drops. Excuse me, come again? Dad is actually asking for my presence? Dinner with all of us—including Sam, I assume—like in the good old times?

I throw a quick glance at Ian, who cocks his head at Sam, a quizzical look on his face.

From an espionage point of view, it's perfect for us: victim and potential assassin in one room and me in between, what could go wrong?

From a needy daughter's point of view… A little spark of hope starts glowing somewhere in the deepest corner of my heart I'm trying my best to ignore. Dad was the target of an assassination attempt. If that doesn't change one's view on life and death... So yeah. Him asking for me doesn't necessarily mean that anything has changed between us.

But then, *he's asking for me.*

I blink once.

Fat chance.

How can I be such a sucker—apparently, I didn't learn anything from the past.

But hope... hope is the strongest emotion of them all, well, maybe trumped by love, but that's it.

Ian beats me to it. "If the President needs you all for dinner, Alix, the President needs you all for dinner." Only because I know him so well do I hear the skepticism in his voice as well as the hidden order.

This is as good a foot in the door as any. We both know it.

"Sure." I stretch my response and wipe my sweaty palms on my jeans.

Ian gives me a thumbs-up. "I'll see you tomorrow then. French vocabularies and grammar can wait." He walks to the screen-turned-normal-whiteboard and wipes off French vocab I hadn't even noticed. Way to go with our cover.

I collect my crutches and work myself up to standing. Within a split second, Sam is next to me, steadying me by the elbow and wrapping his arm around my waist.

Annoyance flashes through me. For heaven's sake, I can do this mysel— Aaand he doesn't know that. Sam's always anticipated my needs, helped me. It's sweet, it really is, and I love that about him, but in retrospect... how helpless exactly did I come across for the last year for him to basically jump at me the moment I try to stand up?

A sting in my mid-section gives the answer.

Yeah. I definitely embraced the victim-mentality.

Sam tightens his hold on my waist, and the gentle pressure of his fingers plus a whiff of his butterscotch-scent kick that annoyance about him helping me out of my system and my heartbeat into overdrive.

Why again did I mind him supporting me if it means he's *that* close to me?

No idea.

Once I'm out from behind my desk and on my crutches, Sam's hand slips from my waist, fingers trailing along my back, leaving sparks along their path.

A shiver runs down my spine. Uhh… did he do that on purpose or an accident?

Carefully, I check Sam out from under my lashes, but his attention is on my crutches, making sure I have them right. Which, technically, I can also do myself.

"All right, good to go. Dinner awaits, my lady." Sam bows, and when he comes back up, he places his hand on the small of my back again, as if it belonged there. "Shall we?"

Maybe I'll become a good spy after all, because the way I'm not twitching from his touch, I'm not dropping my gaze, and I'm not making this awkward by stuttering, is truly impressive.

"Of course, dear sir. I can't wait."

A muffled, odd sound draws my attention to Ian—Ian, frozen in place, eraser hovering over the French *l'amour existentielle*, his gaze locked on Sam's hand on my back. When he catches me looking, he fixes a quick smile on his face.

"Bon appétit, as the French would say."

"Merci beaucoup," Sam replies with a heavy American accent, and guides me out of the classroom.

Every step along the way to the residence I'm hyperaware of his touch, of course I am, it's *Sam*, we're talking about, my forever crush—yet I can't get over the odd look on Ian's face when he saw Sam's hand on my back.

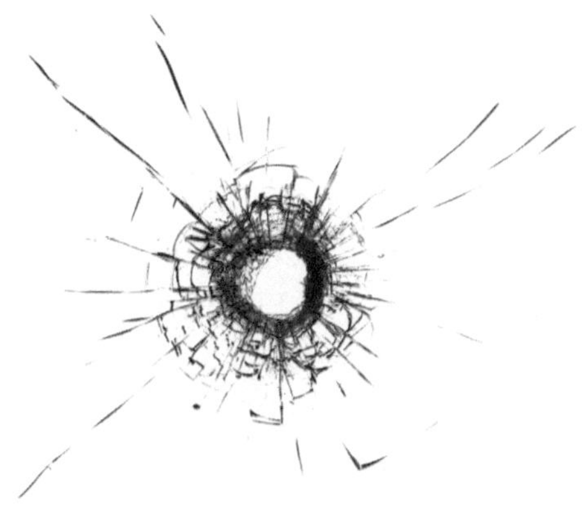

CHAPTER FOURTEEN

Hearts, Hurting

Once we hit the residence, Dad catches us in the hallway. He looks worse for the wear, which reminds me of the time during the primaries, when the stress level was so exorbitant he looked like a zombie: Dark circles under his eyes, skin pasty, and a certain level of tiredness in his eyes, no matter the time of day.

That's what he looks like now.

He nods at us. "Just one second, Alix. Go ahead, Sam, your dad and Bethany are already in there."

Ah, look, Oliver is joining us. Score for Agent Forrester.

Dad waits until Sam has closed the door, leaving him and me alone in the hallway. He loosens his tie and pulls it out from underneath his collar. "I... I need to talk to you for a moment."

Oh. This is new. "Sure." I shift my weight onto the right crutch. "What's going on?"

Dad stays silent, folding the tie into a neat bundle. "There have been a couple of… new developments." He unfolds the tie again. "As much as it pains me, I think we have to talk about it. The last year… you probably know it's been rough on me, but—"

My anger flares. "Excuse me? The last year has been rough on *you*? I almost got killed, my left leg was"—dammit!— "*is* almost useless, you take me out of Harvard, the one thing I've been working for my whole life, and you have the nerve to tell me the last year has been rough on *you*?"

OMG, did that feel good! I suck in a deep breath. Therapeutic, actually.

Hurt flickers across Dad's face. "I'm sorry, that's not what I meant, Alix. Believe me, I know what happened. I know it very well. There isn't a day I don't wish for it to never have happened." He balls the tie into a messy heap of fabric. "But I had to wait and make sure you're strong enough to hear—"

Triggerword. I stomp my crutch into the carpet. That's it. Enough. Once and for all. The same old story, over and over and *over.* "There we go again. *Please* tell me once more how weak I now am, how unable to handle myself, how much I've turned into a loser. Please, Dad. I think you haven't assaulted my ego for at least a day or two, so it really is time." I glare at him, chest heaving with erratic breaths.

His mouth drops open. "Alix—"

Oh, no. No, no, no. Nopedy-nope. All the pent-up emotions, all the frustration… It wants out. "You haven't said a positive thing about me since the accident! All there is—"

"That's not true, I—"

"It is! In your eyes, I'm a disappointment who can't handle her own life anymore, and if it wasn't for Jason challenging me, I would believe you at this point. If he—"

"Jason?"

Pause.

My cheeks warm up. "Mr. Miller."

"You call your teacher by his first name?"

With that one sentence, Dad transforms the hallway's soft, fluffy carpet into slippery ice, but I won't have it. "He offered to call him Jason, and I didn't see a reason to stick to Mr. Miller."

Pause.

"I do. He's your teacher."

I cringe. Yes, Ian is my teacher, but… I haven't seen him as my teacher, or Mr. Miller for a while now. We're too close for that. Ian is… Ian to me. My friend. My colleague.

I sigh. "Dad, he's barely four years older than me."

Dad rolls the tie around his knuckles like a boxer before a fight. "I guess then that's my problem with him."

I jerk back. "Your problem? What—"

"Alix, I'm not blind."

My insides tighten, and so does my grip around my crutches. *Please don't let him know about PRICS, please…* "I don't know what you're talking about."

Dad flexes his tie-wrapped knuckles into a fist. "Maybe the fact that you're spending a lot more time in class with him than I anticipated? Maybe the fact that he's a legal adult, and that he is… how shall I say it, *cute*? Your pick." He unrolls the tie from his knuckles, never taking his eyes off of me.

Oh.

Oh.

I lift my chin up and pull my shoulders back. "What are you saying, Dad? That you don't want me to study, or that you don't want me to study with *Jason*? Because I want to study, no matter what happened last year! And then, correct me if I'm wrong, but I'm sure he was chosen because he was at least able to keep up with my level of education, as you put it so nicely." And I'm more than thankful it's him and not Waterhouse. I wouldn't even have signed up had it been the old grump.

Dad's eyes widen. That's right, I'm not rolling over on my back anymore. Because Ian taught me well, Dad!

"Okay then, Alix. Yes. My problem is not with Mr. Miller, but with Mr. Miller and you together. He is too young for you, a distraction—"

"You just said he was an adult, so how can he be too young—"

Anger flares up in his eyes. "Yes, *he* is an adult. *You* are not. In the eye of the law, that doesn't make it better, if you catch my drift. Especially since he's your teacher."

One-Mississippi, two-Mississippi, three-Mississippi... That's how long it takes me to do the math of what Dad implied.

And it makes me angry. Like, *really* angry.

Forcing my voice into an even tone, I look up at the man who used to literally be a father-figure to me. "I'm going to pretend you didn't say that, because it's an insult to me, Jason, and both our professionalism. He is my col"—I cough once, covering up the stumble—"My teacher, nothing more, and he's teaching me more than anybody has, plus—"

Dad yanks the tie tighter around his knuckles. "And of course that's the only reason why you're putting in extra hours." It's phrased as a statement, but meant as a stab.

That's enough. I ball my fingers into fists around the handles of the crutches. "*Plus* my PT has improved a ton. Of course, you wouldn't have noticed, but I'm actually getting better on my crutches. And I'm sleeping better. And I'm eating." All thanks to Ian. No thanks to Dad.

For a moment, he stays silent. "You know, the fact that you defend him like this..." He huffs. "You're in deep already. You get emotional, defensive, and I don't like it. Maybe you feel like you fit in with the older crowd, but I promise you—"

Oh, jeez, fitting in with the older crowd? Keeping my cool

has never been more difficult. "Dad, Jason is four years older. I'm almost eighteen. A friendship is not unheard of—"

"You're not *almost eighteen*, Alix! You're seventeen and change. And it's not a friendship I'm worried about—"

I throw up both arms, crutches nearly missing the wall on either side. "Dad! Take it easy! I spend a couple of hours working and studying with a guy, my *teacher*, and it automatically means something is going on? *Nothing* is going on!" I shake my head and ram the crutches back into the ground. "Come on, Dad! Seriously? I've spent weeks with Sam and you never—"

"Sam is different." His jaw sets.

"Yeah? Why? What kind of double-standard is that, Dad? Who would even care if Jason and I—"

Dad's fuse blows. "Hold it right there, Fräulein!" He jabs a finger at me, eyes narrowed to slits. *Crap.* Whenever he resorts to Linda's German terms, I'm in deep. "I have to hope that you're not as immature as your last statement makes you seem, because I raised you better than this! An underage girl thinking about hooking up with her four years older teacher? I cannot believe you're this naïve!"

My mouth drops open. This is getting out of hand. "Whoa, wait a second! I'm not thinking about hooking up—"

Ian, holding on to my hand: "Analyze and act accordingly."

Me, wrapping my fingers around his: "I am."

"You better not!" The tie unravels from Dad's knuckles as he thrusts a finger in the general direction of the West Wing. "Because I can guarantee you, that no matter what you may think, abusing his position of authority and trust toward you would be very much illegal no matter the age of consent, and I can also promise you that there's no way I would let that happen, as your father, as a lawyer, or as the President!"

Anger oozes off him and makes me take a stumble-step back.

Where is this coming from? If anything, maybe I have a little or medium crush on Ian, but nothing Dad should've picked up on. Nothing worth this kind of reaction. He's blowing it completely out of proportion. It's nothing. *Nothing!*

His forehead creases. "Now, let me make this crystal clear. You want to be challenged? All right then, you asked for it. From tomorrow on, I will set study goals for you that I expect you to reach. If you don't, you're off to the boarding school, no matter what your mother says. I gave you a shot at the White House hoping it would help with your recovery and bring you back on track, but instead I find you out of the classroom and with a teacher who walked straight out of some kind of teen movie." He shoves the tie deep into his jacket's pocket. "I understand Mr. Miller has been appointed and approved by Mr. Waterhouse, but I guarantee you that I will replace him or remove you if you're not performing or behaving to my expectations, and that does not only apply to schoolwork. Is that clear?"

Replace Ian?

Remove me?

Like he slapped me in the face, my head jerks back, the next breath catching in my throat. "You can't do that." Not to me, not to him.

"Yes, I can. And I will." His features soften, shoulders relaxing the slightest bit. "Alix, all I want for you is to be right where you were before."

Before.

I'm not perfect anymore, and he can't handle it.

I stare at my dad, the man who used to adore me.

The man who has someone trying to kill him.

The man who doesn't know his daughter is actually useful and trying to help him.

Something in me breaks so completely, I'm surprised there's

no cracking sound. "Right where I was before? That's what you want? Has it ever occurred to you that the biggest roadblock is you?"

Dad's eyes widen. "What? Why—"

"Because *you* took that from me, Dad! Not the accident—*you*! The only thing the accident took was my leg. You single-handedly did the rest!" I gesture down to my leg and take a step closer to him. "I was the smart girl with early admissions to Harvard. You took that from me. I was the girl who thought she could take on the world. You took that from me. I was the girl who could rely on her family's support—you took that from me. Screw the leg—it was all you, Dad!" I glare at him, and boy, does it feel good. I'm done offering the other cheek. *Done!*

He reaches for my shoulders. "Oh my God, Alix, no! That's not what's happening, that's what I wanted to explain. I love—"

"Don't you even dare finish that sentence," I hiss. "Actions speak louder than words, Dad."

I push my chin up higher. "I'll be meeting all your goals, or I'll exceed them, but I promise that if you remove Mr. Miller from class or send me to boarding school, it'll be the last time we speak."

And with that, I push past Dad into the dining room, my face schooled into a neutral mask so that nobody sees the horror behind my eyes.

I'm not leaving PRICS.

I'm not leaving Ian.

I'm right where I belong, and I ain't leaving.

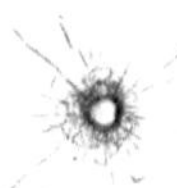

Dinner after that is torture in its purest form.

The shutters are down in front of Dad's eyes, and no amount

of forced easy chatter between Mom. Oliver, and Sam can bring them up again. It doesn't exactly help that I'm not saying a single word, pushing my food from left to right.

Here and there, I feel Sam's gaze on me, waiting for me, checking in with me, but I can't get myself to look anywhere but down on my plate. If I did, the tears would come. At one point, Sam quietly places his hand on my thigh under the table, giving it the slightest squeeze before he removes it again.

My heart close to bursts.

Sam's not stupid. He knows it has to do with Dad.

But he doesn't have a clue how much this has to do with Ian.

And that's the problem right there. Ian. Sam's been in my heart since day one, and over the last months, Ian has wiggled his way right next to him. When I see either of them I'm happy, when I don't, I miss them. I crave every little bit of touch they give me, and yet I fear it, because…

Yeah.

Because this is not the way it works.

I've had a crush on Sam forever, so why am I feeling the same butterflies, the same fireworks with Ian? What a despicable person am I, that I'm falling for two boys at once?

I almost laugh out loud.

No, not two boys. One boy and one man.

A *legal adult* and *my teacher*, as Dad emphasized so nicely.

And somehow, somehow that phrasing makes me feel dirty. As if I did something forbidden, which, heck, I didn't! Unbelievable how Dad turned the conversation that fast and in *that* direction. I'm rediscovering my will to live and doing something he can't control? He's gotta make sure he ruins it— and let's be honest, all this is about is control. Or better, his loss thereof. How dare he taint my relationship with Ian by dragging it into the mud and calling it illegal? Illegal! There is nothing going on that would even fall in that category! And it's ridiculous, because it never will either! It's still *me* we're talking about! Little dorky, hormonal, seventeen-year-old me! Yay.

I actually manage to take a bite of food, but it tastes flat. What a disappointing and depressing outcome for tonight. Should've known. Should've expected it. Still scary how all the progress I made with Ian during PRICS training and Krav Maga, how all that can dwindle down to zero again in a matter of minutes.

Apparently, destroying my ego takes much less effort than building it up.

I force the bite down with a large sip of water.

A knock on the door. Yoshi Nagakawa. "Mr. President? We have the President of France on the line?"

"Of course." Dad is up and at the door in no time, his food forgotten. "Oliver. Sam?" He curls his fingers at Sam, and Sam all but jumps up. Two more Secret Service agents than normal follow Dad, the only sign something is off.

As soon as the door has closed behind them I take the opportunity. "Could I please be excused?" I ask Mom. It's not as if I was still eating, and I need to take a breather.

"Of course, honey, of course." Mom waves a hand at me, already reaching for her iPad. Work. As always.

I fish for my crutches and make my way to one of our one million sitting rooms.

Definitely an enormous waste of an evening. I'm not looking forward to my report to Ian, because not only do I have nothing to show spy-wise, but also a whole lot I don't want to talk about Dad-wise.

I pick my favorite squishy couch and sink as deep into the cushions as I can, willing them to swallow me whole.

Not even thirty seconds later, Sam walks in and leans against the doorjamb.

No matter Dad's words, no matter my own confusion, my heart skips a painful beat.

"Mind if I join you?"

A smile forces its way onto my face despite Dad's shitty behavior. I motion for Sam to sit down. "Please. I thought Dad needed you downstairs." Best friend's son or not, Dad works Sam like any regular intern. Or more.

Shouldn't complain though, which I'm not: Maybe I still have a chance to get some intel. Staying close to Sam, making sure he isn't the assassin—that part I can do.

"Thanks." Sam smiles back and falls into the armchair on my right side. "You know, your dad just said… He told me to—" He chuckles once and shakes his head. "Never mind. Doesn't matter. Anyway. Boy, am I full. Is the chef cooking like that every day? I don't know how you're staying so skinny. I'd be at Sumo wrestler dimensions by now." He pats his stomach, letting out a big breath.

Dad told Sam *what*? But speaking of the devil—I know how I'm staying so skinny. Ian's workout regimen and Dad's psycho terror.

Still, I shake my head. "Nope. This was definitely special tonight. Don't know why, maybe Dad is showing off for you and your dad." I wink at Sam in a feeble attempt to distract from the disaster of tonight's dinner.

"Yeah sure, that's what I thought. It was obvious, right?"

We both laugh at that thought. Dad never ever does anything to impress anyone. He calculates and thinks politically, but he isn't out to impress anybody, otherwise, he probably would've become President a term or two earlier.

"He's definitely trying to get back on *your* good side, I'd say. Not mine." Sam points a thumb over his shoulder in the direction of the dining room.

Excuse me, what? "On *my* good side? Where'd you get that from?" Didn't sound like it before dinner. Or during. Or over the last freakin' year.

"It's obvious."

I huff. "To whom? Not to me. Those days are gone. I'm not his perfect little girl anymore. We don't click anymore." I cross my arms in front of my chest. Great, now I feel like throwing up.

"Easy, Alix. Just saying. I think he's trying. Maybe not during dinner tonight, but overall. You're not giving him much of a chance though. And of course he cares about you. Remember the day in the Colonnades? The lockdown?"

I blush and nod. Well, yeah. I remember, thank you very much.

"He was fighting his security detail about bringing him to safety. He insisted they take you first—"

Not what I saw. "Sam, that's BS. He didn't even look around for me—"

"Well, maybe that was *after* the Secret Service agents had pushed his head down and basically shoved him through the door, but I can tell you that he wouldn't stop trying to get back to you until they got confirmation you were safe."

I frown. That *so* doesn't align with my experience. "Doesn't prove anything." And Dad was always good in putting on a show in public.

Sam closes his eyes and melts into the cushions. "Say what you want. I'm just telling you as it is."

For a while, neither of us says anything, and eventually, I calm down a little. So even if he did worry about me, by now the times have changed—now that I've advanced to a disappointment in yet another area of life.

Somewhere in the room, an old grandfather-clock ticks and tocks. With each click, I relax a little more. This type of silence I don't mind. Comfortable. With Sam. Neither of us feels the need to fill it, although I know I should. The wheels inside my head keep turning, searching for a good start into a conversation that can't give away I know about the assassination attempt.

Sam's cell beeps. He checks it and suppresses a laugh.

"What is it?" I ask more out of reflex than true interest.

"Nothing." He shrugs and slides the cell back into his pocket. "Gianna asking to go out again."

Excuse me? Shot dead, the last bit of positive thinking I had withers and dies. "What?" All my relaxation is gone, chased away by adrenaline pumping through my veins. I'm not quite sure which part of the sentence is bothering me the most: Gianna asking him out, or Gianna asking him out *again*.

Sam shakes his head. "I'm so busy, I always forget to answer her."

"Always?" Geez, how often has this happened already?

"Most of the time. She's very persistent though." Something lights up in his eyes, and it burns me to the core.

Not even here, up in the residence, can Gianna leave me in peace.

Sam reaches over and taps two fingers onto my left knee.

"How's your leg? Is the new splint doing anything for you? How's the pain?"

Is he trying to distract me from Gianna, or is he truly asking about my leg?

I shrug, a frown on my face. "Better. Not good, not perfect, but the splint's doing a good job." I decide to push it a bit further. "I feel like it's helping me more than the others ever did. Plus, they have everything here for me. PT, the Doc. You know, maybe if I'm gonna get better, I'm gonna get better here, with all the resources of the White House."

The warmth in Sam's expression, his undivided attention,

both directed solely at me, make my earlier concerns about Gianna seem foolish.

"Of course you're going to get better," he says. "Let me see that new splint of yours." Before I can even lift up my leg, he reaches down and grabs both of my legs, and just like that, they're in his lap.

Whoopsie.

Both my legs are lying across Sam's lap.

Holy cow. Did that just happen?

My gaze darts to the door, half expecting Dad to barge in and ruin this moment, like he did that one time when Sam held my hand, but nothing.

Sam busies himself feeling around the splint and checking it out, while I try to remain completely still and unfazed by this touch, although I'm not, in any way, unfazed.

Not at all.

An electric tingling runs up my body from where Sam touches me all the way into my fingertips, like he connected me to some kind of power source. I'm pretty sure if I held a light bulb to my head it would glow from the energy he's shooting through me with this simple touch.

For one teeny, tiny moment I allow myself to close my eyes and enjoy this sensation.

Sam checks out the splint some more, before leaning back in his chair and keeping his hands rested on my legs. We sit there like an old couple with my legs across his lap, and while it feels oddly comfortable, it's still… kind of exciting at the same time.

And how convenient at least *he* isn't a legal adult.

The moment I think it, I could kick myself in the butt. Whatever, Dad. Not. The. Point.

I clear my throat. "So, uhh, how's your mom doing? Is she relieved she doesn't have to see you that often anymore?" Sam's about the only person I feel comfortable teasing. He never gets mad at me, unlike other members of my family.

He plays with one of the snaps on my brace. "Yeah, right. Don't know how she's going to handle me asking for three course dinners now after I got used to the chef's cooking."

We both laugh. Liona Brooks is a great and easygoing mom, but we both know her cooking skills aren't going to get her a mother of the year award. Ever.

After another short pause, Sam goes on, only more quietly. "I think she is doing okay without me there most of the time. It's tough on her when Jess is having a bad day, but she's handling it okay. I think. She looks tired a lot."

Sam's sister Jess is two years older than him. When she was born, everything looked all right, but after she turned two, she seemed to forget things she had already learned. She lost all her words, then couldn't walk anymore, or feed herself. From what I know, she turned from an active healthy toddler into a kid with the abilities of a newborn, and has stayed like that ever since: Rhett Syndrome. Since she can't feed herself or even turn herself over in her bed, she's completely dependent on her mother.

There is one day that sticks to my mind clearly, way before my accident, when Sam had just started working for the campaign. I forgot where he and I were supposed to go for something campaign-related, but his mom called, needing help with Jess. We asked the driver to divert and drove to Sam's first. Jess had fallen out of bed and gotten stuck between it and the nightstand, and Liona couldn't get her out and up alone. While I helped Sam and Liona move the furniture and pull a heavy, uncooperative Jess back into her bed, I gained a lot of respect for Liona.

That was the first time I truly understood what being a single mom meant, and what it meant to take care of a special-needs child. Special-needs *teen*.

That was also the first time Sam opened up to me.

After that incident, when the driver brought us back to where we were supposed to be, Sam and I talked—really talked—about life, fate, and everything under the sun. He spilled his heart, and it set mine on fire.

Sam wiggles and twists a different snap on my splint. "They… they laid Mom off at the practice she worked, because she took too much time off when Jess wasn't doing well. That doesn't really help either, you know."

Wait, what? "She got laid off at *the practice*? I thought your mom's a nurse at Children's National—"

"Still there. She's been working two jobs. Has been for a while, since things got… tight."

An ugly feeling spreads through my stomach, like I was missing something I'd rather not hear. "Sam? What's going on?" Yes, I've missed most of the campaign trail, but I've seen Sam. Often. How can I not know what's happening at home?

Sam keeps his gaze down, long lashes fanning his cheeks. "It's frustrating, Alix. The day-nurses for Jess got more expensive, insurance is only covering a few hours per day, Mom's stressed and busy beyond belief with two jobs, and all I can do—" His fingers dig into the snaps and fabric of my splint—the answer to my next question right there.

I know Sam. "You're giving your salary to your mom?" Yeah. That's what he would do.

He nods, and that wordless admission… it gets to me.

With a crack, my heart breaks for him. It's ridiculous somebody would think Sam—gentle, smart, thoughtful Sam— would be out to kill my dad. In fact, at this point, I'm sure a hundred and ten percent, that Dad hired him as a junior intern to help him out. The conversation I overheard between Dad and

Oliver in the hallway comes back: Dad is paying Sam out of his own pocket, although I doubt Sam knows that much.

"Hey." I lean forward and hold out a hand. It comes so naturally that I don't even think about it. Sam stretches his left hand out and drops it in mine, keeping his right where it is, on my legs.

I give his fingers a squeeze. "What can I do to help?"

He returns the squeeze of my hand, and if I wasn't so focused on our conversation, I probably would've dwelled on how soft his skin is. "Thanks, but it's fine. Just a sore topic." The smile he gives me is forced at best, and it doesn't do squat to help with the ugly feeling inside my stomach.

I cock my head. "Nu-uh. What is it?"

"Huh?"

"Sam, come on. I know you. That's not all." Sam's baseline is happy. Balanced. Frowning is not in his regular repertoire.

He busies himself with my splint. "Seriously, nothing. Family stuff. The regular with divorced parents."

Oh. "Your dad?"

Sam rubs one hand across his eyes but drops it right back onto my leg. "Yeah. I… I don't want to talk about it. I know I shouldn't judge him, but sometimes it's hard. It's so damn hard." Frustration oozes from every pore.

Talk about being disappointed by your dad. "No kidding. Sounds like we both have our daddy issues, huh?" I wink at him and drop the topic, empathetic friend that I am. "But kidding aside, you told me once I could always talk to you. Well, the same is true in reverse. You can always call me when you need someone to talk to. You know that, right? Or text. Or email. Or come by. I don't care. Just let me know and I'll be there, okay?" My chest tightens. I'm not offering this as a spy to keep an eye on him, but as a friend.

Finally, his smile cranks it up a notch as he gives a chuckle. "Thanks, Alix. Look at us, sitting in the White House of all places, fed and warm, and still complaining. Perspective, huh?"

"True." As whiny as I am with my leg and crutches, I do know that in the grand scheme of things it's nothing. It could be worse. Way worse. And it could come out of nowhere; Jess is the living example.

Sam squeezes my hand and sticks his tongue out at me. "Doesn't change that fate sometimes is a bitch, right?"

I roll my eyes to the ceiling in wordless agreement.

Yeah, fate sometimes is a bitch all right.

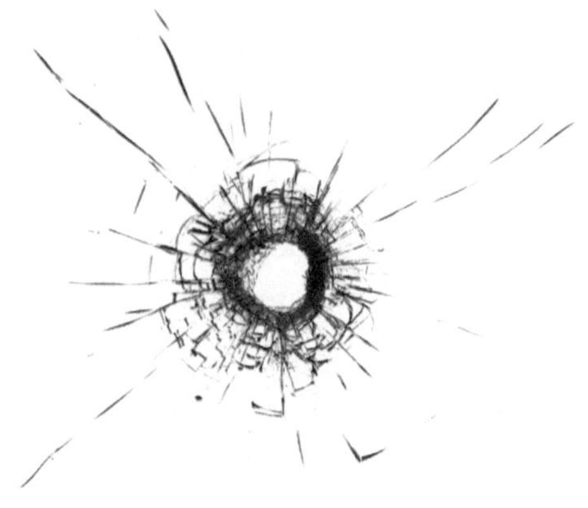

CHAPTER FIFTEEN

Trailing Sam

The next morning, Ian hands me my cup of chai and pulls a thick stack of papers out of his desk drawer. "I had this here in my mailbox this morning, complete with the Presidential Seal and your father's signature." He drops the bundle onto my desk with a *thud*. "Any idea where this is coming from?"

I don't need to look to know Dad followed through. Stat.

"Well, I guess that was why he wanted to see me at dinner." I can't keep the bitterness out of my voice.

"Because he's worried about your schoolwork?" Ian sounds confused. "Besides that you're doing awesome, he said he was okay with you taking it easy, and this is about goals and expectations, listed by week."

I close my eyes. Of course, he would list it by week. I'm surprised it's not a daily schedule. "He thought—" I stop myself mid-sentence.

No.

I know what it feels like to live with Dad's lack of trust. I'm not burdening Ian with it. It's not about him anyway; it's about me.

Only about me.

Plus, it's super embarrassing. What am I supposed to say? *My dad thinks you and I have something going on.*

Right.

Am not gonna get that out without turning tomato-red, and then I'm going to die a slow, agonizing death when Ian starts laughing or something.

Four years older.

Smart as hell.

Green eyes to die for.

A body made out of solid muscle.

Ian could have any girl he wanted.

Let's be realistic here. It wouldn't be me. No matter if I lik—

Nope. Not going there.

My heart misfires once, and I lift and drop my shoulders. "I guess… I guess he just really wants me to succeed." And that's not even a lie. Everything else Dad said is just ridiculous.

Ian's face splits into a wide grin. "That's good, Alix. He cares."

Well, that's one way to phrase it.

Sitting in class with Ian after that is so surreal I have to pinch myself to make sure I'm awake. All the way 'til noon, I'm trapped somewhere in-between the memory of Sam playing with my splint, Dad's latest dagger to my heart, and trying to focus on the intelligence work Ian has laid out for us while *not* focusing on the faint scent of spring soap in the air.

So no, focusing on spy stuff isn't exactly easy today. It's one thing going over reports and looking for data, my mind can do that in its sleep, but whenever Ian mentions Sam, there's that little jolt of electricity distracting me.

And it shouldn't.

I have a job to do, and only part of it is helping and protecting Dad.

The other part is getting Sam—and Oliver—out of this mess. No pressure.

It's already close to noon when we're finally about to take a break from desk work. Ian collects my DUTI-pad to lock it away during my next stint into active duty over lunch.

"Listen, Alix." He takes the second chair, turns it around and straddles it, like he always does when sitting across from me. His arms rest on the chair's back which brings him directly at eye level with me, a wave of his spring soap scent mixed with a little bit of coconut filling my senses. Man, that stuff latches to my olfactory nerve and shoots straight into my limbic system. Meaning, one sniff of it and it hooks me like a drug.

As if he knew my mind wasn't where it's supposed to be Ian gives me a stern look. "Just a reminder. Not that I think anything will, but whatever happens, don't risk anything—you're our eyes and ears, not our fists. Dimitri is always close by, and if he isn't, you can approach any of the Secret Service agents, even if they don't have clearance to know about you or PRICS. There's an override word for you. It's the Secret Service's way of making sure its men and women are being taken care of, undercover or not. You can use it with every agent, and it will grant you executive decision rights and support up to a certain level, meaning: you'll get help and they won't ask questions. Your override word—and I don't need to tell that to the girl with the almost photographic memory, but please, don't forget it—is Apteryx."

An amused smile forms on my lips. "Was that my pep talk? Thanks, Ian." Weirdly enough, it helps. Or maybe it's Ian so close to me. Breathing him in calms me down. And excites me.

But also calms me down.

Gah!

Ian sighs. "Not so much the pep talk, more the please-stay-safe-talk." A shadow crosses his face.

I suck in my lower lip and chew on it. Ian's worry is the perfect reminder that I'm with the Secret Service and therefore playing with the big kids.

I clear my throat. "Apteryx. Got it. Don't worry about me. I'll be fine. I told you Sam didn't do it, so it's not like I'm following and cozying up with an assassin. We'll get to the bottom of this, right?"

Ian traces his finger along the edge of the table in front of him. "We will, but please, don't dismiss any options, Trouble."

"But—"

He holds up a hand. "Yes, I know you think Sam is innocent, and as much as I'd like that to be true, we need to keep an open mind. *You* need to keep an open mind. We can't afford mistakes. It's your father's life on the line."

Well, it's not as if I had forgotten that part. I chew on the inside of my cheek.

Ian scratches his neck. "Anyway. Off you go. See if you can get closer to Sam, Oliver, or your father, or all of them. Everything counts, but ultimately, we're looking for evidence of any kind and motives." He pauses. "Last evening was a good start—"

Good joke right there.

"—but we need more. Report back to me this evening. I've already sent your mother an email apologizing for keeping you busy so much, but that I still need you in class for a while longer. It's a big project we're working on, especially now with the added goals your father set, you know?" The small wink doesn't carry his usual spunk.

At least I won't have to worry about another alibi for my

evening excursions, that's taken care of.

Until Dad finds out I'm working even more with Ian and *not* working on advanced biochem. Then all bets are off.

I grab my crutches and let Ian help me out from behind the desk even though I totally don't need it.

Okay. I'll just have to stay one step ahead of them all: Dad to keep him safe, Sam to clear his name, Ian to keep his job.

Because if I mess up, they all will lose, and so will I.

The way over to the West Wing and Oval Office feels like it's a mile long. I don't really want to start there, but I have to. I need to be able to access both as needed, the Oval Office with Dad, and the Front Office with Sam. That means I've got to clear things up with Dad.

I'm thrilled.

Not.

That little roadblock kept me up quite a bit last night. There's no good way to start the conversation.

Hi, Dad, I have this project for school, can you help me with that? Just like the good ol' times.

Hi, Dad, I'm really interested in politics now, can I stick around for a day or two and watch you? It's also just like the good ol' times.

Hi, Dad, I miss you. Wanna hang out some more? It won't be quite as the good ol' times, but it's good for me.

Hi, Dad, will you please stop being an ass, let me be your daughter again and forget about the f-ing good ol' times?

Yeah, well. Like I said, nothing is perfect. With our history, nothing can be perfect.

Turning another corner toward the West Wing, I pick up on Dimitri's low voice speaking a "Trouble at West Wing" into his sleeve mike before he drops his arm again, staying much closer to me than he normally does.

Even Dimitri is on edge after the assassination attempt.

Usually, I don't even realize he's there, but today, I feel his presence behind me. The new security protocols aren't making his job any easier.

And mine… I might need a minute to focus. The hustle in the busiest hallway in the West Wing is real, and nobody would expect a stationary body in the middle of it, so I find a spot close to the wall and stop.

Deep breath. It's going to be fine.

Go in. Ignore he ordered me to never come to the Oval Office again. Make nice with Dad. Pretend I didn't yell at him and accuse him of scarring his poor daughter's soul. Talk to Sam. See where it takes me.

I take another deep breath of air that's somehow devoid of oxygen and crank my neck.

Show time.

When I pass Dimitri, he gives me the slightest reassuring nod, and somehow, like with the Varen Mission, it helps.

I put on my big girl panties and hobble into the Front Office—the *empty* Front Office.

Now wait a second. Sam isn't at his desk and neither is Mrs. Houser. At least one of them should be here, unless—

I groan. It's Taco Tuesday. What great timing. I'm such a good super spy I forgot it's Taco Tuesday.

Great job, Alix, great job.

Nobody's going to be here for at least another thirty—

Huh. Why is the door to the Oval Office open then? Odd. Maybe I'm in quote-unquote luck after all and Dad is here and not yet to lunch.

"Dad? Are you in? Mrs. Houser is gone to lunch already."

Instead of hearing my dad's voice, someone else's comes from the oval office.

"Alix? Hey girl! Looks like we're both out of luck, I was looking for your father too." The sound of steps coming closer hits my ear, and although I can't see the person because of the angle they're approaching from, I don't have to. I would know that voice anywhere, with that little bit of arrogant undertone.

A second later, James DiBiaso walks out of Dad's office, smiling.

Oh, just great.

"Hey, Mr. Vice Pres—" I catch myself. "James. He's not here, is he?" I nod toward the Oval Office.

DiBiaso shrugs. "It's Taco Tuesday, but I thought I'd catch him before lunch, got even more papers to fight off the Genetic Testing Bill." He flips a pen over in his hand, grinning. "I'll catch him later. He'll be back around one in case you need him." He takes the same pen and playfully taps me on the forehead with it. "Coming with me down to lunch? Like I said—it's Taco Tuesday." DiBiaso wiggles his fingers of the hand not holding the pen, as if Taco Tuesday was a magic word, and taps my forehead again.

Ugh. I use all my self-control to keep myself from flinching and pulling back. I'm not five anymore. If he pinches my cheek next, there's no guarantee I won't use my crutches for one of those pain-inflicting moves Dimitri showed me. If DiBiaso does stuff like that with Gianna, no wonder she turned out such a raging— Well, anyway.

DiBiaso pockets the pen, and my eyes pop wide. This isn't the DMV or whatever. You don't just take one of my dad's pens, especially not one of *the* pens, the imported ones.

Alas, I'm not in the position to lecture the United States' Vice President. So, I force my lips into a smile that I hope seems genuine. "Thank you. It sounds delish, but I'm good. Maybe next time." When hell freezes over. Joining DiBiaso and Gianna for lunch is about as high on my list as getting my toenails pulled.

"You don't know what you're missing, girl." DiBiaso pats me on the shoulder before walking past me out of the front office without another look back.

The second he's gone I release a breath I didn't know I held.

Making up with Dad has been postponed.

Thank God for small favors.

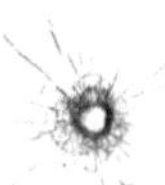

It takes me a while until I finally track Sam down.

He's working on something in the copy room, shuffling papers from left to right and sorting through them.

I knock on the outside of the window right next to where he's standing, but he's so focused that he doesn't see me even when I start making faces to get his attention. I'm pretty sure he didn't have those dark circles under his eyes yesterday, or at least not quite so dark.

As I'm pulling my face into a silly mask, Sam finally looks up, for a second not reacting at all to me distorting my mug at him on the other side of the window.

Three, two, one—Sam shakes his head as if waking up, and the moment recognition clicks into place, a wide grin spreads across his face. Boy, that took him a while.

He waves me in. "How long have you been standing there making faces at me?"

I step into the copy room and close the door behind me, leaving Dimitri outside, guarding it, as always.

"I'd say about an hour, but that would be lying. Felt like it though. You were spaced out completely. I never thought making photocopies could be that demanding for your mental faculties."

I slide up to sit on one of the tables next to the copy machine Sam is using, number three of fifteen, the tag on its side informs me. While usually it's pretty loud and busy in here, it's peacefully quiet with only Sam's machine working at the moment: That's lunch time on a Taco-Tuesday for you.

Sam checks the machine and the papers it spits out. A four-inch stack is already sorted to my right. He must've been here for a while.

"Nope. It usually isn't taxing me to my max," he says with a slight shake of his head. "I don't know. Today's a weird day. Feels like something is off somehow."

Well, I happen to know that he's right. Something is very much off. "You—" I snap my mouth shut. Wait. Is this *my* Sam, just being observant and talking to me? Or is this Sam, the *assassin*, trying to get me to talk to see what I know?

I hate I have to ask myself that question. But while on the outside it looks like we're just two kids talking, it could be that there is an almost-spy trained by PRICS—me—trying to get information from and about a potential assassin—Sam—who in return is trying to get information from the President's daughter—also me.

A frown crosses my face. Heck, spy work is more difficult than I thought.

"You—what?" Sam asks. "Complete sentences please, ma'am."

I roll my eyes at him. "You think, I wanted to say. That something is off, I mean?"

Sam looks up from the machine. "Oh, come on, don't tell me you haven't noticed anything? There are more Secret Service agents here than ever, your dad looks like crap—sorry, but he does—the senior staff interrupts whatever they're talking about as soon as a junior member comes as much as around a corner, and I'm pretty sure my emails are being checked, at least they come in with a small, but noticeable time-delay."

Oops.

Considering the Secret Service wanted to increase security unnoticed I think they've pretty much failed.

Of course, now the question is, did Sam notice all of this because he is perceptive and smart and, well, Sam? Or did he pick up on it because he *is* the assassin and needs to make sure he doesn't get caught? But why would he let me know he is on to the Secret Service?

Argh. This is giving me a headache already and I've barely spoken two sentences with him.

"You know," he continues, "we haven't gone up a DEFCON level, so I don't know what it could be. Maybe it's because of this stupid Genetic Testing Bill that has everyone going crazy. About time we get that off the table for good." He shakes his head. "Or maybe it's just me, and I need to get more sleep—that's certainly an option." He laughs dryly.

Ouch. How hard is Dad working him, salary or not? Judging by those dark circles, it must be a new level.

I give him a reassuring smile. "Meh, you don't look that bad. Nothing a Red Bull couldn't fix."

Sam chuckles. He reaches behind the Xerox machine and pulls out an opened can of Red Bull. "Don't tell anyone. Yoshi would have a heart attack knowing I have *liquids* in the *copy room.*" He raises the can in mock salute and takes another sip. It looks like it's almost empty.

I place a palm over my heart. "Oh, no, what has become of you, Sam Brooks? But seriously, I haven't really noticed anything. That being said, I'm not that often in the West Wing anyway since— Well." I look down at my feet. Since I got kicked out.

Sam hides the Red Bull behind the copier again and comes over to me. I scoot aside to make room, but Sam lays a hand on my knee and holds me in place, his touch rooting me to the spot, drawing my gaze to his hand on my knee.

It's the second time in less than twenty-four hours his hand's on my knee.

The temperature in the copy room must have gone up by a couple of degrees, or why else would my cheeks be burning? I don't know how Sam does it, but I could swear sparks are shooting from his hand, and they all end up in my stomach. He's standing right in front of me, with one of his legs between mine, touching both of them, and so close I smell his aftershave and butterscotch aroma with every breath I take.

This is… unexpected.

Goosebumps pop up all over my skin. Granted, we've been close before, we've hugged before, but this feels more *intimate* than ever, especially when he drops a finger to my chin, the fingertip tracing the outlines of my jaw, lifting up my head to look into his eyes.

I have to crane my neck to do so, and even then, I can barely focus on his eyes at this close distance, although Sam is all I see.

"Hey," he says gently. "Don't let that get you down, okay? He doesn't mean it. He's under a lot of stress. Your dad is happy every time he sees you, and I should know, I'm around him like 24/7 these days." He brushes his thumb over my chin, and hallelujah! If I thought I had goosebumps before, it's *nothing* compared to now.

Sam is so close, his body touching mine in such an innocent yet powerful way, my breath catches in my throat. Every little brush of his thumb brings me closer to a heart attack, but even if it meant going into cardiac arrest right here and now, I wouldn't want him to stop.

Ever.

I don't care my hormones have taken over. Let them. They're fun. Woooh!!

I stare up into his eyes, into a universe made of warm hazelnut brown. Time stretches into an eternity. Two seconds or two hours, I don't know how long I'm locked into his gaze, or how long Sam's gliding his thumb over my chin.

I'm not imagining it, right? Not over-interpreting? There's something between us—

Sam spreads the fingers of his other hand across my knee and curls them back in, like a little massage.

Ohh…!

Such a small, tender touch, but it's flutters-in-my-heart-perfect.

Sam sucks in a little sharp breath and drops his gaze to my lips. I've read enough books and watched enough movies to know what that means: OMG, he's going to kiss me!

And it makes me ridiculously excited.

A surge of hormones takes control of my body. As Sam leans in, I mirror him. The small percentage of my brain still working properly is mortified of making a mistake, but it's zapped into silence by the energy crackling between us. I don't think my brain is getting any oxygen. Don't think I'm breathing. Sam leans in closer, closer—

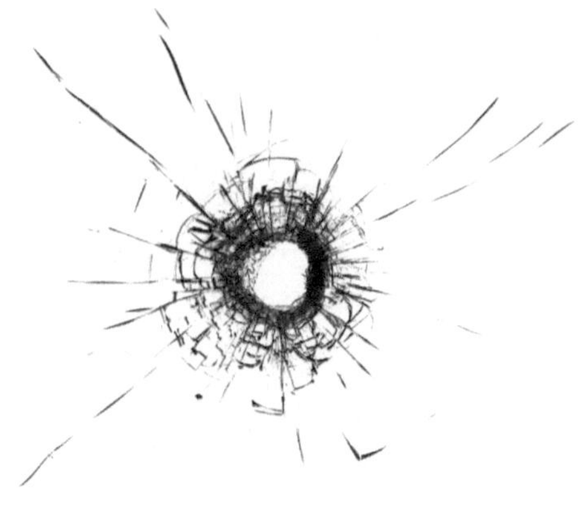

CHAPTER SIXTEEN

Family

The door bursts open with a *bang* and smacks into the wall behind it.

Sam and I jerk apart, the spell broken.

"Here you are, I've been looking everywhere," Gianna chirps as she throws the door into the lock behind her.

Sam takes one big step away from me and straightens his jacket.

All the butterflies in my stomach die from an acute case of acid poisoning.

Gianna.

"Oh, hi, Alix, didn't know you were in here too," she adds so sweetly that I'm convinced it's setting me up for diabetes. Right. Sure. She didn't know I was here—sitting basically in a glass house, visible from all angles, but no, she didn't see me.

Didn't *want* to see me.

"Hi, Gianna," I say past gritted teeth. That woman has a

built-in radar to help her make my life miserable.

Gianna steps behind Sam, and in a move so ballsy I could never pull it off, lays a hand on his shoulder and then rests her chin on top of it.

My jaw drops. She's more or less hugging him from behind. I don't even want to know which parts of her body are connected to his right now, ugh, ugh, *ugh.*

She wiggles her free hand holding a small pink and blue bottle of water. "Dad's busy with a meeting. Wanna go and have lunch? Sam?" She adds his name, just in case there was a misunderstanding whom she was talking to.

She squeezes his shoulder, and when he turns his head they're so close I could barely fit a sheet of paper between them.

Right in this moment, I envy her. I envy that she can just walk up to Sam and be all confident. That she can get close to him without feeling completely inadequate, like I do.

Most of all though, I envy her for the look Sam's shooting at her, and even more the slightly mischievous smile.

That's when I get mad.

I'm right here! She's barging in, obviously interrupting, well, *something,* and yet she doesn't care.

"Actually," I say, "*Sam* and *I* were about to have lunch." I emphasize our names like she did Sam's. Two people can play the bitchy-game.

Sam's eyebrows shoot up, but he covers his surprise with a quick cough, turning his body away from Gianna's, so that she has to pick herself off his shoulder.

Finally. The second the contact between them breaks I can breathe again.

"You were?" Gianna gives Sam a confused look, as if it was completely out of the realm of possibility he was going to have lunch with me.

Sam is back at the copier, feeding more papers into it. He's probably decided to not stand in the middle between Gianna and me, and while that at least means he isn't completely on Gianna's side, it also means he isn't completely on mine either.

"Yeah," he says into the papers, "lunch."

Gianna whips her head around and glares at me, then takes two threatening steps closer to me, hands on her hips.

If I could, I would take a step back, but as it is, I'm sitting, so retreating won't work, and heck, I've gone through months of training with Ian and Dimitri. I've faced down one of the most dangerous men in the world. I'm not retreating.

Gianna doesn't hold any power over me.

Well, I *think*.

"Stay out of my way," she hiss-whispers, enough under her breath so Sam won't pick up on it over the noise of the Xerox machine, "or I'll make this term a very unpleasant one for you." With that, she turns around like a ballerina and all but floats out of the room, head high, throwing her water bottle in the trash on the way out.

Only when the door closes behind her do I notice how much my hands are shaking.

So much for getting better at confrontations.

Sam clears his throat and continues our conversation from an eternity ago as if nothing had happened. No thumb on my chin, no hand on my knee, no almost-kiss. His voice sounds a bit rougher, but that's it.

"No, really, Alix. Go and talk to your dad. I think it's eating him up that he thinks you're mad at him—which you have a right to be, of course."

How can he pretend nothing has happened? I mean, nothing did, and yet everything happened! We shared more than a moment, we almost kissed, and if Gianna—

And that's the problem right there. I'm not stupid. I have eyes. I know how attractive Sam is—and Gianna knows it just as well, judging by the way she's hitting on him. And she's playing the same game with Ian. Seriously, what is it with her hitting on two—

Oh.

My cheeks heat up.

Look who's talking.

And look who's getting a hefty dose of reality.

What an idiot I am. I'm only making myself miserable misinterpreting Sam.

We were so close. *So close.* We could've kissed. We possibly *would've* kissed, but the way he's behaving right now, like it didn't happen…

Not reassuring at all.

If he were into me like that, wouldn't he want to pick up where we left off? I'm right, here, didn't go anywhere!

Maybe he realizes he gave me the wrong signals and regrets it? Maybe he feels he led me on, and now he doesn't know how to clear the air? Because we're friends, and nothing more?

Well, it sure doesn't seem like we're star-crossed lovers.

Disappointment sweeps over me. Story of my life.

"Alix?" Sam looks over his shoulder at me.

"Huh? Oh, Dad. Yes." I swallow all the disappointment and hurt down. Hopefully that won't give me a stomach ulcer later. I pull my ponytail tighter, so my hands have something to do.

Conversation. Continue. Okay. "Nice of you to say our issues are eating *him* up. What about me?" Why would anybody think it's eating *him* up? "He's in such a bad mood with me, all the time, and so opposed to everything I do, it's like he hates me."

Sam loads another couple of papers into the feeder and curls a hand around his neck, massaging it. "Duh, Alix, He doesn't hate you. I think he hates what happened to you, and that's a big difference. Every time he looks at you, he sees his failure to protect you, and your dad isn't good with failure of any kind. In my opinion, you should get it out in the open though, seriously. To me, it feels like you're both trying, but missing each other, like boats in the dark." His hands move past each other twice, boats in the dark.

A sarcastic huff escapes me. "He—"

"I can come with you."

"Huh?" I stare at Sam.

"To the Oval Office, I mean." Sam focuses on the papers once more. "I need to drop off my papers in the Front Office anyway. That way you're not alone, and even if he's mad—which he won't be—I'm pretty sure I can get you in with him before he has a chance to protest." He looks at me over his shoulder. "All you need is a minute, Alix. Don't be mad at him forever. Be the bigger person and reach out. Our families are so close, you're like a sister to me, and I can't stand seeing you like this."

Ouch.

Well, that clarifies that.

Any butterflies or sparks that might have survived the Gianna-induced acid-onslaught are wiped out within a split-second. Gone, gone, gone. Erased from existence without any hope of ever rising up again. The high I was on when Sam was close to me drops me in midair, laughing as I rush down toward the ground.

He just called me his sister.

His *sister.*

That's worse than being friend-zoned. From friends to lovers is a thing, from siblings to—Yuck.

I'm like *a sister.* Not like Gianna. And maybe he's right: Sam and I have been like brother and sister since we've met. We'll never share looks like the one he shared with Gianna, or the un-awkward little touches they pass between them all the time.

Never. It's about time my adolescent brain gets the message.

I've just been *sister-zoned.*

The loss of something that wasn't mine to begin with burrows a hole in my chest as deep as the Grand Canyon.

"What do you think?" Sam picks up the six-inch stack of papers. "It'll make things right, Alix."

Make things right.

I blink twice. "Uhh, okay." Focus. I need to focus. Ian gave me a mission to work on, and so far, I've only done a spectacular job getting distracted by my hormones. "I'll come with you. But"—I hold up one finger, attempting to play it normal—"if he chews me out, I'll blame it on you."

"Won't happen." He hands me my crutches. "Ready?"

I slide off the table and put my weight onto my crutches. No matter Sam's role in all of this, from an espionage point of view, he's helping me tremendously. His invitation lets me keep an eye on him and Dad at the same time—maybe even on Oliver. Plus, I didn't even know how to start reconnecting with Dad. Sam's help is more a necessity at this point.

He takes his Red Bull and throws it into the trashcan, then nods and opens the door for me.

"Okay then. Let's go."

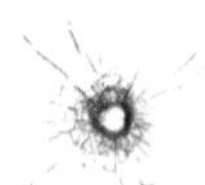

Mrs. Houser is my new favorite person.

She knows Dad's moods and preferences in and out: She could've easily asked me to leave, and yet she doesn't. Instead, she gives me a reassuring nod and wink when Sam pulls a chair next to his desk for me, since Dad's in a meeting right now.

This is what it must feel like waiting for the jury to hand down your sentence.

Sam gets back to work on all the papers on his desk, and soon our whispered conversation dies down.

Still no Dad.

Sam files reports, prints out tables and schedules, and probably forgets about me the second we stop talking. He does tons of busy work one would probably hire a junior intern for, because even the full-fledged interns wouldn't be exactly thrilled with it.

I do my assignment as per PRICS' job description and keep an inconspicuous eye on what he's doing, but it's not like he was dealing with classified information or assassination plans right in front of me.

It's mundane; it's boring.

Sam opens up the fifteenth package and sorts the contents away. "One more," he mumbles to himself. "For the collection." He shoves a sturdy metal box with the image of a pen and a French flag into the top drawer of his desk.

But Sam dealing with Dad's fixation on his expensive pens is about all the excitement there is.

After about thirty minutes, I pull out my phone. One can only gather so much intelligence while watching Sam fill out and file papers.

Eventually, the door to the Oval Office opens, but instead of Dad leading the way, two guys back out, one bearded guy in his thirties leading the other one, who carries a heavy-looking camera on his shoulder with his eyes pressed to the viewfinder.

Right behind them comes the Secretary of State, followed by Dad who's still talking. The camera stays right on him, and I have to agree with Sam: he doesn't look his freshest, courtesy of the pasty skin and bags under his eyes.

"… let's be sure we get that meeting done. Crumbie can just check up on the Hill how the mood is. Maybe we finally get this Genetic Testing Bill out of our way or at least the rider detached and voted on separately, it's—"

The moment Dad's gaze falls on me he snaps his mouth shut. "Hold on." He lifts a finger and moves around the blissfully unaware Secretary.

"I agree, let's get this over with. It's ridiculous the Republicans are still throwing this at us." The secretary keeps talking while going through something in the file he carries, but I don't listen.

I'm somewhat preoccupied by the anger flashing in Dad's eyes and the way his jaw is set in a tight line. He weaves around the camera crew and bends low in front of me, keeping himself between me and them in a somewhat awkward way.

He drops his voice low. More like a growl. "I want you to walk out of here, Alix. *Now.*"

I draw in a sharp breath that gets stuck somewhere inside my throat. "But, Dad, I—"

"No *but.* We've talked about this. No wandering the White House by yourself. You wanted to be challenged, that's what I did. Back to class. Go. Right now. No discussion, no questions." He angles his body some more, completely blocking me from the Oval Office's door.

This isn't happening. My jaw drops. "You're kicking me out?" Is that payback for what I told him last night? That it was all his fault, not the accident's?

Dad flinches and points at the hallway. "No, I'm asking you to use common sense and to leave. You know you've had enough media attention. We don't need this. *You* don't need this."

Ah, okay. That's what this is about. Finally, it's out in the open. I mean, I thought that's what it was, but here's the proof.

I meet his gaze. It's right there, clear as day, written in his face. "You're embarrassed of me." Saying it out loud should hurt, but that's not the part that shoots an arrow through my heart: the worried look my dad throws over his shoulder at the camera crew. *That's* the part that hurts.

"Honey, no. There's nothing you could do that would make me embar—"

Of course not. "Then let me stay. I'd—"

Dad lifts a hand. "Non-debatable. Now. *Please.*" He pinches the bridge of his nose. "And then I'd like to talk to you later. I've got a couple of things to discuss with you." His lips press into a thin line. "I—"

I shake my head. Hell to the no! "That's not how it goes, Dad. You don't get to kick me out and then—"

"I'm not kicking you out, Alix, but my patience is wearing thin. I'll talk to you later." His gaze fixates on something on the floor next to me before he stands up straight again and walks toward the Secretary and camera crew. "I'm sorry, where were we? The Rider?" I get one more pointed look before he completely focuses on the Secretary, and I know what it means.

There's nothing left for me to say right now. Absolutely nothing.

Sam's head swivels from left to right, from Dad to me and back, as if he was watching a tennis match, a puzzled look on his face.

Yeah, he did get that right.

Dad is kicking me out. Again.

Is it me? I mean, clearly it is me, but am I making a mistake by coming here? But heck, I'm not the only teen here! Sam's here. Gianna comes by all the time. So no, it's just me who isn't wanted.

Without waiting for the Secretary to leave, or for Sam to say anything, I grab my crutches and my last bit of dignity that I've left and do as I'm told. I might've taken a bit longer to get the message, but I got it all right.

When I've reached the threshold to the hallway, I pick up on Dad talking to the camera crew. "This gets cut out, understood?"

"But sir, the interaction with your daughter—"

"Gets cut. She—"

The rest gets swallowed by busy noise from the hallway, but I've heard enough.

He's cutting me out of the documentary, just like he's cutting me out of his life.

If I speed up, I'll be out of the West Wing before the tears start coming.

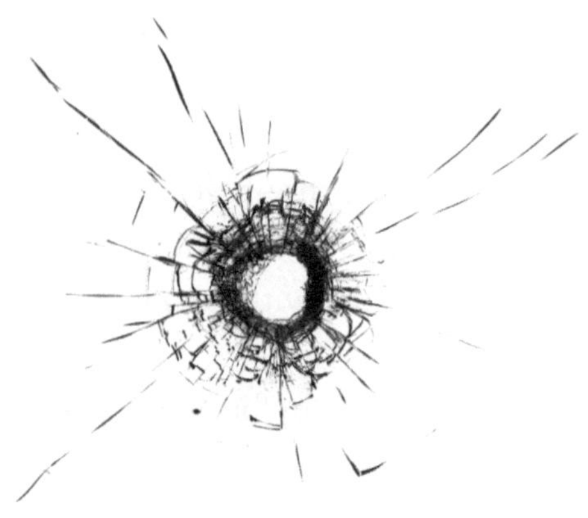

CHAPTER SEVENTEEN

Tough to be a Spy

How I make it back down to the Eagle's Lair, I don't know. It's like I blinked and *snap*, I find myself in front of the holographic wall down in the fake janitor's closet, palming it open for Dimitri and myself. The numbness inside my chest has dulled my senses into nonexistence thanks to the last five minutes running on repeat inside my mind.

And it hurts the same every single, mind-numbing time.

I huff to myself. Well, at least Dad said *please* this time. Maybe that's a step in the right direction. And I didn't cry, that's also a sign of maturity. Or of me getting used to repeated emotional abuse. Who knows.

Ian sits at his desk but grabs his DUTI-pad and comes over to join me on the couch when I all but drop into it, sinking into the cushions and wishing they'd swallow me.

"So, what can you tell me about Sam?" he asks while falling back into his usual seat.

Right, Sam. Almost forgot that was my task.

I rub my eyes and take a shaky breath.

Focus.

"Not much. All he did up to now is make copies and work at his desk—nothing out of the ordinary. Well, he *did* pick up on the heightened security status though, so your Secret Service guys should probably rework their stealth protocols."

Ian rolls his eyes. "How did he pick up on it? Tell me what he said."

Locking all emotions into a safe spot deep inside my chest, I give Ian the rundown. *Without* my voice cracking. It doesn't take me long to describe the whole afternoon, and I even include Sam's sister comment. I could swear something flashes in Ian's eyes with that one, but it's gone as quickly as it came, replaced by a frown when I mention Dad kicked me out of the Oval Office, again.

"Your father is going to need more work than I anticipated. I wonder if something else is going on we don't know about. It feels odd for a man of his intelligence to all but sever the relationship with his only daughter because she's handicapped or doesn't want to go to a boarding school. I can't figure out how that goes together."

He shakes his head and shrugs, and I give a sad little sneer.

"I wouldn't be able to tell you. My shrink and I have been working on this for about the last year or so." Ten long months before I moved here. And I'm still as clueless as before. "You know, let's not talk about that anymore, okay? Right now, I could really use some time in the gym throwing some punches, if you don't mind."

There is absolutely nothing at the moment I want to discuss less than my non-existing relationship with Dad. That is, other than the non-existing relationship I have with Sam—I don't want to talk about that either. I throw Ian a challenging look.

He grins and gets up. "I thought you'd never ask. Let's go and beat the crap out of each other!"

About half an hour later, I question my sanity.

I'm sweaty and exhausted already, and we've only been going at it for about fifteen minutes.

Ian's holding the focus mitts for me, having me throw punch combination after punch combination and duck and weave in between, or I'd get smacked in the head. My bad leg is keeping up pretty well, but despite my recent success, I don't want to take my brace off. It's one thing to do brace-free shuffle steps up in my room, and a completely different one to stay in a fighting stance and avoid getting clocked in the head.

"Let it out, Trouble! Give me stronger punches! Cross! Nice! There you go, best way to let go of your frustration. Jab! Cross! Hook! Keep it up!"

Ian would make a good drill instructor for the Marines: He doesn't let me catch a breath. He's right though; it *does* feel good to let it all out. Strangely enough, it clears my mind, bringing me a peace I've missed over the last weeks since Dad threw me out of his office for the first time.

Jab, cross, duck, cross, weave, jab, cross.

It all flows together into one smooth movement, like soothing meditation—only soothing goes *poof* when the memory of Dad's countless little rejections flood me like a tsunami, and tear down the protective walls I barely held up to begin with.

All I wanted was to be the best daughter to him that I could. *Pathetic.*

All I craved was us being close, like before. *Naïve.*

All I needed was him being proud of me. *Fat chance.*

What a sucker I am. What a pitiful, idiotic sucker.

Why didn't I distance myself more, keep my defense up? Instead, I got myself talked into PRICS, thinking what? That I could actually help Dad and he would let me? Me? The daughter he thinks isn't even strong enough to go to college on her own? Or to the freakin' West Wing? Even for me, that must've been one ginormous ego that got me to join PRICS. To think that *I* could help him, that I could make him proud of me again…

I'm nothing but an embarrassment for my dad.

How Sam can think Dad is blaming himself for my accident, I don't know, because it surely doesn't look like that to me.

Ian barely has time to get the mitts into position after he calls out the shots. I'm on fire. *BoomBoomBoom,* never have I punched faster or harder. He barely blocks a jab sneaking through when he's too slow bringing up the mitt. The next one grazes his cheek.

His eyes widen as he reflexively tucks his head to the side, but I don't see it. I've tears in my eyes and rage in my heart. My breathing turns wheezy, but who needs oxygen? Surely not me.

"Alix—" Ian grunts as he blocks a hook to the side of his body in the nick of time. "Alix—heck, Trouble! Whoa! Easy there, that one— Geez, *Alix*!" He bursts forward when I recoil my punch and hauls me into a bear hug, my arms pinned between our chests. "Breathe, Trouble. *Breathe.* Do I have to make it an order?"

Breathe?

The moment his chest is pressed against me, the fog in my mind begins to clear.

I suck in one large, desperate gulp of air, and when I exhale, all strength leaves my body, leaving behind a hollow exhaustion I've never experienced before—not even when I was told I'd never walk again.

My battery's on empty, and there's no charger nearby.

Locking my knees to keep on standing becomes too much. Gravity becomes too much. *Everything* becomes too much.

My knees buckle, and there's no way I can hold myself upright.

Ian grunts as he gets surprised by my weight dropping onto him, but he doesn't let go. Instead, he lets the focus mitts fall and tightens his arms around me, one around the shoulders, one around the waist, gently massaging my back in small, soft circles.

"I've got you," he murmurs, his breath warm against my ear, and I… I just…

I deflate.

My body is made of rubber, my mind is running on empty, and my soul is splintered and torn. If it wasn't for Ian holding me, I'd be a puddle on the floor.

I got you.

When was the last time somebody got me? That anybody got me?

Ian rocks me back and forth ever so gently. Soothing.

"Reached your limit?" He taps one finger against the back of my head, then brings that same hand back around my shoulders. I'm cradled in his hold and those circles of his other hand are sending waves of comfort through my exhausted body.

But whom am I kidding. His touch might be sending waves of comfort through my body, but it's also sending something completely different: sparks. Myriads of sparks, shooting from my back into every cell of my body. And those sparks, boy, do they recharge me.

Every time his palm or fingers graze a new area, my stomach breaks out in flutters, no matter there's still a shirt between his touch and my skin. A shirt is *nothing*.

"Trouble?" he whispers and gives me a light squeeze.

Oh, right. Question. Talking. Yes. Can do. Totally.

"Uh-huh." I nod against his shoulder, the tip of my nose brushing over the side of his neck. Ian jerks, then swallows hard. Those sparks turn into an electric current.

I clear my throat. Focus. Somewhat, at least. "I think all my issues drained me."

"All your issues?" Humor swings in his voice. "I always took you for even-keeled and on top of things. You *are* on top of things, Alix."

I shake my head the slightest, this time conscious to not make contact with his neck. "*So* not on top of things. My leg still sucks, I suck at spying, and Dad sucks in general." Admitting my inadequacies should make me feel exposed, but the burn of shame doesn't come. In Ian's arms that vulnerability doesn't feel like weakness. It feels like… possibility. Like I'm teetering on the edge of something new, something thrilling.

Ian nods. "I get that. Sometimes the constant drip turns into a flood, and then…" He shrugs.

"Yeah," I croak. "Flood." Especially with his breath tickling down my ear. That's not just a flood, that's a tsunami. A tsunami of sparks, if that makes sense, but even if it doesn't, I don't care. Logic isn't important right now. Ian's embrace is.

I'm acutely aware of every point of contact between us. His arms around me, his fingers on my back, his cheek so close, I feel the warmth radiating from it. Everything inside me twists into a conflicting knot of emotions. I like this. A lot.

But I shouldn't.

Dad's warning echoes in my head. Four years older. My teacher. Ian shouldn't be hugging me. He shouldn't be comforting me other than with a pat on my shoulder. For sure, he shouldn't hold me as if it meant something.

Ian shifts slightly, and for a fleeting moment I think he

might've pressed his lips against my hair. But that can't be right. It can't be, because as much as my body loudly roots for it to be, my brain knows it isn't.

"You'll be fine, Trouble. I know it. You'll be fine," Ian whispers against my hear and pulls me closer, and I... I let myself sink into his embrace, taking another deep breath of his spring soap scent. Might as well enjoy it while it lasts, since—

"Unacceptable! Agents! Stand down!"

Ian jerks once, as shocked by the barking authoritative voice behind us as me, and catapults himself off me as if I burned him. A startled squeak breaks from my throat, because what the—

Oh.

Waterhouse.

"Sir." Ian stands ramrod straight, while I... I need a second to adjust my body and brain to the change in situation.

It's not an improvement.

Waterhouse glares at us, droopy beagle eyes so cold they shock-freeze me to the core. His usual scowl has deepened, tightening his features into an angry mask of wrinkles and irritability. The dark growl that follows doesn't make me feel any better.

Oh, crap.

I don't need an IQ of 160 to know that we're in trouble. Not good.

"Agent Forrester. Get changed. *Now.*" He may point his finger at the room behind him, but his gaze stays on Ian—*drills* into Ian, who hasn't moved an inch.

I step closer to Ian. "But—"

"*Now*, Agent. I do not like to repeat myself," Waterhouse snarls.

That tone brings all the tiny hairs on my body to rise, as if they could protect me from the cold and anger radiating off my boss.

Ian gives me the slightest nod of his chin: *Go.*

Okay then. A dry swallow gets stuck in my throat. "Yes, sir." I guess that's the only answer I can give at the moment. The only smart answer, at least.

I straighten my shirt and limp past Waterhouse toward the changing rooms. With every step, the burning sensation of embarrassment in my neck grows until it's a fire. The heavy silence doesn't help to ease the feeling of anxiety in the pit of my stomach either. Only when I've almost closed the door to the dressing room behind me do I hear Waterhouse hiss at Ian.

"Have you lost your mind?"

I keep the door slightly ajar, not because I'm eavesdropping, but uhh, because Ian taught me to listen. So, I do.

And Waterhouse is going to town on Ian.

"*...is the Commander-in-Chief's daughter, for crying out loud...*"

"*...clearly your genius only applies to technologies, or how should I interpret...*"

"*...what you call PT? Then how...*"

I don't hear a single word from Ian.

Crap, crap, crap.

I work a jittery hand over my face. Great job, Alix. Great job being needy and getting Ian into trouble. If I hadn't lost it, we wouldn't have ended up the way we did and he wouldn't be chewed out by our boss right now.

I should change as I was ordered, but I can't. My attention stays on every sound coming in from the gym, every barked word I pick up adding to the guilt loaded onto my shoulders.

...done with you...

...unprofessional...

...uphold barriers...

…demotion…

Oh, no, no, no.

Not good.

He can't mean that, he's only angry. Nothing happened; it's a complete overreaction.

…breech of confidence, amateur mistake, remove you from her training…

No.

I rip the door open so forcefully it slams into the wall.

Waterhouse stops his rant in mid-sentence, whips his head around at lightning speed and directs his droopy beagle eyed-gaze on me like a spotlight—no, like those laser lights from sniper rifles.

Time to grow a spine, Alix. Ugh, bad choice of words, not that it mattered.

Biting down on the inside of my cheek, I limp toward Waterhouse and Ian, the distance seemingly evaporating between us, like fate enjoyed playing with me, getting me to suffer quicker.

"Mr. Waterhouse? Sir?" Nobody taught me about standing at attention, but I'm pretty sure I'm doing a pretty good job all on my own right now.

Body straight.

Face calm.

Waterhouse presses his lips into a thin line. "Agent Forrester." Not the friendly tone. More impatient, annoyed—at me. Better that than at Ian. He loves his job, and I can't be the reason why he gets fired.

"Sir, I wanted to apologize." Dry swallow. "I behaved inappropriately."

One eyebrow shoots up. "Is that so?"

"Yes, sir. I had a bad day, and Agent Donckers helped me through it." I'm not making the same mistake twice. I'm not calling Ian by his first name.

"I see." The skepticism in his divisive tone is obvious.

"I realize I should have dealt with it on my own, but Agent Donckers has become a friend to me over the last weeks, so I felt I could trust him." Trust is good, right?

"A *friend?*" Waterhouse repeats. "Because let's be honest, Agent Forrester. That's not what it looked like. I have two young genius-level kids here, one barely legal, the other definitely not. Now, both are supposed to be working on preventing an assassination attempt on our President, and instead I find them *cuddling* in the gym." He spits it out like it's a curse.

Ian cringes.

I shake my head. "No, sir, you misunderstand—"

"Alix reminds me of my little sister, sir." The apple in Ian's throat bobs up and down.

Come again?

"Your sister," Waterhouse growls.

"Yes, sir. They're about the same age, and as a big brother I feel responsible. Some of that might have transferred to Agent Forrester."

My jaw drops, but I snap it shut.

Like a sister.

Like a freaking sister.

He holds his *sister* like that? That should worry me, but it's not what feels like a punch to the gut. That would be my own stupidity.

I shouldn't over-interpret what can't be, and I should have learned my lesson from Sam today. I've been sister-zoned for the second time this afternoon, which means I really need to get the hint.

Those feelings… those feelings have to go away. All those stupid butterflies, for both of them. While the ones for Sam at least stood a chance at one point, however small it might've been, the ones for Ian are condemned to death even before take-off.

All I'm doing is hurting myself.

Grow up, Alix.

So, I straighten my spine and lift up my chin. I'll be damned if I let Ian see how much his words have hurt me. "It won't happen again. Sir. Agent Donckers is a great teacher and a good friend, that's all."

Ian coughs with a wheeze. "Agent Forrester is correct—"

Waterhouse huffs through his nose. "I raised three kids. Don't sell me for stupid."

I force myself to meet his gaze, willing my face into an impassive mask. My heart beats so loudly, I wouldn't be surprised if they both could hear it. "Sir, I know how this looks, but I swear it's not like this. My dad…" I hesitate as the words catch in my throat. Ian doesn't know this part, and I wish he'd never have to, but… "My Dad has made it quite clear he'd remove Agent Donckers from his position if he ever thought him and I…" I let that sentence trail off.

Ian inhales sharply. Cat's out of the bag, I guess.

"Dad gave me a more challenging curriculum to work on with Agent Donckers—" to keep me busy—"and he hasn't had a reason to complain." Because there are way, way too many things he doesn't know about and he doesn't need to know about.

Anyway.

"Mr. Waterhouse, Agent Donckers has been nothing but professional. He's been helping me balance everything, and without him there's no way I could've advanced this fast. This here," I motion to Ian and me, "wasn't his fault I just really needed some support for a moment." That's all the adult buzzwords I have in me. All the professionalism. All the genius-level language I can come up with that might convince

Waterhouse to drop this.

As it is, he only stares at me, and not an ounce friendlier than before.

Silence.

The apple in Ian's throat moves up and down.

A drop of sweat runs down my neck, joining the others between my shoulder blades.

After an eternity, Waterhouse nods. "All right then. But"— he whirls around with a surprising speed for a man his age, pointing a finger at Ian—"I expect immaculate behavior. Results. Professionalism." He takes two steps toward Ian, who's still frozen into an attention stance. "This is your last shot. Don't ruin it." He turns around and briskly walks out of the gym, the doors closing on him and on whatever was between Ian and me.

Ian deflates with a sigh, but neither of us moves.

Neither of us says anything.

What a close call.

And what an annoying man.

"He hates me." I'm sure of it, and I can't say the feeling wasn't mutual.

Ian bends down, supporting his upper body on his knees, breathing like after a marathon. "Holy cow. I've never seen him… No, he doesn't hate you. He isn't the biggest fan of me— of me replacing him, to be fair. And he's definitely not the cuddly type." He shudders using the same word Waterhouse dragged through the dirt earlier, then pushes off his knees and stands up straight, one hand working through his hair. "So… Your father wants me removed from duty?"

My heart seizes. In this very moment, Ian looks… young.

Vulnerable. Longing, somehow. I recognize that look, because it's the same one I've been wearing ever since Dad discarded me as a daughter second class.

I suck in my lower lip. Damage control. Because I know how much his disapproval hurts, and because I know how much this job means to Ian. "Well, not like that. He just wants to make sure I focus on studying and don't… get distracted."

Silence. Heat warms my cheeks.

Oh," he says, eventually. "Distracted by me. That's—"

"Ridiculous, right?" I jump at the opening. "I remind you of your sister, and to me you're a really good friend. Parents…!" I roll my eyes as if there was nothing more ridiculous than Dad's imagination.

Ian chuckles, but it sounds different than usual. "Waterhouse, too. We're four years apart. I don't know what he was thinking."

Something breaks inside of me. I don't know what *I* was thinking.

We're friends.

Never been more, never will be more, no matter what.

"Yeah," I croak. "Weirdo, that man."

Ian wipes his hands on his thighs. "Okay then, back to business, right? Uhh, then… let me go and change, and then…" He sighs. "We're changing our approach."

I blink twice. Okay. Quick change of topic, not that I mind it. My face appreciates some time to cool down.

Ian grabs a towel from over the ropes of the boxing ring and buries his face in it for an eternal second before he uses it to wipe his forehead. Eventually he lowers it and clears his throat. "I didn't get to tell you earlier before we came down here, but the Secret Service hasn't come up with anything useful so far, but that's not all bad." He's definitely all back to business, as if Waterhouse never came down here. "They didn't find any intel suggesting a second attempt is planned on your father. I don't think Sam is going to slip if—*if*—he's the assassin. I'd rather you dig a bit deeper into possible motives. For both Brooks. Is either of them unhappy with their work, do they feel unfairly treated, is either being blackmailed by someone to abuse his position close to the President?"

I nod. Makes sense. Sam relies on me to find the truth about him and Oliver, like Dad relies on me to keep him safe and Ian to keep his job. I'm a busy gal these days, and nobody thanks me for it. Rather the opposite.

Ian drapes the towel around his neck. "Regarding your father, try again during dinner. I know it's tough, Trouble. I know. But we have to get closer to him, or we can't protect him."

He reaches for my shoulder, but when *before* he would've touched me, something akin to realization lights up in his eyes. He drops his hand, covering it up with a cough.

Friends.

We're *friends.*

And now I've scared him with Dad's empty protectiveness.

Just great.

I let out a slow breath. "I'll try with Dad, Ian—I'll try, but I can't guarantee anything. If he—"

"Trying is all I'm asking of you, Trouble. I'm not going to ask you to sell your soul."

I huff. "No selling my soul, agreed." I pause. "Let's just hope he won't take me apart again."

Ian's expression softens. "He won't, and you will do great."

A small smile tugs at my lips. "I'll do my best to keep that in mind."

"Good," Ian says, his voice sounding much warmer than a mere minute ago. "And if you ever need anybody in your corner…"

Our gazes meet, and for a moment, the air between us feels charged, like before Waterhouse came in.

"Always," he finishes softly.

My breath catches. There's something in his eyes, something I can't decipher, not after the conversation we just had. Before I can analyze it further, Ian breaks eye contact, scratching his neck.

"Okay then. Take a deep breath, go up there, and get it over with, Trouble. Give me a report before you go to bed, I'll… I'll be up anyway."

With that, he turns away, and for the first time since I started working with Ian, I feel like I was just dismissed.

And I don't like it one bit.

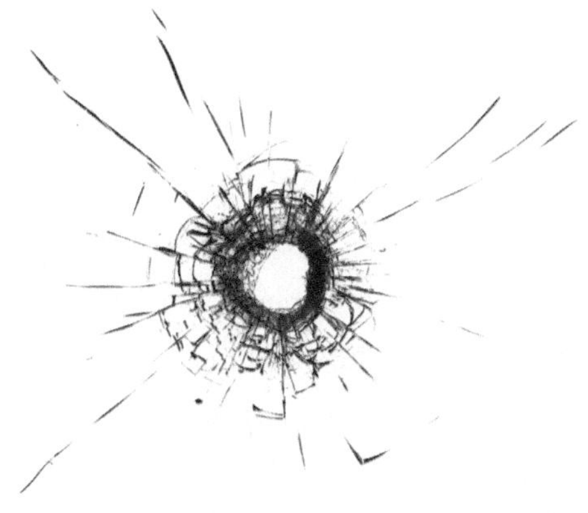

CHAPTER EIGHTEEN

First Kiss

Upstairs in the residence, it smells like chef's delicious cooking. My stomach rumbles despite the nausea that has me.

What a crappy day, on all accounts.

And to top it all off, dinner with the fam.

Awesome.

Before I open the door and limp into the dining room, I steady my grip on my crutches. That shaking of my hands is seriously annoying—aaand dies down the second I realize I'm the first for dinner.

No Mom yet, and, most importantly, no Dad yet.

It's a bit scary how my body relaxes with that.

I sit at my usual spot and drape the napkin across my lap. Odd. At least Mom is never late for dinner. Why isn't she here? Wait—am I missing something? After all, there was one assassination attempt already, who says there can't have been a

225

second one?

The door on my left opens.

"Tadaah! Surprise!"

Sam?

Sam grins as he strides through the dining room and takes a seat in the chair across from me. "I bet you didn't expect *me* here tonight, did you?" He unbuttons his suit jacket, slips out of it and throws it over the chair next to him.

I'm pretty positive I don't look my most intelligent right now with my mouth hanging open, staring at Sam. "Uhh, no? No. No, I didn't. Not really. I thought Dad—"

"Yep. That's what I thought. After you stormed out of the Front Office… Well, let's put it this way. He didn't look happy. It was pretty awkward in there, at least for Mrs. Houser and me. The Secretary of State, as always, didn't catch a thing. He just kept talking while your dad looked like he just wanted to follow you—"

"And do what?" I interrupt him. "Skin me alive? Cause that's what it looked like to me, the way he reacted." I cross my arms in front of my chest and fall back into my seat. Great. Now *I'm* the bad guy who stormed out of the room? Now it's *my* fault?

Sam sighs. "I know. Well, *I don't*. But anyway, what I was going to say is that he can't make it to dinner. For one, he is not feeling well, he looks even crappier this afternoon, and for another there is this—"

"Meeting." I know how it works. "It's *always* a meeting somewhere. Especially when he knows he would have to see me otherwise." I roll my eyes. Dad's tactics are getting old.

Sam shakes his head.

"Nope. Not this time. It's a last-minute visit by the German Chancellor and her team. Your parents, my dad, and Yoshi are taking them out to dinner. So he asked me to join you up here, so you wouldn't be alone. And here I am." Sam wiggles his eyebrows. "I didn't have the heart to turn him down. Just imagine all of the chef's delicious food going to waste, or you sitting here all alone and bored."

He sticks his tongue out at me and I can't help but laugh. If this whole thing wasn't so messed up, it would be funny how for the life of me, I can't get any closer to the Dad-part of my mission, while the Sam-part is happening with a life of its own.

A nice dinner with Sam. Despite the whole brother-sister-thing, it's still the better alternative compared to brown-nosing Dad until he likes me again. And: Talking to Sam is even in my PRICS job description for today.

Score!

As I smooth out my napkin across my lap, I catch the flickering light in the center of the table: Candles. No idea where the next sentences are coming from, but they slip out before I can stop them.

"Wow, Sam," I say, gesturing to the candles. "If I didn't know better, I'd think you're putting on the moves for me."

Sam's eyes widen for the fraction of a second, before he recovers and fixes a crooked smile on his face. "What can I say? I'm a sucker for ambiance." He pauses and tilts his head looking at the candles, then at me. "It's like a date, isn't it?"

My heart does a little flip-flop, but I squash that feeling ruthlessly. Been there, done that, got the *he sees me as a sister*-shirt.

"A date?" I snort. "Whoever wants to wow somebody living in the White House with dinner in the White House needs to overthink their strategies. Have a picnic. Get inventive." I shrug, oh, so casually, but on the inside I'm also oh-so proud of exactly how casual I sound.

Sam laughs, but there's something off about it. "Noted. I'll keep that in mind for future reference."

Wait, future reference? Who—

I all but groan.

Gianna.

Of course.

They're texting, she's clearly hitting on him, and she's another person basically living in the White House.

I just gave Sam dating advice for *Gianna*.

Ugh.

Luckily for me the chef comes into the dining room and serves food at the right moment to give me something to occupy myself with, because I don't know what to say. I wish we didn't have that moment in the copy room. I'm left feeling like a rejected little schoolgirl with a crush on her best friend, who likes the cheerleader instead.

Pathetic.

Coming to think of it, that's become my middle name. Sigh.

But because Sam is Sam and awesome, we quickly drift back into the comfortable banter and playful talk that always was a hallmark of Sam's and my relationship.

"So, have you found out why this day feels so off?" I ask him after another bite of pork chop with cauliflower. About time I start doing my job if I want Ian to keep his.

Sam shakes his head and swallows. "Not really. It's just the senior staff though. Everyone else is normal. I'm thinking maybe your dad is sick and has the flu or something and they don't want anyone to know. He looks crappy enough today, but you know how presidents aren't supposed to show any weaknesses? He can't have it in the media that the President of the United States got knocked down by the flu when the German Chancellor came to visit. Or whatever. Just ball-parking here."

Sam goes for another helping of the pork chops. He's right, they're quite delicious, but I'm a little bit too preoccupied at the moment to enjoy them properly.

"Why do you think it's the flu? I'm pretty sure he got his vaccine this year, like all of us."

"Oh whatever, Alix, just thinking, that's all. It could be something completely else. Maybe they're all bummed about the Republicans playing dirty with the Genetic Testing Bill, maybe it's because today is Wednesday, or the moon is in the seventh house, I don't know. And honestly, right now I don't care. You and I are having a delicious dinner. Great food and even better company. Cheers to that." He raises his glass of water and holds it out toward me.

I raise mine in response and we meet in the middle.

And it's not a date.

After that, we go back to chatting about old times, and soon, I forget my initial awkwardness with the candlelight and dinner. It comes natural to be around Sam, to joke and laugh with him.

At one point, I zone out for a minute or so looking at him while he tells a story about how Yoshi Nagakawa caught him for the first time with a Red Bull in the copy room. The story seems funny, and I laugh when I think it's appropriate, but I don't really listen.

I just look at Sam.

His chocolate eyes twinkle as he tells the story; the candlelight emphasizes his high cheekbones and strong jaw. It must've been a while since he shaved last, at least there's more stubble showing than normally, but it gives him a rugged look. I like it. "You're in a better mood compared to earlier."

He points to his plate. "Uhh, how could I not be?" The grin and wink he shoots at me across the table is so on top of the world, I have to laugh.

There's no way Sam is the assassin. No way. It's only a matter of proving it and keeping him out of the Secret Service's focus.

Would probably help to find the real assassin, too.

Commence spywork. "Do you have to be back downstairs or anything?" He probably has to. I don't think he leaves before 10 p.m. anyway.

"Nope," he says, "your dad kind of ordered me to take the evening off and keep you company. At your disposal, madam." He gives me a mock bow of his head. "By the way, I still haven't really seen much of the residence. Do I get a tour?"

Sam wants a tour? "If you're done eating, sure thing."

When he nods I grab my crutches and peel myself out from under the table. I won't miss this brace and the feeling of carrying a foreign body around with me if I ever get back to normal again.

"Awesome." Sam grins, gets up, and takes me by the arm, making it easier for me to stand. I can tell myself whatever I want—*friends, friends, friends*—the moment Sam touches me, my body betrays me. Goosebumps. All over. Would be nice if my body got the message my brain received loud and clear.

Sam holds out his arm for me to take, so I hook mine into his and give him one of my crutches. He takes it and plays around with it while supporting me with his other arm.

Dad gave him the rest of the evening off… If I didn't know better, I'd say he wanted to do me a favor. Harr harr, good one right there.

All right, grand tour it is. It's fairly quick though, mainly because I can't tell him much about the rooms or their history, and most of them I summarize as "sitting room" anyway. I mean, let's face it, we have about a billion of those. Sam still likes the tour, despite my inadequacies. We both laugh once we hit what feels like the seventh sitting room, and we make a joking effort looking for the nuclear football in my parents' living room.

At the end, we arrive at my room.

I open the door. "Tadaah!" I mimic his earlier fanfare. Sam

goes in first, giving my second crutch back to me. I grab it and follow him in, closing the door behind me. He looks around and walks from wall to wall, looking at my shelves and books, my little study corner with my microscope and chem sets, and stops in front of Stan, my life-sized fake skeleton.

"No way, Stan got to move in with you here?" Sam grabs Stan's boney hand and shakes it. "Buddy! I thought you would have to stay at home with Linda and scare her some more!"

I laugh. "No way Linda was going to keep Stan after what we did to her with him." I grin. That prank…! It got me grounded for a week, but since I never went anywhere anyway, it didn't really hurt that much. Sam didn't even get any consequences, because Linda—and Dad—always loved Sam.

He laughs lightly. "No, you're right. When I told Gianna that story, she said she was surprised your parents still let me come over after that." Sam pretends to high-five Stan.

I flash cold to the core. "You told Gianna about Stan?" That was our thing—*our* prank, *our* time together!

"Yeah." He shrugs, placing Stan's right hand over his skeleton chest, where the heart would be. "She thought it was awesome." He weaves Stan's finger between the ribs to make the hand stay in place.

There are so many things I want to say, yet I stay silent. I want to be mad at him for sharing what is *our* memory, but then, it's not about sharing our memory. It's about sharing it with *Gianna*.

Jealousy is an ugly beast with blonde curls and an impressive D-cup.

Sam taps Stan on the shoulder and then walks over to my desk, looking over my schoolwork. Good thing I kept up the pretense of doing actual schoolwork instead of PRICS assignments.

Since he's standing in front of the only chair in the room, I walk over to my bed and sit. Somehow, my knees are wobbly. Maybe the punching session with Ian was a tad too much for my leg. It can't possibly be because of the sting still shooting through my heart from Sam talking to Gianna, I mean, how ridiculous would that be?

Sam comments on my homework when he glances over it, something about how he made a rap about the Krebs cycle to memorize it easier, but I'm not really listening.

Ian wants me to dig deeper into possible motives, and now's the time. Sam's well-fed, relaxed, and not on duty. This might be my best chance to find out enough information to clear him and maybe even Oliver.

Working on an angle…

"Hey, Sam." I reach and tap against his upper leg. "Sami-boy? Just wondering… How's your dad doing? From what I've seen, my dad is making him work hard for his money. You know how working with him can be." I add a frown and eyeroll to that statement.

Sam puts my chemistry book down and lines it up with the corners of my desk. "No kidding, I know. Your dad can be intense, but mine is fine. At this point, they've been through the campaign together and know how the other one ticks. They're like an old couple anyway, bickering one day and making up the next." He chuckles, but keeps his gaze glued to that chemistry book. "Plus, obviously the job's working out well for my dad, no matter the stress. Remember… remember how I told you things have been tight at home?"

Of course I remember.

Sam walks over to me, kicking my braced leg gently with the tip of his shoes. "Well, they're not anymore. Your dad must've given mine a raise or something, because Dad sent a whole bunch of cash. Mom didn't say anything, but I saw the envelope on the kitchen table with a card from him." He sighs, and it sounds content. "It's good to know he still watches out for us here and there, you know?"

Uhm… "Here and there?" Why does that sound odd the way he says it?

"You… you don't know?"

"Don't know what?" What am I missing? Hello?

"Well…" Sam rubs his hand over his eyes, and sits next to me.

On my bed.

Yeah, tactical error on my part. Should've kept standing.

Sam's leg is pressed against mine, black dress pants against blue jeans. He leans forward and folds his hands in his lap, supporting his upper body with his arms. "Dad hasn't been paying a dime for us, Alix. For a while. Prenup, whatever, no idea. I just know he never paid anything. Nothing."

My jaw drops. "No way." That doesn't sound like Oliver. At all. "Why would he—"

"Beats me. Especially when he knows Mom's working at least two jobs every day."

My mind races. Could that in any way be a motive for Oliver? If he's been struggling financially, could he be desperate enough to… No, that doesn't make sense. If he killed Dad, his source of income would be gone. But what if Oliver resents Dad for whatever reason? That thought feels ridiculous, but what if he felt Dad wasn't giving him the raise he deserved and therefore he couldn't support his family?

I put on a playful tone. "So did my dad give him a raise, finally?"

Sam huffs and his voice hardens. "I don't know, and at this point I don't care. Dad's contributions were overdue."

Ouch. There's the bitterness he doesn't show during the day.

At night though, with his guard down… it does rear its ugly head.

So, how does that make Sam fit into this? He adores Dad. But could he have tried to hurt Dad to pin it on *his* father, who assigned him to limo-duty? Out of revenge? That idea is so far out there, it's beyond ridiculous.

So, let's clear it out of the way. "Is that what makes you sometimes so angry at him? That he not only left you, but didn't even support you?" I give my voice the exact right amount of pity, empathy, and curiosity—I think, at least.

Alas, it doesn't seem to work on Sam.

He turns his upper body and looks straight at me, tilting his head slightly to one side. "Maybe we shouldn't talk about our dads." He scoots around so that he faces me, bringing his knee up on the bed. Unsure if he notices it or not, but I do very much notice it's pressed into mine even more than before.

Nope. That's not distracting me at all.

I swallow hard.

On track. Must get back on track. The poisoning. Information.

"I know, dads, boring." I laugh so high-pitched, even Sam flinches. Yikes. Maybe my acting abilities aren't as good as I thought. "The stuff you do every day is much more interesting. Like, you even got to restock Dad's limo, I heard, right? How did you know what to do? I mean, where do you get the stuff you need? Who gives that to you? I'd be so lost if I had to do any of that." Yeah, I'm rambling. Ugh.

Sam closes his eyes for a second or two and takes a deep breath. When he opens them again, his gaze locks right into mine. His voice is soft and so low that I can barely hear it.

"It's after hours. We've had a great dinner, and finally have some time to just chill. I'm going to get really mad at you, if you say one more word that's work-related."

"But—"

"Shh…!" With deliberate slowness he raises his index finger and presses it gently against my lips, rough skin meeting soft.

Repeat, for emphasis: Sam's pressing his finger against my lips! Oh, holy cow!

My heart is all but hammering inside my chest, as if it recognized the danger of missing a beat. The next breath I take is filled with Sam's butterscotch scent, and boy, it burns me on the inside.

I don't move. I honestly don't know how to react. My first instinct is to look away because this is way, like, waaay too intense and personal, but somehow I can't. Not when Sam's looking at me like… like…

I force down a dry swallow.

Yeah. Like *that*.

A small smile plays around the corners of his mouth. "I thought I'd never get a moment with you alone," he whispers, "this place is crazy busy." He traces the outline of my lips with his fingertip and my stomach contracts as a million butterflies lift off simultaneously. Hello, dizziness. Whoa.

I gasp a raspy breath as my heart skips a beat or two.

Oh. Make that three or four beats, because Sam's sneaking his hand up behind my ear and into my hair.

Oh my God, oh my God, *oh my God*, this is happening! Sam and me, it's happening, it's really happening! It's *allowed* to happen! It *can* happen! It *will* happen!

He moves even closer to my face, so that our noses are only millimeters apart. Every speck of color in his eyes shines like it had its own power source. It's all I see. It's all I can see.

My brain has ceased to function.

At this point I just *am*, I don't think anymore.

For the first time in my life, my body has truly gained control over my brain.

A heartbeat later a storm of sensations erupts in my core as Sam's lips finally touch mine for the very first time.

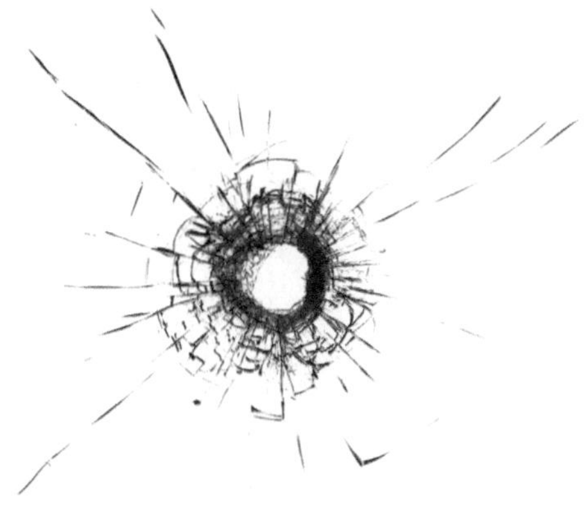

CHAPTER NINETEEN

Kiss, then Tell

wake up early next morning, well before my alarm goes off, and can't fall asleep again. And how could I, with the last evening replaying in my head like the best scenes of a movie?

It really happened.

Sam and I kissed.

Not just once.

Not just twice.

If his pager hadn't gone off half an hour later we still might be kissing!

We kissed! Sam and I kissed! *Waah!*

I squeak out a giggle and bury my head inside my pillow. Mmh, it actually still smells like him. I can't get enough of that delicious Sam-scent. Every breath gives the butterflies more fuel, powering them up until they're soaring high just like last night.

We kissed.

His lips were so soft, and he kissed my lips, my eyes, my nose, and probably every square centimeter of my face at least twice. Thinking back to those tender kisses still gives me goosebumps running down my spine.

Sam.

Hey, happiness, it's me, Alix. I know, we haven't seen each other in a while, but glad you're back. Thanks for clarifying he's into *me* and not Gianna.

I snort once. Who cares about Gianna anyway, when it was me he held?

At one point, before his pager went off, in a small step for mankind, but a giant step for me, I even had my hand under his T-Shirt and on his back. His skin was unbelievably smooth despite the hard outline of the muscles underneath it. Not quite as well defined as Ian, but—

The thought of Ian jerks me right out of my happy place and dunks me into a bucket of ice water.

Crap.

Something weird and heavy settles in the pit of my stomach.

Ian.

I… I guess I made a choice last night.

I laugh out once into the silence of my bedroom. A *choice*. The word choice implies a range of possibilities, and that would be a lie. Ian may like me, but in a brotherly way. He was never an option, for that reason and many others.

He never will be an option.

Sam on the other hand is.

And he chose me.

My chest squeezes tight, as if I messed up, which is stupid. I'm living my life. Puh-lease. As if Ian cared what two seventeen-year-olds were doing. He's focused on our task anyway—

Oops. Forgot to give Ian an update yesterday. I cringe. *Completely* forgot about that. Not very professional of me.

Although, on the other hand, it's not like Sam told me anything Ian would need to know right away. I didn't uncover anything secret or new, so I guess an update this morning is sufficient enough.

Totally.

Ian probably wouldn't have wanted me to waste his time, whether he was up anyway or not. Surely not.

I cuddle deeper into my blanket. One more hour of sleep would be nice.

Alas, sleep won't come thanks to the nagging nip and tuck inside my stomach that lets me neither fall asleep nor go back to my happy place thinking about Sam.

Aww, crap.

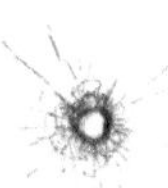

When my alarm clock finally goes off, I'm already showered and ready for the day.

Crossing the hallway to our dining room, I pick up on bits of a heated argument the very second I open the door.

"Leo, all I'm saying is consider the options. The rider—"

"Is tied to a time bomb that'll be our downfall—"

"Come on! Imagine the support—"

Ah, the Genetic Testing Bill. Of course.

"Just let that stupid thing pass and we'll deal with it and modify it later. You—"

"The day I put my signature under a bill like that is the day—"

The door creaks when I enter and both men turn to look at me, neither of them too friendly. They snap their mouths shut the second they hear the door, and I wish I'd stayed in my room longer. I don't feel super confident today is the day to cozy up to

Dad, judging by the way he and Oliver are locked in a staring contest across the table while Mom pretends to be invisible.

Still, she's the first to pretend nothing at all was going on. "Good morning, sweetie. You're up early." She gives me a warm and only slightly fake smile.

Yeah, up early, but apparently not awake enough to use all my PRICS training to properly eavesdrop. *Listen*, Ian said how many times? Great job you did, young Padawan.

"Good morning, *Mom*." I wave at her. "Oliver." Another wave for him, and just because I'm apparently petty, I add the next sentence. "Just up early so I can keep working on my *expected projects*." Like the list of things Dad gave me to *stay focused*.

Mom nods and takes a sip of her coffee—black, to save the calories from the creamer.

Sliding into place behind my chair I glance at Dad and I nearly do a double-take.

Whoa.

Like Oliver, he's already dressed for work in a suit and tie, sleeves rolled up—but those bags under his eyes I saw before? They've gotten company. I wouldn't be surprised if he hadn't slept in days, he looks it. His face isn't only pale, but also pasty, and while he usually sits ramrod straight, this morning he's more slumped at the table than anything.

That's what the worries of an assassination attempt do to you, I guess. Not that I could ask him about it.

Mom on the other hand looks as fresh and made-up as always. Good to see at least one of them is taking this lightly.

I pour myself some OJ, willing my shaking hands to not spill any, then take a deep breath, gather all my courage, and turn toward my right. "Dad—"

"Alix—"

Both of us pause. Awkward.

Oliver clears his throat. "I'll… I'll be waiting downstairs." He nods toward Mom and walks out. Lucky him. Although, he did get chewed out by Dad already, so I can't fault him for getting out of here. Ballsy move to try to get Dad to sign the Genetic Testing Bill, tempting rider or not.

Dad takes his napkin and wipes his sweaty forehead with it. "Why don't you come to my office over lunch, Alix? There's… there's something I need to talk to you about. Waterhouse will be there too, and tonight we won't have time with the festivities and everything."

Oh, crap. Panic shoots through me. Waterhouse. He must've told Dad about Ian and me yesterday. Shoot, shoot, *shoot*. I'm in deep. Ian is in deep—all for ridiculous reasons. I kissed *Sam* last night! Nothing is happening between Ian and me!

Unfortunately, my options are limited at this point. Antagonizing Dad won't do me or Ian any good, and no matter what, I need to patch up my relationship with Dad, even though it might feel like selling my soul.

But in no way am I willing to throw Ian to the wolves.

So I force a very mature shrug, "Sure, Dad. No problem. If Waterhouse is there, should I bring Mr. Miller?" Ian should be there. Together we'll stand a better chance defending us. Plus, Dad *and* Waterhouse against me alone is more than a bit unfair.

Dad frowns. "No. Waterhouse will take care of Mr. Miller afterwards."

Afterwards. My throat is as dry as the desert.

Dad pushes his chair back. When he stands, he wobbles slightly, but steadies himself with a quick grasp of the chair before straightening his jacket and tie. "I have to go. Please be on time." He takes another sip of coffee while standing and walks out of the dining room, leaving me with an open mouth and the very bad feeling that I don't have a clue where to go from here.

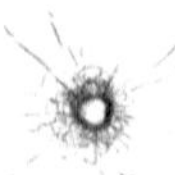

I arrive in our classroom to find Ian pouring me tea.

A smile creeps on my face. However, Waterhouse may have spoiled it and whatever Dad may think about our relationship, at least Ian took the time to get know me. In a pop-quiz All About Alix I'd bet on Ian, not Dad. Sad, but true.

"Hey there." I smile at him, getting a wave back in reply after he fills his cup with tea.

The moment I wrap my hands around that steaming mug and inhale deeply, the tension coiled up inside of me finally relaxes a bit.

"Before we talk about tonight's Fourth of July festivities: How did it go with your father last night? You didn't report to me, so I assume nothing much happened?" Ian takes a sip from his mug.

See, no big deal I didn't report. I sigh. "No talking, not last night. And not this morning either. Although… although he does want to talk later, over lunch." With Waterhouse. I swallow a sip of tea. "Waterhouse is going to be there too, and then…" I can't help my voice turning bitter. "Then he wants to have Waterhouse talk to you." A typical overreaction by Dad. One I'll have to prevent. If he thinks he can ship me off to the boarding school or whatever, he's wrong. PRICS is better for me than Harvard could ever have been.

Ian's eyes widen. "Oh. Well… I wonder what that could be about." He lowers his gaze and his cheeks turn a healthy pink. Yeah, he knows *what that could be about.* "But, uhh, anyway. What was his excuse not to talk to you last night?"

"Oh, last night… Well, my parents weren't home for dinner, so I didn't get a chance to talk to him then either."

Because I was busy with Sam.

My cheeks heat up and I cover it with another sip of tea.

Ian thinks for a minute. "Depending on how your lunch meeting goes, his avoidance of you is turning into a problem. We might have to change our approach. PRICS is founded on the assumption that it's easier for children of the President to be around them. Your father is making fulfilling our job description quite difficult."

"No kidding," I mumble. He doesn't need to tell me that, I know very well why they approached me—it surely wasn't for my incredible talent in espionage.

"Just out of curiosity, what was his excuse for not showing up for dinner last night?" Ian wants to know.

"Sam said the German Chancellor was in town and my parents invited her for dinner." I shrug, because, does it matter? There's always something.

Ian looks at me quizzically. "Sam?"

Oops.

I swipe a strand of hair behind my ear. "Uhh, yeah. Sam came over for dinner. He said Dad had sent him so I wouldn't have to eat alone."

"Oh."

That's all he says. *Oh.*

I take another sip from my tea, staring down into the cup as if I was trying to read the future. Why does it feel so awkward right now? Ah, because I kissed Sam. That would do it.

After a second or two of silence, Ian restarts the conversation.

"Okay, right. So, Sam was there. That's good, that's good. Did you get anything from him? Anything we can use?" Ian raises his eyebrows and looks at me expectantly.

I hesitate a second and hold the cup of chai even closer to my face. "Nope," I don't look up, no need for Ian to see the color in my cheeks. "Nothing earth shattering. He said he noticed that

Dad looked sick yesterday. He thinks he might have the flu. Other than that—nothing, besides that he also said he liked working for my dad." Which I knew. None of that is a huge step in terms of discovering relevant information.

I look up at Ian, who's staring into his cup of tea as intensely as I did a moment ago, turning it in his hands.

"Okay. He's right. The Secret Service officers assigned to him noticed that too. We might make him get checked by Dr. Soong today. Did you get to talk to Sam about his filling in for Amando when stocking the Limousine?"

I answer before I think. "Didn't get to it. Just when I had asked him, he—" Oops. I snap my mouth shut, but the damage is done.

"He 'what', Alix?"

Sorry, but there's no way I'm going to tell Ian what happened between me and Sam, because it was exactly that: between me and Sam.

"Nothing." I shake my head while tracing a line on my desk with my finger.

"*Alix*," Ian says, "*everything* and *anything* he said about the limousine could tip the scale in either direction. I need to know what he said."

"Nothing. He said nothing, okay? We got distracted." I wince the moment I say it.

"Distracted."

"Yeah." My face burns like a super nova.

Ian shakes his head, an expression of flabbergasted incredulity on his face. "Why would you let yourself get distracted—"

"It just happened—"

"—when it's about the safety of your father—"

"Geez, Ian, it's not a big—"

"—and you know perfectly well he depends on us—"

"It wasn't on purpose—"

"Then why didn't you focus—"

Ugh! "Because he kissed me, okay? He kissed me, and that's it!" I throw my arms up, surprisingly not spilling any chai, then set the mug down and cross my arms in front of my chest.

Crap.

That just… slipped out.

And Ian is silent.

I flick my gaze up at him, meeting his. In that fleeting, short moment I glimpse a strange look crossing his features before he masks it: Hurt? Disbelief?

Either way, it's gone as quickly as it came, and maybe I imagined it.

Ian clears his throat. "Well… Okay. Tell me exactly what you talked about at that point."

The only people I would like to discuss this less with than with Ian are my parents, and that's a close call. I groan inwardly— why does he have to make me do this?

Still, I know when I'm defeated. I give him what he asks for. Professionalism, right?

"I was asking him about how he liked the job, about filling in for Amando, where he got all his supplies and who gave them to him. And then…" Then it just happened. He was close and warm and perfect, and it just happened. "… and then he kissed me." And I kissed him.

"And after… you never… never went back to talking?" Ian's voice sounds weirdly flat.

"No."

"Okay… and… how long exactly did he stay?"

"Until his pager went off about half an hour later."

"Okay… anything else I need to know?"

"No." Definitely not.

I pick up my mug again and sip at the hot liquid, trying to keep my hands and eyes occupied. I don't look up, which is why I'm completely startled when Ian slams his hands onto the desk with a loud smack.

He growls. "*Did you ever think—*"

Snapping his mouth shut he sucks in a sharp breath through his nose, then pinches his eyes and exhales slowly. "Did you ever think that maybe, and just *maybe*, you were on to something?" Each word is clipped and precise, with an undercurrent of tension. "You've known him for two years and nothing has happened between you two. He tells you yesterday afternoon of all days how much of a sister you are to him, and then he *can't help but kiss you* later that same day when you were about to get into the assassination attempt? Did you *ever* listen to anything I taught you, and think that he was maybe trying to distract you with the one weapon he knew would counteract your brain?" Ian throws his arms up in anger and marches through the classroom like Rumpelstiltskin. He's beyond mad.

But honestly, by now so am I.

I leap to my feet, shouting, "How *dare* you! I told you from the beginning that there's absolutely no way Sam is the assassin or has anything to do with this!"

How dare he spoil that memory for me!

How dare he suggest in earnest that Sam has to do with the assassination attempts and is using me!

Yes, I got distracted, but by *Sam*, not some ruthless killer! It's different!

A surge of white-hot betrayal shoots through my veins. "I told you *everything* I found out about him, and *nothing* brought up a red flag! Then the boy I happen to like kisses me for the first time in my *life* and you tell me it was a *distraction*?"

Ian stops dead in his tracks.

His body goes rigid and a ragged breath leaves his throat. "The boy you happen to—" He turns away from me, spine stiff. His shoulders heave up and down with deep breaths—deep, choppy breaths that tear something inside me apart.

My heart seizes in my chest. Gone is the anger, the rage, the feeling of betrayal. *Poof.* I swallow dry. "Ian, I— I'm sorry."

He lifts a hand and shakes his head. "No need to apologize."

For a good ten or fifteen seconds neither of us speaks. Neither of us moves. Not sure either of us breathes.

Eventually Ian takes one long inhale and holds it before he speaks again. His voice is softer now, dull, and he's still not facing me. "Alix... I'm the one who's sorry. It's just... Never mind. I didn't mean to spoil this for you, I was just... concerned."

But is it just that? Concern? Or is it this elephant in the room, the one I thought was there when Waterhouse barged in on us, before Ian's sister-comment? Or is there no elephant and I'm way off the mark?

Ian takes a breath like he wanted to say something else, but doesn't. Instead, he turns around, expression neutral and... blank, somehow.

"Concerned," I repeat.

He nods, a muscle in his jaw ticking.

"About the mission." I take one small, tentative step closer to him.

The apple in his throat moves up and down. "About... everything."

"Everything?"

He clears his throat, shifting his weight from one foot to the other. "You know what I mean."

Do I? "I'm not sure I do," I say, my voice barely above a whisper, and take another small step toward him, closing the distance between us.

"We have to be careful." He flinches and shakes his head. "I mean, you have to be careful. Our, uhh, work can be dangerous, even if it doesn't always seem like it."

I nod and keep my gaze glued to his. The tension in the room is palpable, pulsing like a living thing between us. "So you're concerned about me."

Ian's breath hitches. The apple in his throat moves up and down. "B-because you are our biggest asset, of course. I—We can't do this without you."

I tilt my head to the side. "Because without me, there's no PRICS."

"No," he rasps. "Without you there's nothing." He shifts his weight, his hand twitching by his side as if he wanted to reach out for me, but instead he grips the edge of the desk behind him, his knuckles turning white.

Without you there's nothing.

He's completely right. Without me, there's no PRICS. It's a true statement. Logical. But why, oh why then did it sound like he meant something different?

Without you there's nothing.

I look up at him through my lashes, heart racing.

"We should… uhh, we should go back and look at the data," Ian says, his voice strained as he turns toward the desk. "Some tea might be a good idea, too." He busies himself with the thermos, the familiar scent of chai wafting through the air as he pours the steaming liquid into two fresh mugs, as if he'd forgotten he already gave me one.

Eventually he turns around. "Here," he says, his voice low, slightly rough. He cradles the steaming mug in both hands, long fingers wrapped around the curved surface.

"Thank you," I whisper. As I reach to take the mug, my hands overlap his and my fingers slide into the space between Ian's, fitting as if they were meant to be there.

For a heartbeat, the world narrows to just this moment. We're so close I can feel the heat radiating from his body, can see the rapid rise and fall of his chest. And while the ceramic is warm against my palm, it's nothing against the heat radiating from Ian's fingers close to mine. A slight tremor shakes the mug, but for the life of me I can't tell if it's coming from me or him.

And neither of us lets go.

The moment stretches into eternity, filling the space between us.

I glance up, meeting Ian's gaze. His eyes are dark, pupils dilated. The pulse in his neck beats overtime, but my heart isn't exactly taking a leisurely stroll either. It bounces against my rib cage with a force strong enough to bruise it.

I'm hyper-aware of every point of contact between Ian and me, how his fingers rest against mine, warm skin against my cooler one, drawing me in. Nothing else exists. Nothing else should exist when all that counts is that little bit of contact between us. We've hugged before, but this… looking into Ian's eyes as time stretches and neither of us moves their hands… this is way more intimate. Like we're connecting on a different level. The air between us feels thick, charged with possibility and something fragile, yet powerful—frightening as well, in a certain way.

My mind is a battlefield. I was kissing *Sam* last night, but what I'm feeling right now, locked into Ian's gaze and with only the slightest contact between our fingers on the mug is… more. So much more.

Sam.

Yesterday I was happy. *So* happy. And now…

Guilt gnaws on my insides. What is wrong with me? Maybe I don't even know what I want. What my heart wants. Or maybe

I do, and I don't want to listen, because it brings scary to a whole new level.

Nuh-uh. Not true. I know what I want. I just don't know if I can get it.

But I can find out.

Slowly, deliberately, I spread my fingers on the mug until they don't just gently touch Ian's but press against them. It's a small change, but the effect is electric. A shiver runs from my fingers all the way down my spine. Ian's eyes widen and his mouth drops open. He sucks in a short, strangulated gasp—

—and jerks back so suddenly, tea sloshes over the rim of the mug, splashing onto my hand. He all but leaps away from me, chest heaving with heavy breaths.

"Alix," he gasps, "we should—I mean, we need to continue. Briefing. The briefing of course." He coughs into his elbow and turns away from me while I stand frozen, holding the mug and tea dripping from my fingers.

That... wasn't what I expected to happen.

Ian coughs once more, and as if that had cleared his system, turns around with a perfect professional expression: Calm. Neutral. For the life of me I can't read him right now. "So, uhh, where was I a minute ago, the mission, keeping you safe—ah, right. Yes. Uhh, keeping you safe is of the utmost importance, of course. You're like a little sister to me, Alix. In fact, you remind me of her every day. Just the way you talk, you know? So yes, I need you to be safe."

Sister.

We're back to sister. I close my eyes. It's not as if he hadn't said it before. He did. And yet... Yet for a moment, just one tiny moment, I let myself believe. I let myself picture a world where this—us—was possible. I let myself hope. Feel.

Guess I have nobody to blame for that ripping sensation in

my chest other than myself.

Ian steps back and around the desk, his movements a bit too quick to be casual. He runs a hand through his hair, tousling it. A faint blush colors his cheeks, and he's looking anywhere but at me.

Sister.

Right. Is he really—

An ear-piercing shrieking siren rips through the room, so sudden, I jerk my hands up, hitting myself in the face.

What the…? This isn't the proximity alert when someone is approaching our classroom; this one is different. More urgent.

"Oh, no," Ian whispers. He's white as a ghost.

Before I can ask what's going on, Dimitri bursts in from the hallway. To his credit, he doesn't even do a double-take seeing Ian and me across from each other and obviously worked up.

Ian and Dimitri exchange a quick glance, a silent understanding passing between them. Ian's voice cuts through the air, sharp and urgent. "Alix, Dimitri. Eagle's Lair downstairs *now*. It's a Code Red. The President's in danger."

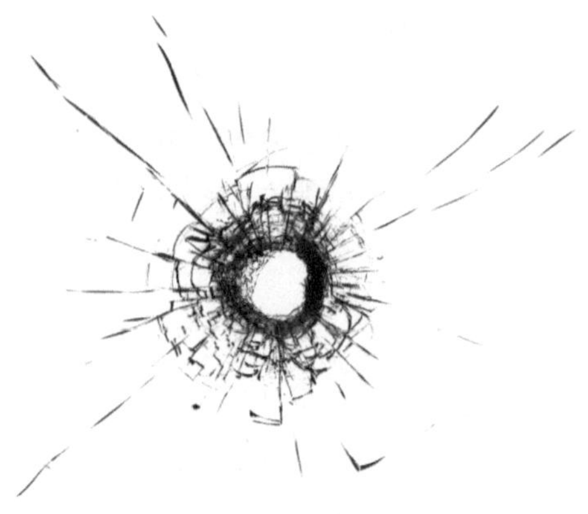

CHAPTER TWENTY

Code Red

The President's in danger.

All the way down to the Eagle's Lair I can barely focus on making my way downstairs without falling. My hands are so clammy, I have a hard time holding on to my crutches. Without Dimitri keeping a hand on my upper arm, I'd break my neck on one of these million steps.

Dad…! Another attack? Is he okay? What happened? Was it Sam? It can't have been Sam. But what if it was?

Dimitri and I make it down the zigzagging staircase about two minutes after Ian, who ran ahead. He's already scrolling on a DUTI-pad with one hand and clicking through stuff on his computer with the other. A frown pulls his eyebrows down into a V.

Nausea rises up my throat. Maybe I misjudged the situation over the last days. Yes, there was an assassination attack on Dad, and Yoshi landed in the hospital for it, but I never realized what it truly meant.

Until now.

I was too busy being mad at Dad, too busy sorting out my relationships with him, Sam, and Ian—and too busy worrying about Sam being wrongly accused. I simply had my priorities wrong. I should've focused more on what was truly important here: Dad's life. I should've worked more, and played less.

Hindsight is twenty-twenty they say. Guilt lodges in my throat. I get that none of it is my fault, I'm not the one attacking him—but I'm the one who's supposed to keep an eye on him, and I haven't done a very good job with that.

Waiting for Ian to come up with a report of what happened to Dad is torture in its purest form. What if he's dead? My knees buckle and I let myself fall into the couch, then lean forward and bury my face in my hands. Come on Ian, faster, faster! "What's happening?" My voice doesn't sound like mine. So raspy. Hoarse. "Ian?" I'm desperate for any bit of news. Something. Anything. I need to know what's going on.

"He's alive, but they don't have the assassin. Give me another minute. This is all coming through via live feed in real time," he says without looking up from his computer and DUTI-pad.

I let go of a big breath, and the world shifts back into view.

He's alive.

He's alive.

Forcing myself to stop hyperventilating brings body control to a whole new level. He's alive. But that also means something bad enough happened that *he's alive* is an acceptable status update.

Bile pushes up my throat.

It only takes Ian the minute he promised before he comes over to the couch. He's not as white anymore, but all the usual smiles and warmth are gone from his face, giving him a look of utter professionalism and seriousness.

"Around fifteen minutes ago, your father collapsed in the Oval Office. They called Dr. Soong, who was able to stabilize him, and he's now in the medical wing. This is all top-secret so far. Not even Mrs. Houser knows they took him. They went through the Emergency Passage." Ian swipes through a couple of screens on his DUTI-pad.

I look at him quizzically. "Emergency Passage?"

"The Oval Office has two secret passageways. One to the medical wing and one out of the White House. Both were installed during the Cold War, when the government feared sudden attacks. Same as with many others, like our lair here. But I digress. The reason they chose the secret route to the medical wing and to keep this under the radar is that Dr. Soong realized immediately why your father collapsed when he opened his shirt to listen to his heart and lungs."

He looks up from his DUTI-pad, turns it around and shows it to me.

"Do you know what this is?"

The picture shows Dad's chest, the carpet of the Oval Office clearly recognizable under his body. His face is cut off in the picture, but judging from the position of his neck, his head is turned all the way to the right. Unconscious? I swallow hard. In the middle of his left chest is an about fifteen centimeters long and one centimeter-wide redness with blisters. It looks angry and inflamed. The area around it is less red but doesn't look good either.

"It looks like a burn," I say, "but why should he have a burn like that on his chest? And why would that make him collapse?"

Ian nods. "True. But you told me he looked crappy when you saw him this morning. Was he pale, with dark circles under his eyes, not quite as steady on his feet, and seemed weak?"

"Yes, exactly, I thought he might be coming down with the flu. How do you—" Oh my God. This isn't a regular burn at all, and neither does Dad have the flu. No. This is much worse. This is something that could've killed him easily, and maybe even others with him.

The implications of what's going on are enormous. My jaw drops.

"It's a radiation burn," I whisper.

A *radiation* burn.

Someone got close enough to poison Dad with radioactive material.

Ian gives me an acknowledging nod. "Yes. It was pure luck your father collapsed this morning. Had he held on longer, the damage would have been far worse. Dr. Soong has him in the Medical Wing, and your father is conscious again. The doc is administering anti-radiation treatment, and your father is expected to recover completely. If he hadn't been so stressed to begin with, he probably would have kept up appearances longer and would have come to medical attention later. I'm thinking another twenty-four to forty-eight hours, and he probably would have died. This way anti-radiation treatment will still work, but only barely so."

Ian takes back the DUTI-pad and keeps on scrolling through the live feed. Chatter-type text boxes and pictures pop up on the screen, and once even a video feed of what looks like the medical wing.

A radiation burn. How cold-war-nineteen-eighties is that? Who would do something like that and— "Wait. This kind of burn doesn't just happen with a one-time touch of something radioactive, does it? How did the assassin get the radioactive device onto Dad? Nobody sees him without a shirt besides Mom and sometimes me, and she should have—" Oh. Error in my logic. I smack my forehead. "No. Mom wouldn't have seen him shirtless. Not lately, I guess. Dad's been working like crazy the last couple of weeks. He usually keeps the light off in the bedroom when he changes, so he won't wake her." That's been his MO ever since I was little. No lights. Which is why he once squished the artwork I made him and put out for him on his bed to find when he came home. There went the toilet paper-roll-turned-butterfly. I was devastated, but not as devastated as Dad when he woke up to the remnants of his four-year-old's artwork.

A small, sad smile tugs on the corners of my mouth. He was so sorry. When Mom got up, she found us in my room, in our PJs, making another butterfly, together.

The thought of Mom wipes my smile right off my face again. Knowing her, she's going to feel guilty beyond belief she didn't pick up on what was going on with Dad. Double-guilty, as his wife and as a physician. I wouldn't put it beneath her to implement regular full-body checks from now on. Fool her once…

Ian sighs and tears his gaze off his DUTI-pad. "Yes, and yes, Alix. Prolonged exposure, and I doubt your mother saw it. But here, this is where the problems start. The Secret Service found this on your father." He turns the DUTI-pad around to show me.

"One of Dad's pens?" That's one of the expensive French ones he keeps in his left inside pocket, right above the burn.

"Correct. When they held a Geiger-counter over it, it went crazy. The amount of radiation from the pen combined with an exposure of days or weeks would be enough to kill a human. It was the pen, Alix. The pen was the radioactive device planted on him. The assassin knew him well enough to choose something he would willingly always carry with him, and, even worse, something that didn't emit enough radiation to trigger our alarms, but would, over time, do its job. This person had an abundance of insider-knowledge." He looks me straight in the eye, regret radiating off him in waves. "And you know who supplies the pens to your father."

I slap one hand over my mouth. Of course I do. Oliver buys them, and Sam keeps my Dad supplied with a steady stream of his favorite pens. I shake my head. "It can't be. It can't be Sam. Heck, it can't be Oliver either. Just because they're supplying Dad with those pens… It doesn't mean anything."

Ian stays silent and raises one eyebrow.

He doesn't need to comment on what I just said, my brain does a good job asking the next question, and I hate it for it: Why was Sam really up in the residence with me yesterday? Did he stay for *me* after dinner, or did he stay so he could scope out the residence for another attempt? Did Oliver tell him to do that? For Heaven's Sake, we looked for the nuclear football! I don't want to think of Sam or Oliver as assassins, but the doubt Ian placed in my heart thirty minutes earlier is still there.

I need more information. Data. Data is good. "Do they know who did it? DNA? Proof?" Clearly, we can't just go on assumptions here.

Ian shakes his head and lets himself fall back into his chair, folding his arms behind his head and looking up to the ceiling. Eventually he lets go of a big breath and leans forward again supporting his weight with his arms on his knees.

"No, nothing yet. And before you ask, they know Oliver orders the pens and Sam provides them for your father. The only reason they don't have either in custody right now is because they're lacking motive and we don't have any proof. We have two assassination attempts on our President, and both coincided with something the Brookses had their hands in. We need one more straw to take them down, just one more thing." He slams his balled fist into his open palm.

I sneer. "What happened to 'innocent until proven guilty'? There must be another explanation. Where would they get radioactive material? It's not as if Sam could go shopping for it in the store around the corner." One serving of radioactive isotopes coming right up. Sure.

Ian suppresses an eye roll. "No, he can't. But his father meets with people from all over the world, many of them political enemies, many of them with the ability to smuggle in enough radioactive material to fly under our scanners. This was well-planned, Alix. Not a spur of the moment attack."

Frustration surges through me. I get where he's coming from, but come on—Oliver, my dad's *best friend,* in an official meeting with somebody, probably tons of people around them including our own, and he gets handed radioactive stuff in what, a gift box? How's that—

Air freezes inside my lungs.

No.

Wasn't it.

Wasn't.

Was *not.*

Ian cocks his head to the side. "Alix?"

I suck in a short breath, my lungs can't handle more. My hands shake, and my heart... my heart limps on every beat, because this cannot be true. Just can't.

"Alix?"

The effort to look up and meet Ian's gaze is equal to moving a mountain. "I... I saw Oliver. In the Green Room. On my first day, when..." I close my eyes. "When I was supposed to distract Lucas. Oliver was there, and..."

A cold stare between the two men. Lucas handing Oliver a small gift box: Full signature, please.

"Lucas gave Oliver something in a little box." I squeeze my

eyes shut tighter. It must be coincidence. Something else. How crazy would it be if Lucas brought radioactive material to the White House and gave it Oliver?

Ian inhales sharply. "Are you sure?"

I wish I wasn't. "Yes. Yes, but it could've been chocolate, for all we know."

Ian gets up and paces, hands folded behind his back. "At this point everything means something, Alix. We have Oliver already connected to the water in the Limousine, and if Lucas—" He halts. "Huh. Could've been radioactive material—or could've been lev-metaminozole. Lucas would have the connections for both."

Oh, crap. It shouldn't make sense. It shouldn't fit. And yet… "But why would Oliver work with Lucas? Why him?"

Ian lets out a slow breath and massages his neck with one hand, staring into nothingness. *Thinking mode engaged.*

When he drops his hand and turns toward me, I know something is wrong.

And it scares me.

"Ian. What am I missing?" He's making me nervous. What am I missing? It's nothing good, that much is clear.

Ian resumes his pacing. "Alix, do you remember the biggest topic of your father's election campaign?"

Of course I do, that stupid thing is still sticking around and making Dad's life difficult. "Yes. The Genetic Testing Bill, that's what you mean, right? What does it have to do with anything?"

Ian sighs. "The Genetic Testing Bill. One of the biggest ethical dilemmas of our time. Should we screen everybody's genome at birth and collect the data? Besides the obvious and questionable implications of how the government could use and abuse data of this magnitude, let's just talk about the medical use. We could tell every person exactly what kind of health they are in at birth, and what will happen to them in the future—apart from accidents and infectious diseases of course. But anything they have a tendency to get—cancer, psychiatric diseases, heart problems, etc—we could predict. Including a tendency for violence, but that's a different matter." He walks around his chair, sitting down again.

"To answer your question of what you're missing. You're missing Oliver's daughter. Jess. She's the connection. Obviously, Lucas wants the bill to succeed, since his company will profit greatly if it passes. Oliver could support the bill to prevent other families from the heartbreak they had with Jess."

That's ridiculous. "There's no way Oliver would support—" I snap my mouth shut. Oh, heck. This morning: Dad and Oliver in the dining room.

Blood swooshes in my ears so loud it threatens to drown out my thoughts. I suck in a desperate breath and lean forward, head buried in my hands. "Crap, crap, crap."

Finding Dad's assassin is paramount, preferably before they succeed. But blaming Dad's oldest friend feels wrong.

"Alix? What aren't you saying?" Ian's voice is soft, and if it wasn't for what happened between us thirty minutes ago in another lifetime, I'd feel comforted by it. Now I'm not sure how to handle it.

I let my hands sink down. No choice but to tell what I overheard. "I heard Oliver this morning. In the dining room up in the residence. He urged Dad to let the bill pass because of the rider."

Ian sits up ramrod straight. "You heard him say that?"

Unfortunately. "I *over*heard him and Dad, yes. And I know what it looks like, but Oliver's the Chief of Staff, it's in his job description to bring up the other side and have Dad consider all the options. And they have different opinions all the time, so there's that. Plus, I'm sure he isn't the only one who ever said to let the bill pass." I snap my fingers. "Take DiBiaso. I could bet DiBiaso doesn't mind the bill half as much as Dad." Where else would Gianna have the opinionated phrases from that she spewed at me on that first day when Yoshi ran me over? Her political interest, as far as I know, is close to zero.

Ian frowns. "Well, okay. Point taken, but that doesn't change the fact that if the bill—and with it its rider—came to pass, Oliver's ex-wife would receive more money to care for Jess."

I hate that it makes sense. "You mean, then Oliver wouldn't have to pay for Jess? Money as a motive?" I can't imagine Oliver sinking so low to even consider selling his soul in exchange for Dad's well-being.

"Definitely money as a motive. Oliver has… issues with money." The way Ian says it… it gives me goosebumps, and not the good kind.

A chill creeps into my bones. "What do you mean?"

Ian sighs. "Alix, Oliver… has no money. His finances are limited, to say the least. Unfortunately."

"Huh?" I shake my head. "Just because he never paid child support? I know that's crappy of him and I must say I didn't expect that, but also I know for a fact that he paid a pretty large amount of money to Liona, maybe a couple of days—"

Ian snaps his gaze to mine. "He *what*?"

Uhh, why is that such a big thing? I shift my weight around. "He gave a huge chunk of money to them. Sam saw a big chunk of cash and card from Oliver at home. He—"

"Cash." Ian curses once, and that curse, it makes my heart stop.

"That's not good?" I whisper.

"No." He exhales heavily. "Alix, if he has money—cash, of all things… The reason why Oliver doesn't have money to give away is simple. He's a recovering gambling addict."

His words hit me like a sucker punch. "What?" My eyes nearly pop out of their sockets. Impossible. I would know—

"Has been for years. I don't want to presume, but it might've been a driving force in his divorce. It for sure was a huge issue when they set up your father's team. Oliver's debt was high, so high that he couldn't have qualified for a government position. We can't have our Chief of Staff be financially unstable and at risk for manipulation and coercion. To your father having Oliver on staff was non-negotiable, so he paid off his debt." He rubs his thumb against his first two fingers, like counting money.

"Your father paid Oliver's debt and is keeping his salary low, so whatever he doesn't need for living, repays your father. It's part of his contract, and so is therapy. And that means… we have a motive, Alix. Not only would killing your father guarantee money for Jess, it would also free Oliver of a substantial debt, and—" He shakes his head. "And the fact that he paid them a large amount as you said, which should be impossible, given his situation… That smells fishy, too. Lucas could've either paid him or bribed him to assassinate your father. Lucas gets the bill passed and makes millions, and Oliver gets the bill passed and his debt and family taken care of."

A muscle in Ian's jaw twitches. "It adds up too well, Alix. We have means, opportunity and motive now, Alix. I have to call it in to Waterhouse. We have to arrest Oliver."

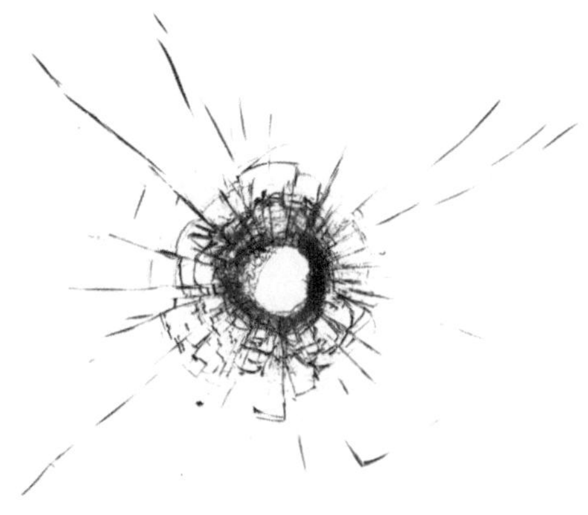

CHAPTER TWENTY-ONE

Unfair

Oliver. Arrested.

I close my eyes. Those two words don't belong together. "Please tell me I heard that wrong."

"You know very well you didn't." Ian sounds genuinely sorry. "And it doesn't get any better with what I'm about to say next. Since we can't be sure about Sam's level of involvement, we'll have to arrest Sam as well."

My heart freezes over. "No."

"Unfortunately, so." Ian presses his lips together. "We have to. Oliver is the main suspect, but at this point most of what we said about him is true about Sam. The Genetic Testing Bill would help his mother and sister. He had means to poison the water or to exchange the pen. Oliver could have recruited him, or vice-versa. Teamwork. Father and son."

If the ground opened and swallowed me, I'd appreciate it.

"We have to arrest them both, Alix. For now. Please, please

don't be mad at me."

Hearing it spoken out loud makes it final. I stare at him open-mouthed. The words make sense, yet they don't.

A charged silence passes between us. Ian clenches his fingers around the DUTI-pad so hard, his knuckles turn white.

My heart is beating too fast, yet it doesn't seem to pump any blood. Can one black out from shock? That's a thing, right?

We're going to arrest Oliver. And worse, Sam. *Arrest,* because we think they're guilty.

I don't know what to feel. Mostly, I hate that all the dots connect too well to be truly coincidental, no matter how much I wish it otherwise.

What did Oliver get from Lucas? Why did he even interact with him? He should've stayed a mile away from that man! Where did he get the money for Liona from? And even worse, why is it untraceable cash? Who the heck gives cash? Ever heard of bank accounts? Venmo? Cash is dirty, cash means hiding things. Why, oh, why does it look so ugly?

And Sam—this one hurts especially bad: Why tell me I'm like a sister to him and flirt with Gianna—and then kiss me when I'm trying to get some information out of him? Why did he never kiss me before? I don't want Ian to be right, but he's got a point. Sam had ample opportunity to declare his undying love for me, and yet he never did until the least opportune moment.

The doubt festers inside my heart, poisoning it.

I rub my palm over my eyes. Think, Alix. Think! Maybe there's something we're missing. There must be! Maybe… I don't know. Maybe we should start with Lucas. He has loads of reason to dislike Dad.

What do we know? We have the poison Lucas could have gotten Oliver. Or it could've been radioactive material. Oliver has access to Dad's pen. Otherwise the Oval Office, and therefore

Dad's pens are tough to get to—

Yellow teeth in an old face framed by white hair. A hand that taps one of Dad's pens onto my forehead.

I snap my eyes open. DiBiaso! He took one of Dad's pens! It's not much, but it's not nothing either. I force myself to sound calm. Reasonable. "Ian. Hear me out. What about DiBiaso?"

"The Vice President?" Ian furrows his brows. "Why?"

I lift both hands up. "Look, I know this isn't the best evidence, but I ran into him when he was coming out of the Oval Office when Dad wasn't there. He had taken one of Dad's pens, so maybe he doctored with it afterwards or exchanged it for a radioactive one." I cringe as I say it. I'm reaching.

Ian keeps his gaze pinned on me. "Humor me. What's his motive?"

"Uhh, becoming President?" I grimace.

"By killing your father."

Yes, it sounds ridiculous. We're the United States of America. We don't assassinate our President. We're democrats by default, even the Republicans. We don't do regicide. "Well, if you phrase it like that…" I deflate, then pop right back up. "But Gianna is supporting the Genetic Testing Bill, which I assume means so is her father."

"Because clearly you and your father are always of the same opinion." He gives me a challenging look.

Ugh, okay. "I know I'm reaching, Ian. I know! But there must be something we're overlooking. What about…" I scramble my mind. Who else had opportunity? Access to the pens? The limo?

I suck a sharp breath as the image of two dark, cold eyes pop up in my mind, framed by a face with a broad chin, bushy eyebrows and a smile that makes hell freeze over.

"Varen!" I snap my fingers. "Ian! It makes sense. It could have been Varen!" I lean forward, my crutches sliding down and clattering to the floor.

What is crystal clear to me, doesn't even make Ian look up from his DUTI-pad. "Can't be. Forget him." He shakes his head.

Huh?

It's right there! It's a completely viable option. "Ian, you're not getting it. He ticks all the boxes. One, he's one of the biggest enemies of the States, and therefore of my dad's, which means he has a motive. Two, he had opportunity. He was in the Oval Office shortly before Nagakawa got poisoned. He could've had access to Dad's pens—"

Something clicks into place in my mind. Yes! Even better! "I'll one-up that. If I'm not mistaken, Oliver took Varen to the airport with *our* limo, at least that's what he said, I heard him: *Let's get back to Limo One!*" I lower my voice into faking Oliver's. See? I listened, for once!

Plus, oh my God, of course! I scoot forward to the edge of the seat. "And one more, in case that wasn't enough. Lev-metaminozole. It's big in Eastern Europe—like in the United Provinces of Talevir." I jump off the couch and limp-pace back and forth. I'm onto something, I can feel it! "Varen is right at the source, Ian! He had motive, opportunity, and he could've gotten the poison! It could've been Varen trying to kill—"

"I said forget him, Trouble." Ian shakes his head again and keeps focusing on the pad instead of me. "And you're not helping yourself. If Varen had had the poison, he was also in direct contact with Oliver Brooks in Limo One." He raises an eyebrow. "That's how Oliver *could* have gotten the poison, *if* we considered Varen at all. Which we're not."

"Nuh-uh." I run scenarios in my head. I'm on to something big, I feel it all the way down to my toes, no matter what Ian says. "This is what happened. Varen was in the Limousine. His assistant could have done it; Oliver could have been distracted.

They could have even done it openly, like asking for water they then didn't open, poisoning the water through the cap with a needle, or whatever. I'm sure they had other more sophisticated options. We need to review the tapes and talk to Oliver."

Surely, they could find a way to get poison into a bottle of water without anyone noticing. Microscopic injection systems maybe? Similar to the one I used on Varen for the tracker? The United Provinces of Talevir aren't as technologically advanced as we are, but don't all countries invest more money in military research than in any other?

That thought brings another moment of clarity. I smack my forehead. "Radioactive material. Eastern Europe, again—the United Provinces of Talevir! He could have brought it with him and could have tapered with or exchanged the pen. Holy cow, Ian, it really could have been Varen!"

I blink rapidly. Whoa. The shoe fits. A shudder runs down my spine when I think about

how close I was to a man who probably tried to kill Dad. I should have injected poison into him, and not a tracker.

Ian, on the other hand, still doesn't seem very impressed by my theory. "Nope. Let it go. It didn't happen that way. We'll have to focus on the leads we have instead of going on a wild goose chase."

My jaw drops. "Goose chase? I don't think this is a goose chase at all. You said we needed to tag him to rule him out as a potential assassin." I use my fingers for air quotes. "Varen was in the Limo, and he was in Dad's office at a time when the pen was probably planted on him! Exchanging the pen quickly during signatures? Shouldn't be a big problem. Ian, we don't just have Oliver-slash-Sam connected to both events, we have Varen connected to them, too! *And* you said once we, as in the United States, we don't trust him, which is why I needed to tag him in the first place" I flop my arms like a pigeon about to take flight; I know I'm right! It fits!

All I get from Ian is silence, and not the good kind.

My heart skips a beat. "Ian?"

He closes his eyes for an eternal second and exhales. When he opens them again, he looks straight at me, the DUTI-pad down in his lap. "It wasn't Varen, Alix. Let it go. It's a dead end. The Secret Service checked him thoroughly."

I snort. "Yeah right. They also vetted Oliver and Sam before they let them near Dad. *Twice.* Once for the campaign and even more thoroughly for duty in the White House." I slam my hands on the table in front of me. Why can't he see what I see? "It's *right there*, Ian. Let me do some research; let me look into it. I *know* I can prove it. I'll figure something out!" I won't let him put the assassination attempts on Oliver and Sam and destroy their lives.

Ian absentmindedly taps a rhythm onto the pad in his lap. "Listen, I know where you're coming from, but I'm telling you Varen is a dead lead. Let. It. Go."

He's still dismissing our best theory besides Oliver and Sam. I clench my fist so hard, my knuckles turn white. "You hired me for two reasons. One, because I'm my dad's daughter, and two, because I can think for myself. I'm thinking like you taught me, Ian, and yet all I get is *let it go*?"

"Yes." He looks up to the corner of the ceiling, like rolling his eyes, and boy, does it make me even madder.

"Just like that." I cross my arms in front of my chest.

He looks up to the ceiling again, and this time… this time I understand.

And it breaks something in me. "You don't trust in me," I whisper.

Ian flinches as if I'd slapped him. "Alix, no. I'm trying to be professional because of the—"

"You think I'm this newbie who doesn't know what she's talking about." Why else would he ignore a lead as good as this?

He doesn't believe me. Doesn't believe *in* me anymore. Since I started with PRICS, Ian's trust and faith in me were the life vest keeping my drowning ego afloat, but not anymore. That life vest is popped, sliced open by words I never thought I'd hear him say.

The tiny hairs on my body rise with the cold shudder running down my spine. All of a sudden, I'm on the outside, looking in, when until a mere thirty minutes ago I thought I was on the inside of Ian's circle of trust.

He exhales slowly, then pushes himself off the chair's back like an old man and crosses the room until he's behind his desk. "I'm not going to discuss this now. I… I literally can't." He cringes as he says it, as if he was sorry, but that ship has sailed.

I don't care if he's sorry, I only care that he's going to call Waterhouse.

Despair floods me.

He really isn't going to listen. The person I thought was on my side, understood me, who *got* me, is ignoring me.

Just like Dad.

Wow.

I'm such a sucker for attention I made the same mistake twice. I let my guard down only to be punched in the face.

Ian's tapping something into his touchscreen monitor. There's the shortest hesitation in his movements, and I take my last chance.

My voice is cold. I'm not talking to my friend Ian anymore. That guy's left the room. "Ian. Give me more time, and I can prove it, I'm sure. Don't inform Waterhouse. I'll figure out a way to prove it was Varen." I just need a little more time to prove Oliver and Sam's innocence. I can get it done—I don't know how, but I will. I owe it to Sam.

Ian's shoulders drop and he chews on his lower lip. His voice is flat as he focuses on the desk in front of him. "First, as your commanding officer, I hereby order you to *not* pursue Varen. Second, not now, not in the future, will you research anything about him. Do not even mention his name outside this room. Let it go. There will be consequences if you don't. Third, as far as our PRICS-missions go, this one is over. I don't want you to bring any more attention to this matter. Let. It. Go."

My mouth hangs open.

Ian is pulling rank on me. Not only is he not trusting me, he's also forbidding me to investigate a potential assassin! He's doing no less than convicting Sam and Oliver without seeing all the evidence.

What's going on here? Am I dreaming and in the middle of a nightmare? I get why Oliver and Sam are suspicious, but so is Varen!

Ian taps once more onto the touchscreen, and two seconds later Waterhouse's image flashes up on the screen behind his desk.

"Yes?" It's a bark more than a greeting.

Ian turns around to face the view screen. "Mr. Waterhouse, we have a suspect. Two, to be correct." He crosses his arms behind his back and stands ramrod straight. "There is a motive for Oliver and Sam Brooks—"

I jump up to standing. "It could've very well been Varen! He had access—"

Waterhouse's droopy beagle-gaze zooms in on me in before he narrows his eyebrows. "What is this, Agent Donckers? A children's playgroup? Make up your mind. Varen is out of the question."

My mouth drops open. Now him, too? "But—"

"Yes, sir," Ian says, but Waterhouse ignores him.

"But *what*, Agent Forrester? It must be the foreigner, because an attack can't possibly come from within our own circles?"

His words hit bull's eye. *Our own circles?* That's what I already said!

Everything I said about Varen is true about the VP.

Everything.

He knows Dad's routines. He had the pen—*he had one of my dad's freakin' pens!* If I look closely enough, I'm sure there's a motive, maybe he wants—I don't know, probably to be the President, even though Ian didn't believe in that.

But then, he also doesn't believe in me, so his judgement went down the drain in my eyes.

And yes, it is a motive not worthy of a Vice-President, but it's a motive nonetheless.

Pushing my chin forward I angle myself so that Waterhouse can see me better. "DiBiaso! It could very well've been DiBiaso!"

A bomb couldn't have shut up the conversation more effectively than I did. For once, both men, Ian and Waterhouse, show the same expression: shock. Ian's eyes are wide, his jaw dropped, and so is Waterhouse's, only in him it looks droopy, like his face was melting.

The stunned silence lasts about half a second before Waterhouse crashes his fist down onto the desk in front of him. "Agent Forrester! Do you hear what you're saying? You're directly accusing the Vice President of the United States of attempted murder—of his President!"

I spread my arms and take a step forward closer to Ian. "So what? You said it yourself! It's possible this came from within our own circles. Why couldn't it have been—"

"Alix." Ian shakes his head. "Stop. We can discuss it once—"

Oh, hell to the no, I'm on a roll! "Stop? Why would I? You're both ignoring evidence—it could've been anybody. Yes, maybe Oliver and or Sam, maybe not. Yes, maybe Varen, maybe not.

Yes, maybe DiBiaso, maybe not. My point is that we cannot afford to overlook anything, and you're about to—"

"I'm getting too old for this." Waterhouse sighs deeply and pinches the bridge of his nose. "What's Brook's motive, Donckers?"

"Money, sir. He received a large sum of cash we didn't know about and paid his ex-wife. Possible connection to Lucas, which is where the money might be from. Plus, his family would benefit from the rider attached to the Genetic Testing Bill if it passed against the President's wishes."

"I see. It's always about money. Makes sense."

I swallow dry. "Sir, I agree there is motive for Oliver Brooks, but we can't ignore—"

"Alix." Ian shakes his head.

"But—"

"Forrester, you heard your superior officer." Waterhouse leans forward across his desk, nostrils flaring. "Jumping to conclusions, an amateur mistake. Unacceptable. Disappointing and unacceptable." He focuses his creepy eyes on Ian. "Get your Agent under control, Donckers. I swear I didn't sign up for this when I hired you."

Ian pales. "Yes, sir."

"And I appreciate the intel about the Brookses. I'll give the go ahead." His gaze darts over to me again. "And now do something about her. *The Vice President...!*" He huffs and rolls his eyes. "And she calls herself a genius." One press of a button, and then he's gone.

No.

No, no, *no.*

The room is dead quiet.

I wasn't convincing enough.

Sam and Oliver are going to be arrested.

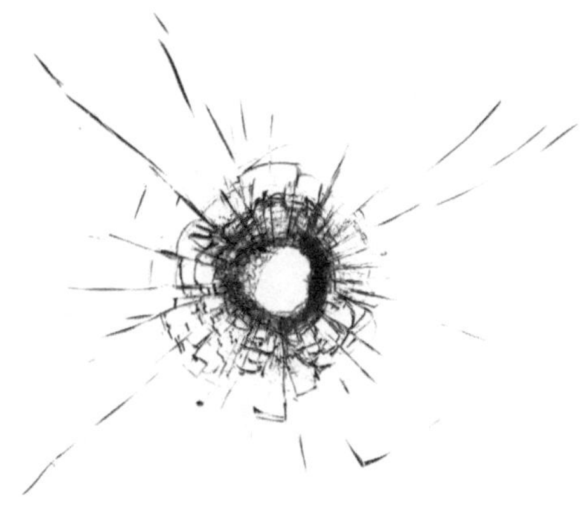

CHAPTER TWENTY-TWO

Betrayed

All of a sudden, I can't stand being in the same room as Ian anymore.

I need air.

I need distance.

As fast as I can, I fumble for my crutches and get up, making my way to the holographic wall protecting the secret passage. The couch won't get out of my way fast enough and catches my crutch, yet I don't fall.

I won't embarrass myself like that in front of the man who won't even give me the benefit of the doubt.

"Alix, where are you going?" Ian's long strides bring him to the coffee table in no time.

"Don't." It comes out harsh. Cutting.

Good.

Ian stops dead in the middle of the room while I palm open the wall.

My eyes sting, the only sensation in my otherwise numb body. I blink once, then twice, into the dusty janitor's closet appearing behind the wall. "I trusted you, Ian. I …" I shake my head. "Why the hell did you recruit me and trust me with this mission when you don't believe me when it counts?"

I glance over my shoulder to my right at the mountain of a man ready to follow me. "Stay away. I can't stand seeing anybody right now." That includes Dimitri. Sorry, big man.

"Alix, wait, I—"

I wobble across the threshold without a reply. With a faint hum, the wall closes behind me, cutting off a whisper that sounded strangely sad.

"Trouble…!"

I don't care.

I have rage in my heart. It might be the only thing holding it together at this point.

Never ever have I stumbled up the myriad of concrete stairs in less time than today.

Every step puts much needed distance between myself and Ian. Can I blame myself for Oliver and Sam getting arrested? No. No, I can't. If they tried to kill Dad, that's not on me, it was their own decision. If they didn't, I still had to report what I found out, so no, I *shouldn't* feel bad about doing so.

Doesn't change that I do, especially since I'm apparently not allowed to follow any other lead that could potentially clear the Brookses.

Only once I'm in the classroom and away from Ian, can I finally take a breath without the suffocating feeling that I'm drowning. The second I close the holographic wall behind me, the security features revert to a normal classroom. Hard steps and loud voices are coming from the hallway outside.

My stomach sinks lower, if that's possible at all.

Opening the door inch by inch to avoid getting smacked in the head by it, I peek around it into the hallway—the hallway that's brimming with activity. Dozens of Secret Service agents are running and crisscrossing in either direction, some with a finger at their ear, listening, some yelling into the microphones attached to their sleeves.

"We're a *go!*"

"Thirteen-twelve, can you read me?"

"… is cleared already. Repeat, it's cleared."

I try to swallow, but can't. This is my doing. They're searching for Oliver and Sam.

An agent stands next to my door in Dimitri's usual spot and holds up a hand. "I'm sorry, Miss. We're on lockdown. No one is to leave the room they're in until the condition is resolved. I'm sorry for the inconvenience." He turns away from me again but makes no move to vacate his position right in front of my door.

Lockdown. The second one we've had since the term started, and the second one I caused.

Not even twenty seconds of chaotic activity later, the conversations and communications between the agents stop, turning the buzzing hallway into the silence of a funeral home. Then, like on command, everyone cheers and pumps their fists at the same time, laughing. Some of them clap each others' shoulders.

The agent next to my door faces me again, his features softened considerably compared to before. "I'm sorry, Miss. Go ahead. The condition has been resolved, we're back to normal."

Normal.

What does that even mean?

Nausea builds up in my stomach; I want to throw up.

It means they have Sam and Oliver in custody.

What have I done?

Or better, did I do that or was it *them* all along?

I hate myself for doubting Sam, for doubting Oliver, but I can't help it.

The sour feeling spreads through my veins like acid, and if I don't get distance, it's going to eat me alive. Problems is, I have nowhere to go.

I can't go to the Oval Office, because Dad's still in the medical wing. Plus, he doesn't want me there. Yay me.

I can't go back down to the Eagle's Lair, because that's where Ian is, and I don't want to see him now. Yay me, again.

I also can't stay in the classroom, because that would be sad. Boo me.

Going home to the residence is out too, or Mom will ask questions I'm not ready to answer. Boo me, again.

Only one option left.

Pushing my way through the sea of Secret Service agents, I limp all the way to the south exit and down the pebble path into the gardens.

Air.

As soon as the door closes behind me and shuts out the noise, my stomach unclamps. A little, at least.

Everything is so surreal from out here. All around me, birds tweet, enjoying the heat of a beautiful day in early July. A bee buzzes past me, probably on its way toward the dozens of rose bushes to my left. Nature is doing its best to impress me in this beautifully kept landscape, but I'm oblivious to it.

After a couple of minutes of mindless crutching, I reach a remote area of the gardens close to the other side of the West Wing, if I'm not mistaken. This place is so huge it's easy to get lost, and I've only been here once. I never had any time.

I'm so deep in thought I don't really watch where I'm going, and unfortunately neither does the Vice President as he's strutting around a bend in the walkway between some man-high bushes. A second before we would've collided, we both stop.

He stares at me as if he'd seen a ghost.

So do I. Of all people, I must run into him. Of course.

I clear my throat. "Uhh, sorry, James. Not watching where I was going… uneven here, and the crutches…" I shrug, dropping my gaze. Not that I was doing anything forbidden, yet I feel like I'm caught red-handed. Here's to hoping he can't read on my face what I accused him of down in the Lair.

Jumping to conclusions, an amateur mistake! Unacceptable! Disappointing and unacceptable!

Yeah, that would be me, genius extraordinaire. In my defense, it still feels wrong he took the pen.

DiBiaso steps aside to let me pass. His usual bubbly and talkative demeanor is gone, replaced by a pale face and jittery hands. Guess that happens with a hunt for an assassin in the White House. It's scary, no matter who the target or the assassin is.

Not Oliver. Not Sam.

The stomach cramps are back.

The VP forces a distracted smile. "Yeah, yeah… All well. I just didn't see you… Oh my, have I been preoccupied." He makes the effort of widening his smile for me, but still barely lifts the corners of his mouth.

I don't really know how to react. All the information about the assassination attempts are highly classified, but of course he would know, being the Vice President. I, on the other hand, officially don't know, so I can't say anything to him.

That's a bit awkward.

"Uhh, yes, it's an odd day today," I weakly offer.

He nods and scratches the stubble on his cheek. That's when I see it: His right thumb and index finger covered in a Band-Aid that has loosened—and the skin under it bright red and infected-looking.

My entire body tenses.

Oh, hell to the no. No way.

A… burn? A *burn* on his right hand? A burn that looks like the freakin' *radiation* burn Dad has? On DiBiaso's *right* hand, he could've held the pen with?

My pulse kicks into overdrive. "Ouch. That looks painful." I nod at the VP's hand, keeping my eyes trained on every move of his facial muscles.

If I thought he'd flinch, look shocked, or hide his hand, I was wrong.

Nope.

He chuckles. "I know, right? Gianna said the same thing." He turns the hand in front of his face, eyes taking on a distant quality. "My wife always told me I was no good in the kitchen. Turns out she was right." A sad smile crosses his face, gone as fast as it appeared.

I cringe. *Disappointing and unacceptable! The Vice President is the most vetted person in the White House!* What a loser I am. DiBiaso's wife died a couple of years ago. I'm such—

"Well, anyway, I can tell you everything in there is back to normal again." He points at the White House. "Don't worry. I know not worrying is a bit of a tall order with all the turmoil going on in there. Gianna is the same." The VP gives me what I bet he believes is an encouraging smile and wiggles his fingers at me. "Well, I gotta get going."

"Me, uhh, too. Have a good rest of your day, James." I wait until he is around the other corner before I continue farther down the way.

Maybe Ian was right: Wild goose chase. I'm so desperate to clear Sam's name, I'm seeing clues everywhere. But what am I supposed to do? Maybe I'm making ridiculous accusations, but at least I'm considering other options.

I'm replaying the conversation with the VP once more in front of my inner eye. Gianna is the same—*please*. As if Gianna and I were similar in anything we did. I blow a frustrated raspberry at myself. The only thing we have in common is being privileged enough to live in the White House with all the opportunities and access that comes with it, but that's about it.

Huh.

Now wait a second.

I stop on a dime. No, I'm being ridiculous.

Completely ridiculous.

Shaking my head, I start hopping forward again, one crutched step at a time. I make it exactly two hops.

But what if I'm right?

One: The day Yoshi ran me over: she was all for that stupid Genetic Testing Bill.

Could be her own delusional opinion, or... could be fueled by her dad's.

Two: The day I tagged Varen: I'm pretty sure I saw her in the hallway, passing him by.

Could be coincidence, or... could have been something else? A meeting in disguise? An exchange of some sorts?

Three: The day in the copy room. She drank from a pink and blue bottle of water, of the brand only used in Limo One.

Could be coincidence, or... could have been something else? A sign she had access to the limo? Or to Sam?

My eyes sting from staring into space. I blink twice. No. It can't have been her I saw at the Oval Office. She was in my classroom, chatting up Ian to let her join my classes.

But she's quick, and I'm slow; she could have... No. Ridiculous. This is just my dislike for her talking, nothing else.

The VP's daughter is not trying to kill Dad.

I'd be so much better at this than you are, and we both know it.

I blink even more. That's not what she meant back at the Inauguration Ball. There's no way she could've implied that she wanted to be the First Daughter instead of me, because… because that would indeed mean Dad was in the way of hers becoming president.

Nu-uh.

Still, I can't help my mind filling in the blanks for means, opportunity and motive.

I groan. She's got all three.

Okay, witch-hunter: Shouldn't I then also suspect, say, Mrs. Houser?

I sigh. Yes, she uses my dad's pens; she has easy access to him…

… aaand yeah, I'm on a witch hunt. Sure, she has means and opportunity, but absolutely no motive.

Back to Gianna. To be fair, the same point I made for Sam would hold true for her, whether I like her or not: Where would she even get the lev-metaminozole, or the radioactive material? Am I really accusing a teen of trying to kill the President, blinded by what I want to see, like Waterhouse?

But damn it, it must have been somebody else but Sam and Oliver, Dad's and my best friends!

I wonder who else knows what really has been happening. Mom probably does. Senior staff? The Vice President's senior staff? What are they going to say happened?

From what I've learned over the last months, I'm assuming everything's going to stay on a need-to-know-basis until they confirm they do indeed have the assassins in custody. So, what are they going to tell Sam's mom? What are they going to tell *me*?

The whole situation is so messed up and wrong that I can't

even begin to *let it go*, or to get over it.

By now, I've reached a well-covered area in the South Lawn, the one part of the gardens with lots of bushes and trees and not only grass or well-designed landscaping. My view of the White House is gone, and thanks to whomever, I'm all to my lone self. Despite being in the middle of the city, the gardens are quiet and peaceful.

Only I'm not.

With one big hurl, I throw my crutches to the ground, a choked scream catching in my throat. The crutches stand for everything that's wrong. My accident. My injuries. Sam helping me through it, Sam kissing me when he never did before, and me providing the intel that got him arrested. Ian inventing the surgery for me, building me up, making me fall—trust in him, and then betraying my trust. Dad pushing me out of his life while I'm trying to save his. Me being such a disgusting loser for not pushing harder to prove it was the VP, or Gianna, or Varen, or, hell, *somebody else* instead of Sam.

Stupid, idiotic crutches! I stomp down on those metal shackles as hard as I can. Who cares if they break? Not me.

I don't care about anything anymore. Nope. Caring is gone. Ciao. My life is beyond messed up on so many levels, I don't even know where to start, ugh, ugh, ugh!

I stomp with my right, I stomp with my left, I stomp with both.

I kick, stomp, grunt, and drive my heel down onto them again. Can I get these things stomped to dust? Into the ground? "Finally break, you stupid things," I grunt at them, but of course the crutches don't even have the decency to scratch. A frustrated grunt breaks free from my throat, carrying all the anger and misery of my life.

Defeated by my crutches.

Again.

My breaths come out in noisy little puffs, resounding loudly through the otherwise silent gardens.

Oh, crap!

With a jolt, I realize what a public display I put on.

Double-crap.

I glance around, making sure nobody saw my little meltdown, but I'm still as alone as a minute before. Thank whomever again, this time for small favors.

I bend down to pick up the completely unharmed and only slightly dusty crutches from hell.

The moment I wrap my fingers around the shaft, I freeze.

I stomped on my crutches.

With *both* feet.

I stood on my right and used my left leg, out of old habits from before the accident.

My hands start shaking when understanding sinks in: I used my bad leg.

The crutch forgotten, I drop it to the ground, using my clumsy, shaking fingers to undo my brace in record time. Stupid little ties and snaps, come on, *come on...*

Finally, it comes off and drops into the dirt where it belongs.

And me... I'm standing.

Freely.

Alone.

Without my splint and without my crutches.

My heart races, making me dizzy with excitement, a spark of hope igniting. Should I be so lucky?

I take a shuffle step.

I'm stable.

I take another one.

Still stable.

I take a regular step.

No problem.

I take a big one.

Still stable.

A grin spreads across my face.

I take a couple of quick steps.

And I'm still standing. Okay, a bit wobbly toward the end, but still no falling, no knee giving in.

Now to the ultimate test: jumping. I haven't jumped in about a year, so I try my good leg first.

One-legged jump on the right—lifts me up about five inches. Not my forte anyway.

Now the other side. I crouch down a bit and then release, jumping up with my left leg.

I gasp. Not a new world record, but I jumped off! My foot left the ground! How amazing is that?

I jump some more, like a happy kindergartner on a day off, and with each time, I become a bit more secure during the jump off and landing, although my strength vanishes quickly. I don't care. By now, I'm grinning ear to ear. A loud, happy laugh escapes me before I slap a hand across my mouth.

Oops.

Way to go keeping a low profile, or my alibi up.

I pick up my brace, brush it off, and put it back on. My hands are a bit less shaky than before, but still so jittery it takes me twice the time it normally does to fix all the little snaps and closures.

The whole time, I can't keep the grin from my face. My leg. It's working again. My face burns from excitement and my chest has this light fluttering, as if a tremendous weight was lifted off it.

The treatment worked! Ian's microchip did what it was supposed to, and it worked. I need to tell Ian, I—

The thought of Ian brings me to a screeching halt, all giddiness and overflowing joy evaporated. *Poof.*

The weight on my chest is back with a vengeance as I bend down to pick up my crutches, feeling very much alone.

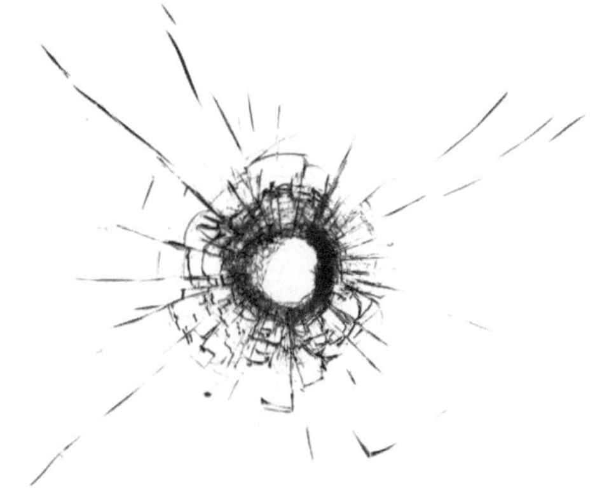

CHAPTER TWENTY-THREE

Decision Time

By the time the crutches are dusted off, I've shoved any thought about Ian into a drawer and locked it. Might've thrown away the key as well.

I've also done my very best to focus back on the matter at hand, finding Dad's wannabe-assassin. That in return means, I've fast-forwarded through all five stages of grief according to the Kübler-Ross model.

The first four sucked.

Denial. It wasn't Oliver. Wasn't Sam. Never. Nope. Didn't happen. No way, Jose. They've got it wrong. *So* wrong.

Anger. How could I ever think I could do spy-work? I'm useless. Useless! And it's all Ian's fault—all of it! Recruiting me, making me believe I was a good agent, and then choosing to not believe me when it's convenient. Gah!

Bargaining. If only I had struck a deal with Waterhouse. Something. *Anything!* Anything that would've made him see reason. Or if only I had looked harder for the real assassin, maybe then we wouldn't be in this situation then.

Depression. It's all my fault. Everything. Sam's life is ruined, thanks to me, and so is Oliver's. Probably even mine, the way I behaved in the Lair. I screwed up. Majorly.

Yeah, that Kübler-Ross stuff is no fun.

The fifth stage though, acceptance… it brings a strange kind of peace. And even better, an idea.

I stood. I stomped. I kicked.

I freakin' walked.

Sooo… Maybe I don't need to be passive here and take whatever comes at me. Nu-uh. I can get things done myself. Not only am I somewhat smart, I do have some training in stealth operations *and* I'm the daughter of the President of the United States, granting me access almost everywhere in the White House.

And, despite PRICS only being for information collection, Ian trained me much more than planned.

Hope extends its fragile tendrils until it takes root. It's crazy, but it could work.

The gears inside my brain move quicker and quicker, until my heart beats at the rhythm of a steam train.

I blow out a puff of air.

I can get this done without the help of PRICS. They already gave me all the help I needed. I'm not the scared girl I was when Dad became President.

Working under the assumption that Sam and Oliver are innocent despite the—most likely coincidental—accumulation of evidence for opportunity, means, and motive, my priority is to get them out of this mess.

I chew on my lower lip. If Sam is innocent, it would also mean he didn't just kiss me as a distraction, and that would mean… Butterflies take flight inside my stomach.

That would mean a world of opportunities ahead.

I push my chin up and forward. It doesn't matter if Ian wants me to back off Varen or not—I *will* start digging into everything and everyone.

And no matter how stupid it is, DiBiaso will be on that list.

I don't care if I step on toes. It's my duty as a, uhh, *friend* to help Sam and my duty as an agent to not let the real assassin run free.

Always easier to ask for forgiveness than permission, right?

When I make it back to the classroom's terrace, Dimitri is already outside waiting for me. He isn't even visually scanning the area for me—he looks straight in my direction like he had a built-in Alix-radar. I bet he knew exactly where I was the whole time.

I should've known he wouldn't really and truly leave me alone.

"Feeling better?" he asks.

I nod. Funny what a little melt-down can do for mental clarity.

"Ian is still in the Lair. He says to resume class after lunch."

I'm about to say something not so nice, then snap my mouth shut. "Okay, then I'll go up to the residence until then." I shrug, like, no biggie. It does come in handy though. I need time to think, and the last thing I want to do right now is face Ian.

I squeeze past Dimitri and make it through the classroom and crutch into the hallway. Half an hour ago it bristled with Secret Service activity, and now… Now everything is back to its normal level of activity, which is strange. How can the world continue to function despite what happened here today? How can life continue like it was any ordinary day?

It makes my stomach churn, and not in a good way.

If I could, I'd dump my crutches and sprint up to the residence to get away from the West Wing, my classroom, and anything that connects me to it. For the first time in over a year, I actually could go faster than I do, and it makes me unbelievably impatient.

Up at the residence, Dimitri stays in front of the entrance while I walk inside, closing the door all but in his face.

Sorry, Dimitri. Not personal.

I lean against the door and close my eyes. Okay. Deep breath.

How do I best play this? I can't be too obvious, which means… As little as I want to, I'll have to go back to class after lunch. I use my fingers to check off my to-do list. That's point one, playing along. Two, fake that I'm not doing well and leave class. Three, start some investigations. Without making it too obvious, obviously.

Sounds easy.

I roll my eyes. Yeah, super easy—until the point where I need to explain to Dimitri what I'm doing. There's no way he is going let me stroll around and do my, uhh, *research*. I'm sure he reports to Ian, and frequently so.

Well, I guess I'll have to put those IQ-points of mine to work. But first things first, as always: keeping up appearances. It's noon—the chef should have lunch ready by now. With an effort that's equal to moving a mountain, I push off the door and wobble over to the dining room.

Only Mom sits at the table. She has an iPad in front of her and browses through something, but looks up when she hears me, gracing me with a smile.

Well. I should put smile in quotation marks. It's more a grimace pretending to be a smile. It's no match for the worry-lines etched onto her face. "Sweetie. You're, uhh, here. No lunch in the cafeteria?"

Translation: I didn't expect you.

I hold her gaze and shrug. "No. There was too much going on down there." Not even a lie.

Mom fidgets with her hair, a dead give-away she's uncomfortable. "I know, it's…" She sighs once. "Anyway, sorry I missed you this morning. I've been *so* busy. How have you been? Are you still working on your projects with Mr. Miller?"

Hearing her mention Ian makes my stomach cramp. Still, I force myself to nod at her. "Yeah, it's been busy."

The chef brings in the food, interrupting our conversation just in the nick of time before we run out of inconspicuous things to say. Mom and I both eat in silence while she taps on her iPad. We usually don't talk much anyway, but today I realize for the first time how little we have to say to each other, despite everything.

Even when our life was normal, we weren't the best buddies to begin with, but now that she's keeping secrets from me—two assassination attempts on Dad, Dad in the Medical Wing, Oliver and Sam arrested, and I'm keeping secrets from her too—I know all of the above plus there's PRICS she doesn't know about—we literally have nothing to talk about.

After a while of moderately awkward silence, Mom looks up from her iPad, sighs and pulls her shoulders back into the straight posture I'm used to. "Dad… got sick today."

The little bit of appetite I had is gone. "Oh." I fake bored interest. "What happened? He looked off this morning."

Mom flinches. "He did. Dr. Soong said it's the flu." Her cheeks take on a pinkish hue.

And there would be my answer what the official story is and what they're going to tell me.

She forks up another bite. "He's getting meds as we speak and should be out of the medical wing later today. More treatments tomorrow, IVs, a couple of blood tests. Maybe… maybe you could spend some time with him tonight. I'm sure he'd appreciate it." Her voice stays exceptionally level, and if I didn't know what happened I'd take this for nothing else but a wife's worry about her husband.

Not the worry of a mom whose daughter could've lost her dad.

I rub a hand over my face. That part, it gets to me. "Mom, I… I'll try, but… Every time I try to talk to him, he shuts me down. He sees me in the West Wing and he literally kicks me out of the office. I don't know… lately, he just seems not interested in me or in anything I do. I know he's disappointed in me, but…" I push a couple of peas from left to right on my plate.

Mom's brows furrow. "Sweetie, I don't know what you're talking about. You're in your father's *every* thought. You should hear him when he comes back from work. Most of the time it's 'I wonder how Alix's leg is doing', 'do we need more security detail for Alix?', 'do you think Alix likes her new room?' I don't know how you can say that your father isn't interested in you, sweetie." She shakes her head, her attention already back to her iPad, before she lifts her head once more. "And he is not disappointed in you. If anything, he is proud how you're handling yourself. Worried, yes. Disappointed, never."

I stare at her open-mouthed as she continues reading her iPad.

Have I just crossed into a parallel universe? He is *proud?*

I fold my arms in front of my chest. "I don't see that. He kicked me out of the Oval Office in front of everybody. Twice. He was mean." It feels odd calling Dad—the man who's currently getting anti-radiation treatment in the medical wing—mean in front of Mom, but it's the truth.

Mom tears her gaze off the iPad and shakes her head, swallowing her bite of food. "Sweetie, again, I don't know what you think you're seeing, but I can promise you, nothing could be further from the truth. Your dad *adores* you. He always has. You know that. And like I said, he's been worried. I think that's what he wanted to talk to you about today, before he got... sick."

Right, today's lunch meeting with Waterhouse. Yeah, that didn't happen. *Thanks,* assassination attempt.

Mom gives me another smile and then goes back to her work, swiping quickly a couple of times, and I know the moment of mother-daughter-bonding has passed.

I can't make sense out of her replies though. It's like we're talking about two different people.

Maybe I've been looking at this from the wrong angle?

Maybe it's all me.

I'm the one who's having trouble with everybody in my life, it appears.

Maybe it's all me.

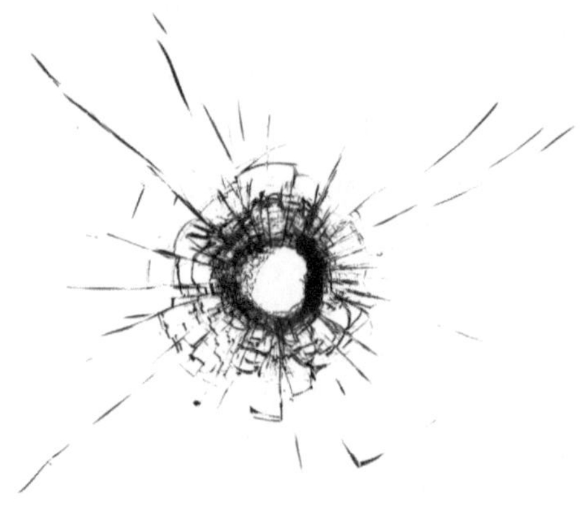

CHAPTER TWENTY-FOUR

Torn Apart

The closer I wobble toward my classroom as if I didn't stomp my crutches into the ground a good two hours earlier, the more I wish I had eaten more lunch.

Who knew nausea could be that bad on an empty stomach. Or maybe it's performance anxiety. Pressure. Angst.

It's paramount I play this right. At each and every point, something could easily throw me off and derail my attempts of finding the true assassin.

Dimitri opens the door for me, leaving me no choice but to walk right into the classroom, ready or not.

Not.

Ian sits on his desk, mug in his hand and dark circles under his eyes.

My heart seizes inside my chest, betraying me.

Biting down hard, I maneuver through the door and to my desk. "Hey."

Ian gives me a careful smile. "Hey." He lifts his cup and takes a sip.

I sit. The obligatory cup of tea is already on my desk.

I don't touch it.

It's a peace offering I'm not willing to accept yet.

I unpack my block and pen in silence. When I don't say anything else, Ian sighs and reaches for his DUTI-pad.

"Right then. Let's get started with the situation report. Your father will be released later today in time for the festivities. He is considered stable and expected to recover fully within a couple of days. Dr. Soong has everything under control. In the matter of the assassins…" He looks down and brushes some imaginary lint off his pants.

The assassins, he said.

I don't look up from my doodling. "They have names. Sam. Oliver."

Ian stops in mid-sentence and hesitates for a second. "*Sam* and *Oliver* have been taken into custody and are being interrogated. So far, neither has admitted to anything."

My heart skips a happy little beat hearing that.

I keep doodling on my pad. If possible, I'd like to avoid eye contact.

Ian stops talking.

Neither of us says anything.

Ian sighs and takes another sip of his tea.

I still haven't touched mine.

Silence.

I have nothing at all to say to him right now.

At the point the silence starts to stretch and become unbearable, he clears his throat.

"Okay, alert level, let's talk about that. We're down to Condition Green now that the threat has been eliminated. It's just in time for the festivities and fireworks this evening, under Condition Yellow or Red we would've had to cancel."

I groan inside. The festivities. Now that he mentioned them twice, it clicked for me. Look at me, I almost forgot about one of the biggest parties of this year, our Fourth of July event. The White House Gardens are going to be filled with over fifteen hundred visitors tonight, first listening to one of Dad's speeches, and then enjoying the fireworks from the South Lawn.

They won't have a clue how close they came to attend a wake instead of a party tonight.

Ian points outside toward the lawn in front of our classroom. "Secret Service agents are roaming the perimeter already and special posts have been established, but during the event itself, after everybody has been admitted, we will downsize security. The Vice President has requested scaling down security measures to Code Green again, and at this point, the Secret Service feels strongly that with good preparation and the assassins… *Sam* and *Oliver* in custody, we'll be able to have a Fourth of July celebration with a normal level of security."

I don't need to look up to feel his gaze on me.

"Remember that for tonight you're back to your role as First Daughter. You're expected to be up on the balcony with your father and your mother during the President's speech at 2100 hours, and also out seeing the fireworks from up there together with your parents at 2130 hours." He interrupts himself for a second, and the next question is much gentler. "Do you think you can handle those two events together with your father?"

Handle what? Seeing Dad, or not messing up anything for PRICS? Something inside of me turns ugly and chooses to misunderstand Ian.

"Yes," I say coldly, "don't worry. I'll follow your orders. I won't say anything to Dad. I won't let anything *counteract my brain* this time."

Ian takes a sharp breath in. "Alix, that's not what I meant."

I know.

But I can't help it, I want him to feel the same pain I felt earlier—the same pain I *still* feel, from his comment, and from not believing in me.

"Hey," he says gently, "I brought you some chai. Added a bit of honey, thought you might like it."

I don't know why, but him trying so hard and being so nice makes me a complete ass. Oh, and childish—because without looking up, I push the cup of tea as far to the end of the desk as I can and keep drawing on my pad.

Silence.

Nothing else.

Ian doesn't say anything, and neither do I.

The silence stretches and I'm still not lifting my gaze off my pad as I draw another jittery doodle and my throat dries out to desert-level.

Why did I just do that? I know I'm pushing it, but I can't help it.

The tension is so thick in the room, I could cut it with a knife. Cliché score one, Alix score zero.

Ian sets down his cup. From the corner of my eye, I see him fidgeting around with his hands.

When he finally speaks again, it's not much louder than a whisper, but it is so dead quiet in the classroom that every word is as clear as if he shouted it.

"Is this how it's going to be, Alix? I… Look, I don't know what to say. You know I had to call it in. If I'd had a chance to avoid it, I would have. Don't be mad at me for doing my job. *Please.*"

The *please…* it tugs on a heartstring.

I ignore it and speak down into my pad, keeping my voice as level as I can. "You could have trusted me. You could've given me at least a couple of hours to verify or disprove my theory. *Any* theory. It could have made all the difference." To Sam, and to me. "Instead, you and Waterhouse overruled me, and I don't get it. Varen. Someone. Anyone." I throw my hands up. Gone is my somewhat calm demeanor. "Hell, even pretending to look into the VP would've helped. I know it sounds ridiculous, but now he's downscaling security—"

"In agreement with the President's team, Alix. That's according to protocol and not just the VP's doing."

"Well, I don't care! You have circumstantial evidence for Sam and Oliver, so don't ignore the same for the VP! Or Varen! Or—" I don't know. Any-freakin'-body! I rub both palms over my eyes. Damn it. "You could have trusted me," I repeat. That part hurts the most. "You could have believed in me." Finally, I summon the courage to look straight into Ian's eyes.

Big mistake.

Gone is the usual spark in his green eyes. They seem dull, like somebody forgot to switch on the light behind them. Together with the dark circles under them, he looks miserable, to be honest.

I swallow dry, my throat a desert on a hot summer day as my heart seizes and then cracks a little bit.

Oh no. We're not getting emotional.

Clearly, it's time to remove myself from this situation, planned or not. I take my crutches and maneuver myself out from behind the desk. "I'm not feeling well. If you don't mind, I'll rest. The flu is going around, I heard. And…" And I won't get emotional. "…you won't have to worry about my unprofessional behavior much longer. I'll… I'll ask Dad for a new teacher. Obviously things didn't work out between us if there's no mutual trust involved."

As soon as last sentence is out, I regret it.

Before he can see the shock about what I said registering on my face, I move toward the door, not waiting for a reply.

Only when I don't hear him say anything do I realize how much I was waiting for one.

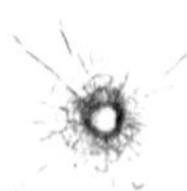

Dimitri falls into step behind me as soon I leave the classroom.

I don't even close the door, because it would've meant turning around and possibly letting Ian see that I'm close to tears. It would've meant seeing the look on his face, and that… Too much.

Why did I say that? Why?

I crutch ahead down the center hall until I reach the Palm Room. My stomach's an impossible mix of lead and acid, but I've taken the first step to set my plan in motion. Well, at least part one of my plan worked out fine: I got out of class.

It doesn't feel like a victory at all.

Dimitri's large hand covers mine on the terrace's door handle. "Wait." He raises an eyebrow toward me.

"You know that Ian had to report what you told him, don't you?" he asks in his quiet baritone. "Under Code Red, everything in the Lair is recorded. The second you told him what you did, there was no going back for him. It would've cost him his job once Waterhouse reviewed the tapes."

The job he loves with all his heart.

The job I just promised to have him removed from.

I push that thought away.

Don't want to think about it.

So I focus on the other part of Dimitri's explanation. "Why

didn't he say anything about the recording?" Sounds like something I should know.

"He tried." Dimitri rolls his eyes up to the corner of the ceiling, like Ian did in the—

Oh. My cheeks heat up. "He hinted at the cameras."

"All he could do. Because guess what Waterhouse will do once he reviews the tapes—and he will review them, given that it's Ian's first Condition Red—and hears him warn you about the recording? One, he'll know something is up, and two, behaving suspicious is the last thing Ian needs. He told you, he literally couldn't discuss any of your concerns and accusations. He meant it."

Understanding sinks in, and it doesn't feel good. "Because Waterhouse isn't a fan of his."

"Exactly. Anything other than pure professionalism, and Waterhouse would fire Ian from his position."

I chew on the inside of my cheek, then let go of the doorknob, adjust my crutches and face Dimitri. "I understand that. I do, Dimitri. But it's not just that. Ian neither listened to me, nor let me investigate anybody else. It's a slap in the face, Dimitri. I had good ideas, yet he doesn't take me serious. How can I trust him after that?" I twist a strand of hair around my fingers. It sounded bad in my head already, but saying it out loud…

Dimitri scratches the back of his head and takes off his sunglasses. Huh. This is the first time I see him really up close in bright daylight without them, and his eyes are striking. They're so light, I can't tell whether they're a very light blue, or rather a clear grey tone, but no matter which one it is, he looks much softer without his glasses, and also much less intimidating. Come to think about it, that's probably why he never takes them off.

"Alix, I've been working with Ian since he joined the Secret Service and PRICS. We've been through a couple of missions together, and I would say I know him very well—as well as you get to know someone when your and his life may depend on it. I can tell you, he *does* trust you. You've already moved through PRICS training faster than anybody on record since the program was started. He's shown you more and given you more access to information than anyone at your level under any head instructor ever had, be it at PRICS or at the Bureau. He does trust you *and* your judgement."

Over the last couple of months combined, Dimitri hasn't spoken as much to me as he did just now. I appreciate hearing what he said and maybe he's right, but it doesn't change that when it counted, Ian did *not* trust me. My judgement did *not* count for him. And here I thought Ian and I…

Yeah, or not.

I deflate.

"Dimitri… I…"

"If there is anything to what you said, I can guarantee you Ian will be on it. He doesn't neglect evidence, no matter whom it pertains to." He pauses. "That being said, you're not going to like my next piece of advice, but you need to let go of your theory about Varen. If Ian says it's a dead end, it is a dead end. I know it's tough, but he has his reasons. He ordered you to drop it, so drop it."

He tilts his head and lifts both eyebrows, waiting for my reaction.

I put on a mask of embarrassment to hide the shock surging through me.

Why? Why is now even Dimitri insisting I drop it? It's one of our best leads. I can't be the only one seeing this.

While on the outside, I fidget with my hair to buy some time, my insides are working on a plan. Reverse psychology is working overtime on me: *Don't look into Varen.* Okay, I *will* look into him. *Don't you dare accuse the VP.* Oh, I *am* accusing him.

Yes, Ian ordered me to drop it, but no way I'm giving up now. Order or not, I *will* get to the bottom of this.

It's time I start to play the game myself instead of just being a pawn.

The tip of my shoe draws a pattern on the spotless floors. I suck in my lower lip and sigh. "I'm sorry, Dimitri. It's all… quite a bit to swallow, maybe that's—"

Dimitri pulls me into a gentle sleeper hold. "Naah, blame it on those hormones going crazy, Trouble." He rubs his knuckles over the top of my head, a wide grin on his face I swear I've never seen him pull off before.

"Ow." I protest and pretend to push him away. In truth, I'm glad I'm trapped down here, so Dimitri doesn't see me blush.

Hormones.

Maybe I can use them as an excuse for some of my stupidity over the last months, but I can't use them to excuse what I'm about to do: disobey a direct order from my commanding officer.

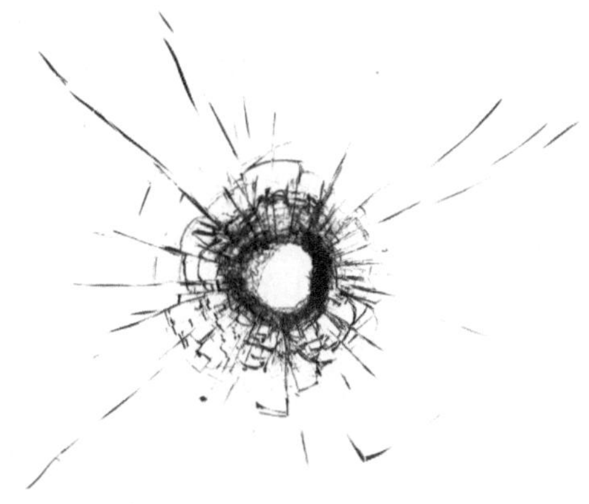

CHAPTER TWENTY-FIVE

Going Rogue(ish)

Getting rid of Dimitri is close to impossible.

I kind of knew that, but it doesn't do anything to lessen the sting of frustration. Seriously, how am I supposed to gather intelligence if I have a shadow clinging to my every move? Checking out my main leads is going to be a challenge anyway, but doing it under observation?

Grr.

On the other hand, it doesn't really matter. I'd draw more attention without him, and let's be honest: it's all about stealth anyway, only that I'll not limit that to my suspects, but extend it also to Dimitri.

My IQ and spy-skills are getting a workout today.

For now, I'm *taking a walk* through the gardens to make it less obvious I have a destination: Crime Scene #1, so to speak: the limousine, hopefully including its driver. After that, I have a couple of other ideas, although the execution is still in the works.

Dimitri or not, getting useable intel from DiBiaso, his team, and whomever else I can come up with, is a whole different animal. But then, that's what I was trained for. The inconspicuous teen with a different approach than the Secret Service. That's what Sam needs now. Someone who doesn't play by the rulebook.

Turning a bend close to the pergola in the Jackie-Kennedy-Garden, I freeze in mid-step.

Right there, sitting on the corner of a white, iron-wrought bench, is the next-best thing after DiBiaso himself, her arms crossed in front of her chest, face pulled into a frown that doesn't suit her Barbie-doll appearance at all.

My spirits do a little jiggly dance, for once revived.

Today luck is on my side, especially with her security detail keeping watch from the flower garden, about twenty yards away from the bench. This is as private as it'll get.

I stop and look over my shoulder. "Dimitri, do you mind?"

His response is a curt nod before he joins his colleagues over at the rose bushes. Aww look, they're keeping our leashes loose.

I hobble closer. "Gianna." I let myself fall onto the other side of the bench, leaning the crutches against it.

Her frown only deepens, and somehow that makes my heart leap in excitement. Anything that makes Gianna frown is worth my time—uh, investigative skills, I meant.

"What's going on?" I fumble with a plastic part on my crutches. "Odd day today, huh?" Playing it innocently is probably the best way to go.

Gianna huffs and throws me an angry glance. "Shut up, Alix."

Ouch. And, excuse me?

Now, my usual MO would be to retreat into the shell that kept me safe all those years in school, but I don't. I'm not that girl anymore. The accident changed me. Ian— I mean, PRICS changed me. Kissing Sam changed me.

So instead of blushing and shutting up, I twist to the left while pulling my bad leg up onto the bench so I can face her and the problem head on, because I'm done with turning the other cheek. "Not shutting up, sorry. But good buzz words, why then don't we talk about why you don't like me?" And I'm sure I'll wing it somehow to get some useable intel from her. *Of* her, maybe. Hate is a powerful motivator.

Gianna's eyes widen as her eyebrows shoot up. "You're kidding me. Right? You're absolutely kidding me."

"Actually—"

"You have the nerve to ask me why *I* don't like *you*?" Gianna also twists her upper body toward me, keeping her arms crossed in front of her chest, holding the barrier between the two of us in place. "After everything you've done?"

I jerk back like slapped. "What? I haven't done anything! You—"

"Oh, please, don't play the simpleton, we both know that's not you, *Miss Professor*," she sneers, lifting both palms up in a mocking calming gesture.

Okay, this is getting a bit out of hand here. Also, not at all in the direction I was going for.

"I—"

"Yeah, you. It's always you, Alix Forrester, First Daughter, genius extraordinaire. You were bad enough before your accident, but ever since, there's just no getting along with you. It's all about you, you, and again: you." She glares at me. "And thank you for getting Sam fired."

"*What?*" My jaw drops. I can't have heard that right.

Gianna looks at me down her nose, disdain clearly written all over her face. "Didn't know it yet, did ya? He's gone, thanks to you, I assume." She falls back against the wooden backrest. "But since it's all about you, you probably don't care what becomes of

Sam." She jerks her head away from me and stares into the gardens.

It takes all the self-control I have to inhale, exhale—and keep my voice calm. "That's not true," I say past clenched teeth, "I very much care about what happens to Sam." So much that I'm trying to find the real assassin to clear his name. Granted, after I got him into this mess, so maybe she has a point, although I'd rather die than admit that.

Gianna huffs.

"What?" I ask and throw up my arms. "What is it? Please enlighten me!"

She whips her head around, her eyes shooting daggers at me. "*What?* You don't get it? And yet it's so simple. You get Sam into trouble, and he gets fired. Period. I've been looking all over for him today, and all I get from Mrs. Houser is that he's not working here anymore. Neither is Oliver. Just like that." Her eyes fill with tears. "I can add one and one together, it doesn't need your precious advanced college classes for that. He lets you stay in the Secretary's Office. Your dad gets mad. Sam gets blamed, and since he's his dad's responsibility, they both get fired. Easy."

My eyes make a good attempt at popping out of my skull. "That's what you think?" How in the world did she come up with that? My fault? "You're crazy. Dad's not going to fire Oliver—or Sam—for something like that! Nothing of what you said has anything to do with Sam not—"

"How would you know? Are you your daddy's assistant now, Mrs. Know-it-all?"

Geez. I roll my eyes, more from her interrupting me all the freakin' time than from the idiotic nickname. Pulling on all the self-restraint I've left, I take a deep breath. "*No*, I'm surely not my dad's assistant. *Yes*, I do know it had nothing to do with me." Kind of. I look her straight in the eye. "And why would you even care? The only reason you go after Sam is because he and I are friends." And more, I think. *I hope.*

Gianna's mouth opens and closes again, and then a tear falls down her face. She wipes it away before I can be sure. "Yeah, you of course would think that."

I don't understand anything anymore. What's going on with her? With her and Sam?

Pushing my ego a gigantic step back, I force myself to stay calm. "Gianna, help me out here. What am I missing?" Obviously, it's something.

For a moment, she looks at me like she was going to lash out again, but then something in her eyes turns dull. And it makes her look miserable. "I didn't want to move to D.C.," she whispers, "not at all."

Oh. Okay… "I didn't know that."

"I wanted to stay home, or move in with one of my siblings, but Dad insisted I come. So I did, and everywhere I go, everything's about you. How Alix is doing after her accident, Alix here, Alix there. Alix is taking advanced college classes and you'll be too stupid for those," she mocks, "and worst of all, you're not even interested in any of this." She keeps her gaze trained onto her hands in her lap. "You don't come to any fundraisers, to any campaign stops, to—"

"I was kind of busy recovering from a broken spine." I interrupt her for a change. "Priorities, Gianna."

She shrugs. "Maybe. All I'm saying is that I'm chopped liver to everyone, and I'm the one actually *there*. So I started talking to Sam, and Sam… was awesome. He helped me through it. We became friends. That is until you started putting me down in front of him."

"I did not—"

"Of course you did! Inauguration Ball—could you've been

any colder toward me? Whenever we meet—ever thought you could actually look at me? When I tried to pick up Sam for lunch—you going all territorial on him? So yeah, thanks to you, Sam didn't meet with me anymore, and thanks to you, now he's fired. But whatever." She waves dismissively, only to pull her hand back up to her face and wipe her nose.

Holy cow. She really is mad at me for the same reasons I'm mad at her.

I adjust my position on the bench. "Inauguration Ball—you basically ignored me, only to tell me then how much better you'd be than me. Whenever we meet—you look for something to rub into my face. When you wanted Sam for lunch, he—" I stop right there.

He was just about to kiss me, I was going to say, but I don't. Too much.

For the first time since her outburst, Gianna meets my gaze. "I know," she whispers. "And I couldn't let it happen."

A lump forms inside my throat. "Oh," I breathe. Well. I did and didn't expect that.

"Yeah." She plays with her hair, looking down. "Do you… do you like Sam?"

I grimace. This isn't really my kind of question, but Gianna looks as un-hostile as she's ever been. Open. *Vulnerable.*

I take a deep breath. Whatever. Here goes nothing. "Yeah."

A small smile pulls the corners of her lips up. "Yeah. Me too."

And somehow, these couple of words, they bring us peace. She gives me a shy smile that I return before I shrug. "All over misunderstandings and a guy, huh?"

She giggles. "All over misunderstandings and a guy. But not any guy. Sam."

"True."

The lump inside my throat grows. Sam, who's still in custody, because I haven't made any headway. Well, besides kind of ruling out Gianna as the assassin. Not that she was a serious contender for that title.

"Is that why you came to the Oval Office that day that I was there? With the foreign Minister?" I'm *sure* those were her blonde curls I saw there, no matter how fast she made it to my classroom thereafter.

Her cheeks turn color. "Looking for Sam." She tugs a strand of hair behind her ear. "I've really been alone, you know? I needed a friend, like Sam. Someone, like, even your teacher. He's kind of cute too." She blushes, and my spine stiffens. Not thinking of Ian now.

Gianna plays with one of her silver creoles. "I didn't want to be left out. Every time I see you, you have it all. You're the President's daughter, the smartest girl in probably all North America, and—"

"Wait, what? That's coming from you?" I ask. My jaw drops to the floor, literally. Okay, not quite literally, but what the heck? That's how she sees me? That's definitely not how I see myself! Her, on the other hand... "Look at you! You're a model, and what am I? Wherever you go, people look at you, wherever I go, they look right through me."

We both stare at each other. Mind blowing how two people can be so different, yet so much alike. This is the closest we've come to bonding since I met her. Which means... if I ever wanted to get information from her, now's the time.

"Hey, Gianna?" I try out a small smile. Doesn't feel too weird. Huh. "Can I ask you something? Living in the White House... still takes some getting used to for me. How's *your* dad holding up with all this stress? Mine..." I drop my gaze and chew on my lower lip. Acting 101. "Mine is not in the best mood. So busy." *Please talk about your dad, please talk about your dad...!*

She draws up her legs until both are crossed on the bench in front of her. "It's okay. He's okay. Considering his age. The workload is crazy, right? He gets frustrated sometimes too, it's not just your dad."

I laugh once. "I was hoping you'd say that. Sometimes I feel I can do no right." Truth, right there. "What does yours get frustrated about?"

"Ugh. Everything. Sometimes I think he has OCD."

Digging further, bait coming right up. "Genetic Testing Bill. That's my dad's Achilles heel."

"Sure. Not bad though. I don't think he'd mind it as much as your dad if it passed. Plus, the rider is nice."

"Yeah, I agree." About the rider, at least. "Why do you think he wouldn't mind it?"

Gianna leans forward, supporting her weight on her elbows. "Don't know. Just something he said, and that he likes the CEO from that company. They used to play Golf together, like, years ago."

Wait, DiBiaso played Golf with Lucas?

An alert tone chimes from her jeans' pocket, making her twitch. Gianna pulls out her cell and rolls her eyes. "Speaking of: My dad. My cab's ready."

"Your cab?"

She gets up and pockets her phone. "After I've been whining for the last months that I want to see my old friends, today of all days Dad allows me to go, so no fireworks and celebrations for me. The cab is gonna bring me back home. He couldn't even spare his limo and Gary." She makes a face.

I tilt my head. "What do you mean?"

She kicks at a pebble on the otherwise spotless red brick pavers. "To you, it might be superficial, but it's the only benefit this has for me. The White House. The limo. Press. Dinner invitations. Dad knows that. Like I said, I rather wanted to move in with my sibs, but this is how he convinced me. The glamour and swag that comes with *my job*." She puts the last two words in air quotes. "Anyway. Dad knows I hate going by cab. Usually, he sends Gary and the limo for me, but apparently not today." Bitterness colors her voice.

"Gary?"

"His favorite Secret Service agent. Has been with us for years, had some special training or so. And…" She chews on her lip. "I feel more appreciated when Dad does that. Bit more special."

Look at that, I wasn't quite wrong when I diagnosed her with spoiled-princess syndrome. And the funny thing is, I get what she's saying, it's just not my cup of tea. "You really *do* like all this stuff," I say. She may miss her friends, but she likes the limelight.

Another shrug. "I like the attention it brings me and the fact that Dad goes the extra mile for me. So yeah, you talk about stress, and today he's super-stressed, because he *needs Gary. We're working here, honey.*" Gianna's next air quotes carry the same punctuated irony her intonation does. "Last time he didn't have me driven was during the campaign when your dad ran late and we had to give up Gary and the town car to pick you up."

I draw in a breath that gets stuck on the lump lodged inside my throat. "My accident."

She flinches. "Oops. Sorry, yes. Didn't mean—"

"It's fine." I wave her off.

Awkward silence hovers for a moment before Gianna stuffs her hands into her pockets and turns toward me. "You know, Gary felt so bad about it. It wasn't his fault. I hope you know that, Alix."

"Y-yeah. Of course." Investigations concluded there was nothing the driver could've done to prevent the accident. Now, it would've come in handy had my seat belt held. *His* did—mine gave, and that's why I wound up like this. I still have the scars on top of my head and the brace on my leg to prove it.

"Well, anyway, I've gotta go… It was… nice talking to you, Alix." Her smile is the first real I have ever gotten, and I return it. Guess I'm getting used to it, because this one also feels less awkward than I thought.

"Same here. See you later, okay?"

"See you later."

I watch her cross the perfectly manicured lawn toward the White House and give myself another minute before I get off the bench.

DiBiaso and Lucas played golf together. Granted, it was years ago and it might not mean anything, but at this point, I'll gladly take it as a lead.

I tighten my fingers around the crutch handles. Next step, Limo One. If I can find the slightest bit of evidence that'll bring some doubt to Ian's and Waterhouse's narrow-mindedness, then my rogue mission will have been a win. Anything that shows a connection to somebody else, be that DiBiaso, Varen, or whomever. Anybody but Sam and Oliver.

Anybody, who could still be out there, planning to kill Dad.

Yeah, sorry. Not on my watch.

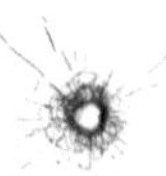

Pretending I have nowhere to go is tougher than it should be, especially when trying to be inconspicuous.

I stop and—literally—smell the roses.

I take out my cell and check… something.

I walk in circles, only to make Dimitri think nothing of me eventually arriving at the limousine garage.

He's keeping a couple of feet distance, as always, and I haven't heard him announce anything so far. Doesn't mean he isn't at one hundred and ten percent attention, but that's okay. I can work with that.

I crutch along the smooth asphalted street, my head kept low, but my eyes trained on the limo's garage at two o'clock another thirty yards away. Calling it a garage is maybe an understatement, but it's also not quite a hangar either. It's a massive space with pull-up doors that houses the two state cars, i.e. presidential limousines, as well as enough equipment and tools to dismantle and put them back together again.

When I get closer, I notice the garage doors are wide open. Cadillac One, Dad's limousine, is parked in front. We named our BMW at home Georgie, this one's name is The Beast. Aptly named for size and equipment. One of the Secret Service agents is getting in and out of that monstrosity, checking whatever people check in cars and noticing us way before I would have expected it.

Good for me.

The agent first straightens his sunglasses on top of his nose, then his black suit jacket. They all must buy at the same outfitters. I've yet to see any agent wear something different. Maybe their socks. And no, I don't want to know about their underwear.

He nods at us. "Dimitri," he calls over, raising a hand.

"Amando."

I stop and turn. "You know each other?"

Dimitri folds his hands behind his back. "I know everybody who is important to your safety."

My mind scrambles. "And he is?"

"Amando drives your father's limousine, which means he might be driving you at one point."

Lights, camera, *action*: I frown and push out my lower lip. "*Great*. I haven't even *sat* in the limo yet. I—" Dramatic pause.

A questioning glance at Dimitri. "Do you mind if I…?"

"Go ahead."

Yes!

Amando chuckles as he comes closer. "I heard that. Hi, Alix. Officially—Amando. I'm the one who gets your father from A to B when he needs me." He points his thumb over his shoulder at the limousine.

And we are *on.* "Very nice to meet you, Amando." I put my weight on my left leg and transfer my right crutch over to free up a hand. I even take care to not forget supporting myself with my crutches. I'm not messing up. It's part of my disguise and job.

I hold out my freed right hand to Amando, who takes it and gives it a firm shake. "So you've never sat in the Beast, huh?"

"No, never. It's supposed to be really cool though." I do my best to look appropriately enthusiastic.

Amando grins widely and nods. "Indeed it is. I'll give you the tour. Well, I'm going to skip the top-secret parts, or I'd have to kill you." Before I can make up my mind if he means it or not, he snickers. "Kidding. Even I don't know the top-secret parts, and I've been driving this lady since she came off the factory line."

Okay, Amando is a jokester.

I force a laugh, but I don't think it's funny.

Not at all.

Not with what's been going on. Making jokes about killing me after an assassin was around—or is around, if I assume Sam is innocent—is not the smartest idea. Either Amando doesn't have the clearance to know about the assassination attempts, or he has really bad taste… or he actually *is* the assassin.

So far, I don't have reason to believe my last assumption could be true, but I'm here to find that out, am I not? No clue is too small to be dismissed.

Witch hunt.

No. Nope. Not witch hunt. Following evidence.

As we're approaching the limo, Amando dives right into telling me Limo One's stats, and after a couple of seconds, I have myself enough under control that I can actually listen.

I'm not a car person, but even I can tell this limo is impressive, despite—or because of—its massiveness. Night vision, sealed against biochemical attacks—the whole shebang.

Amando opens the rear door for me. "Ready for your first contact? Have a seat."

"Awesome." I fake excitement and get into the limo.

It's pretty big on the inside, but not as big as I thought. Two forward facing seats are in the back, a folding desk in-between them. Three more seats face the other ones, their backs against a glass partition separating the front from the back of the car.

I sit in one of the forward-facing ones and look around. Amando gets in diagonally across from me, leaving the door open and one leg outside, while Dimitri stays a couple of feet away in the shade of a tree.

Time to wing it.

I look around, the poster-girl for wide-eyed curiosity. "Whoa. Huge. Impressive."

"Indeed again. You're sitting in your dad's seat." He points at me. "No one else is allowed to sit there when we ride, even if he isn't coming with us. He has a desk at his disposal, and we carry extensive communication arrays right under there." He points to a compartment hidden under the seat next to where I'm sitting and keeps on listing details about the types of antennas the limo carries.

Not what I'm here for.

I nod my chin at another storage compartment under the rearwards facing middle seats. "What is this over there? More communication stuff, or is that the blood bank?" That innocent look, I've got it down.

Amando interrupts his monologue. "Actually, no: you found the most important part of Cadillac One. It's the mini-bar." He grins and reaches down with his left hand. Conveniently, he doesn't even need to get up in order to open it.

Ta-daaah.

A whole array of pink-and-blue-striped bottles smiles at me, neatly lined up and framed by an OJ on each side.

Commencing questioning, treading carefully.

"Nice," I say giving it my best that's-so-cool-voice, "I bet that is the one compartment that needs the most maintenance, i.e. refilling." Wink-wink, grin-grin.

Amando grins back in return, grabs a water out of the bar and throws it over to me. "Yep, it does. Here you go. Nice and chilled. Cheers!"

I catch the water in midair and my throat goes dry. I don't want to drink this water. What if... What if this one is poisoned too? Yes, the Secret Service checked, rechecked, and replaced everything after Yoshi landed in the hospital, but if I'm working under the assumption that Sam is *not* the assassin, then Amando could be. He could've poisoned the water again, second time's the charm, and who knows, he could have just handed me another tampered bottle.

No, wait. Why waste a perfectly fine assassination attempt on me if he wanted to get Dad? Even if Amando was the assassin, he'd gain nothing but unwanted attention by poisoning me.

Plus, I have Dimitri *right there.*

"Thank you," I say and unscrew the cap. Here's to logical conclusions. "Cheers." I tip my head back and take a tiny sip of my water. It tastes normal, without the slight acidic sting the lev-metaminozole would cause. *Good.*

With a quick glance under my lashes, I check on Dimitri:

Attentive and focused on us, but relaxed. Back to business.

"So, wait, is that part of your job description too? Stocking the bar? I thought as the Secret Service agent, you know, you got your gun and stuff…" I drop my gaze to the holster visible under his jacket.

"Yeah, I know." Amando pats the gun through the fabric of his suit. "You'd think life would be more glamorous as a Secret Service agent, right? Actually, I don't mind that part. The President appreciates it very much, and it's just one of many things that have to be checked upon before every trip. It's priority three, so it doesn't have the same importance as let's say, the security checks. Those are priority one and two."

I bet that changed recently. "So that means—"

Someone comes around the open rear door and bends down, peeking into the limo through the open door, dressed in a suit just like Amando's. "Man, I've been looking for you everywhere, you're supposed to—oh!" He freezes when his gaze falls on me. His eyes widen in recognition and he quickly switches to a more polite tone. "Hello, ma'am." He nods toward me.

"Uh, hi." I recognize him instantly—that crooked nose is hard to forget. He's the Secret Service agent from the Green Room during my first, screwed-up mission to keep Dad from meeting Josiah Lucas. The same one who had to witness the whole OJ-debacle after Lucas talked his ear off.

Amando does a quick gesture between myself and the other agent. "Alix Forrester, meet Gary, my backup driver. Gary—Alix Forrester, the President's daughter. I'm explaining to her everything about Limo One."

"Gary?" As in, Gianna's Gary?

"Yes, ma'am." Crooked-nose Gary gives a crisp nod, like he was responding to a superior officer during a military drill.

Now look at that. Fate delivers me another connection to

DiBiaso, and on a silver platter.

I stretch out my hand to Gary. "Nice to meet you." I only give it a light squeeze, since it's wrapped in a white dressing. Still, he flinches from my touch.

"Sorry," I say. Looks painful.

"It's all right." Gary squats in front of the door, facing us without having to bend down. "Burned myself. Lesson learned, never grab a hot pot by its handle. Anyway, sorry for interrupting. Central was looking for you." He taps Amando on the knee, who groans.

"Hey, I'm kind of busy with the First Daughter. Can they wait? Although…" He pauses. "Alix, do you mind if Gary takes over? He's the backup driver for this limo anyway and the main driver for the Vice President's one. He can tell you all about either limo just as well as me."

He swings his other leg out of the limousine.

Click. Now wait a second.

My blood pressure spikes up a notch. "Uhh, oh, cool. Gary drives both limousines?" As in, Gary had access to the water?

As in, Gary is *DiBiaso*'s favorite Secret Service agent, according to Gianna?

As in, Gary has a burn from a *kitchen accident*, like DiBiaso?

In the deepest corner of my mind, a connection falls into place, and I'm not sure I truly want to look at it, because this is more than me *jumping to conclusions*: this is real.

And it's scary.

A drop of sweat runs down my neck. I could be looking at the assassin. Maybe it's not so bad Dimitri is close by.

Amando freezes in mid-motion and falls back into his seat, resignation on his face. Maybe it's impolite to walk out on the President's daughter.

"Yeah. Gary gets called in when I'm sick or need to be

somewhere else. Everyone gets bumped up one step: Gary from being the VP's driver to your father's, and the backup driver gets to work for the VP. Gary is a lucky slacker though, he only needs to do priority one and two checks when I'm gone, priority three gets reassigned by the Chief of Staff."

Damn it. That would be Oliver, who tasked Sam. Another strike against them, and one off Gary's list. Doesn't make me feel any better about him though. Still too many coincidences.

A muscle in Gary's jaw pops once. "I wouldn't call myself a slacker, 'Mando. And no matter what"—he gets up and straightens his jacket—"Central is making quite the ruckus, so get your butt inside. Have a great day, ma'am." He gives me a disinterested nod before he walks away.

Crap. There goes my chance to dig deeper, to—

Amando peels himself out of the limousine. "Sorry to have to cut it short. At least you got to sit in it, right?"

I nod like a bobble-head figure. "Yes. Sure. That was great. Thank you so much."

Amando helps me out of the limousine when my right crutch gets stuck. Out of the corner of my eye, I notice Dimitri coming closer.

This is my last chance, and I better speed it up.

"Hey, Amando? Is Gary always so grumpy? Or is he just not a fan of my dad's? No hard feelings, believe me, I know he can be curt with people sometimes." Sue me for not coming up with anything better, but at least this angle made Gianna open up.

And it works again.

Amando sighs and scratches his head. "No, it's not that. It was wrong of me to call him a slacker. He lost his wife last year, and he's working harder than any of us to get his daughter through college. Take today. He's off, but he still chooses to come in as backup. That's dedication. And by the way, your dad is very nice, with all of us, but Gary hasn't exactly had a lucky streak when it comes to Limo One. You remember Mr. Nagakawa having a seizure in the limo? That was when Gary was driving. And he didn't realize what was going on in the back until he arrived at the destination."

No way.

Gary was driving that day? But then, if he had poisoned the water, wouldn't he have tried to keep Yoshi from drinking it? Actually, I can answer that question: No. Too obvious. Yoshi drinking the water was a risk he had to take if he wanted to stay under the radar.

Amando waves at Dimitri to come over. "And then Gary had the pleasure of driving a foreign minister and his entourage, and that didn't quite go per protocol either."

I narrow my eyes. "What do you mean?"

He shrugs. "It was a last-minute thing, so it got stressful. Their limo wasn't secure enough; there were huge concerns about that. We see lots of foreign dignities, but usually we don't take them in Limo One. This time we had to, or this whole thing would have blown up in our faces, maybe even literally. They—"

The puzzle pieces click into place. "Are you talking about Varen?" Foreign minister and Limo One together in one sentence aren't really a common occurrence, even at the White House.

"Indeed I am." Amando nods once, slowly, one eyebrow raised. "You met him?"

"Unfortunately." I shudder. "Wasn't a fan."

He huffs out a short laugh. "Neither was Gary. Or anybody on the team. Can't really expect us to like foreign security searching Limo One for listening devices for an hour." He rolls his eyes. "Listening devices, please. If we want to know what they're saying, we have better methods."

A thrill runs down my spine. Varen's goons could *totally* have poisoned the water while supposedly 'searching' the limo. They had the opportunity right there and then. But then, why would Gary freak out if he worked together with Varen? For show? And if it was a last-minute thing, could they have planned for it, or am I seeing things?

A bad feeling seeps through the walls of my stomach and into my intestines. That's not it. There's a connection—

Dimitri's shadow falls in-between us. "Alix?" There's a warning in his tone, one Amando picks up on as well, only he mis-interprets it.

"No worries, Dimitri. I'll let her go now. Anyway, nice to meet you."

"You, too."

I get one more nod, and then he's gone.

Without waiting for Dimitri, I hobble away from the garage back to the gardens. Au contraire to his usual habit, Dimitri walks next to me. "Varen, Alix? Again?"

I stomp my crutches into the ground harder than technically necessary. "Hey! I didn't ask him. He started—"

"Ian ordered you to drop it. I told you the same."

"And I didn't start it! Gosh, is that so hard to believe? All I wanted is to have a seat in the limo!"

"Really."

"Yes, really!" Frustrated, I crutch ahead. I need time to *think*, but time is the one commodity I don't have. Not with Dimitri on my heels, and not with the assassin still out there.

After another minute or two, Dimitri breaks the silence. "I will have to report that to Ian, Alix."

Oh heck, *come on*! I stop and turn. "Nothing. Happened."

"You went against a direct order—"

"I didn't! I wanted. To sit. In the stupid. Limousine." My knuckles turn white, that's how tight I'm clinging to those crutches. "You said it was okay! He brought him up! Am I to pretend I didn't meet him? Dad knows, Mrs. Houser knows—people know!" If he calls it in to Ian, I'm… I don't know. Out. On house arrest. Detention. In any case, I won't be able to investigate, and Sam's and Oliver's fate will be sealed.

Dimitri's face stays infuriatingly calm. "It is still my duty to call it in."

I snap my mouth shut.

His duty.

It's mine to protect Dad, to help Sam and Oliver, and I'm messing up left and right. The more I try to figure this out, the more I'm losing touch. I have nothing that can sway Ian, nothing tangible that would make a difference. All I can go by are assumptions. Wild accusations.

Tears of frustration prick my eyes. "Dimitri, Ian—" I suck in a deep breath and hold it. "Can you… can you wait a couple of minutes? I need a minute to… I don't know, collect my thoughts?" Because I will need all my wits together when he chews me out, all my emotional barriers in place and fortified. "A minute." I nod at a bench hidden behind bushes close to the spot where I stomped my crutches into the dirt earlier.

Dimitri sighs. "Alix, I—"

"Please." My voice is so pitiful it breaks. "I need a couple of minutes before I can face him again." The corners of my mouth twitch, and not in a good way, more in a I-might-cry-kind of way.

Dimitri deflates. "Okay. I'll be waiting at the rose bushes. Ten minutes. It's getting late, and if we want to have you up on the balcony in time for your father's speech and talk to Ian before, we've got to get going."

He turns away, but pauses. "You've got to start trusting in him, if you want him to trust in you." Then he's gone, swallowed by the bushes and trees, leaving me alone a couple of feet from the bench.

I swallow down the tears, but the lump in my throat stays.

Over the last year, I always thought the feeling of disappointing Dad was the worst.

Turns out it stings even more when you're disappointing yourself.

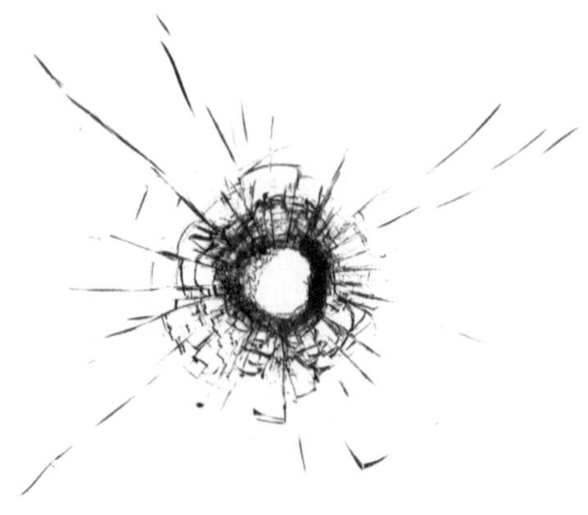

CHAPTER TWENTY-SIX

Screwed Up

I fall onto the bench without realizing I'm bruising my tailbone.

The buzz I felt a mere couple of minutes ago is gone, replaced by anxiety. Panic.

If I want to have a winning closing statement ready for Ian I don't have much time, but I need as long as I can get, because… it's my last chance before becoming the girl who cried wolf.

But am I crying wolf, or am I onto something? My heart speeds up its pace. It's too easy and too elaborate at the same time. I try to swallow, but the apple inside my throat refuses to move. What if I take Varen out of the equation and focus on DiBiaso and Gary? What if it's still all connected? *Everything?*

I squeeze my eyes shut so hard stars are dancing in-between my view of trees and bushes when I reopen them.

The first time I saw Gary was in the Green Room, together with Lucas. They were talking and—

I face-palm my forehead. "Of course." Of course! Lucas spilled the OJ and I *saw* him hand a pill box to Gary—but I never saw him take it back. *That* could've been the lev-metaminozole! Not the gift box for Oliver. The pills for Gary!

Excitement pulls my shoulders back and spine straighter. My first piece of evidence. That must be on video. We can look at every freeze-frame of that messed-up encounter and check exactly what Gary did with the pills. Ian must believe me when he sees it.

Score one, Alix.

Score two: I bet DiBiaso replaced Dad's pen with the tampered one. Maybe even on Taco Tuesday when I ran into him. At that point, DiBiaso's hand looked already red, so he must've held on to it for a couple of hours at least I would think. We could run a Geiger counter over his hand. Look at the radioisotope, rate of decay, residual contamination. In short, full radiological forensics. Boom. Check, connected.

Score three: Gary's burn on the other hand—no pun intended—is probably because he got the radioactive material for DiBiaso. Or handled it. Or something. Why else would he have a burn on his hand too? It can't be coincidental that Gary burned himself on a quote-unquote hot pot when all of this is going on. Enter Gamma-Spectroscopy and science.

Score fou—

Oh, for the love of all that's holy! No, no, no, no! "Shit," I whisper into the silence of the gardens. "F-ing shit." My heart skips a beat, no, several beats, as if the magnitude of what I just realized was too much for it to handle.

I wheeze on my next inhale. Gianna said, the VP needed Gary today because they *were busy*, hence he couldn't spare him to drive her. But Amando said, Gary was off and here as backup, which means…

I work on a dry swallow. Which means he isn't officially assigned to any position, and he would've had time to drive Gianna. So if he's here and working, why not do his boss a favor and drive his daughter, as always? Why break the routine?

Little droplets of sweat build up on my neck and run down into my shirt.

Because he is busy today, like Gianna said.

Only it's not work, it's another assassination attempt.

He's going to try again.

He's going to try to kill Dad again.

Tonight.

Holy cow. I try to swallow, but can't. My throat's too dry, too parched all of a sudden.

It makes sense—the most sense any of this screwed up convoluted mess has made so far. Today is ideal: Security is lax—

A loud groan escapes me and I smack my forehead. "Of course, security is lax. The VP scaled it down himself. To make it easier to kill Dad." The gardens answer with a rustle of branches and the annoyed chirping of a couple of birds as they fly off.

Okay. Okay. Deep breath. This is not just my imagination running wild, right? I mean, it sounds completely crazy, but it fits.

If I'm right with this… *if I'm right*, I have to act quickly. I need to let Ian know. He was right all along; it wasn't Varen, but I was right too. It wasn't Sam. Wasn't Oliver.

The *Vice President*.

Ian needs to know the assassin is still out there—and not just somewhere, but in our direct middle.

My mouth feels full of ultra-dry saw dust.

What if I'm wrong? What if I charge into PRICS and wrongly accuse the VP of being the assassin we're looking for? Again?

I wince. Should've thought about the consequences of my

actions before I went behind Ian's back, but stupid me was too busy being mad at him.

It doesn't matter now. If I'm wrong, I'll have to live with that. If I'm right… Dad is still in danger. Ian needs to know. DiBiaso could succeed—and I couldn't live with *that*.

A gust of wind whips my hair into my face and I shiver. The sun's going down behind the trees at the far end of the gardens. It's late already, and if I were an assassin… "I'd kill him during the festivities," I whisper. Enough distraction.

A hefty curse leaves my lips as I fumble for my phone inside my pocket.

I don't care if I'm wrong, Ian needs to act on this. Now. He needs to hear this now and from me. No time to explain to Dimitri and have him call it in, no time to walk me down to the Lair. Dad's life is on the line, and every second counts.

My fingers are so jittery I miss the print sensor twice, and facial recognition takes twice as long as normally. What use is a super-safe government phone if it doesn't do what I need it to do, damn it? Gah, finally it unlocks! *Scroll, scroll, tap, tap*—I lift the cell to my ear.

"Come on, Ian, pick up. *Pick up.* I really don't want the VP to kill Dad," I mumble. Seriously, now's not the time to ignore my calls. I drum a fast rhythm onto the bench with my other hand. "Pick up!"

"Beep. Please leave a message. Beep."

Oh, crap.

Okay. Okay. Can't leave a message—if this doesn't qualify as sensitive information, nothing else will. On the other hand, he *must* know. Leave me a clue, he said, on the day that feels like a lifetime ago. Okay then.

I take a big breath. A couple of birds fly up behind me, complaining. "Ian, it's me. Alix. I…" Damn it. Deep breath.

Again. *Again.* Don't screw it up, Forrester. "First, I'm sorry. You were right, but I was right too, and sometimes things aren't what they seem. I'm sorry I disappointed you—"

Smack!

Something hits my head like a steam train, whipping it around like a ball on a string.

Fire explodes on my left temple and eyebrow. *Pain, dizziness, nausea*—a confusion unlike I've ever felt before, and then…

Nothing.

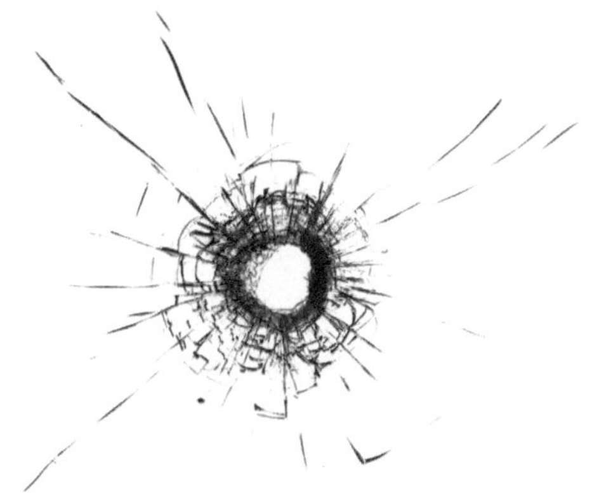

CHAPTER TWENTY-SEVEN

Unexpected

The world sways around me.

Up, down, up, down, up—

"—sniper shoots him straight into the head. Want it televised—"

I groan. *Fog.* Fog's everywhere. Can't think, can't—

"Shit, she isn't even truly out anymore."

"It's enough. You should be able to handle a single girl. Set her down, damn it!"

The world stops swaying and instead tilts. My bare feet hit cold floor and my knees buckle. Somebody catches me, turns me around, and twists one of my arms onto my back so hard, my shoulder's about to pop.

I groan again, although for a long moment I don't understand that sound came from my throat. What… where… wh—

Screeching. A door. I think. I manage to force my eyes open for a half-second, before they roll back into their sockets. *Bright ceiling lights, neon, a bare concrete room, no windows—*

Somebody pushes me forward into two stumbling steps, and the pain in my shoulder explodes. Out of reflex, I twist my body—

"Easy there. Every move you make costs you." The person digs their fingers into my hair and yanks my head back. The pressure in my shoulder also cranks it up a notch, and that pain, it slices through the fog with no problem at all. I let out a yelp. This isn't good. Not good at all. My next breath comes out raspy.

I get turned around and pushed onto something cold and hard. A chair. My butt hits the seat and a moan escapes my throat. *Dad.* He—

"Get the hands!"

"On it!" Rope is being wrapped around my wrists, rough against my skin.

And like a switch was flipped, the last of the fog lifts and reflexes I didn't know I had take over. No tying me down. I wrench my hands up and throw my body forward—

Right into James DiBiaso. "What the—!"

Before my sluggish mind or body can react, he slaps me across the cheek so hard, my head whips to the side. I yell out from the unexpected attack and stumble back into—

Gary.

From behind, he slams me down into the chair again, and this time he tightens the rope before I have a chance to free my hands. The taste of blood seeps through my mouth, bringing nausea to my stomach and tears to my eyes.

DiBiaso.

DiBiaso and Gary.

I'd feel some kind of satisfaction my theory was correct if I wasn't trapped by Dad's assassins. Trapped and tied to a chair.

The bitter sting of failure and despair shoots through my

heart and soul. I messed up. I failed. How could I not have checked my surroundings? Somebody—DiBiaso or Gary—followed and overheard me. I panicked and called Ian without precautions, and no good ever came from panicking, in case I didn't know that.

A drop of blood runs into my eye, tinting everything in a faint pink hue. The mother of all headaches takes up residence behind my skull.

Concussion. That's probably from a concussion. Under normal circumstances that would scare the heck out of me—my brain! I need that!—but now it's the least of my problems.

Gary gives my bound wrists one more testing tug and then gets up. "Secured. I'll get more for her legs."

DiBiaso shrugs out of his suit jacket. "No. Get the stuff instead. Time's of the essence."

Gary hesitates for a moment.

"Go." DiBiaso rolls up his sleeves.

"Yes, sir." Gary walks out of the room, leaving the thick metal door a tad open behind him. No knob on its inside. Yeah, this is a prison cell, and who knows where.

Another wave of despair washes over me when reality hits like a tsunami: It's too late. I can't fix this, and it's not going to end well.

Neither for Dad, nor for myself.

DiBiaso takes a handkerchief out of his front pocket and pats his forehead with it. He's much paler than the last time I saw him, the clamminess of his skin and dark circles under his eyes doing nothing to improve his looks. "Little Alix Forrester. I've got to admit, I didn't expect you here."

Acid roils inside my stomach. "And I didn't expect you to try to kill my dad." Thanks to my swollen cheek from his slap, the words come out slurred.

The VP laughs drily. "Point taken, although it wouldn't be necessary if you had done me a favor and died in that car wreck." He stuffs the handkerchief back into his pocket.

I choke on a gasp. "Wha—"

Of course.

I pinch my eyes shut when yet another puzzle piece falls into place: The one time Gianna had to spare Gary was when he drove me on the day of my accident. Accident—please. Assassination attempt. He almost killed me. Unbelievable. DiBiaso planned to have me killed.

"Why me?" I croak, my voice breaking on the last syllable. What did I ever do to him?

He shrugs. "Easiest way to get rid of your father. You weren't as well protected as him. All I needed to do was delay him and offer Gary and my town car with the prepped seatbelt to pick you up. Get the stunt driver in place to crash into you—check, check, check. Five minutes of work." His face darkens. "Undone by that idiot Brooks."

More blood runs into my eyes. I blink once, then twice, trying to clear my vision and hoping it'll do the same to my mind.

That idiot Brooks. Sam, who saved me. Who crossed the VP's plan.

It makes sense. Had I died, Dad would've dropped out of the race. For one, even a man like Dad, who buries himself in work, wouldn't have been able to function had his only daughter just died. For another, let's say he did try to overcompensate for his grief with work, nobody elects a man whose daughter just died and who puts work over family. DiBiaso would have taken over and most likely become president. Done deal.

Only Sam kept me alive, crossing DiBiaso's plans. And that leaves only one conclusion. Geez. I was right: Everything is connected.

"You framed Sam," I whisper and spit out a bit of blood that ran into my mouth from nowhere. "Revenge."

DiBiaso smooths a hand over his hair. "Him and his father. I'm not the type of man who forgets his enemies, my dear. All it takes is some planning and set-up, done. Someone to take the fall. Two, to be precise."

I shake my head. "No. Whatever you're planning tonight, you can't blame it on Sam. He's in custody, and so is his dad." And for the first time, I'm glad for it.

DiBiaso chuckles. "Oh, honey. So naïve for a genius. So little faith." He kneels in front of me. "See, I have a sniper ready to go—a sniper, who'll kill you father—"

A strangled yelp breaks from my throat. *Straight in the head. Televised.* I overheard that, kind of, when I was out. It still doesn't prepare me for the shock wave racking through my body, wreaking havoc like an arrow to the heart. This is fear turning physical.

DiBiaso looks at me down his nose. "Well, anyway. My sniper is going to find a sudden end when Gary quite accidentally runs into him and shoots him. And guess what Gary will find on the sniper? Sam's keycard to the back entrance, connecting him to the murderer and keeping him in prison. And, coming to think about it, his dad probably too. That gambling history and sudden influx of cash he sent his wife… Tah-tah."

The floor opens and swallows me whole. Part of me is impressed by how clever DiBiaso thought it through. Everybody tapped into the pitfalls he laid out for them. Everybody saw what he wanted them to see.

In the end, Sam being in jail is even more my fault than I knew. If Sam hadn't helped me, I would've died—but he and Oliver would've never gotten onto DiBiaso's radar.

We were all pawns in a game that was played around us.

That thought flips a switch inside me and pumps acid up my throat and anger through my veins. "You son of a bitch!" I snarl at DiBiaso. He took so much from me—from my family—I wish I could spit at him right in the face, or better, punch him in the face, but I'm too far away and too tied up.

DiBiaso laughs, and something in his eyes changes. He takes a lock of my hair that's stuck to either blood or saliva on my face and tucks it behind my ear. I flinch away. His touch is worse than a punch. No one is allowed to do that, it reminds me of what Ian did with a similar lock of hair, and I don't want that memory spoiled by a slime bag like DiBiaso.

"Don't. Touch. Me." I breathe through my teeth. His skin on mine makes my stomach turn.

DiBiaso drops his hand, chuckling. "You can protest all you want, it won't do you any good. Life as you know it will be over in—"

Gary shoulders the door open, a big cardboard box in his hands. "Got everything. Should be all you need."

A freaky smile creeps over DiBiaso's face. "Perfect." He fishes a gas mask out of the box, throws it up in the air and catches it. "Gary."

"Yes, sir." Gary clears his throat and steps closer to DiBiaso.

"I want you to start with butane." DiBiaso turns the gas mask over a couple of times and unscrews the lid at the end of its snout. "Then you work your way through the paints. When in doubt, give her another round." He hands the mask to Gary and points to the cardboard box on the floor.

Panic curls around me. "No," I whisper. I know what that means. He's going to make me sniff solvents and gasses. A short sniff would make me high, but the undiluted dose that I'll inhale through the mask with every breath… If it doesn't kill me, it'll give me irreparable brain damage.

The panic lashes out and wraps its tendrils around me.

No, no, no. Not *this.*

Even if I survive, I won't be *me,* I'll be a shell and nothing of me will be left.

DiBiaso chuckles. "Ah, I see you're getting it. Somewhat smart, after all, eh? But me too. Can't really kill you, dear. So difficult to explain why you're dead. So difficult to get rid of your body. Too many questions. But then, can't have you talking either. This here"—he nods at the box—"takes care of it though. *So* tragic. On the day of her father's death, the First Daughter is found unconscious in a janitor's closet with an open can of solvents, trying to drown her sorrows." He chuckles. "That being said, thank you so much for that voice message you left for whomever you called. I don't care who it was, I just love that you *apologized.* Apologizing before killing yourself. Aww, teenagers. So dramatic." He makes a fake sad face at me and pats my cheek. "Say goodbye to your brain, sweetheart."

His touch is poison on my skin, and while I want nothing more than to flinch away, I don't.

I have an even better idea.

Screw you, DiBiaso! Instead of pulling away, I tear into his forearm with primal force, locking my teeth down with crushing pressure until I taste blood.

DiBiaso yowls out and rips his arm back, leaving skin and blood between my teeth. Yes, disgusting. But also, exactly what I wanted.

"Fucking bitch!" he yells, cradling his bleeding arm embellished with a good impression of my dentition.

I grin and spit his skin and blood out onto the floor.

First rule of a dog fight: You don't pull back.

DiBiaso winds up like an MMA-athlete before a knock-out punch and backhands me in the face. This time, the force is so great it knocks me over with my chair. I hit the floor on my side, the impact driving the air out of my lungs when I can do nothing to brace my fall. The side of my head hits concrete, a sound like a gong reverberating through my skull, the only noise I can hear over the ringing in my ear where DiBiaso hit me.

A silent moan escapes me, and even that one hurts.

DiBiaso bends down to me on the floor, grabs my hair, jerks my head back, and growls. "That was your final mistake, sweetheart." He shoves my head back onto the floor and I hit concrete. Again. Not that it mattered.

"Gary. Get going. You got fifteen minutes until the fireworks. You know where to be later, and if you want to keep your daughter alive, you better be on top of your game," DiBiaso snarls at Gary, while unrolling his sleeves to cover the bite wound. He crosses the room with large steps and leaves, the echo of his dress shoes on the floors becoming fainter with every second until they're gone.

Game over.

It's done.

I am done.

There's no way out of here for me, and no one else knows about DiBiaso. I didn't nearly leave enough info for Ian to figure it out, and Dimitri—

Yeah, Dimitri is probably searching for me like crazy, but that doesn't mean he's going to find me. If it's only fifteen minutes to the fireworks, I doubt they're going up an alert level because they can't find me right away. I could be in the bathroom, or whatever.

Instead DiBiaso will have Gary fry my brain, and then a sniper shoot Dad. And there's nothing I can do about it.

Absolutely nothing.

The magnitude of that truth is overwhelming. If I thought my accident or joining PRICS changed my life, it's minor compared to what's about to come. Nothing is going to be like it was before.

I can't see Gary from my angle down here, but judging by the rattle of metal cans, he's preparing the gas mask. A carpet knife clatters to the floor, followed by some kind of lid.

My throat is too tight to breathe, so every breath rasps on its way in or out of my lungs. My heart flutters instead of pumping blood. Nausea roils inside my stomach, so strong I might throw up.

I'm so unbelievably afraid of what's going to happen.

Afraid of dying, but mostly afraid of surviving without my brain.

Afraid that my arrogance and near-sightedness over the last day or two were the final straw in Dad's death.

Afraid that I won't see him, Ian, Sam, or even Mom and Dimitri again.

Ian.

My heart seizes once and stutters along.

I shouldn't have said those things to him. I did it to hurt him, and now the last words I'll have spoken to him will be lies. *Never* would I want him replaced with somebody else. Not if he said a million times I was like a sister to him. If he told me he appreciated me for my smarts only, and nothing more. If he stayed out of reach to me forever. If he felt nothing for me.

None of it matters, because… I'm feeling enough for the both of us.

I only wish I had been stronger and shown it more, like the one time when we were training in Krav Maga, and he had Dimitri in that ridiculous padded suit attacking me. My defenses sucked, but afterwards I gathered all my courage and held on to Ian's hand.

The hint of smile tugs on the corners of my lips. When I

wrapped my fingers around his and he didn't pull away… For a moment, the world was open with possibilities.

The scene re-plays in front of my inner eye: how Dimitri had taken me down, how—

I suck in a short, sharp breath that goes nowhere: Dimitri. Dimitri taking me down over and over, then taking me aside. What did he say? *The fight isn't over until it's over.*

But he didn't mean a situation like this.

Or—

I bite down on the inside of my cheek until it hurts, squeezing my eyes shut so hard stars dance in front of them.

I'm tied to a chair lying on the ground. I'm basically out of time and about to lose my sanity and intellect to Gary and the gas mask. If this doesn't mean it's over, I don't know what does.

No matter how bleak the situation, you finish the fight.

I pop my eyes wide open. *You finish the fight. You use logic. Your brain.*

My heart skips a beat, but it's a skip of hope.

This fight is *not* over.

The flicker of hope flares up and spreads like a wildfire.

Dad is still alive, and as long as I am, there's a chance. We've only lost already if I give up.

I draw in a shaky breath.

And I'm not giving up.

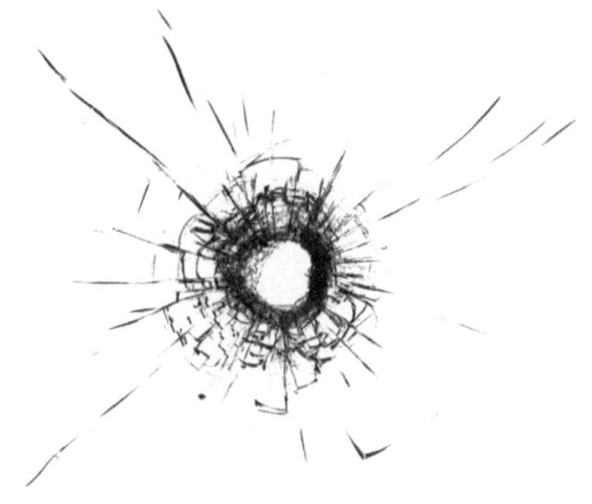

CHAPTER TWENTY-EIGHT

Fourth of July

Not even a minute later, Gary is done with his preparations. He stands from his crouching position with a loud sigh, like he was carrying the weight of the world on his shoulders.

Cry me a river, why don't you?

I on the other hand stay motionless on the floor, my head tucked to my chest as much as possible, the only active defense I've got. It needs to be difficult for Gary to put the gas mask on. If he gets it on my face, I'm done for sure.

It must stay off me at all costs.

My heart beats so rapidly I'm afraid to pass out. Strangely enough, while my body is showing signs of a classic panic attack, my mind is focused and sharp. That's the way it's supposed to be. My brain's always been my biggest asset, not just after the accident.

And I don't intend to lose it.

Gary comes closer. He sighs again at the sight of me all curled up. "Crap," he murmurs before grabbing me by the shoulders and the chair by its seat to get me in an upright position.

My muscles scream as I clench tighter, making myself as small as possible. *Stay curled, just stay curled.* Even as he maneuvers me upright, I keep my body locked into this little protective ball. I'm not making this easy for him, and it shows in his sharp bursts of breath and strained movements, despite his strength.

I force my eyes to keep track of him through my blood-crusted hair. The gas mask dangles from his fingers like some kind of grotesque trophy. My stomach lurches as he pours a liquid into the mask's snout.

"There we go," Gary murmurs, and my pulse spikes as he turns back to me, carefully balancing the death-contraption in his hands.

Good.

Now, get closer, Gary.

As if he heard me, he steps in front of me. If my hands were free, I could probably touch him.

He fidgets with the strap on the gas mask. "Listen… I'm sorry. It's not personal. I know that doesn't make it better, but I'm sorry. It's you or my daughter, and I have to choose her over you." His voice is apologetic.

Oh, so maybe he *is* carrying the weight of the world on his shoulders.

His daughter.

I hear him and I think I understand, but right now, my empathy for him is limited.

I choose this moment to look up in his face. Every fiber in my body burns with anticipation. Wait for it… Wait for it… Our gazes meet, and something in mine makes him take a small step back, putting him exactly where I want him.

Adrenaline floods my system. *Let's dance!*

I launch myself upward, the chair scraping against the floor as I use my good right leg to drive me into the air. My splinted left leg does its very best to cooperate as I force it up, up—and *boom*! The impact against Gary's groin lands with a satisfying, meaty thud, reverberating through my bones.

Gotcha.

"Ngh!" A strangled sound escapes his throat, somewhere between a wheeze and a scream. His eyes go comically wide as he throws his hands down to his crotch to cover and protect.

Which, conveniently, brings his face much closer to me.

Thank you, Gary. How convenient of you.

"Surprise," I snarl, then drive my head forward.

Bone meets bone with a thickening *crack* as pain explodes along my forehead.

Gary crumbles to the floor like a marionette with cut strings, motionless, blood streaming from his broken, and now even more crooked, nose.

Silence.

"Whoa," I wheeze.

I suck air into my lungs in heaves. My head hurts like a mo— well, bad. Doubtful a head butt is a good idea with a concussion, but *OMG it worked*!

Ian was right: *Click—lights out, simple biomechanics.*

I can't believe it worked! I set him up for what I needed, and *it worked*!

Thank you, Ian, for *upping my physical therapy goals.*

I huff out a laugh. They should've tied my legs too, but they didn't expect poor little me to be able to use them. Shows to never underestimate your opponent. Speaking of: Gary.

Time to start the second part of my plan.

Gary's crumpled form lies motionless at me feet, but my heart slams against my ribs as if it wanted to remind me we need to start running, we don't have much time.

Tick-tock.

A minute, maybe more? How long does one stay unconscious?

This next part is going to be tricky. I rise on trembling legs, bending my upper body when I stand, inching my bound hands up the chair's high back. My shoulders scream, but I ignore them. Just a bit more, a tad higher—and yes! I pull my arms free.

Thank you again, Ian, this time for getting me out of my self-pity and teaching me I can use my body and trust it.

I jump to the ground, landing securely on both legs, grinning with satisfaction.

Yeah. I need to thank Ian more for this. Much more.

Twenty seconds gone.

I drop to the floor, keeping one eye on Gary's still form. His chest rises and falls steadily, but that doesn't mean anything. He could wake up any moment.

Move faster.

Listening to my own advice, I twist and writhe like a contortionist, forcing my bound hands beneath me. The rope tears at my skin as I drag my body across it. *Thirty seconds.* One leg threads through, then—crap!—the other one catches. Of course, the left one. My pulse spikes. No, no, no! I wrench it free with a desperate heave, and finally have my hands in front of me.

Forty seconds. He could wake at any moment.

With two quick steps, I'm over at the box Gary brought, aka my beacon of hope. *There.* I grab the carpet knife Gary used to pop open the cans, manage to extend the blade with shaking fingers, and sit. Careful now. I trap the knife between my feet, clamping my soles together like a vise.

Don't slip, don't slip, please don't slip...

I won't. Resolve washes over me. I got this. As carefully as possible yet also as fast as possible I rub my bound wrists over the blade. One wrong move, and bye-bye radial artery. I can almost hear DiBiaso's smug voice: *Such a shame about her suicide.*

Heck, no.

Fifty seconds.

My hands tremble as I work the rope against the blade. That's what an overdose of adrenaline will do to you—or maybe fear, because it's taking a small eternity, the fibers parting with agonizing slowness. My lungs burn—oh, right! *Breathe, idiot, breathe!*

Sixty seconds gone. Dad's out there with a sniper's crosshairs on him.

The rope finally snaps with a soft and underwhelming *ping*, and a half-hysterical laugh bubbles up my throat.

I'm free! Remnants of the rope still cling to my bloody wrists, but who cares? I'm free, I can fight!

Speaking of: Gary.

I creep toward Gary's sprawled form. Three feet away, I freeze. What if he's only faking it? My heart thunders in my ears. A trained agent like him would have me down in half a second—

And there is my answer: Unlike me, he doesn't need to fake it to surprise his opponent. In a fair hand-to-hand combat he'd win, no questions asked.

Okay then.

With shaking hands, I pat him down. Feels absolutely weird to touch him like that, but desperate times…

My fingers brush over cold metal. His gun. My stomach cramps. I don't want to take it, but leaving him with the weapon is a mistake that could turn deadly for me—or Dad. I unlock the hook-safety-thing and slide it out of the holster under his arm pit. It feels alien and wrong in my grip. What the heck do I do with it now, besides not pointing the shooty-end at myself?

I keep it in my left hand, arm stretched out and shooty-end pointed away from me. I don't trust that thing.

Pat, pat—there! The keycard!

I breathe a sigh of relief. Finally!

There we go. One key card. One gun. No phone, which sucks, because my phone is gone.

And no time to lose.

I dash to the door, get out of the room, and let it fall into the lock behind me. It clicks with satisfying finality. Gary is trapped, like they tried to trap me. Sorry, not sorry.

Okay, part two of the plan—check. Now I need a way to either contact Ian, or to get out of here, or preferably combine those two. Ian and Dad must be warned. But how?

I blink twice. Thinking is hard with this headache, but at least I still have my brain. Can't complain. The fluorescent lights above buzz mockingly, making my headache spike.

Then it hits me.

Of course! I pump my fist and a grin spreads across my face. The puzzle pieces fit. Every villain needs their lair, right? Where was I when DiBiaso-slash-Gary found me? In the gardens, close to where I ran into the VP once before. He didn't have much time to get me somewhere safe, plus, he needed to be at the fireworks within a short amount of time, he can't just show up the minute they start. That suggests that I was taken somewhere really close. Why should only PRICS have a secret underground lair and an elevator that comes out in the trunk of a tree? I already know there are secret passages out of the Oval Office, like the one they used to get Dad to the Medical Wing after he collapsed from the radiation. It's only logical to think that the VP has access to similar catacombs.

And this hallway, the sterile white walls, the non-descript doors, they could be mirror images of the Eagle's Lair. Same contractor, different evil mastermind, so to speak.

So if this is the VP's lair of underground tunnels… How do I get out?

I compare the left side of the hallway to the right. Nothing is a dead giveaway, soo… I pick the left.

I dart down the hallway, keeping the hand with the gun comically extended and the weapon pointed away from me. It makes for awkward running, but tucking it into my waistband and accidentally shooting myself would make for way more awkward running—or dying—so I'd rather not.

My footsteps echo off the sterile walls. *Faster!* Must run faster! Either I'm going to find the office and entrance that brings me back to the stairwell and connects to the VP's office, or I'll find an elevator. I just hope the exit isn't one of Ian's holographic walls, or I might just run past it and never know it.

I skid around another corner, then—*there*. My heart leaps into my throat. About five meters ahead gleams what can only be elevator doors, super slim and familiar like the ones in the Eagle's Lair.

I dart forward. Slim doors are good, right? Maybe they also lead to a tree, and hopefully not to the VP's conference room or something.

I skid to a stop, ripping Gary's key card form my pocket. Frisking that guy did at least do something good. I swipe his keycard across the reader, and a soft rumble starts somewhere behind the closed doors.

The elevator's coming.

Relief floods me. I'm almost out. Breathe, Alix, breathe…!

The rumbling gets louder—

Oh, crap!

With one quick spin I flatten myself against the wall next to the doors. Who's to say the elevator is going to be empty?

The rumbling stops, the doors slide apart with a squeaky hiss—

Silence.

I whirl around, gun extended like in the movies—empty.

Holy cow.

I exhale with a loud puff. Maybe espionage isn't for me. I was this close to a heart attack.

I breathe another sigh of relief and lower the gun—wait. My gaze falls onto the gap between the elevator cabin and the hallway.

Why not?

I drop to one knee and try to squish the gun through the gap into the elevator shaft, barrel first, in case it discharges. Come on you stupid thing…! It gets stuck after not even three centimeters. Ugh. Typical. Those gaps eat bundles of keys by the dozen, but you can't get them to swallow something you actually want to get rid of.

Okay, Adjusting. That gun needs to go. I can't handle it, so it could be used against me if I got disarmed, and I can't very well run around the White House grounds with a gun in my hands. I'll be shot sooner than I could drop it.

There must be a button for… Gotcha. Not that I'm an expert, but there are only so many options where the release for the magazine could be. As soon as I hold it in my hands, I shove it down the elevator shaft's throat. Ammo? Gone. Alix? Safe.

I let go of a breath I didn't know I held. No more losing time. I leave the rest of the gun behind and jump into the elevator, Gary's card at the ready. Come on, reader, take it…!

The doors close and the elevator rumbles back to life. *Yes!* My left leg buckles a bit from its jolt, but that's it. I can't even let myself think about how fantastic that is, because I have one heck of a task in front of me. *Focus, Alix.*

Within seconds, the cabin slows and I get ready to exit. Aww, darn it—maybe I should've kept the gun until I arrived up here and then gotten rid of it: Who knows where the doors are opening to? So much for playing it smart, genius.

Like a ninja, I press myself against the wall of the elevator, heart pounding. Hiding isn't going to give me much protection, but hopefully at least a little bit.

The doors open with a hiss at the same time the lights snuff out, leaving me in complete and utter darkness.

Crap.

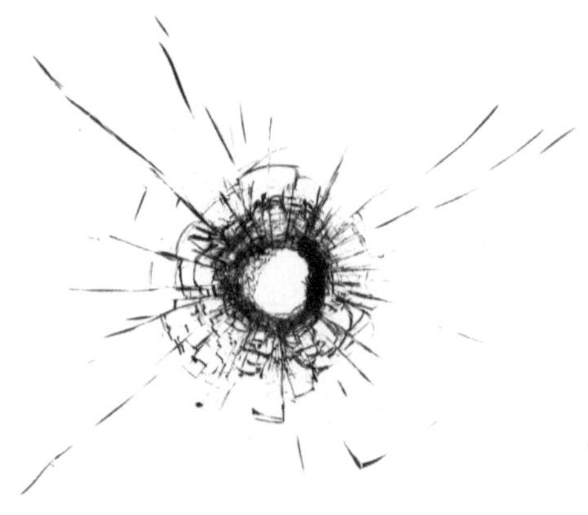

CHAPTER TWENTY-NINE

Fireworks

Like a weighted blanket of about five-hundred pounds the darkness wraps itself around me, choking my throat to the diameter of a straw. Every breath wheezes, although I'm doing my best to keep it quiet.

Anybody there? Anybody…?

Nothing happens.

No voices, no steps, no nothing.

Only pitch-black darkness in front of me, and the slightest whiff of fresh air.

And… the sound of birds? A gust of wind?

Oh, thank whomever—I'm outside!

It takes my eyes several more seconds, but eventually they adjust. I'm surrounded by trees. The gardens, as I hoped.

With one big step I'm out of the elevator, which is housed in a wide, old American Elm, like ours at PRICS. The doors hiss shut behind me, as if they only had waited for me to finally get on with it.

And right they are.

Dad.

Fear freezes every cell in my body: Am I too late already? Did the sniper—

No. No sirens wailing, no helicopters circling: No one has tried to kill Dad. *Yet.* This place would be locked down tighter than Fort Knox otherwise.

Relief washes over me in an intensity unlike anything I've ever felt before.

Dad is still alive.

Let's keep it that way.

Where am I? I whip my heard around, trying to glance anything useful to orient myself. Stupid darkness! Trees and bushes all look the same—

No, wait. Looking back at the Elm tree, something shifts in my brain and I know exactly where I am: On the other side of the White House. The bench I tried to call Ian from is right around the corner. Theory proven: DiBiaso and Gary didn't take me far.

Okay then: Showtime.

I break into a sprint faster than anything I've pulled off in a long time, and not only in the last year. Who cares if somebody sees me running, screw my alibi, this is life or death.

I crash through the manicured gardens like some kind of wild animal. Paths be damned, the shortest connection between two points is always a straight line, and I'm sticking to mine! Branches claw at my face, thorns snag my clothes, but I push through.

Faster, *faster!* The fear of losing Dad, of being too late, acts as rocket fuel. I need to get to him, or at least to a Secret Service agent, so they can lock down the White House and protect Dad—and where the absolute hell is everybody? There should be more agents here, no matter that we went down to Code Green—

Some stupid plant or root trips me, and I stumble, arms flailing. Crap! Can't fall, can't lose time—

Somehow, I stay upright and continue my mad dash toward the South Entrance looming ahead across the vast lawn. My lungs feel like they're filled with broken glass. Something warm and sticky trinkles into my eyes, but I don't dare slowing down and wipe at it. My left leg feels like jelly, but it doesn't buckle, and that's all that counts.

The distant pulse of music and laughter floats around the building's corner. That's good. Voices are good.

I reach the South Entrance, and not even there is a Secret Service agent watching the door. What the—? During an event of this magnitude, with hundreds of visitors? Plus, what about cranking up security once they realized I was missing? No? I don't count?

I slam into the door and yank on the handle—and nothing happens.

It's locked, which explains why no one is guarding it.

"Damn it!" I yell and kick the door. Another couple of seconds gone.

I curse under my breath. My hands shake as I fumble for Gary's key card. If it doesn't work, I'm screwed. Not all agents have access everywhere, as far as I know. It's a definite sign for the lax security tonight that no one comes running after my kick to the door. They must have even scaled down the in-house security.

Please work, please work, please—

The reader blinks green. A soft click reaches my ears like a gift from heaven.

I burst through the door and sprint right. My footsteps echo through the empty halls like gunshots against the polished tiles. Where is everyone?

Should I call Ian? No. No time to stop. Find him, Dad, or an agent. Someone with a radio, an earpiece, something!

Turning one more corner, my classroom door appears ahead, and a wild idea hits me.

Change of plans. Might be riskier, but at this point risk has become my business.

I rip open the door and rush across our classroom toward the fireplace. Thanks to the semi-darkness, the whole room looks spooky, sinister. Fits the mood.

The map of the world nearly tears off its hinges as I wrench it aside and slam my palm against the reader with enough force to sting.

For one heart-stopping moment nothing happens. Then, a soft hum dies and the holographic wall dissolves, revealing the secret staircase beyond.

Move it, Forrester! I duck inside and the hum resumes behind me as I pound up the stairs toward my room, taking two or three at once. The silence in here is deafening—cut off from the party sounds, from any sign that Dad is still alive.

Once I reach the end of the stairs, I slam my hand against the palm reader. The holographic wall poofs out of existence and I stumble through the opening into my room, lungs burning.

I leap back into motion, and dash over toward the door. The voices from the inside of the residence get louder with every step—until they're tuned out by a PA announcement.

"Ladies and Gentlemen! May I present to you: The President of the United States!"

My blood turns to ice as the crowd on the South Lawn starts cheering and clapping.

The countdown to Dad's assassination has just been announced via PA.

I rip open the door and sprint across the center hallway

toward the Yellow Oval Room.

"Now let's get ready to start our annual White House Fourth of July Fireworks!"

Dad will be out on the Truman Balcony by now. *Almost there, almost there, almost—*

"…the National Anthem!"

I burst through the doors into the Yellow Oval Room—which is unfortunately the first room that's not empty at all this evening.

The second I set foot into it, three Secret Service agents are on me, grabbing my arms and shoulders, nearly yanking me off my feet. Pain shoots through my shoulders.

"Miss, no one enters this room!"

"Ma'am, who are you?"

"Post 33-15—we have a runner!"

I thrash against their grip, but it's like fighting stone. Through the windows I see Mom and Dad, dark silhouettes illuminated from behind against the black sky. *So close.*

"Dad! Dad!" My scream tears at my raw throat. Hear me, come on, *hear me!* He tilts his head as if he picked up on *something*, but doesn't look back. The music is too loud.

"Ma'am, stop struggling!" They start dragging me backward and out of the Yellow Oval Room.

No, no, no—not after I came so close!

The Anthem comes to a finish and the audience applauds, cheering some more.

"Everybody please join us. The countdown is on!" the PA announces.

I scream, I fight, I buck and try to shake them off. "Let me go! Someone's going to kill the President!" I catch my reflection in a gilded mirror—blood-streaked face, swollen cheek, rope burned wrists. My hair sticks to my face and neck, and my eyes…

I look like a deer on its way to the hunters' party. Not like the President's daughter.

"*Ten…*"

The agents waste no time. "Condition Red-3, Condition Red-3, we have a breach! All eyes, we have a breach! Aggressor in custody! Repeat: Aggressor in custody!"

"*Eight…*"

Oh my goodness, no, not me! *Not me! I'm not the threat!*

I give it all I got against the strength of the agents hauling me away—away from Dad, away from any chance to save him. Unless—

"You got the wrong one! Sniper! There's a sniper! Let me go! It's not me, you idiots! I'm his daughter! I… *Apteryx! Apteryx!*" The word rips from my throat like a prayer.

As if I had pressed a release button the agents let go and I drop to my knees. The pain barely registers, because Ian's safe word, it worked.

I breathe heavily and push up from my knees. *Please let there still be time.* "Sniper, high ground!" I shout over my shoulder, already sprinting.

From the corner of my eye, I see them talk into their wrist mics while I'm springing into motion.

"*Four…*"

The world narrows to a tunnel as I bolt through the room. Just Dad's silhouette against the night sky. Just the countdown hammering in my skull.

"*Two…*"

My muscles coil as I hit the doorway. No time to yell, no time for anything.

"*One…*"

I launch myself forward like a missile, yet everything moves in slow motion. The distance closes—

"*GO! Happy Fourth of July!*"

Impact. My chest slams into Dad's shoulders, my face cracks against his skull. We spin like in a twisted dance as his body crumples under me and—

WOOSH!

A bullet tears through the air where his head was a heartbeat ago.

Pop! Pop!

Screams rip through the night. We crash to the ground, Dad face-down beneath me. The collision drives every molecule of air from my lungs.

A firework blooms overhead, painting us in red light as the audience's delighted *oohs* morph into terrified shrieks.

Dad struggles underneath me and rolls over on his back as I'm grabbed and dragged off him.

Is there blood, is there—

The balcony erupts into organized chaos as dozens of agents in suits or full black SWAT gear including face masks swarm the balcony.

"AOP! I repeat: AOP. Attack on Principal! Crash the White House!"

"Trailblazer secured, Trailblazer secured."

"337-1-19! Now!"

"AOP! Crash it—*now!*"

"Helicopter 1 through 3, you are a *go*. Repeat, you're a *go!*"

Mom and Dad vanish behind a wall of suited bodies. *They're walking! They're both walking!* Relief floods my system for one brief moment—

Somebody grabs me by the waist and throws me over their shoulder like a sack of potatoes.

"Wait! No! Dad! My—"

I pound my fists against their Kevlar-protected back, but it doesn't slow the agent down. He charges through the mayhem of the Yellow Oval Room, dodging the flood of tactical teams and bomb dogs. Sirens wail, panic spreads below the balcony like wildfire.

"Put me down, I have to——" My voice breaks as the agent sets me down, pushing me against the wall, away from the chaos.

I surge forward. "I need to——"

The agent slams his hands into the wall, one to the left of my head, the other to the right. "Trouble!"

That voice—that hint of spring soap… I freeze. "Ian?"

Green eyes flash behind the tactical mask. "Yeah." He starts to remove his mask, then glances back at the chaos behind us, and leaves it in place. His chest heaves with heavy breaths, his fingers trembling as they brush my hair aside. "What the hell were you thinking?" The words catch in his throat when he finds the gash. "Shit. This is big." There's a near-panic edge to his voice I'm not used to.

He moves with desperate speed, probing my skull, racing his hands down my neck, shoulders, ribs. "Where else? I can't see blood on your dark clothing. Talk to me, Trouble!" Raw fear bleeds into his voice.

"Nothing else," I whisper. "I'm fine." *Ian is here. Ian came.*

He cups my face, thumbs ghosting over my cheekbones. "You're not fine. What. The. Hell. Were. You. Thinking?" His breath is warm as it dances down my cheeks.

"I needed to clear Oliver and Sam." I swallow hard. They didn't do it. It was the VP, Ian. DiBiaso——"

"I know." He tightens his hold of my face, anchoring my gaze to his. I can't see anything else but him, not that I wanted to. My entire world zeroes in on Ian, the green of his eyes, the worry clearly recognizable in them, face mask or not.

Focus, Alix. "You know?" I give the slightest shake of my head.

Wait, but—

"I agreed with you, Trouble. DiBiaso was worth investigating. So I did. Your voice message did the rest. I have men out to arrest him right his very moment."

A wide smile breaks free, and it has nothing to do with finding the true assassin, but everything with the fact that Ian believed me. Believed *in* me—and trusted me. Dad is safe because we both played our part, no matter how close the call. "You got my message." He got it, and he acted on it. Me, knighted. Right there.

Ian cringes. "I barely figured it out in time, but I wish nothing more than having picked up when you called." Pain threads through his voice. "I was already investigating DiBiaso after you left, and—" He closes his eyes, and when they flutter open again, I'm blown away by the raw emotion in them. "You were gone. I thought… I thought I was too late. I—"

Wind rips on the golden curtains draped to the side of the door toward the balcony. The deafening *chop-chop-chop* of a helicopter mixes with a cacophony of voices from the South Lawn.

Ian pauses for a moment, giving my cheekbones one more sweep of his thumbs. "I thought I lost you." It's a whisper, yet it screams at an impossible volume.

My heart does a backflip. *He likes me.* I feel the truth of it in every cell, powered by the way he cradles my face in his hands. By how he looks at me. I feel it in the electricity between us, hear it in what he is and isn't saying.

And I act on it: I bring both my hands up to cover his.

The movement of Ian's thumbs across my cheekbones freezes, and a choked sound escapes him. "Trouble…!"

My turn. This time taking all my courage isn't hard. It comes naturally.

I stroke my thumbs across his knuckles, first in small circles, then wider and wider. His skin feels soft, but strong, different than mine.

The chaos and noise around us fades away—the shouting, the helicopters, the sound of running feet. The lockdown is in full progress. None of it matters.

It doesn't concern us.

None of this does. The world has shrunken down to the two of us, and in this universe of two I have all the courage I need. I peel his hand from my cheek and angle it the slightest bit away from my face. My heart stumbles inside my chest, kicking wildly, as if it wanted to tell me it's now or never.

I turn my head and place the smallest, most gentle kiss on Ian's palm.

The moment my lips connect with his skin, time skids to a halt.

A small gasp escapes him, and it ignites something in my soul. He curls his fingers around mine as he leans forward until our foreheads touch.

We've been close before. Hugged. Trained Krav Maga. But never has it been this intimate. This personal. This connected.

His forehead against mine is heaven. It's us. Us against the world. Us together.

"Trouble," he whispers, voice rough. He squeezes my fingers entwined with his. It feels right. Perfect. Meant to be.

"Ian." Our breath mingles. Where his forehead touches mine, face mask or not, my skin burns. Not that it mattered, because my whole body is on fire from his proximity. Every cell is about to explode, or at least about to light up like a neutron star.

He brings our hands together between us, trapping both of mine under his, massaging them, caressing them. When he speaks, his voice is low. Hoarse. Raspy.

"I'm only going to say this once, and then I'm going to step away." He swallows hard. "In another life, this would go different. We'd be different. In another life, I'd kiss you right now, consequences be damned. But in this one, I can't. You and I… we can't be. You hear me, Trouble? We can't." His voice breaks on the last word, and so does something inside my heart. His hands hold on to mine so hard they might fracture something, and I wouldn't mind. Better the physical pain of a broken bone, than the destructive force of a broken heart.

My next breath is wheezy. "But if—"

"No." He shakes his head, rubbing his forehead across mine. "No *if.* We don't get that." His shoulders move up with his next big breath. "I'm giving us five seconds before I step away and this never happened. Teacher. Student. Colleagues. Nothing more. You hear me, Trouble? Nothing more."

No, no, no. I just found him, we haven't even become an *us* yet! How can we be doomed and done for before we've even had a chance? "It's not fair," I whisper.

I hear the small smile that comes with his next words. "No, it's not. But that's life." He squeezes my hands once more and brushes his thumb over the back of my hand. "Five—"

"I'm sorry I said those things to you. In the classroom." A small sob catches in my throat.

"Four—"

I press closer. *More.* I need more contact, even if it's for no more than a handful of wonderful seconds. "I didn't mean what I said, I—"

"Three—" His voice trembles.

"I don't want to let go, Ian."

But I have to let go. I know that. He knows that.

"Two."

He lifts away, then—through the mask—kisses my nose.

"One."

My heart splits in two as he steps back, gaze locked with mine. For one more precious moment, we exist in our own world, our world of two.

Then he takes a deep beath in: "Medic!" he calls out. "Agent injured! I need a Medic!"

Pop goes the bubble as it bursts around us.

Not even two seconds later, agents appear out of nowhere, all clad in black. They guide me to the floor. "Ms. Forrester, sit down. Sit. Can you hear me? Do you know what date it is today? How many fingers?" Somebody feels around the cut on my forehead, somebody else holds up two fingers in a victory-sign. I can't get them into focus. My body has forgotten how to function. It refuses to acknowledge anything or anybody else besides Ian—Ian, who steps back farther, making room for the onslaught of agents.

"Trouble secured! Repeat, Trouble secured!"

"Medic at the scene! Need backup, come on, come on!"

"Ms. Forrester, again: How many fingers? How many?"

Like insects they swarm around me, feeling my head, my body, wrapping a blood pressure cuff around my arm, and jabbing a needle into me. The Secret Service machine whirls to life around me, patching up my physical wounds.

But my soul… My soul breaks into a million pieces as Ian fades into the crowd of black uniforms, taking a part of me with him I'll never get back.

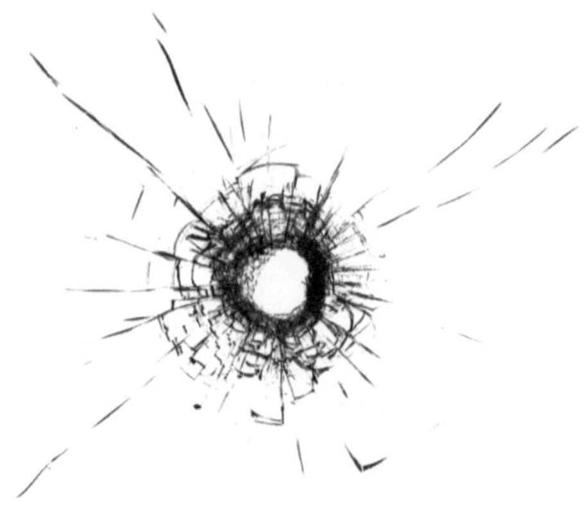

CHAPTER THIRTY

Still Alive

The world is quiet around me and my brain is slow, so agonizingly slow.

It's like coming back from deep sleep, only without the sense of peacefulness. I'm not quite sitting and not quite laying down in something nice and soft, with a faint sterile medical smell and some spring soap mixed in.

Ugh. I'm dizzy, and that's already *before* I've opened my eyes.

A rhythmic beeping noise resounds in my head. I flinch. Ouch. That hurts, too. I groan, and in response, something rustles next to me before I hear a very soft and gentle voice.

"Hey."

It takes me all the strength in the world to open my eyes, and when I finally get it done, everything is uber-bright. *Ow.* Stings in my eyes. After a couple of seconds, my senses adjust to the light and focus on the person sitting in front of me.

Ian.

The moment I recognize him, we both smile. Smiling doesn't hurt.

"Hey," I croak. Wow. Was that my voice?

Ian winces. "Don't stress it, Trouble. You fell asleep again. That's what concussions tend to do to you."

I groan. "Again?" How much can one person sleep after a concussion? As soon as the Secret Service took me out of the Yellow Oval Room's chaos and brought me down to the medical wing, my body went into recovery mode. That was the first time I fell asleep: standing up.

The second time was when Dr. Soong stitched up my laceration, and I can't say I minded being out for that one.

The third time was annoying though, because it made him keep me for observation, heart monitor and frequent neuro-checks included.

The fourth time… is a whole new category, because Ian is here, and that fact alone makes me feel better already.

He's out of his SWAT-attire and back in a suit without a tie, the tightness around his lips the only give-away that the last few hours were anything but routine. No, not true: his eyes are the biggest give-away something has changed between us. His gaze is fixed on me, but even warmer than normal, fired by a serious intensity thanks to those fateful five seconds.

Five seconds.

Something tugs on my insides and makes them melt a little.

Ian shoots a pointed glance at my stitches. "Feeling better?"

"Kind of." Physically, yes. I mean, my head really hurts, and with nothing to distract from it, like, Dad's impeding assassination and stuff, I feel it way worse than right when it happened. But I'll heal.

Ian leans forward in his chair, elbows supporting his weight on his knees. "Your father got briefed. Well, partially."

I cringe. "Oh." That can't be good. "How much does he know?"

"Too much and not enough at the same time. He knows it was you who tackled him, he recognized your voice. Nobody else identified you because of the darkness, the dirt and blood on your face, and the angle of the impact. You were hidden behind his back."

I nod as if I planned it that way. Super-spy. Yup, that's me.

Ian sighs. "Waterhouse has asked him to keep it quiet for now, although I don't know what cover story he's going to come up with for your father." Another sigh, deeper. "Officially, and for anybody else, an anonymous female Secret Service agent protected the President from a bullet to the head. And your cover story is moderately close to the truth: The VP abducted you as his contingency plan—to fake your suicide and get your father to resign."

A shudder runs down my back. Flying into the windshield broke my spine, but DiBiaso's plan would've ruined my brain. At this very moment, I could be in the medical wing in this very same bed on life support or with a flatlining EEG. Brain activity? Not worth mentioning.

Ian lowers his voice. "By the way, as a little get-well gift, I requested authorization to bring you in on Varen, and I got it granted. I know you were frustrated that I didn't follow this lead, and I want you to understand, so that in the future you can maybe trust that I know what I'm doing, at least most of the time." He winks at me and my cheeks heat up, for more than one reason.

"Ian, I—"

"Never mind." He holds up a hand and keeps his voice down when he goes on. "Alix, we know exactly what Varen is up to, because—and this is top secret information—his second-in-command is our guy. He is ours and has been planted in Varen's deepest circles for years. The only thing missing to bring Varen down was proof of what he was up to—he needed to be tagged. Problem was, we couldn't get the technology to our mole to do it, and that's how PRICS came into the picture. But once our sleeper came through, we eventually knew it wasn't Varen this time."

Ugh. I close my eyes. It's very much possible I'm the most ignorant, foolish, and dull-witted person with an IQ of 160. *That's* why he behaved so oddly. Not because of Sam, or me, but because he knew the true reason why it wasn't Varen.

I asked Ian to trust me, and yet I never trusted him. Dimitri was right.

Time to apologize. I sit up straighter in bed, glad I insisted on wearing a White House-issued shirt instead of an open back hospital gown. "I'm sorry I behaved the way I did. I should've trusted you, and not made blind accusations. And while I'm at it, I'm sorry about researching on my own. I understand…" Deep breath. This one's a tough one. "I understand if there are consequences." After all, Ian ordered me to drop it. I didn't.

Ian shakes his head. "No need to apologize for the accusations. I get it. I know where you're coming from, I've been there myself when I started out with the Secret Service and PRICS. Need-to-know-information can make things really complicated." His voice turns serious. "In regards to you going off alone and violating a direct order… It can't happen again, Trouble. Dimitri spoke to Amando, and from his point of view, you guys were only chatting. He was the one who brought up Varen, you didn't ask." He folds his hands. "Officially, you are cleared and all you get is a warning, but you and I, we both know why you were really there. Well played, but still against orders."

That weight falling off my shoulders? It's real. My stomach

muscles unclench and I can breathe again—until Ian lifts his head and his green gaze pins me to the bed.

"All I ask for is that you never do that again, Trouble. Never." The last word is said with an urgency coming close to the tone in his voice when he patted me down in the Yellow Oval Room.

All of a sudden it's pretty hot in here.

"I won't." I drop my gaze to the blanket covering me and smooth it out. Too intense. Too intense for *teacher and student*, because that's all we'll ever be.

Change of topic needed, stat. "So, uhh, how come you were up in the balcony in SWAT gear?" Yes, Ian trained with the Secret Service before Waterhouse assigned him to work with me, but despite his mad skills in Krav Maga, I never thought of him as professionally trained in hand-to-hand combat. I guess the geek-stereotypes sit too deep.

"Long story." He sighs. "Once you took longer than Dimitri gave you, he went to check on you. Obviously, you weren't there, so he assumed you'd gone back to the garage. When he didn't find you there, he notified me, and that's when I checked my phone and heard your voice mail. That plus your accusations against the VP..." He lifts and drops his shoulders. "Couldn't locate your cell either, so probably turned off. I had people out for DiBiaso and was about to inform your father of what happened when you turned up, and—"

I sit up straighter, pulled up by morbid excitement, because I haven't heard the ending of this story yet. "So you did get him? DiBiaso?" Ow, dizzy. Dang it. I fall back into the pillows. "You got him, right? Did he confess?" Please don't tell me he got away.

Ian closes his mouth and nods. A short flicker of *something* crosses his face, gone as fast as it came. "Yes, eventually. Confessed to everything, including framing Sam and Oliver. He'd gotten himself a pretty good alibi, but he obviously didn't take your mad genius into consideration. At first when we confronted him and found your teeth marks on him, he said he ran into you earlier and that you seemed under the influence. Aggressive. Biting him. But once we searched the VP's Lair, we had a willing witness in a very headachy Gary—"

I grimace. "Yeah, about that—"

"He deserved it. Has a mild concussion from your head butt. Not as bad as yours. Believe me when I say he'll take that gladly to be out from underneath DiBiaso's thumb."

"The daughter?" Not difficult to come to that conclusion after I heard DiBiaso threatening Gary.

Ian nods. "I feel sorry for Gary. After all he's been through, DiBiaso exploits him and blackmails him. Well, anyway. We had evidence tying both you and DiBiaso to that jail cell. Biting him and spitting his blood mixed with your saliva on the floor? Great idea, Alix. No, seriously, I mean it. Great idea."

"You noticed." I give a little squee as my cheeks crank up their heat level. I love that Ian gets what I did—right away. My whole plan hinged on hoping DiBiaso would disregard the bloody saliva, a.k.a. his and my DNA, on the floor, being too cocky to cover his tracks and get rid of the evidence.

"Of course I did. Trouble, you're the smartest girl I know—" His cheeks redden, just like mine.

There's an elephant in the room, carrying five little seconds on its back.

Ian clears his throat. "Uhh, anyway. One little safety FYI: Next time you take a gun apart, you might also want to take out the bullet in the chamber."

"Bullet in—"

"The chamber." Ian makes a sliding motion with his hands. "Gary's gun had one shot left. In the chamber."

Crap.

Color drains from my face. What an idiotic mistake. That could've gone *so* wrong. "I—"

Ian holds up a hand. "You couldn't have known. I guess I'll add weaponry to our topics for the next couple of weeks." He winks at me, but it does nothing to lessen the sting of my idiocy. Smartest girl he knows my a—

"Oh, speaking of next few weeks. Judging by the fact that your crutches were leaned against the bench you were kidnapped from and you did a pretty good job taking down your father, I'm assuming your leg is better?" Ian playfully taps my leg but pulls his hand back right away.

My leg. I almost forgot about it. So much happened; so much was more important. I couldn't have done any of it without a functioning leg though. The kicking, the fleeing, the running and jumping. If Ian hadn't fixed me and built me up, I would've failed miserably. A wave of gratitude washes over me.

"Yes," I whisper, "thank you for fixing me. Without my leg working, I would've never pulled any of this off. Thank you for coming up with that chip. Thank you for training me more than you were officially allowed to. And most of all, thank you for—"

His gaze crashes into mine, bright and sparkling like two emerald gems.

Thank you for those five seconds.

Neither of us says anything. With words, that is. The hint of a smile plays with the corners of his lips, and to anyone who saw us, we'd be nothing but two people looking at each other. But we're more.

So much more.

Shivers dance across my skin as I'm locked into Ian's gaze. That connection… it occupies ninety percent of my brain's activity, and about ninety-nine of my heart's.

I wish he'd sit on the corner of my bed and hug me.

I wish I was older.

I wish we were like any boy and girl meeting anywhere but in here, the White House.

As if he could read my thoughts, Ian's smile turns kind of sad and he shakes his head. "No, Trouble."

I sit up and reach for him. "But—"

He captures my hand with one of his and holds on to it.

Neither of us moves.

Our connected hands hover between us like a bridge we have to tear down.

His throat works on a slow swallow—and he leans forward, bringing his lips to my knuckles.

The moment they touch my skin, one of those electricity surges shoots through me, of the kind that energize every cell and light up every neuron.

The heart rate monitor speeds up its beeping from normal pace to rabbit-speed.

Ian's smile widens. I literally put my heart on display for him, not that it wasn't obvious before. "Ian—"

He lowers my hand and covers it with his. "Trouble—" Ian sighs and whispers, "Teacher. Student. Nothing more. Five seconds." His fingers close around mine once more before he lets go of me. The moment he does, my hand feels cold, like something was missing without his touch.

Silence hovers, charged by the last minutes and the choices that will never be made.

Five seconds aren't enough. They can't be.

The door thunders with three quick knocks—then crashes open before the echo fades. A Secret Service agent materializes in the doorway, his practiced gaze mapping out the room and taking in every detail.

"Clear," he announces via his sleeve microphone, and stands

with his back to the wall.

Two seconds later, footsteps approach, and Dad walks in.

The instant Ian and I recognize it's him, two things happen:

One, Ian jumps off his chair and to attention next to it.

Two, I all but choke on my own spit and start coughing like crazy, wincing from the pain inside my skull.

Ian's gaze darts from me to Dad and back, torn between wanting to pat my back but also by not wanting to get too close to me with my dad in the room.

Luckily for everybody involved I catch my breath after two or three seconds, just in time for me to see Dad dismissing his Secret Service agent with a nod and a hand wave.

And… I blink, then blink again. There's a smile on his face; the relaxed kind I haven't seen in at least a year, and he looks… good. Still with dark circles under his eyes and kind of pasty, but a lot better than when I last saw him.

Ian shoots one more glance in my direction, but then focuses on Dad. "Mr. President."

Dad stops at the end of my bed, lays one hand on top of my foot under the blanket, and… squeezes it once?

Is that really happening?

Holy cow.

All those strange, warm and fuzzy feelings…!

Dad turns toward Ian and releases my foot. His smile cools the slightest bit. "Mr. Miller. Good to see you again. Or should I rather call you by a different name, if my assumptions are correct?" He holds out a hand, and for the tiniest moment, Ian hesitates before he gets himself back under control and shakes it.

"Actually, Mr. President, if you don't mind, Mr. Miller, or Jason, will do just fine for now." Ian's brows furrow just the slightest bit.

Dad gives Ian's hand another slow, controlled shake. "Fine

with me. Let's keep it at that. Before I politely kick you out of the room so that I can have an overdue heart-to-heart with my daughter, I would like to thank you." A muscle in his temple twitches once. "If I'm not mistaken, it was you who got Alix to where she is now, and… while I might not have had the most open-minded attitude toward you, I can see what you have done for her, especially during *physical therapy*. Thank you."

I'm about to stroke out, for more than one reason.

Ian nervously tousles his hair. "Uhh, thank you, Mr. President. Alix's been the best student the White House Teaching Program has had to date."

Typical Ian. Quick recovery. He's so much better at this than me.

Dad chuckles once. "That's what I expected of her. But now, if you don't mind…" He doesn't need to finish the sentence; Ian knows exactly what he means.

"Of course not, Mr. President." He gives Dad a short nod, then looks at me, waiting. I can't explain what exactly I'm feeling for Ian right in this moment, only that it somehow makes me complete that he knows me well enough to not just leave when the President asks him to. He cares.

For me.

Whatever distance I put between us by my own stupidity, Ian bridged single-handedly.

I give him a short smile and nod. I'll be all right.

Ian's stance softens as he reads me. He gives me one last look—the kind that speaks louder than words—before slipping out and gently closing the door behind him.

And just like that I'm alone with Dad, something that hasn't happened in almost a year.

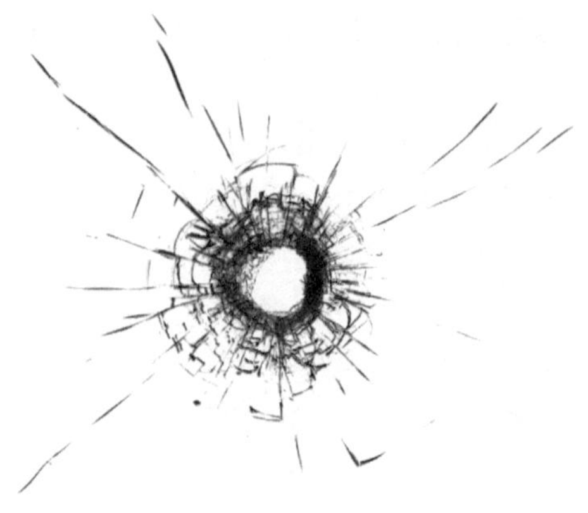

CHAPTER THIRTY-ONE

Reset

Dad watches Ian leave, a pensive expression on his face, brows furrowed. Only when Ian closes the door behind him does he shake his head and turn toward me.

He doesn't even ask, but pulls Ian's chair closer and sits down, leaning back like he owned the room. Guess that's something that comes with the job description as the President.

There's a moment of silence between us while we look at each other, neither of us saying anything. Should I start? I mean, I already did my fair share of trying that over the last couple of months.

After half a minute, he gives me a sad smile and sighs. "Alix, I don't know how and where to begin." He leans forward and looks me in the eye. "There's so much to talk about, and it's all complicated."

Sounds like a description of my life over the last year or so. Yeah, I get it, life as the President is probably a million times more complicated than mine, but just stop messing with me! *Talk*, for crying out loud!

I cross my arms in front of my chest, and the first thought coming to my mind bursts out of me. "Do you think you can look at me now with something else than pity in your eyes? Because, I'm not as broken as you think I am? You know, since I saved you and all?"

There.

I refuse to lower my gaze. Not anymore. I'm stronger than that. No. More. Tears.

Dad's eyes widen and his mouth drops open. "*Broken?* Alix, I—"

Ugh. "Come on, Dad! I saved you from a sniper, I think I deserve a little honesty."

"I'd never—"

"Just say it. Get it over wi—"

He slaps his thigh, hard. "Geez, Alix, will you stop? That's *not* what I think of you! At all! Never have and never will!" He glares at me, shaking his head for emphasis, and it feels… genuine.

Dad's smooth in phrasing things politically correct and in bending the truth. Ian would've had a blast with him. That reaction, the anger and bewilderment, means we moved beyond the political and into the private, and I'm talking to my *dad*, not to a politician.

It's a start. I force down a swallow and keep my head high. "Okay. Then what's been going on? Because from my end…" Now I can't help my voice cracking once. "… from my end, it sure looked like I could do no right."

Dad stares at me with his mouth open before he shakes his head and buries his face in his hands, taking a shaky breath. "No, Alix. *Never.* Don't you ever think that. I…" He drops his hands from his face and covers my right hand on the blanket with his, sighing deeply. "Listen, this… this isn't easy for me."

I open my mouth, but Dad holds up a hand. "Wait. I know it wasn't—and isn't—for you either, but that's what I'm talking about." He leans forward, supporting his upper body with his elbows on his knees, my hand folded into his. "Right after your accident, I was ready to drop out of the race. It was clear you'd need months or even years to recover, and I didn't think a father who wasn't there for you would be beneficial. I talked it through with Oliver and DiBiaso, and after a while, both supported me dropping out. My head wasn't in the game, and how could it have been?" He slowly shakes his head. "A day or two before I wanted to announce quitting, one of my personal Secret Service agents came to my office. He made a big deal about checking for listening devices and even after that, we mainly communicated in whispers while Spotify was blaring."

For a second, his eyes drift to the stitches under my hairline and his jaw tightens. Then, he forces it loose and continues his story. "Alix, I don't know how to say it. Your accident… wasn't an accident. The belt was tampered with. It was supposed to tear. Somebody…" His eyes close. "Somebody tried to kill you."

Holy everything! My jaw drops. "You… you knew?" *He knew* it wasn't an accident? He knew? All these months, and he *knew* somebody tried to kill me?

Dad looks at me, brows pulled tight. "Wait—you know?"

I roll my eyes. "At this point, yes, I do, but please continue: You knew?"

He opens his mouth, then snaps it shut, swallows once and nods. "Yes, I knew. That's why I took you out of Harvard. That's why I wanted you in the boarding school, or here instead, closer—"

Ohh wait a moment! I grip my blanket and roll it into my fist. "You *knew* and you didn't tell me? Did you ever think that maybe I should've known somebody tried to kill me and that someone was still out—"

"*Nobody* knew, Alix!" The words explode from him. "Not even Mom! The Secret Service was sure this was aimed at me, and you were a means to an end. It looked like somebody wanted me to leave the campaign! It was personal, and you weren't the primary target. *I* was, which is why—"

I bounce off my pillows and sit up straight, steel in my spine. "Which is why, what? Why you treated me like a delicate flower, like I was too fragile to handle the truth? Or *life?*" I shove my balled fists into the mattress or else I'm not sure what I would do with them. "Did you ever think what effect that would have on me? How much that would hurt? I thought you were ashamed of your broken daughter! I could've handled it, Dad!" Better than I did his rejection. His babying.

Dad presses his lips into a tight line. "Don't you ever say those two words again, Alix Forrester. You are not my *broken daughter*, and I am *not* ashamed of you!"

I huff. "Right." So obvious. *Not.*

"Yes, *right!*" He pauses. "I was ashamed of myself, Alix. Myself! Never you. I'm your dad, I'm supposed to protect you, and because of me…" He bites his lower lip and shakes his head. "Because of me you were in that wheelchair! *I* took that from you! Every day since the accident I've blamed myself. Had I picked you up as planned, your accident would never have happened. Would something else have? Maybe. But you wouldn't have nearly died because of me! Every time I saw the wheelchair or the crutches, I saw my own failure to protect you."

The words knock the air from my lungs.

He truly blames himself, like Sam said he did. My voice breaks. "None of it happened because of you, Dad. It happened because of DiBiaso." I can blame Dad for a lot of things, but this wasn't his fault.

Dad growls. "Yeah. DiBiaso. That was… unexpected."

No kidding. "Dad? You could've told me about the accident. How you felt. It would've made a difference." All the difference, actually.

He pauses and leans back in his chair, rubbing his palms over his thighs. "To be honest, I tried, Alix. I tried to tell you. A couple of times. You wouldn't listen though, and then—"

"When was that supposed to be?" The words come out sharper than intended, but I can't help it.

Dad gives me an arched eyebrow. "Once before dinner. That didn't go so well, and I ended up giving you goals for your classes with Mr. Miller instead. Then again when you came into the Oval Office when the camera crew was there."

Oh.

Oh.

I remember. He said he wanted to talk and I… "I thought you wanted to chew me out again for something." I cringe.

A small smile graces Dad's lips. "Not this time, Alix. But anyway… then I finally wanted to let you know the day I collapsed—"

One and one equals… oh. "The lunch meeting? With Waterhouse?"

"Correct. He knew more of the details of your quote-unquote accident, and he would've briefed Mr. Miller afterwards with the necessary details."

A small laugh gurgles from my throat, relieved from the weight that had been holding it in. And here I thought it was about Ian and me in trouble. Darn jumping to conclusions, seriously.

Dad looks at me curious. "Well, but anyway, here's something else for you to know. I wanted you to come to the

White House."

I raise an eyebrow. Somehow I remember that differently. "Not the boarding school?"

"Well, at first. But then I heard rumors. People talk. There are hints and winks, sentences left open full of implications. I heard that if I became the President, there might be a secret organization that would keep you safe. Your very own branch of the Secret Service. Dedicated to you as the First Daughter."

I don't breathe; I don't move.

Holy cow, Dad truly figured out about PRICS on his own? What do I say? What do I not say?

Dad scratches his neck. "Rumor had it they would keep an eye on you and even train you to recognize dangerous situations. My hope was that this organization truly existed and would take you under its wing. Keep you safe. So yes, I trusted your life on a *rumor*, because I didn't know what else to do." He huffs out a laugh. "Crazy, right? I doubled my efforts to be elected President, so you could get *the* best protection from this unknown enemy, in case the Secret Service was wrong, and you were still a target."

He takes my hands between his, regret shining from his eyes. "And here I was thinking you'd be safer at the White House, and instead I brought you right into the lion's den." He pauses and gives my hands a squeeze.

I shake my head. "I'm okay being in the lion's den if it means you're not dead, Dad."

Something flashes in his eyes. "I don't want to hear that ever again, Alix. Ever. I'd gladly take a bullet if that meant you're safe! Gladly! Nothing is worse than seeing your child hurt, nothing besides knowing it was your fault. And it was mine. Everything. If I hadn't run for the presidency, you'd never have become a target. You'd be walking. Every time I saw you in your wheelchair, it was a punch to the gut. My fault. You have to understand how guilty I felt—how guilty I still feel. And then I take a step forward, hope for this organization to be there—"

I make a spur-of-the-moment decision. "PRICS. They're called PRICS." What the hell, he figured it out on his own anyway.

He whips his gaze up to meet mine, a slow smile pulling at the corners of his lips. "They exist?"

"They do." I nod. "They're called PRICS."

"PRICS?" The smile widens, and I nod once more, before Dad chuckles. "How fitting." "Anyway. I was hoping for this organization to be there and keep you safe, and then I see you out and about. Alone. Not in class. Not protected." He counts off his fingers. "The Colonnades. At the Oval Office—"

"Dad!" I sit up straight in bed, never minding the pull of the tubes and cables on my chest. "That was all for PRICS! Dimitri was never far away and—"

"Well, I couldn't have known that, could I? All I saw was you out and unprotected and at risk." He reaches for my hand again, but hesitates ever so slightly before he takes it. "I'm sorry I didn't talk to you sooner. I'm sorry I hurt you, I'm sorry I didn't see what I was doing to you. My only apology is that I wanted what was best for you, and that… well, frankly I was overwhelmed with what happened. I don't mind handling a crisis in Eastern Europe, or whatever, but this… Too close to home." His gaze meets mine, serious. "And just to be clear about that: you *are* welcome in the Oval Office. Anytime. The timing was inconvenient with the camera crew. You don't want to know how much manpower it takes to keep press about you under control. And I… uhh, one could say I lost it a little bit when I saw you approaching Varen. I'm assuming now in retrospect it was for PRICS?"

I nod.

Dad rolls his eyes. "Well, I wanted to rip that guy's face off.

I didn't want my daughter anywhere near that bastard's radar, Secret Service protection or not. So yes, I'm sorry about that. I behaved like an ass."

A laugh bursts free from my throat, and it feels heavenly. "No, you didn't just say that!"

Dad's light, free chuckle gives me wings. Paternal protection. Nothing else.

The revelation floors me.

I spent the last year mentally distancing myself from Dad to avoid the pain that came with his rejections, and it was all to *protect* me, to keep me safe.

The shackles burst off my wings and I take flight. "You're not disappointed in me." I have to say it out loud, because… it's hard to believe after I indoctrinated myself for the last months that Dad couldn't stand me.

Dad grins—he actually *grins*. "Alix, whatever you do, I'm proud of you. You don't have to do anything to impress me, because from where I'm coming, you're perfect."

I'm weightless and flying, the love radiating off Dad picking me up like a gust of wind and making me soar. If it wasn't for the slight steady pulsing pain inside my head, I'd have to pinch myself to make sure I'm awake, because Dad… Dad is giving me everything I've yearned for over the last year.

He clears his throat. "And now that DiBiaso is under lock and key, we can get you to Harvard, and you can work on your PhD. Remember how we always said you wanted to be the youngest—"

I crash right back onto the hard ground of reality. "Dad?" I squeeze his hand once, and his tightens around mine in response.

"Yes?"

"I don't want to go to Harvard."

Confusion flickers across his face. "This year?"

I shrug. "For now. I'm happy where I am. With my family. With PRICS."

The confusion turns into skepticism. "You're not going to stay with them. There's no need. You're safe, you—"

I let go of his hand and lift both my palms up. "Hold on, Dad. I *will* stay with them. It's what I signed up—"

"Alix, you almost got your brain destroyed! What's so difficult to understand about that? You could've died, and why? Because you're meddling in stuff you shouldn't—"

Oh, hell to the no! "Yes, bad stuff happened to me, yet here I am! And for emphasis, if I hadn't been there, you'd have gotten shot! So yes, sue me, I'd do it all over if it kept you alive! You said the same thing vice versa! And don't start again with that you-can't-do-this-crap, cause I've had enough of it over the last year!"

Dad slowly closes his mouth.

But I'm not done. Not by a long shot. "I'm telling you, I will not leave PRICS. Ian—Jason Miller—is the reason I can walk again and jump and tackle you, in case you didn't notice. PRICS is the reason I don't feel like a failure anymore! I don't want to give that up, and I won't!" The moment I say it out loud, I know it's true. I couldn't leave Ian or PRICS even if I wanted to, and I wouldn't even if Dad tried to make me.

"But—"

I hold up my palm. "No. This is how it's going to be. I'm going to stay with PRICS, and I want more duties. We're an important branch of the Secret Service, and we can do our part to keep you safe. To keep *us* safe. I want you to talk to Waterhouse and make sure Ian stays my partner, and that we're allowed more active missions."

Dad cringes. "Alix—"

"I'm not talking dangerous things, Dad! I'm talking stuff where I can help you. Like putting a tracker in Varen. I *want* to do that. Ian is challenging me more than I have been in ages. More than Harvard would. And we can work on credits from here, like we have already." It won't delay my PhD by much, and if it did, who cares: This here, this is the opportunity of a lifetime.

And I won't leave Ian.

Dad groans. "You're asking me to put you in danger."

"No. I'm asking you to put your faith in me like you should've done over the last year. Like you should've done the moment you knew my accident was anything but." Low blow, but necessary. "And I'm asking you to trust me and Ian that we know what we're doing."

That shoots his eyebrows up to his hairline. "Trust you and… Ian."

I nod so hard, my headache spikes up. "Mr. *Jason Miller*. Correct."

"Your… partner." A muscle in his temple twitches.

Oh, for crying out loud. Not again. "As in *my fellow agent*, Dad! Nothing else." A swarm of butterflies lifts up inside my stomach, calling me a liar.

Dad massages his temples and groans. "You're asking me to take two steps at once, and—" His shoulders heave up with a big, silent breath. "Alix, we've had this conversation before, and I don't want to repeat myself, but… I can't exactly say I'm comfortable with you and him working that close—"

"Dad!" Gosh, that makes me angry! *Five seconds* was all I got, and Dad doesn't even know about that! *Five freakin' seconds*, because I'm too young by a few precious months, and because he is my teacher. Which… he isn't. Not really.

Oh.

I sit up straighter. "And you know he isn't my teacher, right? We're colleagues." No need to mention he's my superior officer. "We're colleagues, and we can work together like professionals."

Dad cringes. "Alix, somebody your age—"

"Nu-uh. Don't even go there, Dad."

He sighs with the weight of paternal discomfort behind it. "How can I convince you not to stay with PRICS?"

"You can't."

"I can send you to Harvard. To boarding school. Somewhere."

My stomach tightens. "If you don't want to ever talk to me again, you can."

He lets his head fall down to his chest. "Alix—"

"Dad." I lean forward and reach out for his knee. "Believe in me and trust in me. I can do this. I *want* to do this. Ian is the last person to place me in danger, and you know me. Believe in me. Trust me." That's all I ask. Not much, yet it's everything.

I can practically see the gears turning inside his head. All that's missing is some steam coming from his ears.

"Okay. *Okay.*" Dad slaps his thighs and sits up straight. "Okay, Alix. Under certain conditions. I'll need to talk to Mr. Miller—Ian. And to Waterhouse. I need clear guidelines, or else I won't be able to sleep for the remainder of my term, for more reasons than one. But if that's what it takes for us…" His eyes brighten as he looks at me, although a bit of trepidation stays. "If that's what you want to do, I trust you. I believe in you, Alix."

He believes in me.

My eyes begin to sting. After a year of crappiness, those few words are a Band-Aid for my soul. "Dad." My voice cracks at the last second.

Dad surges forward and gathers me into his arms, wrapping me in a hug so fierce, it steals my breath. I cling to him, digging my fingers into his shoulders. He feels like childhood, like home, like safety, and all these feelings only drive home how much I've missed him—so much, I didn't even let myself realize how much it was.

I hold on to him and breathe in his Dad-scent.

I don't care what happens next.

I'm home.

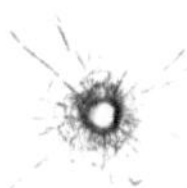

We stay like this for a long while.

When we pull apart, his eyes are moist, and boy, if that didn't make me all emotional again: He cares.

Dad squeezes my shoulders, his warm gaze gliding over me. "By the way, nice moves tackling me. I didn't know what hit me, at least at first."

I grin. "Thank you. You were my first tackle, but I think I did okay." Although I'd also be okay never ever repeating it.

Dad's blinks several times in a row. "That you can walk again…"

My cheeks heat up and I drop my gaze. Too much emotion in that one sentence. "Uh, Ian did that. Ian's treatment idea."

He ignores my comment. "And I haven't said it yet: Thank you for saving my life out there. But please, no matter what happens with PRICS, if you ever put mine or anybody else's life over yours, even to save that person, I will personally lock you into your room and ground you for eternity. Is that clear?" He looks at me sternly, but there's that twinkle, alive and dancing around in his eyes. I know what he's saying though. Anything iffy and he'll pull me from PRICS.

Still, I answer with a smile and fake salute. I have absolutely no intention to put myself in true danger. Work smarter, not harder, or, uhh, safety first, prevents the worst? Okay, crappy rhyme, but still. "Yes, sir, Mr. President. No more bullets. That's fine with me." I give him a second mock salute, and he playfully salutes back.

There's a knock at the door, and his smile is getting even wider. "I think my surprise for you might be here." He turns toward the door. "Come in!"

The door opens and the Secret Service agent from before walks in. "We'd be ready then, sir."

Dad gets up and straightens out his suit jacket. "All right then. I'll be on my way—but don't even think you'll have peace and quiet. I'll be back later today to check on you." He squeezes my hand and bends down to kiss my forehead. I close my eyes and enjoy this moment.

When he straightens up, he nods to the agent. "Bring him in."

The agent speaks into his microphone. It's too soft for me to hear, but after he finishes, steps approach, and another person comes in.

I'd know that outline anywhere.

"Sam." I only get out a whisper.

Sam.

My heart drops and meets the knots forming in my stomach.

Sam with his chocolate wavy hair, his bright and warm light brown eyes.

Sam, who's looking unbelievably smart in his suit.

Sam who kissed me.

Sam, who doesn't know about those *five seconds*.

Sam who made me chase a killer all by myself.

Sam.

He wiggles his eyebrows and waves at me, but first shakes hands with Dad. "Mr. President."

"Sam. Can't tell you how glad I am you and your dad are back."

Sam stuffs his hands in his pockets—a typical Sam-gesture.

"Yeah, me too. Probably even more than you." He smirks.

Dad laughs and claps Sam's shoulder. "Most likely, yes. All right, I'll give you two some time. But don't slack off, Sam. I expect you back in the office and ready to rock 'n roll later today." He holds out his fist, and Sam bumps it. I don't think his grin could get any broader.

"Sure thing, Mr. President."

Dad bends down to kiss my cheek. "Go for it, baby girl," he whispers into my ear. "Can't set up dinner for the two of you every week." He winks and blows me a kiss before he leaves, the Secret Service agents following him.

Now wait a second, set up dinner for—

The door closes and I'm alone with Sam.

I don't know how he makes it over to the side of my bed so quickly, but I only blink once and there he is, sitting next to me.

Uhh, awkward.

Neither of us knows how to react once he sits next to me. For a second, I think he wants to hold my hand, but he doesn't go for it, and I'm frozen in my bed. Still haven't processed Dad's words, and nope, I don't need to be a genius to read his intentions. Dad is trying to set me up with Sam.

Once more, for emphasis: *Dad is trying to set me up with Sam.*

I smooth out my blanket again, only to do something with my hands. Doesn't happen often, but I'm at a serious loss for words. I don't know where to start. *Glad you're back* doesn't really cover it. *Things have gotten weird all around* would be better, but still doesn't do it. After a moment, I notice Sam's looking right at me. His eyes are so big and warm, heat rushes to my face. His oh-so-pleasant Sam-scent is wafting over to me and it makes my insides tingle, no matter those five seconds.

I guess a crush this big isn't undone by the flick of a switch.

"You got hurt."

Although he's sitting right next to me, I have a hard time hearing him, that's how calm and soft his voice is.

"Yes," is all I can come up with, because, heck, I don't know how much Sam knows and what I can tell him.

"Crazy days, huh?"

"Yeah. Totally." *Cringe.*

A small smile creeps up the corners of his mouth, but he hesitates. "You… You know that your dad… he talked to me?"

"Huh?"

Sam huffs out a laugh and glides one hand through his hair. "Yeah. Twice actually. First a couple of months ago. Told me to keep my hands to myself." His cheeks turn red, and so do mine.

"He… *what?*" No, he didn't. Who does that? And if he did, why now have Sam—

Sam nods. "Yup. So, I did keep my hands to myself. President's orders, right? But then… stuff happened, and next thing I know he takes me aside and tells me…" He closes his eyes, chews on the inside of his lips and shrugs once before he opens his eyes again. "He tells me that if you were interested, I'd have his blessing. If I was responsible." He laughs out once, shaky. "Weird conversation, I can tell you."

I'm at a loss for words. I was right. Dad… is trying to hook me up with Sam. Has been, for a while? Something hardens inside of me. "When was that?"

"That day you and him didn't get along during dinner." He keeps on talking about that evening, but I don't listen. Oh, I remember just fine: Dad chewing me out for using Ian's fake-first name, telling me I was in too deep already. Giving me goals to uphold, so I don't get distracted by Mr. Miller.

Sam scoots closer. "So, since we didn't get to talk much since… Do you… do you want to pick up again where we left off?" A slow, mischievous grin spreads across his face.

"Rephrasing. Do you want to be *not* responsible with me?"

Do I…? Oh my God.

A week ago, he would've gotten a wholehearted yes. The same two days ago.

But ever since our kiss—

No. Ever since I let myself believe Ian was an option. Since the five seconds that changed everything.

Since then the world doesn't only consist of Sam—but yet it does, because from where I'm standing, Ian might as well be in another universe.

Sam leans forward and drops his voice to a whisper. "You know what else your dad said? And I really think that flu got to him more than he lets on, but… He said he needed me to keep you out of trouble." He chuckles once. "As if you'd ever be trouble."

Trouble.

I *am* Trouble.

But not to Sam.

Only to Ian.

And maybe to Dad, but then with a lower-case t.

I don't know what to say. I don't know how to handle either of it: Sam. Ian. Dad. The chaos they cause for me, the turmoil of emotions—conflicting ones, contradicting ones, ugly ones.

Beautiful ones.

My crush on Sam's been epic since forever, and now that it finally is working out, it feels… forced. Forced by circumstance, by law, by paternal… *protection*.

But come on, it shouldn't feel forced. Not at all.

Ian and I, we're not together. Will never be together. And being together with Sam is not *wrong*.

I'm. Not. Doing. Anything. Wrong.

"Hey." Sam reaches for my hand, turns it over and slides his fingers in-between mine.

The heart monitor's rhythmic beeping cranks it up a notch to Salsa-rhythm. Seriously, Dr. Soong's over precaution is not doing me any favors here.

I grunt in annoyance and grab the cables coming from my chest without taking my eyes off Sam as I yank them from my skin, suppressing a tiny wince when the sticky pads protest their forceful removal. They held better than I thought.

The machine gives off a couple of even more annoying beeps, but then seems to realize the cables are no longer attached to any patient and shuts up. Thank you.

Sam smirks. "Treacherous equipment." He leans forward a little, waiting. "You okay?" he gently asks, gaze bouncing over my face.

I put on a quick smile. "Yeah. Yeah. I just… The last day was a lot to deal with."

Decision time.

I give his hand a squeeze. "Can we… like, take it slow?"

Something lights up in his eyes. "How slow would you like it?" Sam tilts his head to the side, inching his mouth forward until his lips brush the corner of mine. An onslaught of sensations whips through me. He brings his hand to cup my chin, thumb ever so slightly brushing my skin, adding fuel to the fire. My body vibrates from head to toe, then settles with a sudden heaviness.

For the second time in my life, Sam presses his lips against mine. He kisses me like he's savoring every moment, but unlike last time, my mind doesn't go blank. No, it stays crystal clear—clear enough to remember that in what I thought were my final moments, every single thought was of Ian.

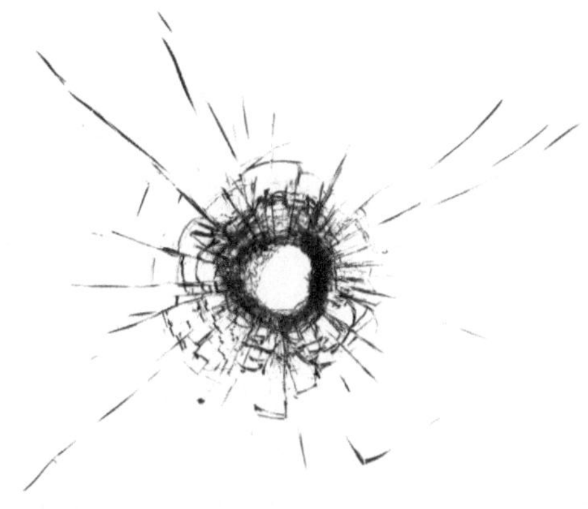

CHAPTER THIRTY-TWO

Routine Again

Getting out of the Medical Wing is more of a challenge than I thought it was.

Turns out Dr. Soong is rather conservative when it comes to concussions and my brain, and well, can't say I mind that. I've kind of grown fond of that marble of mine. Plus, I don't have time to get bored, because either Dad, Ian, or Sam are there basically any time of the day. Mom too, and even Linda makes it in two or three times, although she doesn't like to come to the White House if she can help it.

This morning, Sam has snuck in from work. It feels forbidden, although Dad's been knowingly ignoring Sam's frequent absences from his desk.

Rephrasing: Dad has been *encouraging* Sam's frequent absences from his desk.

At the moment, he's on my bed, his knee on my mattress so his dress pants ride up above his socks. Scant inches separate our faces—scant inches I could bet are going to be annihilated pretty soon.

I reach up and fumble for the top buttons of Sam's dress shirt under his tie, popping open the upper three.

Sam's eyes twinkle like stars on a clear night. "Feeling bold today, my lady?"

Well. Yes. Somewhat. My cheeks start flaming and I nod as I brush my fingers across the skin I uncovered. So soft.

"Mmh, me likey." Sam leans forward the slightest bit, his lips caressing mine, nibbling on my lower lip. I flatten my hand on his chest and he groans into my mouth, and boy, if that didn't overload my senses.

"Is this a bad time?"

Like doused in cold water, Sam and I jerk apart.

"Because I can surely come back and start class later."

Ian.

Ian's got a bookbag under his arm and something akin to a smile on his face, green eyes blank and trained to somewhere next to my head.

That look, it shoots straight into my heart and *boom*, out the back. Clear through-and-through.

Sam's face burns dark crimson. "Uhh, sorry, Mr. Miller." He leaps to his feet, straightening his jacket and buttoning his shirt up. "We—"

Ian waves his hand, dismissing him. "Don't worry about it. And call me Jason, please."

Sam's crimson turns even deeper. "Sure. Uhh, thanks, Jason. I… I think I need to get going then." He hesitates but bends down and gives me a quick peck on my cheek. "I'll see you later," he whispers, before he's out the door as fast as humanly possible.

Which leaves me alone with Ian.

Which also shouldn't be a big deal, only… only it is.

I pull my blanket up higher, willing time to go back and undo the last minute. Why couldn't he have knocked, or—

Ian clears his throat. "So. You and Sam, huh?"

He hasn't moved from the foot of my bed. Not an inch.

I can't get myself to meet his gaze, like he caught me doing something wrong. Which I didn't.

I'm not with Ian.

I'm not.

"Yeah," I whisper. "Dad, he…" Dad what? Wanted me together with Sam? Wanted me away from Ian? How pathetic can I be using Dad as an excuse?

Ian shakes his head and clears his throat again. "No need to explain, Trouble. He's your age. You like him and he obviously likes you. This is between the two of you."

Between me and Sam—but is it? Isn't it also between me and Dad, between me and Ian? Between Dad and Ian? My gaze flies up to his. His face is neutral, with a little bit of something else mixed in. Disappointment? Sadness? "But—"

"No." A small sad smile crosses his face. His voice drops to a whisper. "Remember, it never happened."

It never happened.

Us.

Our five seconds.

We never happened.

And by the looks of it, we never will.

"Ian—"

Ian pulls the chair closer to the edge of my bed and rubs his palms together as he takes a seat. "Nope. Work. I wanted to update you. I spoke to your father."

"You saw Dad?" I'm sitting ramrod straight in my bed like propelled forward by rocket boosters. "What did he say? Are we a go?" Only because that news is huge do I let Ian get away with changing the topic. And, well, maybe also because… it's awkward. The whole Sam-Ian-thing… It feels like a betrayal that has no ground to stand on, because I'm doing nothing wrong.

Nothing. Wrong.

Right?

Ian gives me a thumbs up. "Yes. We're a go."

I ball my hands to fists and pump them in the air. "Awesome! I knew he'd stick to it!"

Ian laughs once and it chases away the tension. "Yes, he did, but he sure went over our job description with a fine comb. Plus, I'm pretty sure there were a couple of death threats at me hidden in his demands today. That man is very protective of you, Trouble." He reaches out to pat my leg, but withdraws his hand, instead scratching his head. "So yes, we're active, and more independent from Waterhouse."

And I can't say that's a downside. Would've been difficult to pull off if he hadn't dug his own grave there by completely ignoring my accusations against DiBiaso. Ian came around and did his research. Waterhouse didn't.

"And speaking of active." Ian taps my braced leg once, but withdraws it faster than a lightning strike. "We're dropping the crutches. The—"

"Yes!" I drum an excited staccato-rhythm onto my blanket. "No more crutches! Can I—"

"Nope." Ian holds up a hand. "The brace stays on for a while longer. Can't have you go from zero to a hundred in no time. Slow advancement, Trouble. Your father will have Jenna Altman include a one-liner about your improvement in one of the next briefings, and we'll take it from there. Dr. Soong already spoke to your mother."

I'd like to have been a fly on the wall for that conversation. "What did he tell her?"

"That we're still working on why you're better, but that it doesn't matter as long as the outcome is good." Ian sighs. "I feel like I've just been hit by a car—no offense. Your father is an intense man. My lie detector test for the Secret Service wasn't as tough as answering your father's questions."

I make a face. "Sorry. I know. But—he didn't remove you, and he stuck to his promise." Because he trusts me to do my job. *Because he doesn't perceive Ian as a danger anymore.*

In a way, Sam is the reason we're allowed to continue.

Sam, who had a crush on me for a while, and wasn't sure if I felt the same. Who tried to cover up his almost-kiss with the sister-comment, starting this whole mess—not that he knew that, but still. Who sometimes seems to know something is off, but who's Sam enough that he doesn't ask.

Not that I'd tell him anything anyway. PRICS is mine, and I'm not endangering Ian or the organization by blubbering to my boyfriend.

I shoot a quick glance to Ian on my side, in his white dress shirt, complete with tousled hair and the most mesmerizing green eyes I've ever seen.

I'd never do that to Ian.

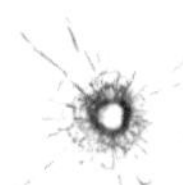

Two weeks later, I'm finally back to normal life and classroom work.

Today is my fourth day back at PRICS. Ian and I spent the morning going over intelligence briefings and working on my decoding skills, and honestly, I needed the desk work, because yesterday… Yesterday, a furious Dimitri worked me during Krav until I was too sore to breathe: Defending against a crutch attack. Something tells me he might've been the slightest bit miffed that

I got him to give me privacy and then got kidnapped from under his watch, at least that's what I take from his comment toward the end of class, something about me not being able to go pee alone anymore if I ever pulled this crap again.

Well, I think we made up and are happily walking beside each other in silence again, or better, him a couple of steps behind me, like now.

He might be a grump, but he's giving me privacy. Again. Sam and I are coming back from lunch, courtesy of Dad. Really, he's been… quite accommodating when it comes to Sam and me spending time together. It's almost a bit embarrassing, although I must admit spending time together has done us well.

While Sam and I have been great as friends for years, the last weeks have brought our relationship to a whole new level. More intimate. Not in a get-down-and-dirty-kinda-way—because, let's be honest, no matter how much Dad likes Sam, he'd have a heart attack and kick him out faster than I could protest—but in a getting-to-know-each-other-way that makes me proud to be the girl Sam trusts.

Of course being the girl Sam likes to kiss isn't bad either.

But: When out and about-slash-visible in the West Wing, we try to keep it down to a minimum. It's not professional for Sam to be seen hooking up with the President's daughter.

Today though, we make it back to the classroom, giggling. Happens when you watch Sam pull Yoshi Nagakawa's leg over lunch. Sam comes up with the craziest stories, and Nagakawa… best victim ever.

Sam drops me off at the classroom but blocks me from entering. "Not so fast. I won't see you until dinner." He wraps me in a close embrace. He's been staying a lot more for dinner recently, like the good old times during the campaign. Had somebody told me a year ago that today I'd be walking and together with Sam, I would've asked what they were on—yet here I am. *Squee!*

Sam leans in and kisses me, and while it comes with butterflies and tingling all the way down my spine, I wish he wouldn't do it right under our PRICS surveillance camera. Ian is getting a first-row view to our smooch thanks to the Human Nervous System monitor: *Brooks, Sam'mear, junior intern* and *Forrester, Alix, First Daughter*

Sam doesn't know that of course, but I do, so yes, I break the kiss.

"Eager to go back to studying?" Sam grins and winks at me. "That's how I know you."

I swipe a strand of hair behind my ear. "Got me. See you later—"

"At dinner."

I open the door to the classroom and Sam catches a glimpse of Ian sitting up on his desk, as always.

"Hi, Mr. Miller." Sam waves into the classroom. A short flash of something crosses Ian's face, but when he looks up from the book he's holding, he smiles at Sam, easygoing as always.

"Hi, Sam. Told you to call me Jason."

Sam gives him the thumbs up. "I'll remember one of these days." He waves goodbye to Ian and me before he takes off toward the Oval Office.

I step into the classroom and close the door. The scent of chai wafts over, my usual cup already filled to the brim and on my desk.

Ian frees his DUTI-pad out of the book's sleeve. Smooth. He's so much better at casual cover-ups than I am.

I hurry over to my desk. Last thing I need is to open up a conversation regarding what he most likely saw on the monitor.

"Had a good lunch?" Ian wants to know and yup, there we

go, I blush. Well, I guess he has firsthand knowledge about the ending of my lunch.

"Yeeaaah." I stretch it as long as I can and buy more time with a sip of tea. "So, what are we going to work on this afternoon? My language skills could use some brushing up." It's true. Kind of mean that natural sciences, mathematics, and computer sciences are no problem at all, while speaking more than one language is.

"Actually, I have a couple of updates for you first." He swipes across his DUTI-pad. "The Secret Service completed the report on DiBiaso. Just as we expected."

I raise an eyebrow. Took them long enough.

Ian holds up one finger. "One new development: we confirmed where the lev-metaminozole came from."

"And?"

"You were right."

"Wooo! I was right!" I hold up both hands, fingers forming the victory-sign. "I was right!"

Ian laughs, stretches out, and playfully smacks me over the head with the DUTI-pad. "And so humble. But anyway, yes. Turns out Lucas' company manufactures it somewhere in Romania. He gave the drugs to Gary during the reception in the Green Room. The package he gave Oliver…"

I tilt my head. "Yes?"

"Was a newly-developed drug, not yet FDA-approved, but with great potential." He cocks an eyebrow at me.

"For Jess?"

"For Jess. Oliver's way of helping his family, when all he had were connections instead of money."

Aw… And I was the one turning that into the proverbial rope he almost got hung with. I drop my head onto the desk in front of me.

Ian gives me another light smack with the DUTI-pad. "Forget about it, Trouble. It was a good first pick-up and it led to your second one. Anyway, Lucas is in jail, probably DiBiaso's cell neighbor. The money he bribed DiBiaso with into supporting the Genetic Testing Bill and killing your father has been secured in Switzerland."

I lift my head. "So we have enough to get them prosecuted?" I never ever, ever want to see any of them again.

"More than that. We have Gary's statement of DiBiaso blackmailing him as well, and we have the sniper."

The sniper who only survived because I locked Gary into the catacombs, or else he would've shot him. Elimination of witnesses. You're welcome, sniper. No hard feelings, right?

"So yes, we have more than enough evidence, even if Gary and DiBiaso didn't have the radiation burns matching your father's. Or if DiBiaso hadn't downscaled security for the Fourth of July fireworks to give his sniper easier access. No worries. DiBiaso is in prison and… we'll see about his punishment."

I cringe. Don't want to dive into what he means by that. While it doesn't make me shed a single tear for DiBiaso, to my surprise, a sting of sorrow for Gianna pierces my heart. I know what it feels like to be disappointed by your dad. Maybe I should give her a call. She's with one of her adult siblings now, as far as I know.

I swirl the tea around in its cup. "So the Genetic Testing Bill is definitely history?"

"History," Ian says. "With all that backstory, not even the most hardline Republicans will want to touch it. Too hot to handle."

Good.

Ian slides down his desk, shoves the DUTI-pad into the drawer, and locks it. "Let's go down to the Lair. I really need to keep you on track with grad school, or your father is going to serve my head on a platter." He shoves his hands into his pockets. "Plus… you have another mission."

All my senses come online at the same time, adrenaline rushing through my veins like Porsches on the Autobahn. "A new mission?" That's what I've been training for! "What is it?"

Ian chuckles. "You're way too excited about this, Trouble." His face turns serious. "This mission is easy. Mostly desk work."

Oh. Okay.

Ian sucks in his lower lip and comes over to my desk, holding out a hand. "And if I have anything to do with it, we're going to keep it at that as much as possible."

I take his hand and have him pull me out of my chair. "But—"

He interrupts me with a soft sigh. "I'm all for cranking it up, Trouble. But I'm all against you getting shot at again. Ever. Or anything close to it. Gary and DiBiaso almost *killed* you. And you're only seventeen. Still a minor."

Ouch.

Yes, I know I'm only seventeen. I know it and Dad knows it.

An ache opens up in my chest. I'm too young for—

Ian's eyes lock with mine, and the world around me fades into nothingness. "No one will *ever* do that to you again, you understand?"

I nod. The way Ian says it, I know he'd throw himself in front of me if it meant he'd keep that promise.

"Come." He holds on to my hand and leads me toward the secret entrance behind the fireplace. The palm reader recognizes his print and the holographic wall vanishes for us. Both of us step into the opening, the wall zipping back to life as soon as we're through.

I look down the spiraling staircase of a hundred million steps.

"We need an elevator here, seriously."

Ian gives me a sideward glance. "Well, you definitely still shouldn't put too much strain on that leg, Trouble." He steps next to me and drapes his arm around my waist. "Hold on to the railing on that side, I'll stabilize you from here." He looks at me with one of those smiles that make me question my sanity.

The words form on the tip of my tongue, but I don't say them. When he gives my hip a small squeeze, I don't care if I can walk by myself or not. I nod and let him guide me downstairs, his hand on my waist sending goosebumps all through my body.

I didn't know how right I was on that day several months ago when I met Ian for the first time.

It was a game changer.

A major one.

ABOUT THE AUTHOR

Micky O'Brady is a pediatrician-turned-writer living in beautiful, dry Southern California with her husband and two critters (one son, one dog). Micky loves to write YA thrillers and sci-fi with a romantic twist, mainly because she wishes her life had been such an awesome mix of action and cute guys when she was a teen.

When she isn't up at around 3 a.m. (with a cup of tea, Earl Grey, hot) drafting stories she can't get out of her head, she can be found at a martial arts dojo, though maybe not at 3 a.m. She holds a first-degree black belt in Krav Maga and a second-degree black belt in Judo, and is convinced every girl should know how to kick some butt.

Micky also is a firm believer in the healing powers of Nutella eaten straight from the glass and in the magic that can happen on a rainy day, as long as there are fuzzy socks and a cup of hot tea involved.

Before diving into YA fiction, Micky published several academic works including a doctoral thesis, medical articles, and a book on emergency communication. None of them are as fun to read as her YA novels though.

Through Snowy Wings Publishing, Micky has released an impressive collection of award-winning YA fiction, including "The President's Daughter" series (THE PRESIDENT'S DAUGHTER and its sequel TRIAL BY ICE, originally published by Curiosity Quills), the "Time Warped" sci-fi romance trilogy (TIME WARPED, TIME BOUND, and TIMED OUT), another YA sci-fi romance BETWEEN WORLDS (award winner), the multi-award-winning contemporary romance-slash-pro-wrestling-story PLAYING WITH #FIRE, and the standalone novels ANGEL DOWN, 33 DEGREES, as well as the award-winning CRISPR—CRIS PARR. All titles are available on Amazon and at mickyobrady.com.